Harper
Monogram

A Bed of
Spices

⊰ BARBARA SAMUEL ⊱

HarperPaperbacks
A Division of HarperCollinsPublishers

To my mother, Rosalie Putman Hair, who taught me to dream and dance instead of clean and cook. And to Ram, for heroically eating whatever I happen to burn for dinner.

This is a work of fiction. The characters, incidents, and dialogues are products of the author's imagination and are not to be construed as real. Any resemblance to actual events or persons, living or dead, is entirely coincidental.

HarperPaperbacks   *A Division of* HarperCollins*Publishers*
10 East 53rd Street, New York, N.Y. 10022

Copyright © 1993 by Barbara Samuel

Cover illustration by Bob Berran

First printing: September 1993

Printed in the United States of America

HarperPaperbacks, HarperMonogram, and colophon are trademarks of HarperCollins*Publishers*

❖ 10 9 8 7 6 5 4 3 2 1

BLAZING TORCHES
OF PASSION

"Are we mad?" Rica asked with a tremulous smile.

"Utterly," Solomon said in a raw whisper. A need welled up within him, rising until it broke the threads of restraint he'd held over himself. Moving slowly and deliberately, he pushed gently at her shoulders until Rica lay amid the grass and buttercups, her hair spread out below her like an Arabian carpet.

"I am mad," he murmured. "But I care not—for if madness brings such visions as these, I willingly leave the world."

Closer and closer Solomon moved, until their bodies touched from ankle to shoulder.

"Rica," he said and could think of no more. He touched her cheek only for a moment. One moment, stolen from all time, was little enough to ask.

"Please," she whispered hoarsely. "Please kiss me, Solomon, or I shall die of wanting."

Author's Note

   Two thousand Jews perished in the Strassburg fire of February 14, 1349, but the sacrifice did not, of course, halt the advance of the plague. Within a few weeks, the city fell prey to the Black Death.

   Throughout that summer, plague and pogroms raged through Germany. Some Jewish refugees fled to the east, some were successfully protected by the ruling princes of their territories, some converted to escape the flames.

   In Mainz, a curious thing occurred. Throughout the summer of 1349, the Jews of that city secretly collected arms with which to protect themselves. When the killing mob descended in August, two hundred of them died over several days of fighting. The Jews, at last defeated by the greater numbers, retreated to their homes and set fire to them.

   Within twenty years, Jews settled in nearly all the communities once more, but they were under much stronger restrictions. Thus did the era of the ghetto begin.

Part One
Strassburg—Summer 1348

I should like to hold my knight
Naked in my arms at eve
That he might be in ecstasy
As I cushioned his head against my breast.
　　　　　　　　　—Countess of Dia

My poor heart she has caught
With magic spells and wiles
I do not sigh for gold
But for her mouth that smiles;
Her hue it is so bright
She half makes blind my sight.
　　　　　　　　　—Judah ha–Levi

Prologue

Charles der Esslingen stood near the embrasure of his chamber and looked to the courtyard below. His solar filled the top floor in the keep of the old castle, and the builders had been generous with light so high, where arrow slits and protection were no longer necessities. Buttery May sunshine splashed into the room, warming the sweet herbs in the rushes beneath his feet.

It was a glorious view, and all he surveyed belonged to him; all had been won with his sword in his youth. There was the keep and the manor, the upper and lower baileys with their whitewashed walls. Beyond was a meadow dotted with sheep, their newly shorn bodies oddly naked. There was a forest, thick with game birds and animals, a vineyard where grew some of the finest Rhenish grapes in the empire, and an orchard where apple and pear trees flourished. In the distance, beyond his eye's reach, was a smattering of peasant dwellings and the fields with their new crops.

In the greening baileys, the morning bustle had begun. Scullery maids washed pots in a tub nearby the open kitchen door. Another girl gathered herbs in her apron from the garden close to the wall. A vassal paced the walk in obvious boredom.

As Charles lifted his cup, his daughter Frederica bustled from the kitchen, headed with purpose across the grass. Taking in the busy swish of her skirts, he half smiled, feeding his hawk a crust of bread. "On her morning rounds," he commented to the bird, who cocked an eye toward the yard.

The vassal on the walk called out to Rica in some jest Charles could not hear. She paused to laugh over her shoulder, and the sound rang through the hazy morning, teasing and ripe, like the girl herself.

Charles stepped closer to the embrasure to watch her progress. Chickens scurried in alarm before her, squawking in protest of the flying skirts. Within the confines of the bailey, she was bareheaded, and her hair glistened in the morning sun as if laced with silver and gold, the tresses flowing well past her waist. The dark woolen cotehardie she wore clung to the curves of breast and hip that had been so long in coming, and even the billowing surcoat hid little of the final result of her long wait for a woman's body.

The vassal on the walk had kept pace with her, calling out. Ignored, he finally stopped, but looked after the girl with such wistfulness and frustration that even her father had to laugh.

Rica slipped into the brewhouse. Charles turned from his post, still smiling softly at the besotted youth on the walk. Poor fool was hardly alone.

He sipped from the cup of wine his servants had brought him, along with a dry bit of stale bread from last night's supper. Rica teased him over his indulgence in early morning food—she teased everyone about something—but Charles grappled with weakness enough as it was. Without food in the morning, he sometimes shook like an old woman.

A soft sigh came from the corner. Charles eyed his second daughter over the rim of his wooden cup. Head bent over her needlework—her endless, endless needlework—she was utterly still but for the flying fingers.

Etta. Her hair, too, streamed over slender shoulders and a fine, lush woman's form. The face was oval, as pale and flawless as a field of fresh snow at evening, her lips red and tender. As if she sensed his gaze, she lifted her eyes to her father. Fringed with almost unnaturally long lashes, the irises were a deep purplish blue.

His daughters. Twins. So utterly identical that no one would have been able to tell them apart but for the tragedy that made the physical similarities almost a parody. The tragedy that was, perhaps, his judgment from God for the violence of his youth.

Etta, for all her shining loveliness, had no besotted youths trailing in her wake. She rarely went abroad. She never spoke to anyone except Rica, who swore that Etta was not simple-minded, only deeply wounded somewhere in the darkest heart of her.

Without a smile or any acknowledgment, she lowered her gaze back to the tapestry on her lap. A familiar pluck of grief touched his heart. To have lost his beloved and beautiful wife so violently ten years before was sorrow enough. That his six-year-old daughter had been so brutalized was beyond his imagination.

The dark thoughts were interrupted by the appearance of a vassal at the door of his chamber.

"Ah, Rudolf," Charles said in greeting. "Come in. Tell me what you have learned."

The young man settled on a bench nearby the wall

and rubbed his hands to warm them by the fire. "The pestilence is widespread, my lord. They say there has never been such as this."

Charles grunted, chewing his hard crust of bread.

"They say that India is gone, so littered with bodies the stench travels for a hundred miles. Italy has suffered the same fate for nearly a year. France is in chaos . . . now the pestilence moves north."

"And what, pray tell, have the famed doctors and astrologers to say?"

"A demon in the air and an alignment of planets," Rudolf said in disgust. "It should be plainly obvious it is a punishment from—"

Charles raised a weary hand and pressed with the heel of his palm to his chest, trying to ease the ache there. Thin rumors had wound through the countryside for many months, telling of the disease. With the rumors came grim prophecies of death for all mankind. "Heard you a tale of its look?"

"Yes, the sufferers—"

"I need no more gruesome stories. Tell the guards to watch for it in travelers along the river. We will admit no such victims here."

"Yes, my lord." Rudolf stood, and he cleared his throat. His nerves were betrayed by the clutch of his fists at his side. "Have you given thought to my suit?"

"I have." Settling himself upon a stool, Charles waved toward a bench and Rudolf sat, back straight. Against the sunlight, his hair took on a glorious blaze of yellow, the ends curled at his shoulders, his handsome face earnest. Rudolf had served him well. The link to his powerful family would help erase the less noble blood running through Charles's own veins. Beyond that, Rudolf was the most besotted of the field of Rica's admirers. He would make a good husband to her. "I will agree to the betrothal—"

Rudolf jumped to his feet in exuberance. "Oh, thank you, my lord!"

Charles forestalled any further display. "There is a condition."

"Anything."

"She is headstrong," he warned.

Rudolf gave him a rueful smile. "Of that, my lord, I am all too aware."

Charles walked to the embrasure. Rica stood now in the gardens, conversing with a servant. He gestured to Rudolf, who joined him.

"She is also a romantic girl," Charles said slowly. "Her head is filled with the tragic poems written by the ladies and knights of the courts." He paused. "I want you to take the summer to woo her, so I am not forced to wed her against her will."

"And if I cannot capture that wild heart?"

"I think I know a little of the romantic dreams of young girls." Charles inclined his head. "You are not without your gifts . . . I watch the eyes of the women here."

Rudolf flushed darkly. "Foolish wenches with only coupling to fill their brains."

"Seemed a lovely pastime when I was a youth," Charles said mildly, but raised a hand once again to forestall Rudolf's protestations. This was the only flaw of the young man—a certain grim piety that manifested itself at odd times. "Speak not to Rica of religion and God," he cautioned. "She is not concerned with matters of the spirit at this point in her life. Women grow more serious when their bellies swell."

"She is all I wish as she is," Rudolf murmured, leaning out to watch her, his eyes glowing. "Whatever I must do to win her—" He straightened and clasped his hands behind his back. "You need not worry. For the summer I will be a model of courtly love."

"Good." Charles turned away. "If summer's end finds her still reluctant, I will tell her of the betrothal and you will be wed. By All Saint's Day, you will have a wife—willing or no."

From the corner, the ordinarily silent Etta cried out, and Charles started. Both men stared at her, but she ignored them, her gaze fixed on a cut on her palm. She whimpered in terror as blood trickled over her hand and began to run down her arm.

Charles sprang forward, for once not annoyed with the girl. Her aversion to blood was well known and understandable given the trauma of her childhood.

"There, my sweet," he murmured, taking her arm. He plucked a length of fabric from the basket beside her and twisted it around her hand. "Your scissors slipped, that's all."

But as the blood soaked through the cloth, Charles felt a tremor of foreboding pass through his belly. As Etta fixed terrified eyes on his face, he felt as if there were something he should be seeing, something just beyond his reach.

He dismissed it. "Rudolf, fetch Olga." To Etta, he added, "She will attend you quickly. All will be well."

1

Rica knelt in the confessional, smelling the sour, sharp scent of beeswax that had been rubbed into the wood. Stone flags met her knees. Beyond the screen, blocked with sheer white linen, the old priest wheezed, as he always did in the spring.

She clasped her hands together. "Forgive me, Father, for I have sinned," she murmured. "It has been six days since my last confession."

Pursing her lips, she tried to remember the pockets of wickedness that riddled those six days. She had nearly forgotten to be shriven at all, and now, breathless with the run across the courtyard, she found her mind a blank. "I borrowed my sister's scarf without telling her, the good one she embroidered for Assumption."

"Mmmm." The priest coughed, the sound shallow but wheezing.

Beginning was difficult, but once reminded, she seemed to recall an avalanche of transgressions to confess each time—there were so many ways to err! "I spoke sharply to Cook this morning and disobeyed my father's order to wear my hat when I leave the castle grounds. It was too hot."

A murmur came through the screen. Rica shifted on the flags, uncomfortable with the need to confess the next sin. It had been told and repented a hundred times—and would be told a hundred more, for she could not overcome it. Her voice dropped. "I dreamed I slew my mother's murderer."

A short pause marked the air. He was supposed to be anonymous, a figure of shadowy authority, although he was the chapel priest and everyone knew it.

"Is there nothing else you would tell me?" the priest prodded. Obviously, he had some concern she might have omitted something.

Swallowing a smile, Rica realized what it would be. She did not help him. The priest had been in her father's chapel for most of her life. He had given her instruction in the catechism and taught her to read Latin. It was the gentle old priest who supplied Rica with her beloved texts, and although he disapproved of the path her thoughts took at times, she knew he was fond of her. Now he was worried that the poems of the courts, those passionate avowals of tragic love, would corrupt her completely.

More worried, she thought with a frown, about her reading those stories of illicit love than he was about her repeated dreams of revenge.

Bloody dreams they were, in which she was armed with only a dagger and her hatred. In light of such, the romances in which she so delighted carried little weight. "I have read no more of the literature you forbade me," she said quietly.

"Ahhh." Relief soughed through the word. He gave her prayers of penance. "God bless you, child. Pray for me, who sins as you do."

He coughed and Rica promised herself she would prepare a tea to soothe that ticklish hacking. Her father, too, needed a fresh batch of his medicine. She would go see Helga this afternoon. Perhaps even Etta could be persuaded to go along.

Her spirits rose in anticipation. She hurried from the chapel into the warmth of the spring day, her limbs lightened with confession and the promised break in routine.

But in spite of her eagerness to be away, it was the middle of the afternoon before her duties allowed her to set out for Helga's cottage. Her sister, Etta, walked silently alongside her, a serene expression on her beautiful face. Although they were said to be identical twins, Rica knew Etta was far more beautiful than she. Her heart was pure, and that virtue shone in her complexion, in her eyes, in her almost unbearably sweet smile.

Their dog, a monstrous wolfhound, knew it, too. Leo trotted steadfastly at Etta's side, licking her fingers every few steps as if to assure himself of her continued presence. He loved Rica, and always came with her as protection when she walked alone to the cottage for herbs, but it was to Etta he was devoted.

Rica slipped her hand into the bend of her sister's elbow. "The day is beautiful, is it not?" she said, gesturing toward the Vosges Mountains standing blue to the west. The river Ill rose from a secret spring in those hills, its path lined with thick trees.

To the east wound the great Rhine. Nestled against a bend in the waterway spilled the city of Strassburg, its rooftops piled one atop the other like a tumble of chess pieces. At some times of day, the city glowed with a magical, rosy wash, but this afternoon the walls wavered in a haze of heat.

Faintly from the monastery on the river came the echo of monks at prayer, a melancholy song Rica loved in spite of its sadness. "Listen," she said to Etta. "Do you hear them?"

Etta cocked her head toward the sound and smiled

softly, but she made no reply. Rica had not really expected one. Etta was not mute—nor simple-minded—as
the servants and her father were wont to believe. She
spoke to Rica, usually about God, if the truth were
known, when Rica would much rather have discussed
a new fabric she had purchased from a wandering
peddler, or a bangled belt she'd found in the city.
God and embroidery proved Etta's only topics, however, and Rica had learned to live with that.

Her vivid, bloody dream flitted through her mind
again. Gone now was the contrition she felt in the confessional. She always told the priest it was her mother
she was avenging in her dream, and perhaps it was in
some small way. But when she lifted her hand, dagger
shining in the moonlight of her dream, it was Etta who
was in her mind; Etta who was avenged in the murder
of the man who had brutally handled Rica's twin. One
day, she promised herself grimly. Perhaps then, the
wounded spirit of Etta would be freed.

Rica led them around a muddy hole in the road, lifting her skirts. It made little difference, for the hems
dragged the ground as fashion insisted. For the hun-
dredth time, Rica swore to shorten her tunics and coats.

The dog whined suddenly, ear cocked in alertness.
Rica smiled. "What is it, Leo?" She scanned the trees
along the road. A flurry of sparrows danced through the
branches of pine and birch, but the dog cared little for
birds, though he snapped at them as a matter of course if
they got too close. He made a soft whimper in his throat.

Rica spied the squirrel at the same instant it began
to chatter and scold. Its tail flicked indignantly at the
intruders, and it scrambled for the safety of a branch
from which it kept up its haranguing.

Three months ago, nothing would have kept Leo in
his place beside them, but Rica had worked with him

patiently, rewarding him when he did not give chase to some succulent little animal in the fields and forests. With a pang, she realized she had forgotten to bring treats with her today.

She nudged her sister. "Etta, bend down and give Leo a hug. Tell him what a good dog he is for not giving chase."

For a moment, Etta only looked at Rica with a blank expression in her wide, lavender eyes. Then she knelt, unmindful of the mud in the road, and buried her face in Leo's gray-and-brown fur. "Good dog," she said quietly. Leo made a small, grateful noise in his throat and licked Etta's face.

A wild, searing sense of hope unfurled in Rica's breast, an almost painful sensation. It was the first time Rica could remember Etta ever speaking to any human or animal save Rica herself. Were the demons passing, then? Or was the dog a link to the world that Rica had never thought to use before?

Biting her lip to contain her excitement—for anything sudden or unexpected sent Etta scurrying behind a mask of silent terror—Rica watched them, dog and girl in the humid warmth of a late spring day. "Good dog," Etta said again, and offered her face for his licks. A bubble of laughter slipped from the pale throat.

Rica's hands shook. Out of a need to move somehow, she tore the barbette from her hair and tossed it above her head, catching it just as Etta stood up again. Her face again held the slight, virtuous smile, but Rica didn't miss the way her hand lingered on Leo's back, protective and loving.

Sweet mother of God, Rica thought in joy. *Thank you.*

It was only then she realized she had sinned twice on this walk, the same sins she had confessed this very morning. It seemed she could never keep a day clean of them.

And yet, she didn't replace her hat. It was too hot, and the damage, after all, had been done.

Helga's cottage squatted at the edge of a thick stand of trees, a plain thatch-roofed dwelling surrounded with neat beds of herbs, the medium of her commerce. The widow of a minor squire, Helga had raised seven healthy children with her concoctions and potions. It was a miracle so near to the river, and some said she was a witch, but when needy enough, even they sneaked through the woods to her cottage.

It had been Helga who had delivered the twins; Helga who had nursed a six-year-old Etta back from the edge of the grave; Helga who had kept the old priest healthy and had even put a stop to the worst of Rica's father's bellyaches.

Rica thought she might also be her father's mistress but knew better than to ask either of them.

The twins approached the cottage, their hems tangling in stands of borage and lavender alongside paths covered in red clover. The pungent odor of dill wafted through the air as Leo waved his eager tail into a stand of it.

Rica heard voices from behind the cottage, where Helga worked in warm weather. Helga's was one, of course. That throaty, rich sound was unmistakable—"the voice of a bawdy," her father always said. Rica liked it.

The other one was deeper, thick with laughter, unfamiliar. Rica hung back for a moment, trying to place it, wondering if she ought to put back her hat and smooth her hair before she appeared. But what if it were only some peasant come for Helga's spring tonic?

She peeked around the corner. The midwife's broad body blocked Rica's view of the male visitor and she bit the inside of her lip, waiting. A fly buzzed nearby her ear and she shooed it away distractedly, setting the tiny bells on her bracelet jingling.

Helga's broad figure swiveled with more grace than one would have suspected. "Rica!" she said, beckoning with one hand. "Come, girl. No need to hide yourself."

Rica slid around the corner, tossing a handful of hair over her shoulder as she came forward, her eyes downcast as befitted a maid—even if her hat was gone, she thought with a flush. In her wake trailed Etta and the dog.

"Ah!" exclaimed Helga. "Both my pretties are here today." She kissed them soundly.

That ritual finished, Rica looked at the man in the yard. At first, she only peeped through her lashes to see how embarrassed she ought to be, but one glance astonished her so fully, she opened her eyes wide and stared.

His voice had led her to expect a man, full-grown and burly. And in ways, she supposed he was a man, as much as she was a woman. His hair tumbled over his head in thick, unruly curls, the color black as a starling's tail, and glossier still. His brow was high and wide above black eyes that twinkled with the lingering humor of the joke he and Helga had shared.

Her stomach squeezed. She pressed her palm to the place, dumbstruck for once in her life. His skin gleamed with color: a fine ruddiness in his cheeks, a warm walnut on his hands and neck.

He was beautiful, as beautiful as a fallen angel or a pagan god. And he stared back at her as if he could not believe she stood there, as if he knew her, as if he were as dazzled as she.

She turned in panic toward Helga. "My f-father sent me for some tonic," she said breathlessly. "Oh, and I need yarrow and lungwort for the priest."

Helga gave her a curious look. "Did you run all the way?"

"Er, w-well," Rica stammered, then realized what a

good excuse it made for breathlessness. "Only through the meadow."

Helga laughed. "Our Rica is not a lazy girl—she's been seeing to the kitchens and gardens since she was ten—but she loves to escape when she does."

The visitor laughed and Rica glanced sideways at him. His teeth were big and strong and white, his lips red as apples.

A little ache bloomed in her breast. Like a lady stricken with the beauty of a knight in one of the poems the priest had forbidden her, Rica felt faint and star-struck and bewitched.

She smiled at him.

He swallowed, then glanced away quickly, a dusky stain on his cheekbones. "Is that so?" he asked.

Having lost the thread of conversation, Rica frowned. "Is what so?"

"That you like to escape when you have finished your chores?"

"Er, yes." She looked at Helga. "Shall I get the tonic? I know what to do."

"Oh, I'll fetch it, child." She patted her shoulder. "Stay here and keep the young man company while I get it. He is a good student. Tell him about your thoughts on sickness."

Rica nearly bolted, followed after the robust old woman no matter how odd it seemed. But the stranger's voice halted her. "Please," he said in his resonant voice. "Do not go. It is rare enough a girl thinks at all. I would hear your thoughts, if you would tell them."

"It is nothing," she said. "I only see that my father is much better when he does not eat certain things."

"Oh? What sort of things?"

She twisted the stem of a stalk of chamomile lying on the table. "Goose and duck, old mutton, beef. Even frumenty seems to sit ill with him." With a slight shrug, she again glanced at him shyly. "He growled a lot at first, but he no longer gets the bellyaches he once did."

"And how came you to this thought?"

"I watched to see when he grew ill." She frowned. "Not such a difficult step to take."

He leaned forward. "But not a step all would see." He met her eyes and Rica, unwillingly, saw a glimmer of respect there. A man who would listen to the thoughts of a woman?

She inclined her head and felt her hair fall over her arm and wrist. "Anyone with any intelligence would see it."

"Ah," his grin was swift and devastating. "And we all know how widespread intelligence is."

His phrasing somehow made them a unit, two apart from the teeming masses. It was the first time anyone had thought to recognize her ability to reason.

"Common as tamed boars."

He laughed. What a beautiful mouth he had, Rica thought. Generous, as if it could give—

Startled, she flushed with a painful intensity. A third sin in less than an hour—perhaps four if she counted thinking of the poetry that the priest had forbidden her to read.

But, as with her hat, the damage had been done. Her gaze caught on his throat, long and brown. His shoulders were broad beneath the dark jupon, his calves well shaped in his hose.

The small ache in her chest bloomed as wide as a poppy, touching her breasts and belly.

Then her wandering gaze fell upon his hands. Powerful they were, with the look of hard work in the long dark fingers. But it was the cleanliness of them that struck her. No dirt clung beneath his neatly trimmed nails. The knuckles were scrubbed.

And she became aware of a heady, warm scent the wind blew toward her, a scent of clean male skin mixed with a unique, elusive smell. His smell.

"Who are you?" she asked, suddenly frightened.

"Has your Helga not told you of her student?" His voice dropped to a rough, low tone. "She has told me of you."

"You?" Rica's eyes widened. She sought and found the round yellow patch on his chest, the mark of his Jewry. Her heart squeezed painfully and her words came out on a disappointed note she could not control. "I thought you a burgher's son, by your clothes."

The black eyes hardened a notch. "My father is a merchant," he said. "A rich one—but I am his fourth son and he has granted permission to let me study medicine." He turned his face toward the city. "The pestilence chased me home, but as I wait for better days, Helga has been kind enough to share her knowledge of herbal cures with me."

"And a bright, quick student he is," Helga interjected, emerging from the cottage with several packets of muslin tied in string. A fat black-and-white cat wound around her ankles, and somehow she avoided tripping. "Solomon has learned in a few months what's taken me four years to teach you."

Piqued, Rica lifted her chin. "Perhaps he has better reason." The words came out on a rather more annoyed note than she had intended, and she caught the tail of a grin hidden behind Solomon's hand.

"Oh, now, sweet," Helga said with her husky chuckle, "I meant no harm."

Rica clasped the packets close to her chest and lifted her skirts. "Come, Etta, it is time to return."

Etta rose from the ground, where she had squatted to stroke the cat's wild long fur. Next to her, Leo whined jealously and licked her hand. "Good dog," she said in a clear, high voice.

Helga gasped. Rica glanced at her in alarm, shaking her head quickly once. Then, unable to stop the swell of joy in her chest, she crossed the yard and hugged the midwife. "It's the third time today," she whispered against her ear.

"You must come tell me about this soon," Helga whispered in return, squeezing Rica's arms.

Rica smiled and lifting her skirts, hurried after her sister, who was heading back toward the castle.

In spite of the fact that Rica watched her sister almost continuously, there was no further manifestation of the strange, alert behavior until late afternoon.

Upon returning to the castle, Etta bent over her tapestry frame and with monotonous concentration, poked the needle in and out, in and out of the fabric. The dog flopped next to her on the rushes, content to sleep nearby his mistress if nothing else were required of him.

Rica leaned restlessly against the embrasure, waiting for her father. There was a newer wing than this two-hundred-year-old keep with its damp walls, but Charles clung stubbornly to his solar, giving the newer quarters to his guests. The lower-slung addition could not hope to compete with this eagle's view of the courtyard and all its goings on.

Below were kitchen maids in the garden, collecting new greens for supper. From some unseen place, a musician plucked a lute, readying it for the evening's entertainment. The priest sneezed his way across the courtyard. Along the walk, two men-at-arms paced slowly, their lackadaisical attitudes shouting of the peace that had reigned since the new emperor had taken his throne. There were always dangers so close to the river, but the reckless, bloody days of Rica's childhood had settled now in this simple peace.

Charles came in, his hawk on his arm. His face was pale and beaded with sweat. "Papa!" Rica exclaimed. "Come sit down."

"Do not flutter so, child," he grumbled, but did not shake off her hands. He allowed her to remove his outer garment, then wash his face with a cloth dipped in cool water.

"You are too fat, Papa," Rica said with a frown. "If you do not stop putting food in your mouth every minute, all summer you will suffer thus."

He waved a beefy hand. "You have taken all my favorites from me. I eat only what is left."

Rica smiled as the color began to return to his cheeks. He was not, in truth, terribly fat, although a round belly filled his tunic well enough. But even the moderate extra weight had him billowing as he took the stairs, flushing in the heat of a summer's day, and sleeping poorly. "It will be easier now we have fresh food. I will go pick cherries for you tomorrow."

He winked and patted her hand, his good humor returning with his wind. "As you wish, *liebling.* You have been right thus far." He shifted to pour a cup of ale. "Did you bring me some magic potion from Helga?"

"I gave it to Matilda. She will send a girl up with it." She kissed his cheek. "I will leave you," she said with a smile, knowing he would nap until supper and that he hated admitting to an old man's weakness.

Charles caught sight of Etta and frowned. "Take

her with you, girl. I am weary of her sitting like a stone in my corner."

"She is not deaf, Papa." Rica whirled, furious at his bad-tempered words, and touched her sister's slim shoulder. "Come, I will dress your hair and you may do mine."

As Etta complaisantly settled her threads in a basket, Rica shot her father a look.

He lifted one bushy gray eyebrow, unapologetic.

Before they left the chamber, one of Charles's vassals appeared, Rudolf der Brumath. A tall man with the grace of a young stag, he smiled genially toward the girls. "I hope I do not interrupt."

"No." Rica smiled. Unlike most of the rest of the castle inhabitants, Rudolf always included Etta in his greetings and she liked him for that.

He bowed now over Rica's hand, then Etta's, turning the latter's over. "I see your wound has healed," he murmured.

Etta bent her head, and a rosy flush of color stained her pale cheeks. "Aye," she whispered.

Startled, Rica glanced quickly at her sister, then toward Rudolf, who smiled gently into Etta's face. Although she knew Rudolf extended his kindness toward Etta in order to win Rica's favor, she thought now there might be a way to use that kindness.

Giving him her broadest smile, she said, "Perhaps you will sit with us for the entertainment tonight."

Rudolf bowed his golden head. "It would be an honor and a pleasure."

Rica smiled again and took her sister's hand. "Till later, then."

Out in the passageway, Rica noted Etta's flush. "He is handsome, is he not?" she whispered.

"Yes," Etta whispered, looking with wonder at the hand he had kissed.

Rica hugged her sister. "Come. I will dress your hair with lavender flowers. Tonight, you will be a beauty such has never been seen before."

The meat was already upon the table before Rica and Etta appeared, and by that time Charles was fuming. The scent of braised pork taunted him with savory fingers, plucking at his belly with teasing temptation. Around him, the faces of other diners were smeared with the grease of the fat, rich cut.

He picked without interest at the broth and bread before him, torn between the bellyache he would face if he indulged his hunger and the deep satisfaction of chewing hard.

So when Rica, then Etta, appeared in the great hall, he frowned. His gaze darted from one to the other. He frowned outright. Rica always led, always. But was that Rica?

For the first time in his life, he could not tell them apart. Both wore richly embroidered surcoats over pale gowns, their identically creamy shoulders displayed. One girl had braided her hair with ribbons, the other had left hers free to tumble in a glory of silver and gold over ripe breasts and graceful arms.

As they took a place at the table, Charles heard the awed stilling of speech that grew below the buzzing of the ladies. Every man in the room had fallen completely, absurdly silent—no doubt, Charles thought grimly, contemplating all manner of ménage à trois with his nubile daughters. Elbowed by wives and nudged along by his own warning glance, the men quickly lit again the flame of chatter.

Charles ate slowly, watching his children. The one with the braid . . . now, that must be Etta, for she was the more modest of the two. That one's gown skimmed the edges of her collarbone, and she wore no bangles about her wrists or waist.

So it was Rica who had left her hair loose save for a small weaving of gillyflowers and lavender, Rica whose womanly curves swelled above a low-cut gown, Rica whose hands made bells ring on her bracelets. He smiled to himself in satisfaction. For though her head was demurely lowered as Rudolf next to her whispered something into her ear, he saw her smile in the strangely ripe way she had, even as a flush stained her cheeks.

A queer release rippled through him. Perhaps there would be no trouble over this betrothal. He'd not even known he was worried until the pair had met in his chamber this afternoon.

What a fine marriage they would make! Both were so strong and fair, and Rica was sturdy, unlike many of her class. She would bear fine sons. Rudolf, in spite of his wearying piety, was healthy, and he carried the blood of the noble Brumaths in his veins.

Charles looked at Etta, sitting quietly. Perhaps there was even hope for this girl. Surely there would be some lad willing to trade her silence for her beauty. Someone gentle but a bit stupid.

He scanned the trestle tables. Ah, he thought, spying the son of a squire—a black-haired youth of some bearing. Hugh was famed for his handling of difficult horses, but even his mother admitted that was the extent of his intelligence.

Charles lifted his cup. Perhaps. There was not only the matter of her silence, however, but that of her virginity. Sobering, he touched his belly, aching now even with the bland food he was allowed.

He must somehow see them both settled before the year was through. Then he could die in peace.

2

"Solomon," said his brother Hershel, leaning his elbows on the good embroidered tablecloth their mother spread for Sabbath meals. "A game of chess?"

Replete with the rich food of the midday feast, Solomon merely shook his head. "I am no match for you at my best. Today I am too sleepy."

"A walk then?" Hershel never stopped moving. The notion of rest was alien to him, as it was to their father, who chuckled with a friend in a corner of the sumptuous room. Together the old men shared a joke in Yiddish.

The air was still and close with the heat of the afternoon. A walk by the river might awaken him. To his brother, Solomon nodded.

They carried bread crumbs for the birds, and once beyond the walls of the city, scattered them for pigeons and wrens. Hershel was unusually silent, a faraway expression on his strong, dark face.

"Dreaming of your wedding night, brother?" Solomon teased.

A telltale flush lit Hershel's cheeks. "Ah—well," he protested. Then he smiled. "Perhaps a little."

"Raizel is beautiful," he said. "She will make you a good wife."

"I had the good luck to claim her before your travels brought you home."

"Nay." Solomon tossed a handful of crumbs toward a waiting pigeon, who then warred with a squirrel over the choicest chunks. "I have told you—I will not marry till I am finished with my studies."

"You cannot wait so long," Hershel protested. "The women will be old and used by then. Who knows how long the pestilence will last?"

"It has always seemed cruel to marry then leave a wife to manage all." He shook his head. "When I marry, I will be there."

"You never forget Benjamin's poor wife. She was only one of many."

"She worried herself to an early grave without him. It was unkind to leave her as he did."

"He had no choice. A man must do what he must."

Solomon shrugged, dismissing the subject. "I will not marry until I am finished at Montpellier."

"A man should marry," Hershel persisted. "It is your duty and without it, who can resist sin?"

Solomon chuckled. "Your mind is filled with visions of your beloved. I have no such dreams to torture me."

Hershel planted his feet on the banks of the river. "You are the one Papa beat—when you were seven!—for kissing girls. Have you forgotten?"

"How could I forget?" He lifted an eyebrow wickedly. "He beat me at ten and thirteen for the same. What of it?"

"Such a nature does not just go with the mist. It may be buried, but it will be your death if you do not marry."

"Pah! I have a heart, but I have also a mind with which to rule it."

"It is not the urgings of your *heart* that concern me."

With a small shake of his head, Solomon touched Hershel's shoulder. "Truly. You need not fret."

Hershel let go of a breath, then nodded. "Perhaps it is my own thoughts that vex me. I tell you I cannot even close my eyes for waiting."

"The time will pass soon enough."

They began to walk again. From the monastery came the faint sound of monks singing dirgeful prayers. A wide barge loaded with barrels floated by on the current of the Rhine. Wine, perhaps.

Traffic on the river this spring had been light. Solomon sobered, thinking of the plague that had so thinned the boats traveling to and fro on their busy errands.

As if reading his thoughts, Hershel asked, "Think you the pestilence will fly so far north?"

"Who knows?" Solomon shrugged. "They say it spreads on the fogs—perhaps we should pray for winds that blow southward." He shuddered inwardly. "It's a gruesome blight."

The pestilence had struck the school at Montpellier with swift and devastating consequences. The students and physicians and priests had swelled and blackened. The smell of them foreshadowed their fate: a smell of rot and death so powerful Solomon had been forced to tie a cloth about his face.

As he fled the evil, traveling home to Strassburg, he had seen whole peasant villages littered with too many bodies to bury. Survivors had begged blessings from him, dressed as he was in his priest's guise. Twice, in sympathy, he had nearly given them, but his conscience had not let him.

"They say there are hangings in France over this plague," Hershel said quietly. "They say the Jews are poisoning the wells."

"Ignorance and terror—they know not whence the

pestilence comes." He tossed crumbs to an eager magpie. "But the pope has issued a bull to protect us, and the emperor has warned he will fine his subjects if they try such."

"You have forgotten, Solomon." Hershel looked at his brother. "These peasants have nothing, no thoughts. They are like cattle—when they are afraid, they will stampede."

"What would you do? Gather your bride and run?" Solomon frowned. "Where? Here we are many. We have allies in the town council and the emperor—weak as they may be, they are better than no allies at all. At least the council will lose our taxes if we are harmed." He stepped closer. "You leave Strassburg and you will die of the pestilence."

"You did not die."

There was no answer to that. Solomon had puzzled over it a dozen times, a hundred—not only his own survival, but that of others who stood in the midst of the victims and never fell ill. What protected them? And what of those who sickened unto death, then recovered? Was it something they ate or some blessing or a way of breathing?

It was the kind of question he longed someday to answer, the kind of question that made medicine endlessly fascinating. He had learned much at Montpellier, but Helga had taught him in a few short months more than he dreamed an unschooled woman could know. There was a logic in her herbs and potions he had missed in his studies of humors and purging.

Beyond Helga's knowledge were the Arabians, with whom he had a burning desire to study; their excellence was renowned.

"Ah, Solomon," said his brother in disgust. "You dream and leave me when I speak to you of pressing things." He stalked away, calling over his shoulder, "It is no wonder you cannot play chess! You have no brain!"

Smiling at Hershel's impatience, Solomon let him rush ahead while he lingered, watching birds pick along the banks. His gaze fell upon the silhouette of Esslingen's castle, nestled on a hill alongside the Rhine. From this distance it looked small, a toy for a child, and beyond it rose the Vosges, blue against the sky.

It was a reassuring sight, torn from a more peaceful, less crowded time. Long ago. Solomon smiled, thinking of the beauty contained now within those walls—a princess or an angel, with lips lush and ripe as strawberries . . .

His flesh grew warm, and for a long moment, he let himself dwell upon the beauty of the girl he'd seen in Helga's garden. After only one glimpse of her, she haunted him at odd moments.

He thought of Hershel's warning. Solomon knew he was weak in matters of the flesh. Women. He sighed. There were so many beautiful women! He found them endlessly alluring—their eyes, their hair, their swaying bodies, their lilting laughter. There was a promise of pleasure in their soft mouths and clean hands and white breasts.

And it seemed as long as he could remember, there had been girls willing to share their glories with him—the daughters of merchants and stray gypsies and pretty peasants and lusty married women, bored with their lot. Precisely because he'd been approached so often, because he knew himself to be weak in matters of lust, his brother need not have worried. Solomon allowed himself to think of the treasures of women, of *many* women, happily and hungrily, but he never allowed his attention to be fixed upon one single beauty for more than a little while. Thus were his passions satisfied and thwarted all at once. It was a simple matter of discipline.

So as he walked back through town, even though it was Sabbath and he should have at least tried to keep his thoughts pure, he admired every girl and woman he saw, covertly but thoroughly. Thus was the beauty of the angel in the castle purged again from his mind.

Three days flew by before Rica could find leave again to return to Helga's cottage. She was eager to tell the old woman about Etta's triumph at supper one evening, about her response to the handsome Rudolf, ah—about all of it.

It wasn't until she entered the yard that she admitted she had also hoped to find the young man Solomon there. Upon seeing only Helga grinding rosemary on a stump, she felt an irrational sense of disappointment.

"Hey, my pretty," Helga greeted her. "Sit down and help me, girl." Her red face shone with a film of perspiration, and her skirt immodestly showed her calves. "Oh, and don't be looking at me that way. If you were an old woman like me, you'd lift your skirts to the wind, too."

Rica smiled, sinking down upon a stool. "It is a hot day," she agreed, then lifted her surcoat over her head and hung it on a tree. Even in her tunic, her skin felt sticky. She envied Helga her age and freedom.

"What will you have me do?" she asked. "I am yours this whole afternoon to do your bidding." The words were teasing, but both knew how Rica prized her forays to the cottage.

Helga handed over the mortar and pestle. "Grind away. And when you've finished, I could use a bit of weeding in the gardens. My old back ails me."

"Mmmm." Head bent, Rica asked innocently, "Where is your helper? Have you chased him away so quickly?"

"Well, I'll not be working *him* that way. Too many

things to teach before he goes back to his fancy school." She heaved her considerable frame upright. "You know my thoughts on physicians, you do. If I can send one off with some knowledge of true healing, I've paid for a goodly number of my sins." She grinned, showing a mouthful of broad white teeth, teeth of which she was inordinately proud. Still had every one she'd grown, she was fond of boasting.

Rica smiled, breathing the pungent scent of crushed rosemary. "Of course," she teased, "it is *painful* for you to have such a healthy young man in your clutches for hours each day."

"Oh, it's a sore trial," Helga agreed, shaking her head. "Were I a maid . . ."

"Were you a maid, you'd keep your skirts down like the rest of us."

Helga pinched her cheek. "See that you remember it, girl."

Rica flushed. So her interest had been noted. "I am no fool for men, like some I know," she said, piqued.

"It only takes one man to make a woman a fool," Helga returned, her voice light. "None are above it." With that, she bustled toward the cottage.

Rica ground the rosemary, staring off toward the mountains, hazy blue beneath a heat-whitened sky. Sweat trickled over her scalp and between her breasts, both tickling and annoying. A fat old fly buzzed and lit upon her shoulder; apparently liking the taste of the salt on her flesh, he returned persistently. In the forest beyond the cottage, grackles and merles and starlings twittered and sang. It was hot, but peaceful, too.

Away from the castle, she always felt a sense of lightness. Here, in Helga's simple yard, she could just sit and be, without worrying over Etta or her father, or wondering whether the girls in the brewhouse were ruining the ale.

The rattle of a harness reached her. Helga's voice, bawdy and teasing, boomed out. It was the peddler, no doubt, come to flirt and talk awhile with the midwife. Helga would fetch him a cup of ale and together they'd while away an hour or so, exchanging ripe faux invitations that neither would ever act upon. A safe and pleasant entertainment, Rica supposed, and wondered if she'd flirt with peddlers when she was old.

She leaned against the tree, feeling rough bark against her back. Dappled shade fell over her skirts, looking cool, but providing little shield from the heat. She blew a strand of hair from her eyes.

She had no idea how long she sat there, with the mortar between her palms. From time to time, she stopped to push her dampened hair from her face and pull the linen of her tunic from her slick skin. She was in the act of lifting the fabric from her flesh when someone held out a cup of water to her.

"Your face is flushed, *fräulein*," said a deep male voice in concern. "You must have some water."

With a shiver, Rica recognized the voice. She'd heard him speak no more than a handful of sentences, but the rich sound was burned into memory. She looked up to find Solomon standing alongside her, a faint smile on his mouth, a wooden cup grasped between his extraordinarily beautiful, clean fingers. She accepted the offering without looking away. "Thank you."

In deference to the heat, he carried his heavy jupon, wearing only a light tunic, loose at the throat to show a brown chest and dark curls of hair. "You should take care with this heat, you know," he said, settling on the stump Helga had vacated, his hands clasped loosely between his knees. "Perhaps the work would wait until another day."

The water slid down her throat, deliciously cool. It

seemed she could feel it all the way into her belly, and for a moment, the sheer pleasure of the feeling outweighed even the glowing presence of the young man.

"Ah, no," she said when she'd drained the cup. "If I leave this work, there is only more awaiting at the castle—most of it hotter and more boring than this. I'd rather sit here."

He smiled, pulling a plume of grass from its sheath to chew on. "So it is with me." A tumble of black curls fell over his forehead. With a careless gesture he tossed them back. "My brothers tease me for walking out here every afternoon, but otherwise my father would find some unpleasant task for me to attend."

"Yes." She felt a swirl of awareness and looked away, afraid her thoughts would show.

He seemed to be perfectly at ease. "I saw Helga with the peddler. Do you wish for help?"

"Oh, it is a job for only one, I think."

"Well, then, do you mind if I sit with you until Helga is finished?"

"I do not mind," she said quietly. But perhaps she did. Perhaps she would do something foolish if he stayed, talking so easily to her. "You have been studying medicine?" she asked politely.

"For almost five years at Montpellier."

"And what brings you home so soon?"

He bent his head, using the feathery end of the grass to brush a beetle away from his toe. "Have you not heard of the pestilence, *fräulein?*"

"Only a little. Is it so bad?"

"They say ships with the whole crew dead washed to shore in Italy," he said. "From what I saw, I know it to be true."

Rica frowned, turning the mortar in her hands. "My father's vassal believes it is a punishment from God."

"Do you share his belief?"

"No. Do you?"

"No." A slow smile spread over his beautiful mouth, giving a warm glow to his dark eyes. Rica suddenly saw a flicker of something hot and pointed, an expression he hid quickly behind lowered lids—so quickly Rica wondered if she had imagined it.

"Where is your sister today?" he asked, twirling the grass between his fingers.

"She stayed behind to do her tapestry. She does not come abroad with me often."

"Helga said she will not speak."

"She is very timid. She speaks to me, and to our dog. I think she will begin to speak to a vassal because he is beautiful." She bit her lip, realizing she had said more than she intended. "Did Helga tell you also what happened to her?"

He shook his head and sunlight glossed a hundred loose curls.

"When we were six," Rica said, "my mother and sister had been out to gather blackberries and my mother turned her ankle, so they were slow getting back." Between her palms, the mortar turned slowly. "Soldiers found them just after dark and carried them to a meadow. There were six of the soldiers. They took my mother by force, over and over until she died, and then began on my sister."

Rica looked at him, seeing in his face not the aghast horror she saw so often when the story was told, but a resigned and terrible sorrow.

"So," he said, "her timidity has reason."

"Yes."

He looked at her steadily. This time, his gaze softened. She felt it trail like the tip of a finger over her cheek and jaw, and slide over her mouth. Without thinking, she returned his exploration, seeing the plumpness of his lower lip and the fine brown skin at the neck of his loosened tunic.

The bowl of rosemary slipped from her fingers and fell to the earth. With a small cry of embarrassment and chagrin, Rica bent over to retrieve it at the same instant Solomon also reached for it. Their hands brushed. His hair swept her cheek, smelling of sunshine and heat. Rica wanted to press her mouth into it.

Endlessly, the moment stretched, with his fingers over her own, his head bent over her breast, his hair upon her face. He looked up.

Rica met his eyes almost against her will, feeling a thready pulse in her veins. Up close, she saw there was no break in the color of his eyes at all—the black irises faded into the black middles, giving them the look of a pond at night.

Yet, like a pond, his eyes glimmered and shifted. A puzzled frown touched his clear, wide brow. "If it did not seem mad, I would swear I knew you," he said.

A ripple of the same recognition had whispered through Rica upon seeing him the first time, and in an effort to hold to sanity, she tried now to recall where they might have met. Perhaps it was only as simple as passing in the roads of the city.

She shook her head infinitesimally.

Flushing, Solomon stood and handed her the pestle. "Forgive me," he said with a short, formal bow. "But it would be best if I find some other task for my hands."

Rica did not raise her eyes. "Yes," she said softly. "That would be best."

It was only when he had turned away, flinging his jupon over his shoulder, that she allowed herself another glimpse of him.

It only takes one man to make a woman a fool.

Rica knew how foolish this particular attraction was. Poets and poems aside, to indulge even a fleeting fantasy would be a lunatic's move.

In sudden panic, she gathered the herbs and donned her surcoat, and found Helga still chatting with the peddler. Rather than interrupt them, she gave a little wave as she passed a few feet away, knowing she would have to explain the next time she came. In the morning. He came only afternoons.

But as she whistled for Leo, she felt Solomon's gaze once more. She turned to find him standing in the shadow of a grove of pines, watching her. She lowered her head and kept walking.

For the first time, she realized all the poems she so loved were grounded in tragedy. Of tragedy, she'd already had her fill.

From his shadowy post, Solomon watched her stride away toward the castle that loomed atop the hill, all whitewashed stone and bleakness.

There had always been talk of the great beauty of Charles der Esslingen's twin daughters, the sort of lusty talk men indulged while in their cups.

Once more, he was stunned. This afternoon, leaning against the tree, staring so dreamily toward the hills, she had been the most singularly beautiful creature he'd ever seen. Her tunic, damp with the heat of the day, clung to her breasts and waist and long thighs, revealing her form in a manner that seized him fiercely. He had watched, stricken, as she tugged the fabric from her flesh; watched as it settled back like a fond hand over her graceful curves.

He swore under his breath. Too much. In two meet-

ings, he absorbed more deeply the details that made
her than of dozens of women he saw every day. Tearing his gaze from the sway of her hips, he focused upon
the cool blue mountains. Discipline. His few moments
of admiring this beauty were ended.

His father would have been proud. Solomon had
always been the mote in his father's eye, the son he
chased down from rooftops and yanked away from
fights and punished for sneaking away to the river. It
had been Solomon that Jacob had found kissing a
cousin when they were seven, just as an experiment;
Solomon that Jacob whipped for less innocent
explorations when he was ten and thirteen.

His father no longer had to intervene and Solomon
took pride in his discipline. Not even a beauty so
great as Rica's could tempt him.

But into the glow of pride slipped a vision of her
ripe breast, poised inches from his mouth a few
moments before—as if in invitation. For one blazing
instant, he had allowed himself to imagine tipping
forward to kiss that rise of soft white flesh.

Instead, he'd swallowed his desire, only to look up and
find himself ensnared in the lure of her wide and innocent
eyes. Remembering now, he sensed a ripple passing over
his skin. In her eyes had been the most alluring and curious combination of innocence and seduction; her mind
did not know what her body promised.

Henceforth he would arrange to come in the morning to Helga. It was only a few months until the pestilence spent itself, surely. Then he could return to
Montpellier.

Relieved, he wandered back to Helga's yard to grind
the rosemary that Rica had begun. Discipline and
avoidance. Together they would protect him from this
dangerous attraction to a forbidden woman.

3

The sound of the cock crow filtered into Rica's chamber along with the first, faint light of day. A drizzling mist fell from low clouds. Rica shivered a little as she unshuttered the embrasure and pulled her wrap more closely about her.

On the river, a barge passed slowly on the current, and peasants from a village to the north walked already toward the city, a wagon loaded with wool behind them. Rica wished she were among them, walking toward the bustle of the market, toward the noise and color and bargaining. From her narrow window, she could see Strassburg, obscured somewhat by the mist. It looked like a fairy kingdom, soon to disappear.

It was her conscience she wished to submerge in that noise and confusion, in the pleasure of baubles and fine fabrics. That same conscience had awakened her long before cockcrow.

As if to bring the point to bear, the sound of the bells for Prime rang softly in the air. She sighed and pressed her forehead to cool stone.

Today she must make her confession. Although it had been several days since the disturbing encounter with Helga's student, she had not yet solved how best to accomplish her ablution.

It was not only the afternoon in Helga's yard that concerned her, for that had happened quickly and she had carried herself quickly away from temptation. Even the old priest would laud her effort. There was, she thought wryly, no sin in the act of being tempted, only indulging.

Or was there? Thoughts were sins—she had confessed and been absolved of many evil thoughts.

Moving from the window, Rica began to pace. She had deliberately taken herself to Helga's in hopes of seeing the beautiful young man again, even knowing he would never be her husband. Was there sin in that action? Was there sin in looking upon a beautiful person? God had created all beauty, even that of men. Would not admiring the perfection of a man be giving glory to the Lord, much as admiring the perfection of the sky?

Here she let go of a snort. There was the small matter of the difference in her thoughts as she admired the sky and as she admired the man. They somehow kindled quite different visions.

So how to confess it? She pursed her lips and settled the matter, knowing even as she did so that there was a certain duplicity involved. It could not be helped. Priest he was, and as such sworn to keep her private thoughts private, but if she were in danger or he perceived her to be so, she had no doubt he would alert her father.

And Rica would find herself married in a trice.

It was not that she did not wish to marry. She simply did not wish to do so *yet*. Marriage would mean leaving her father and her sister, would mean leaving all she knew and found dear. Forever.

Restlessly she leaned on the embrasure, looking down toward newly planted fields and the vineyards sloping down a hill. Everything was covered with a faint greenish gray mist.

Every night since the afternoon at Helga's, Rica had found her thoughts upon Solomon. Each night as she closed her eyes to sleep, she remembered the brush of his hair upon her cheek and the hot black eyes and the wide, apple-red mouth. His rich laughter hung with ghostly insistence in her ear.

The first night, she had pushed away the ribbons of memory. But no matter how she guarded the gates of her mind, persistent visions of him slipped through. Finally she had yielded to the pleasure they gave, the warm tingling they spread through her, night after night. It seemed a small sin.

Why did this man stick so ferociously in her thoughts? There were many men who flirted with her, men of great virility who had made plain they would take her gladly to wife for the pleasure of bedding her.

She had never given a moment's thought to any of them. None of them had spoken to her as Solomon did, as if she were a creature of reason with thoughts in her own right. No man had ever expressed curiosity over her musings.

He spoke with her as if she were his equal.

Even the thought of his voice sent a lingering ripple of that dangerous restlessness through her limbs. Perhaps the priest was right. The illicit poetry of which she'd grown so fond had left the mark of lust upon her.

She straightened suddenly. Brooding would certainly give no help. Shivering in the dampness, she washed and dressed quickly. There were chores to be done before mass.

* * *

"Forgive me, Father, for I have sinned." Rica knelt upon the stone flags, taking pleasure in the cold of them against her knees. Through the thin linen screen, she could hear that the old priest's breathing had eased with the cooler weather and perhaps the tea she had brought for him to drink.

She twisted her rosary between her fingers and found herself confessing a multitude of minor sins— losing her temper with the worse-tempered cook, who refused, once again, to listen to Rica about her father's diet and had given him a rich pasty. She confessed to the small duplicity she and Etta had practiced at supper one evening—she playing Etta, Etta playing Rica with bangles and a low-cut gown.

The memory made her smile. Etta, under the rich attention of Rudolf—who thought himself to be charming Rica—had bloomed. She said nothing, but Rudolf seemed to think little of this; wine had made him full of himself.

Father Goddard made a small noise and Rica knew he, too, was amused.

There had been no dreams of bloody revenge this week, for which Rica silently gave thanks. And she had read none of the forbidden poems.

"I have another sin to confess, Father," she said softly, bowing her head. A rush of heat stole into her cheeks. For a moment, she wished desperately to spill all of her wanton longings, to tell the priest and be absolved of her sins.

Her pause stretched so long the priest prompted her gently. "There is no sin so deep the Savior cannot cleanse it."

Rica squeezed her eyes closed. In a rush, she said,

"I think my thoughts have been overtaken by the demon of lust, Father," she said in a mortified voice. "I have entertained many impure thoughts about a certain man this week."

"Ah." His voice was gentle. Perhaps even understanding. "It is a common enough sin for a girl of your years," he said. "It is time you married. Have you any other sins to confess, my child?"

Vastly relieved, Rica sighed. "No, Father."

Her penance was remarkably light, Rica thought, emerging from the chapel into gray day. For a moment she stood just beyond the archway, uneasy with the knowledge that she had not fully confessed.

The drizzle had eased a little. In no hurry, Rica wandered toward the kitchen gardens, which lay wet and perky at one end of the bailey. Against the gray day, the green of the plants fairly hummed. The sight eased her. She bent to pluck dead blossoms from a tangle of beans, smelling wet earth and decaying leaves as her hems dragged the ground.

To one side were the modest herb gardens that served the ordinary needs of the castle. Peonies thrived, their bright pink heads dotted with lingering moisture. There were fine stands of lavender, the blooms gloriously purple, their leaves a soft gray-green. Rica pinched a stalk and lifted her fingers to her nose.

"Mistress?" said a voice behind her. "Cook's ailing. She sent for ye."

Rica followed the girl to the kitchens, where the cook sat in a corner, holding her belly, an unearthly moan cutting through the clatter and noise. Rica knelt beside her. "What is it?"

"A terrible pain in my gut," she said, then in a lower voice, "and blood in my piss this morning."

Stones, Rica thought. It wasn't the first time Matilda had suffered thus. "Go to your chamber and I will fetch Helga." Distractedly, she patted the woman's shoulder as she scanned the faces assembled. "Gertrude," she said, and a small, buxom woman stepped forward, her hair contained beneath a tightly tied scarf. "See to the morning meal and I will come help you later with supper."

To another girl, she said, "Help her to her room. Give her some chamomile if she'll take it."

Lifting the hood of her cloak, she made for Helga's cottage, pleased that whatever the means, she could be abroad on such a gloomy, soft morning.

At the cottage, it was plain Helga had already been called away. The cat rubbed Rica's skirts, meowing hungrily. Churned mud in the yard told of horses riding through some time ago, for the edges of the hoofprints were blurred and softened by the rain. A birthing, no doubt. At a loss, Rica picked up the damp cat and let him curl against her as she scratched his ears. He meowed again, as if to tell her that he enjoyed the ministrations, but it was only an ephemeral expedient.

Rica grinned. "Oh, you'll surely starve, you poor thing. A meal or two missed would be good for you. She spoils you—cats are supposed to chase mice for their meals."

The cat opened one yellow eye in censure, and Rica laughed. Enjoying the silence and the comfortable companionship of the animal, she wandered through the wet gardens, trying to jog her memory. What did one do for stones? The sad faces of pansies caught her eye. Yes, that was right. Pansy and yarrow. She frowned, trying to remember the rest.

A crack of branches came from the forest and Rica turned, hoping it was Helga. Instead, a hooded man emerged. Water from the sodden trees clung to his shoulders and hood. Not until he was nearly upon her did he lift his head.

Solomon.

She could not quell the sudden, quick leap of her heart. In the dark cloak, with the hood framing his face, he looked somehow mysterious and dangerous. He was a large man, and sturdy. For the first time she realized that his thick tumble of hair was all that made him seem youthful. Now those curls were hidden and she saw that his face carried the unmistakable hard lines of a man full-grown, a man well acquainted with the foolish fantasies of maidens.

As if he could read her mind, Rica flushed.

He paused a foot or two away from her. "What brings you out on such a dark day, *fräulein?*"

Rica let the cat go and gestured nervously toward the cottage with hands that felt suddenly clumsy. "The cook has stones, I think, and I came to fetch Helga for her. It appears she has been called away."

Solomon looked at the cottage and back to Rica, his lips twitching. "So it appears." With his hands folded before him, he said, "Perhaps I may be of assistance."

She hesitated. If she did not accept his offer, she would either have to wait for Helga—and a birth could sometimes be a lengthy thing—or send a messenger into Strassburg for another doctor. "If I send to town, the physician will likely kill my cook with purgings and bloodletting," she said and measured him. "You've not yet learned the more serious butcheries of your trade."

He laughed, tossing his head back in genuine amusement. The hood fell away from his hair, and Rica found her eyes on the even brown skin of his throat. "A smooth and terrible insult," he said. "But perhaps there's some truth to it."

His rich smiling eyes sent a memory of her imaginary kiss through her mind. She bowed her head. If she walked to the castle with him alone, would her traitorous impulses lead her into another sin?

And yet, there was no help for it. "You will come?" she asked, striving for a formal tone.

He inclined his head, then paused. "What have you to treat her?"

"Nothing very much." She frowned toward the gardens. "I was trying to think—yarrow and pansy is all I remembered."

"So, you *are* a lazy student," he remarked.

Rica nearly bristled, but she caught the gleam in his eye. How could she keep herself aloof if he teased her? She smiled reluctantly. "I am content to learn only what I must."

"Lazy and honest," he said with a grin. "Hmmmm." He gestured toward the cottage. "Helga has what we need."

They walked to the cottage and he lifted his chin toward the eager cat. "Find him a morsel to eat while I gather the herbs."

The cottage was dim in the gray day, but homey enough. Herbs in various states of readiness hung from the beams on the ceiling, their scent agreeably mingling with the old smell of a cook fire.

With an air of confidence Rica found reassuring, Solomon riffled through the jars and bottles and boxes on the shelves. In her turn, Rica found a pot of stew left from the meal Helga had cooked and spooned a bit into a battered wooden bowl, shaking her head as she did so. "Truly spoiled, you are," she said to the cat and patted his haunches.

Solomon finished and waited at the threshold of the open door. A wash of pale light touched one side of his face. "Shall we?" he said with a courtly gesture, indicating Rica should precede him.

Refusing to allow herself the smallest of hesitations, she picked up her skirts and bowed her head to pass him. But even before she reached the door, she could smell him—freshly washed with undernotes of something she thought might be frankincense.

Determined, she stepped forward. Holding her breath, she began to move by, feeling the press of his cloak against her body, the brush of a hard thigh against her hand. Again the size of him surprised her—her head barely met his shoulder and she was no small girl. She glanced up at him for an instant, simply to measure his height.

Or so she told herself. As soon as she did it, she knew it was a lie; she wanted only to see up close again the depths of those immeasurably black eyes and the curve of his lip.

As if she had swayed, his hand came up to guide her safely through the doorway. But instead, Rica stopped, almost against her will, to look at him face-to-face.

For a long moment, neither of them moved. His breath touched her cheek, and she felt the cushion of layers of wool between them. His gaze was somber.

It was he that gently turned away, motioning with one hand for her to proceed.

Blinded with humiliation over her boldness, Rica stumbled, and only his firm grip kept her from dumping herself ignobly in a puddle of mud. Flushing, she righted herself and shook his hand away. To hide her quick, unaccountable tears, she strode toward the muddy road, hearing him follow more slowly behind.

After a moment, Rica managed to take control of

her wild embarrassment. Stiffly, she slowed and allowed him to catch up with her.

They were shrouded in mist. Trees along the road were barely visible ghosts of black. As if they had been sealed inside a bubble, the world beyond them disappeared. It was oddly still and intimate.

She took a breath. "You must think—" she began, unsure how to phrase her apology.

"Oh, I do," he cut in smoothly. "I think a great deal about a great many things. Have you ever noticed, for example, how many fevers follow weather like this?" He looked at her, a gentle light in the black eyes, a light that told her he did not mind, that she need not embarrass herself further.

Grateful, Rica smiled her encouragement. "It had not occurred to me to think in such ways."

"What then do you think of in idle moments?"

"Idle moments?" she echoed dryly.

"Or when your hands are busy and your mind must wander."

"I think of ways to make my sister well," she began. "And remember all the legends or poems I have read." A long thick branch lay in the grass alongside the road, and she bent to pick it up to use as a walking stick. "I think about what other places must be like."

He smiled. "Which other places? England and France? Do you wish to sit in the courts of the monarchs?"

"No." She looked at him. "I wonder about the places where the Crusaders rode."

"Do you?" A quizzical expression crossed his brow. "How came you to wonder of those places?"

"My father told me about them. He heard the stories himself as a child."

"I have a painting of Egypt," he said, "brought by one of the merchants to my father."

Rica quelled a quick bite of envy, then laughed. "I am jealous!" she exclaimed. "Tell me, how does it look?"

"Hmmm. How does it look?" He inclined his head. "There are white spires of the mosques, and a cruel warrior with a scimitar." He cut her a teasing look. "Bloody."

"Do you think that frightens me?" she asked with a smile. "Do I seem to you a foolish maid, prone to fainting away at a little blood?"

He stopped and stared at her. The hot, pointed expression filled his eyes, and Rica saw him swallow. "No," he said. His voice was low and intimate.

In the silent gray fog, they were alone. The knowledge rippled between them as they stood face-to-face, a fearsome and dangerous thing.

His eyes swept her face, and he lifted his hand, as if to touch her cheek. Then he dropped it again. "Perhaps I will leave the painting with Helga for you," he said.

Rica nodded, afraid her voice might waver with emotion if she tried to speak.

He glanced away, in the direction of the castle, then back to her. "I will come mornings to Helga. Come you in the afternoon."

Her heart soared and plummeted as his meaning sunk in. She was not alone in her longing, but he knew the foolishness as well as she. She squeezed her eyes closed once, quickly. "That would be best."

They began to walk again, and the castle walls appeared suddenly through the mist. Rica led him to the cook in silence, ignoring the curious glances of the men on the walk and the covert glances of the serving girls.

The cook's cries rang out as they reached her quarters. Solomon looked at Rica. She gestured with a sweep of her hand for him to enter the room.

Neither spoke. Solomon knelt next to the pallet and asked questions of Matilda in a gentle voice as he touched her belly and sides with his clean hands. Somehow, watching him, Rica was reassured. He had the same calming effect upon the ruddy-faced, bad-tempered woman on the straw mattress. Rica turned away, calling to a kitchen girl to bring hot water for an infusion.

Solomon heard the order and glanced over his shoulder with a minute shake of his head. His eyes cut toward the bloody stain showing on the cook's skirts. Rica nodded her understanding. The stone had been passed, and for now, at least, no tisane would be necessary to dissolve it within.

"You've done my work for me, *fräu*," Solomon said quietly. "In a day or so, you will be good as new."

The cook nodded wearily.

Solomon rose in a billow of wool. To Rica, he said, "Can you spare her for a few days, my lady? She will be weary."

Quelling an impulse to put the bad-mouthed bat right back to work, Rica licked her lips. "I suppose that depends upon whether she will offer me a promise."

Matilda's eyes flickered cannily. "*Ja*, mistress. No more tidbits for the master."

"Do you promise?"

"*Ja.*"

With exaggerated care, Rica bent over her stout figure and tugged the coverlet over her shoulder. "Rest as long as you need, then, Matilda. I will see to the kitchen."

To Rica's surprise, the cook's brilliant blue eyes softened. "Bless you, mistress."

Rica only nodded, realizing the woman was no

longer young. Creases and loose flesh marked her face. More kindly, she said, "I will send a girl to help you wash in a bit."

Outside, Rica led Solomon to the bailey gates, then reached into the pouch on her girdle for a coin.

"No, lady. I did nothing." He bowed formally. The drizzling rain dotted his curls with silvery beads, and Rica once more felt a painful catch in her chest.

"Thank you," she said.

For a moment, he held her eyes and she felt the heated pulse of his maleness through the cold mist; sensed once again that she was not alone in her wish to be less polite and more tangled. He tugged his hood over his head and stared down the road toward Helga's.

Then he turned back and Rica clasped her hands, hoping for she knew not what.

"Give her the tisane. It may be there is more than one."

She nodded.

Still he paused. Rica waited. When he still said nothing, she asked, "Is there more?"

"No." He turned and walked stiffly into the mist, disappearing like a specter. Rica watched him go, an odd stinging pain in her heart.

There was more. But he, no more than she, could say it.

4

The rain lasted only a few days, and summer returned with sunny azure skies and warm, thick afternoons. After the morning meal a week following her encounter with Solomon, Rica packed a loaf of bread and a chunk of cheese, fetched a large basket, then went in search of her sister and the dog.

Etta sat on a stone bench in the lower bailey. As Rica crossed the grassy enclosure, she smiled at the picture her sister made. Behind her stood pear trees with their offerings of young fruit. Vines climbed the stone walls. A stand of blooming lavender circled the trees, catching the color of Etta's gown. Her hair, loose below her barbette, shimmered silvery gold in the sunlight, and the ends trailed over the edge of the bench to brush a stand of gillyflowers. At her feet were a basket of fabric and her ever-present Leo, snapping at flies.

Rica settled on the bench. "What work have you found this morning?"

"A christening gown for Gertrude's niece." Etta displayed the tiny garment made of snowy linen. Embroidery in white silk edged the collar and sleeves.

"It's lovely."

Etta smiled softly at the praise.

"But," Rica said restlessly, "surely it will wait for another day? I promised Papa some berries for his supper. Will you go?"

"Not today." Etta sucked a bit of silk and rethreaded her needle. "I will sit here."

Rica nearly missed the flutter of her eyes toward the walk. A black-haired vassal paced there, but Rica knew Rudolf often appeared to converse and give direction to those below him in rank. She touched Etta's arm fondly. "So be it. I will take Leo for my company."

She bent with a jingle of bells and took up her basket. Her meal was tied snugly in a square of cloth at her waist. She whistled at the dog.

Etta stroked his ears and gave a single command. "Go."

From the gates, Rica took a slim path through the long grass that grew in the fields. Against the sky, the mountains were a dark, hazy blue.

Her task was a pleasant one. The bushes were heavy with their offerings of ripe, plump blackberries and she ate fully half as many as she picked. Leo snuffled around in the undergrowth, following the trail of some small creature, and dug on occasion through the earth for delectable tidbits.

She smiled at the monstrous animal and wiped her fingers on the grass. Leo suddenly went rigid and barked fiercely, the sound low and full of menace. A shiver of gooseflesh crawled on her arms. She whirled— and let go of a sigh of relief. It was only Rudolf.

Rica touched Leo's back in a gentling gesture. He sat down, but his ears remained alert.

"I have not approved of your father's wont to let you wander abroad alone," Rudolf said as he rode close. He smiled. "I see there is no cause to worry as long as your beast is with you."

Rica nibbled a berry, wondering what his purpose

might be in following her to this isolated grove. "He will tear the throat of a man if I give the word."

He laughed. "I pray thee, lady—say no word."

"What brings you so far abroad this morning, my lord? Are there bandits hereabout?"

"'Tis my duty to your father to oversee all his holdings." He gestured with a richly garbed arm and again gave her a smile, as if to belie his words. "I am only seeing to that which I am required by vow to do."

"Ah." Rica inclined her head. "'Tis duty that brings you out. I will not keep you then." She picked up her basket in one hand and caught her skirts with the other.

"I would have you stay a bit," Rudolf protested, and Rica glanced at him. A blush lit his cheeks.

She paused, wondering if the chatter of the servants was true. The rumors held that Rudolf was yet a virgin, more inclined to the priesthood than knighthood, though his valor was unquestionable.

The maids spoke scornfully of him, of the manner in which he rebuffed their flirtatious glances. Looking at him, Rica thought it was their longing that made them speak so sharply. Mounted upon a fine stallion and lit by a broad finger of sunlight that fell through the trees, he was nearly as beautiful as Etta had been, sitting upon the stone bench in the bailey. The chin and nose were strong, his eyes clear. Only his mouth flawed his face, for his lips were thin, reflecting the severity of his nature.

He was not to her taste, but she could see why Etta might love him. As Rica stood there in the dappled shade, with blackberry stains on her fingers, she made up her mind that Etta should have him.

She bit her lip, knowing the dimple in her cheek would appear, and lowered her eyes as befitted a shy maid. "It would be more seemly to speak in the company of the hall."

"Perhaps. But always you rush hither and thither, lighting only as long as a butterfly. I would have your whole attention."

She felt a little rush of nervousness at what she was about to do. Did she dare? And could Etta possibly follow through?

"You speak of my sister, I think," Rica said without raising her eyes. She leaned to retrieve the basket, knowing as she did so that his eyes would be fastened to the neckline of her gown, as they had been upon Etta's that evening at supper.

"No," he said, his voice a little hoarse. "I left your sister darning in the bailey. You are not so handy with a needle as she."

Rica bent her head, letting her hair fall forward, shielding her from view as she mulled how best to answer. He was no fool.

Finally, she lifted her chin and tossed her hair over her shoulder. "Not even my father knows who is Rica and who is Etta, my lord." She smiled. "How can you profess to know what a father does not?"

His gaze slid over her shoulders and the upper swell of her breasts, licking with lasciviousness at her young flesh. Rica felt a moment's pang. It would be unwise to miscalculate this man. Virgin he might well be, but a man nonetheless, with the lusts and passions of any man. Even now, there was a dark flush over his cheeks, a hard sheen in his eyes that Rica found frightening. Mayhap Etta would be consumed in such a fire.

She would find a way to ask Helga about such things. For now, the seed had been planted. "Come, Leo," she said to the dog. As if to reinforce her thoughts about the mounted man, Leo sent one last growl in Rudolf's direction.

"*Fräulein,*" Rudolf called from behind her.

Rica turned.

"Whichever you be, perhaps the two of you will sit with me at tonight's entertainment."

Rica gave him a smile, then walked with Leo into the shadow of the trees.

She walked a long time in the warm sunshine, her basket over her arm, her barbette in her hand. In a high meadow she paused to eat her meal of cheese and bread. It was hot and she shed her surcoat. She carried it over her shoulder.

Seduced by the warm day and the peace of the hours spent alone with no one to please but herself, she wandered toward the river Ill, to an isolated stretch surrounded by stands of pine and birch trees to which she came often when time permitted. Leo leapt joyfully into the water, and Rica settled in the shade of a pine to watch him.

It was a lazy, bright day. Much too warm. After a time, she shed her clothes to bathe in the cool water, as both Leo and she had known she would do.

Wading out to a deep pool, she submerged herself, shaking her hair to loosen the dust, glorying in the icy fingers over her scalp. She rubbed the sweat of her long walk from her arms and from between her breasts, then leaned against a submerged boulder and closed her eyes against the sunshine, hearing the call of crows and twitterings of sparrows and the chuckling of the river over stones.

The current swirled around her, cupping a breast here, stroking her belly there, circling an ankle and splashing her shoulders. At her feet, it was cold as ice, but warmed as it moved higher. The sun shone on her shoulders and through the water to her torso.

'Twas Paradise, she thought, and moved her arms lazily. Her thoughts drifted toward Solomon, with his thick tumble of hair and generous mouth. She called forth the memory of him outside the castle walls, turning to tell her just one more thing—the one thing he could not utter.

What would it be like if he were here in the water, too, swimming and bathing with her, his skin shining with water? What if he were laughing here, showing those fine white teeth? What if he were as naked as she—

She opened her eyes and straightened abruptly, sending water splashing outward. A short sound of frustration and dismay escaped her throat, and flushing, she buried her face in her hands, feeling shame sweep through her.

Sweet Mary, could she never escape her thoughts of him?

Hidden on a hill not far away, Rudolf crouched low in the shadow of a bush, watching the woman below. He told himself he had only followed her to puzzle out which sister she might be and to keep her safe should danger appear.

Had he known she sometimes escaped here to bathe? His crouching now in the trees would then be a sin. He frowned. Nay. Once he'd seen her return to the castle with wet hair, but he had not known she bathed, or that she wished to do so this fine warm afternoon.

In the water, she dipped her head backward to wet her hair and the ruddy tip of one slick breast broke the water. A rigid heat rushed to his loins. He closed his eyes.

But was she not his betrothed? Whether or not she knew it, her father had promised her to him. Therefore, it was no sin to look upon her with hunger. For his wife, a man could—nay, *should*—conceive a passion. Had not Saint Paul himself extolled the virtue of marriage?

He straightened and stared. As if to display her womanly treasures for his full approval, she stood up to wade from the water. Wet tendrils of her hair trailed over her arms and clung with exquisite accuracy to the swell of her hips. Her breasts were full and high, her belly smooth and flat, her legs slim and long and white. He groaned and touched himself once, then fisted his hand against the temptation. Soon enough, he'd bury himself between those long legs and swell her flat belly with his child.

A flash of white in the trees downriver caught his eye and Rudolf saw there was a man approaching the spot where Rica stood, naked and glorious. Wildly, he mounted his horse, cursing his choice to hide on this hill. Now he had to ride down it again.

Rica waded toward the bank and donned her kirtle. Her dog had disappeared. Unalarmed, she whistled for him. Almost immediately, he came crashing through the trees, noisy as a bull, his tongue lolling joyously. He paused by her a moment, then raced for the water's edge and plunged with delight into the river once more.

She laughed at his unadulterated pleasure, then abruptly stilled as she became aware that he had not returned through the forest alone.

For an instant, a deep and penetrating terror overtook her—until she realized it must be someone known to Leo, or he'd not have been so free and quiet. Slowly, she turned.

Solomon had stopped less than two feet from her, his jupon hanging unbuttoned over his tunic, his strong legs bare. In his hands he carried his shoes. His skin shone with the rosy gleam of a good scrubbing.

He stared without speaking and Rica became aware of the water streaming from her hair, wetting the soft cloth of her kirtle.

And yet, she could not move. His eyes, fiery with

desire, trapped her where she stood, as if he had cast a spell over her. Or perhaps, she thought, he was caught within the same evil net as she, and acted no more upon his own will than Rica did.

His gaze washed over her, lighting upon her shoulders and waist. The heavy curtain of her wet hair hid her breasts, but Rica felt them grow weighty with a sudden, restless ache.

She stared back at him, seeing a silver rivulet of water trail over the smooth flesh of his neck and through the curls of hair upon his chest.

He stepped toward her and Rica could see he was as moved as she. His chest moved with quick, shallow breaths. "It seems," he said in a low voice, "we share a favor for this part of the river."

Rica swallowed. "So it would seem," she whispered.

He stopped bare inches away from her. "I have cursed you," he said in a husky tone. He glanced away, then back again to her, and shook his head. His breath soughed over her face, smelling of mint. "You haunt my dreams."

He touched her cheek and Rica nearly swooned. She closed her eyes and caught his hand, pressing it between her cheek and her palm. It was hot and strong. "I will never be able to confess this," she whispered almost desperately.

"Tis madness," he agreed, his voice a low rasp.

The sudden, fierce barking of the dog shattered the moment. Solomon snatched his hand from her as if he were burned. "Dear God," he muttered, and stared at her as if she were a witch.

A sound of hooves in the forest reached them, and Solomon bent to retrieve Rica's clothes and basket. He hastily shoved them at her as she whistled for Leo, who bounded toward her, shaking water from his fur forcefully.

Terrified, Rica glanced at Solomon. He didn't hesitate, but dragged her, clutching her clothes, into a thicket of bushes. Leo struggled in behind them, and though he whined almost inaudibly, he shushed even that small noise at Rica's touch.

They were crowded hard in the small space, but neither moved. The hoofbeats came nearer, thudding in some hurry, then passed no more than a few feet away. Rica smothered a gasp as she spied the white boots of Rudolf's stallion. He had come after her.

As the sound faded into the distance, Rica became aware of Solomon once more. His knee was pressed against her thigh and a loop of her hair rested on his arm, soaking his sleeve. His side was pressed into hers and his body seemed extraordinarily warm. She stared at his hands with their scrubbed knuckles and clean nails, at the long gentle fingers and the hot strong palm that had lain against her cheek.

Abruptly, Solomon pulled away. "He is gone."

She followed him from the thicket of bushes into the lowering sunlight of the grove. Suddenly aware of her near-nudity in the thin wet shift, she donned her tunic. Nervously, she steepled her fingers and listened for the sound of hooves in the forest. "It was a vassal of my father's on that horse."

Solomon's face was grim. He pointed to a bluff. "He watched you—there. When I saw your dog, I thought it might be you he watched."

Rica lifted her chin. "Were you coming for a look yourself?"

His nostrils flared. "Perhaps you should not bathe in the forest again, lady."

"It has always been deserted here," she protested. Then, remembering the pagan thoughts of him that had filled her mind at the caress of the water, she bowed her head. "Perhaps I should not," she said softly.

With a low, growling sound, Solomon moved close. He stood before her and tipped up her chin. "Have no shame, Rica, for you are as God created you." A blazing light glimmered in his eyes. "I would give many years to be able to lie with you honestly."

She swallowed, pricked at his admission. "Men will often give much to have knowledge of a woman that makes their cock rise," she said, and turned her head from the grip of his fingers. "It was for the lust of men that so many laws were given women."

Shifting her skirts away from his feet, she bent to pick up her basket.

His hand curled around her arm. "Lust?" he said softly. "Is it lust that sends me dreams of you? Lust that makes me think of naught but the shimmer of your hair and the curve of your lips?"

Her mouth went dry. "I know not of those things," she whispered.

"Have you never tasted passion, Rica?" he whispered. "Nay, innocence is your cloak, for all that you drive men mad." His fingers brushed her cheek. "Lust is an evil thing, ugly and dark," he said quietly. "Lust is a word too small to speak of the dreams I have."

He stepped closer. "It is passion, Rica, that I feel when I see you, passion that haunts me when you are gone."

His breath, moist and warm, brushed her cheek. Rica raised her gaze. And it was again the day in Helga's garden, when his face had been so close.

"Forgive me," he whispered, but his head tilted and he moved slowly closer, until the full lips were poised a hair's breadth above hers. "I have never known a woman who moved me so," he murmured. He kissed her.

His mouth was mobile and firm, as luxurious upon her own as the water had been upon her body. He explored her lips with a curious mixture of hunger and hesitancy, expertise and caution, nibbling now, pressing and moving until Rica found her mouth parting of its own accord. Even then, he only used the tip of his tongue to taste her, to ribbon around the edges of her lips and parry with the tip of her tongue.

The heavy feeling returned to her breasts and spread thickly to her middle. Rica gave herself to the splendid taste of him. Her hands lit upon his arms for steadiness, and her basket bumped his hip.

In a hundred poems, she had read of kisses. She had not dreamed it would feel thus, so deep and swirling, as if her body had swelled and lightened, until she was near to floating in his loose embrace.

At last he lifted his head. His palms circled her cheeks, tender and powerful, and his eyes swept her face hungrily. "I would teach you passion, Rica."

"There are penalties," she whispered, riveted in the darkness of his eyes.

His jaw hardened. "Aye," he said with a bitter twist of his lips. "And I am a fool."

He backed away, watching her. Rica lifted her hand in wonder to touch her tingling lips. He froze, then turned and left her.

As if his presence had been all that held her upright, Rica sank to her knees on the ground as he stalked into the trees. Her mouth burned with the press of his lips; her tongue tingled with the ghostly image of his. Her heart skittered in her chest, as wild as a panicked bird.

Wanton.

In a crush of shame, Rica buried her face in her hands, her flesh burning with humiliation. She thought of Solomon looking at her as if she were some kind of demon, a she-devil come to torment him. She thought of him turning away in disgust.

Madness. 'Twas all madness. Her mind had been overtaken by some force outside herself the moment her eyes had fallen upon his face in Helga's garden.

And how she would free it, she did not know.

In the streets of Strassburg, the merchants and butchers were hawking the last of the day's goods. A ball of gold sunlight settled over the mountains and lent a gentle gilding to the scene.

Bemused, Solomon wandered through the streets toward home, admiring the hues of the stone walls and the dull gleam of thick glass in some of the windows. Two snaggle-toothed old women chuckled together near the well, and even they seemed beautiful.

The very air glowed with a sense of Rica. The gold light made him think of her hair, flowing in streamers over her shoulders. He passed the open door of an apothecary, and the scents from within momentarily blotted out the riper city odors; these, too, gave him a moment's pause, for his senses were flooded with the taste and scent of the woman who had kissed him.

No. He swallowed. Let him kiss her.

He was bewitched. He could not stop the burning he had for her. She haunted his every step, his every dream.

Only the plain walls of his father's house sobered him. As he approached the wooden gate, he smelled chicken and garlic thick in the air. The ring of his mother's voice, light and happy, floated down to him.

Even before she ushered him through the courtyard and into his chamber, her eyes bright with excitement, he knew visitors had arrived. Relations from Mainz, come for the wedding feast of Hershel and Raizel. They would sing and dance, laugh and gossip and eat.

Solomon sank to a bench in his chamber with a

sigh. He had no wish to join them. Their talk would be of weddings and sons, of business and survival. As it always had been, as it always would be.

Without enthusiasm, he shed his tunic and from his trunk pulled a freshly brushed velvet surcoat and the small embroidered hat he wore at home. As he took it out, the miniature painting of Egypt tumbled loose from its spot.

It was only a camel with white pointed spires of Cairo behind. Women in black veils gathered to one side, and a proud Muslim warrior with a scimitar stood victorious over a slain Christian knight. His father thought it grim.

Solomon inclined his head, and holding his coat on his arm, picked up the painting. The exotic promise of a faraway land was what had first drawn him to it. Even as a small boy, he had heard tales from the traders who sold his father his goods—fine carpets and spices and exotic woods—tales of elephants and camels; of pyramids and deserts and snake charmers. The traders spoke of the wisdom of the East, of knowledge only just dreamed of in the West. The tales had filled his young heart with wanderlust and a longing for adventure.

Now he still longed to travel there, but it was for the physicians he would go. At Montpellier, even the priests had been forced to admit the excellence of the Arabian physicians. Fully half the body of medical knowledge had come from the Moors.

He fingered the painting. One day he would stand in this street and see for himself. One day he would train with the finest physicians in the world.

So perhaps he would take Rica this little painting. It was forever emblazoned upon his brain, and she, perhaps, had never seen such a thing.

His brother Asher called to him. "Solomon! We shall starve waiting for you!"

Hastily, as if burned, he tossed the painting back into its place, then dressed. At the door he paused, trying desperately to remember how he usually went down, how he behaved when he had nothing to hide. He felt as if the impression of Rica had branded him obviously, as if her mouth hovered in a ghostly image over his own.

He cursed himself. How could he have let himself go so far past his promises to himself?

For a moment, he pressed his fingers to his brow. How could he not? In the deserted meadow, damp and fresh from the water, she had been more beautiful than a vision. His heart ached at even the memory.

Madness. Perhaps there was some clue in the stars. He would consult the astrologers on the morrow. They often had much to offer.

Thus steadied, he descended.

But the evening was cursed, as the day had been. There were too many people, too many aunts and uncles and cousins and friends, all crowding in, laughing and talking and teasing.

The instant Solomon took his place at the richly laid table, he spied the girl. She sat nearby his mother, who fluttered around the girl with an oddly protective air.

Raizel's sister, no doubt. And like Raizel, a beauty. Rich dark eyes and rosy cheeks; a glorious weight of hair and fine, clear skin with the shimmer of moonlight. She blushed when she looked up to find Solomon's eyes upon her, and her pretty mouth trembled.

He set his jaw and bent over his plate, knowing there would be a proper introduction, and pressure from his father. *"It is your obligation to marry!"*

Perhaps his father had grown weary of Solomon's insistence upon waiting. Perhaps there would be no choice this time—and he could not protest that she was ugly. He looked at Jacob, who sat at the head of the table, viewing the assembled guests with the pride and bearing of a monarch.

And why not? There were few Jews as rich as Jacob, few who could boast such finery as the gold-embroidered jupon that he wore, who could display such treasures as spread all around them in the lavishly furnished room. It was a plain house from without, even ugly, so as not to incite the jealousy of Christian neighbors. Within were luxuries even many of the petty barons of the town could not afford.

Not only was he rich, but Jacob had also sired five living sons—a wealth of children. His wife was beautiful, even in her age, and Jacob himself was yet a fine, handsome man with the same curls of his sons and a black beard only now showing signs of silver.

As if he felt Solomon's eyes upon him, Jacob turned. His mouth pursed in a speculative gesture, and his shrewd eyes narrowed. Solomon, alarmed, hastily bowed over his food.

Could it be that his father somehow knew of his attraction to Rica? Had someone seen him kiss her in the meadow?

No force in the world could have stopped the deep flush of shame that rose up his neck. It had been the thing that often gave him away as a boy; it had not so humiliated him in years.

With a sense of horror, he realized it was his own guilty thoughts that had put the color in his cheeks. He would go no more to Helga's, he vowed. He would not stray from within the walls of Strassburg itself. Surely, if he had no glimpse of her, this lunacy would burn itself clean.

For, dear God, it must.

5

Etta sat motionless as Rica wove flowers through her hair and tied her braids with golden thread. "You must listen to me, Etta."

"Yes."

"I see how you watch Rudolf and it is a good thing. A woman needs a husband." She frowned for a moment, remembering the white boots of Rudolf's steed as they flashed by the hiding place in the bushes. He had watched her, Solomon said.

And yet, perhaps he was only perplexed over the puzzle she had offered. "A man must be coaxed," she continued. "Do you understand?"

Etta raised her eyes. "Yes. I must not be shy."

"You may be shy, but not silent. A man will always talk about himself, but you must do the prompting." Pleased with her handiwork, she stepped back to admire Etta's hair. "Good," she said, and turned to the trunk by the wall that held her clothes. A blue velvet surcoat, trimmed with fur and embroidered with morning glories, was folded on top. She took it out and then pulled out a pale cotehardie as well. "Wear these," she said, and fetched out for herself simpler things, in dull colors.

"It is you he wishes to bed," Etta commented.

How often had Rica sworn to her father that Etta was not simple? And yet she had made the same assumption herself. She bit her lip, turning to meet her sister's eyes. "I know."

"You do not love him."

"No."

Etta reached for the rich blue surcoat. "He knows I am not you."

"He will not know anymore. I promise you, Etta. You shall have him, not I."

Nodding to herself, Etta shook her shoulders gently to let the fabric settle low, showing her creamy neck and shoulders, and the enticing swell of white breasts. "This is what men wish to see, is it not?"

Rica felt her heart thud once, uncomfortably, remembering how Rudolf's eyes had fastened upon her neckline this afternoon. Even Rica could see the enticement the low cut of the gown offered. She saw, too, the innocence that shone in Etta's serenely beautiful face. The combination might be dangerous. "Beware, little sister," she said softly. "He is a man."

Etta raised her eyes and a strange, secretive expression flashed over them for an instant. "Aye," she said.

She left the room, her skirts swishing upon the rushes, bells jingling softly. Rica stared after her, disturbed.

They were twins, identical to the dimple in their left cheeks, to the length of their lashes and the sound of their voices.

Could it be they had similar hearts, as well? Had Etta been roused from her long silence by passion?

Rica frowned in concern. Her own newly awakened passion was wrong, and she must find a way to resist temptation. She could not indulge her attraction to Solomon, especially after the kiss they had shared this afternoon. It still shamed her that she could have acted in such a way with him—and it was truly, deeply dangerous for both of them.

Buried in the heart of her sister was there such wantonness?

Was it the force of the stars that made Etta awaken to the passion of her heart, as Rica had also awakened?

Distractedly, she combed and braided her hair and donned the plain clothes. An astrologer could tell her what fate awaited them, what the stars of their birth had to say about the strange new events in their lives. Perhaps she could find leave to go to Strassburg on the morrow.

For suddenly, she felt uneasy.

Charles stayed in his room, and in his absence, Rudolf felt free. He ate well and drank readily of mead, filling the cups of Etta and Rica as often as he filled his own. Surely a little wine would loosen those tongues and trip them in their game—which girl was Rica?

The minstrels assembled in the gallery and Rudolf leaned toward the girl next to him. Rica, he thought. Her face was soft with drink, her eyes deep violet. "I sought you in the forest this afternoon, lady," he said quietly.

"No, my lord. Today I did not go abroad."

Puzzled, he glanced toward the other girl, who stared at the lute player with glassy-eyed fascination. "It was you in the garden?"

She lowered her gaze to look at her hands, folded in her lap, and dimpled prettily. "Perhaps."

"Nay," he said hoarsely, remembering the proud, uplifted breasts shining with water. As if drawn against his will, he measured that same flesh now with his eyes. His loins grew heavy. "'Twas you I saw bathing in the river."

Her eyes flew open to meet his, startled. An odd, fleeting fury crossed her features.

Contrite, Rudolf cursed himself. His caution was gone—insanity and lust had taken its place. "I sought only to protect you."

A flush crawled over her delicate white skin and she lowered her lashes once again. "I am ashamed to have been seen so."

"You are as beautiful as—" he struggled, trying to think of suitable words, "as our Holy Mother. You have no need to be ashamed."

A servant bent to the other girl, toward Etta—he was sure it was she now—and whispered. Etta nodded and murmured something in her sister's ear. There was a quick exchange of words between them, then Etta rose and departed.

"My father is not well," Rica said quietly.

The lutes and drums banged to a merry start. "Shall we begin the dancing?"

Gracefully, Rica rose. "As you wish, my lord."

Ah, what a wife she would make! As he held out his arms, smelling lavender on her skin, he congratulated himself heartily. Today he had played the courtly lover well. Charles would be pleased.

Rica hurried up the circling stairs toward her father's chamber, worried that his illness had taken a turn for the worse. In truth she was glad to escape the hall. It was a strain to be silent at the meal, to listen to each word Etta spoke for fear she would misstep herself and give the game away.

Wine had loosened her sister's tongue, and

Rudolf was well into his cups. All would be well now.

As she entered her father's solar, he looked up and scowled. "Where is your sister?"

Rica glanced at her drab tunic and sighed. "I am my sister, Pappi. I am Rica." She settled next to his bed on a small wooden stool, looking in concern at the flush in his cheeks. "What say you? Was it a goose or a fat cut of pork? And who gave it to you?"

He waved a hand. "'Twas neither. I hunted with my hawk this morning and grew overtired."

The room was too warm. A bright fire blazed on the hearth in spite of the season, lending a reddish glow to the walls.

"Papa, you must—"

"Ah, girl, do not preach at me!" he roared. "I asked for your company, not your shrewish lectures."

Rica narrowed her eyes. "A tantrum will only make your chest ache all the more." With a swish of her skirts, she stood up and restlessly poked at the fire. "I'll not stay if you take your temper out on me."

He glowered at her a moment more, then a reluctant smile spread over his broad, handsome face. "You were born a queen, *liebling*," he said with a chuckle. "It wearies me so to be trapped here, I fear I do you an injustice."

Rica relented. Chin in the air, she settled back upon the stool. "Company I have. Will you play dice?" she offered.

"Nay. Just sit with me." He touched the brown hem of her mantle with a frown. "What game perform you with your sister?"

Rica was wise enough to know her father would not approve her plan to win Rudolf for Etta. "'Tis only a diversion, meant to amuse."

"Ah, well, it brings light to your sister's eye," he conceded. "No harm in that."

From below came the faint echo of music, a haunting pipe, and lutes, and a drum. As Rica listened, the music stilled and a single voice rang out, the rich tenor of a troubadour.

"What think you of Hugh for Etta, daughter?" Charles asked suddenly.

"Hugh, the horseman?"

"The one."

Rica plucked at the buttons on her sleeve, mulling her answer. "He is fair and good, but think you it wise to offer her?"

Charles fell silent. After a moment, he reached for her hand. "I am ailing, child. I would see you both well settled before—"

"Do not say it!" Rica cried, gripping his sturdy fingers.

His sharp blue eyes flickered. "Very well. I am pleased to see you are so fond," he said, amused.

"Pappi—" she began, and stopped, wondering how to tell him, to hint to him that Rudolf might make a better mate for Etta.

"Have you some burden, *liebling?*"

For a moment, she peered into his face in the flickering light, trying to discern the future on his beefy features. "Nay," she said at last. She would wait. Her father saw how improved Etta seemed to be; in time, perhaps, he would see that Etta would make a fine wife to the knight. There was time.

Instead she coaxed him into a hand of cards, then when he wearied, left him with a kiss to his brow.

Faintly the music floated through the halls as Rica made her way through the passage. On the stairs, she paused, thinking she ought to see how Etta fared.

But in truth, her heart was heavy. The world seemed a sad dark place this night, and she could not say why. She made for the quiet of her own chamber.

As she neared the doorway, a shadow emerged from the other direction and Rica started, then saw it was the priest, a candle held aloft, a thick book in his arms.

The mere sight of him was enough to bring a rush of guilt to her heart. "Good even, Father," she said quietly.

"Rica. I had hoped to find you."

She smiled. "Not even my father knew which girl I was tonight—and yet, you, in the gloom, name me rightly."

"Perhaps God lends me clear sight." He shifted to lift the bound manuscript from his hands. "I have come to ease your heart, my child." A twinkle in his eye betrayed the solemnity of his words. "You have no mother. I took the liberty of finding that which might prepare you for the glory of your marriage."

For an instant, Rica was certain he saw her sin burning on her flesh. Then she realized he referred to her confession of lustful thoughts. How small that sin now seemed! In a whisper, she accepted his offering. "Thank you."

He winked. "There is more to God's wishes than prayers, child."

Rica watched him amble away, candle aloft and flickering in the drafts of the passage, his rotund figure rocking. At least he no longer coughed.

With a sigh, she entered her chamber and touched her candle to the rushlight before she sank to her bench. As he often did, Father Goddard had marked pages for her to read from one of his precious volumes.

For a moment she was thankful for his presence in her life—kindly and sprightly and wise. He had given her all the treasures she deemed powerful by releasing the secrets of Latin. Had she been a son, he would have begged her father to send her to a monastery.

It was not uncommon for high-born ladies to read, for there were many tasks required of the mistress of a household—one must tend the books of the kitchens and read the records of harvests, brewings of ale, and mixes of grapes for the wine they made. Where Rica knew she differed was in her longing for the knowledge Father Goddard gave her. She gulped mathematics and Latin, the philosophies of the masters and the words of the Holy Book itself. There was a magic in the words written upon a page that she had yet to find equaled elsewhere, a magic all the more precious for its rarity.

She owned two books. One was a book of hours, a devotional her father had given her, lavishly illustrated with vines and devils and soldiers. The other was a brisk manual of household rituals, duties, and directions for all manner of things Rica found useful.

But the bound manuscript the priest had placed in her hands tonight was the Bible, a text he had used more than once for her edification. Rica frowned perplexedly as she slipped her fingers into the place he had marked with a silk ribbon, wondering what illumination he hoped to give her now.

As the pages fell open, her breath left her. She closed her eyes and a rush of emotion bolted through her. The dear priest, wishing to reassure her that her thoughts were normal, had given her a sacred poem of love to read, unknowingly releasing within Rica's soul a renewed and pounding ache of hunger.

The words had been written thousands of years before, but they rang with freshness for Rica.

With a trembling heart, she began to read the Latin aloud in a whisper, "The song of songs, which is Solomon's. Let him kiss me with the kisses of his mouth: for thy love is better than wine . . ."

As if burned, she dropped the bound pages, terrified of the visions crowding now into her mind.

But even as she knelt, bowing her head, she could feel his mouth upon hers, could feel longing like honey flow sweet through her veins. The song of songs, her mind whispered.

Solomon's song.

Rica set out for Strassburg early the next morning, pleading a need for fabric and sundries. Riding with her was Olga, the red-faced servant woman who had been in Rica's father's employ for nearly twenty years, and the ever-faithful Leo.

Olga had a sister married to a blacksmith, and they stabled the horses there. Olga and her sister climbed the stairs to the solar above, waving cheerfully at Rica as she departed. It was a secret between the old woman and the young girl.

Out in the street, free of servant and father and house, Rica felt a sudden, soaring sense of happiness crowd through her chest. Leo loped along beside her, tongue bobbling, his ears alert as he examined the wondrous array of sights around him. A snorting, muddy pig ran past, and hard on its heels came a boy, calling and cursing after him. Leo whined and glanced at Rica.

"No," she said.

He lowered his head and kept trotting along beside her. She smiled.

It was early yet. The sun had begun to penetrate only the widest of streets, but the exhilarating noises of the city had already begun in earnest. The sounds of workmen's tools rang out—the clang of a blacksmith's hammer against his anvil; the rasp of a carpenter's saw.

Harnesses rattled and wagons squeaked and horses clopped on the stones of the streets. Bells rang from both cathedrals to mark the hour, their music echoing and bouncing through the narrow canyons between the half-timbered houses overhanging the streets and shops.

Rica made her way toward the new cathedral, knowing there was an astrologer nearby whom she could trust. Perhaps, too, there would be some fine fabric or bangles for sale in the square to give weight to her shopping excuse.

She passed great houses surrounded with walled gardens. Outside the gates huddled clumps of beggars, waiting for the soaked trenchers left from the morning meal. A pair of nuns passed her, heads demurely lowered as if to remind her of her place as a woman. There were seven nunneries in Strassburg—a fact her father had threatened her with more than once.

Near the cathedral, the streets were warming in the sunshine, the stone walls taking in heat. Rica loosened her cloak in relief.

The astrologer's shop was dim and smelled of something foreign. Parchment charts, intricately detailed and colored, covered the walls. On a stool near the front of the room sat an elderly man with a long beard. He nodded at her respectfully. "Good day, my lady," he said.

Rica smiled. "Good day." Hastily, she sketched the urgent nature of her request, without actually going into any detail that would give her away. She asked for a reading or guiding indicators for the coming months.

The astrologer had pale blue eyes growing rheumy with age, but they were shrewd as they measured Rica. "Is it a matter of love that concerns you?" he guessed. "I might save time by looking only in those quadrants and houses if it be so."

Rica blushed. "Yes."

He chuckled. "'Twould have surprised me greatly

had it been another matter, given your youth and beauty."

Rica grinned reluctantly. "Are all maidens so foolish as to ask the heavens for guidance?"

He pursed his lips. "Is it foolish to try to divine the workings of our fate? Is it foolish to try to avoid disaster?" His gnarled white hand lifted and he pointed at her, not unkindly. "For it is a disaster you fear, is it not?"

Rica swallowed, but lowered her eyes before she gave her fear away. She tossed her hair over her shoulder and with a regal straightening of her skirts said, "I will pay you double your fee if you will find the answer I seek by afternoon."

"It shall be done."

She left the small shop. The square was filled with booths and trestle tables and makeshift counters made of overturned wagons. The peasants were prosperous this year, and business was brisk. A musician banged a drum and blew a pipe as a tumbler flipped by him. Rica paused, watching with awe the limber leaping and flipping of the acrobat, amazed at the fluid nature of his body. The small knot of onlookers cheered when he completed a double back flip and landed solidly on his feet, his grubby face beaming as he bowed.

A wandering Franciscan friar, garbed in a rough robe tied about his waist with a length of rope, approached her. His face was gaunt. "Your heart is heavy, my lady?" From his sleeve, he pulled a small bundle. "Perhaps a relic will ease your heart? The tooth of a saint to stave off the evil you fear?"

The friar had no doubt seen her enter the astrologer's shop. "I fear no evil," she said.

"But there is evil all about. The Black Death marches toward us. Will you not take the tooth of Saint Blaise for healing?"

"Saint Blaise?"

"Aye, my lady. 'Tis said this very tooth saved an entire family in Florence when the pestilence swept through."

Rica thought of her father's precarious health; Blaise was said to have healing properties. "Let me see it."

Obligingly, the friar unwrapped the relic. Nestled in the length of linen was a very old, very yellow tooth. "All right," she said, taking a coin from the pouch at her girdle. "Let me have it."

Next to her, Leo made a small whining noise of greeting. Curious, she glanced around to see who it was that Leo would know in this teeming city.

Solomon.

Her heart shivered in both guilt and joy. *Solomon.* He walked with easy grace through the square, his black hair spilling from beneath his hat in glossy disarray, his figure lean and strong. He had a faint smile upon his mouth, as if he contemplated something secret and pleasurable. He did not see her.

But Rica was not the only woman in the square who saw him. Matrons turned as he passed, speculative gleams in their eyes. A young girl, perhaps eleven, stared after him long after he had passed, craning her neck until her mama yanked her dress.

As if struck by his beauty, a pietist rang his bells. The musician struck up a tune on his pipe. The tumbler began to sing a soft ballad.

The friar wrested the coin from her fingers, dropped the relic in her waiting palm, and disappeared in the crowd. And still Rica stood unmoving, as if turned to stone.

In contrast, her black-eyed Solomon seemed extraordinarily alive in the bright day. When he spied her, his expression sobered. For a moment, he paused. Then as the old cathedral bells began to ring the hour, he moved toward her.

Rica looked at her hands.

"Rica," he said in quiet greeting. "What brings you abroad today?"

"I came to see the astrologer," she said, gesturing toward the building behind her.

"Ahhh." He made a gentle sound of wry amusement. "So did I."

Rica raised her eyes. "Did you?"

A faintly ironic twist of his lips lent his face a harsh aspect for a moment. Then his black eyes softened. "It seems we are fated to meet, my lady. What are we to do?"

Warning and fierce excitement rippled through her. "I know not," she whispered.

He lifted his chin toward the astrologer's sign. "Perhaps he will have answers for us," he said. "I came myself here to ask him my fate."

Rica couldn't help herself—she laughed. It was all too absurd to be ignored. "Perhaps you have learned it," she said, spreading her hands. "Every corner you turn, you will find me standing there."

A hot light flared in his eyes and he quickly shifted his gaze away from her. "Are you in a hurry today, *fräulein?*"

Rica knew she should say yes, that she must rush to meet her servant. To stay in his company was to sin once again. But in spite of this, she found herself shaking her head. "I do not meet my maid until Nones."

"Will you wait while I ask the astrologer what he sees?"

Softly she said, "We will be in the square, Leo and I."

"I will find you."

6

The astrologer dutifully recorded Solomon's request and said it might be late afternoon before the information was ready. Solomon impatiently nodded and rushed back out into the day, knowing he was mad. He should wander these busy streets today and admire every beauty he saw, to take his mind from the one. But he could not.

He had tried. Filled with the wispy, erotic memories of his dreams of Rica, he had admired every woman with even a single beauty to her keeping. But the eyes of one, the lips of another, the breasts of another, all seemed to echo some unforgettable part of the whole that was Rica. No matter how he fought it, it seemed every dry corner of his mind had been given new life with the presence and shape of her.

Outside the shop, he scanned the throng of people in the square anxiously and spied Rica haggling with a peddler over a belt. Her hair was caught back from her face under her barbette, and the dark blue eyes snapped with quick wit as she bargained. She laughed, showing her white teeth and the dimple deep in her cheek, as the peddler gave in with a bow.

Before she saw him, Solomon sprinted through the streets to a cookshop he knew, and paid for a pasty and a loaf of bread for them to share. He could not eat the meat, but the bread would do him no harm.

In a trice he was back, holding the meal in his hands. He slipped up beside Rica and murmured quietly, "I should not like to think people will put us together, my lady. There is a gate to the east of the city and from there a path leads along the river."

"I do not think—" she began, turning to look at him. Her fear was plain.

"We will only walk, Rica. And eat." He lifted the food to display it to her. "Just for today."

"All right," she whispered. Her throat moved as she swallowed. She shifted away, twitching her skirts from a pile of refuse in the gutter.

He bowed, his heart pounding hard in his chest, and led them through tiny alleyways and past stone dwellings with walled gardens. Another turn took them into a dark, deserted stretch near the east wall.

Once they had passed through the city gates, Solomon felt his tension begin to fade. The east gate was busy with the traffic from the river. Soon he and Rica were able to peel apart from the crowd to seek shelter in the trees.

They walked some distance in silence, Leo trotting happily alongside. It was a bright day, humid and filled with insects. Rica waved at a flurry of gnats that swirled around her face and swatted at mosquitos. "I have never seen a year with so many bugs," she said with annoyance.

"It is the decay to the south that breeds them so thickly."

She looked at him with horror in her wide eyes. "I had not thought—"

He glanced over his shoulder. They had left the main road, and the path they followed toward the grove of trees was deserted. He took her hand. "You could not know, Rica."

For a moment, she let him hold her hand, then gently eased free of him. "I wonder how long it will be until Strassburg is laid low with this pestilence."

"Perhaps it will not come at all."

With a bitter twist of her lips, Rica looked at him. "Perhaps, Herr Doktor, the peasants might believe your soothing noises. I do not." She plucked a silvery leaf from the low-hanging branch of a beech tree. "It will come."

"No, Rica. It may not." He gestured toward a sun-dappled stretch of grass. As she settled, he went on. "We do not know why or how the plagues come, or why they leave one place alone and destroy another. Perhaps Strassburg will be fortunate. We have been untouched thus far."

"Perhaps." Rica broke a hank of bread from the loaf. "Will you eat with me?"

He smiled and nodded, taking the bread she offered. "You do not believe me. Why?"

"I do not trust the word of *any* of you." She tore into the bread with her fine white teeth and chewed lustily. "Do you know what the physician from the city said about my father's condition?"

He chuckled. "Tell me."

"He wanted to bleed him when the moon was in Jupiter." Her gaze showed the idiocy with which she regarded this suggestion. "I didn't let him. Now he will not come to us."

"How did you come to such odd ideas about medicine?"

"Odd ideas?" She fished a chunk of beef from the

pie with her fingers and held it ready near her lips. "Do you, Solomon, believe in the practice?"

"There is nothing that will break a fever more quickly," he said, "though I see little else it helps."

He shifted, stretching his legs out before him. On the river a barge passed, and the strong afternoon sunlight glinted on the coppery head of an oarsman. "You did not tell me where you came by your ideas," he prompted.

"I came by mine as you did yours—by thinking."

He grinned. "Such a strange pastime for a girl."

"So it may seem." Brushing crumbs from her skirt, she answered him more seriously. "I read what I could procure from the priest and watched my father to see when he grew ill. He cannot take much exercise, nor heavy foods. He improves when his diet is light and filled with fresh foods. He gets very hungry for berries."

In her voice he heard the same sense of puzzlement he himself felt over the mysteries of illness and cures. He leaned forward eagerly. "It is no secret that fresh foods are better than salted and dried, but I've not heard of berries in use for a problem of the heart."

"Heart?"

He glanced at the bread in his hands, cursing himself for talking freely. It was, after all, her father about whom they spoke. Restlessly, he pinched out the soft center of his bread and mulled his reply.

"Do I seem to you a fainting maid? What do you mean?"

He lifted his head and smiled. "I forgot myself, Rica." There was a glint of steel in her eyes and he sighed. "Helga told me it is his heart. The tisane she makes for him helps to keep it strong, but it will not keep him so forever."

She jumped up. "He is no invalid. He hunts and rides and oversees all of his holdings."

"Yes. And will do so for many years to come." He stretched out a hand. "Come. Do not fret—he is a hale man from all I hear. You need not worry."

Her brow yet creased with a frown, she nonetheless settled back in the grass, her skirts pooling around her like water. A swath of gilded hair spilled over her shoulder and torso. For an instant, Solomon imagined his hands buried in that silken texture; he saw himself smoothing the shimmering tresses over the curve of her arm and the lush rise of her breast and the sway of her waist.

With effort, he willed his gaze away. "How came you to read Latin, Rica?"

"There is a priest in my father's chapel who loves to teach," she said. "Since my father had no sons, I am all he has to work with. He is not always happy with the turn of my thoughts, but he cannot resist teaching me anyway."

Solomon laughed. "How well I can imagine! Do you torment him over matters of religion, as you torment me over matters of medicine?"

"'Tis daunting enough to challenge you," she said and lifted one perfectly arched brow, giving her face again that odd mix of knowledge and innocence. "He is patient, but if I say too much, perhaps he would take away his books—and that I could not bear."

"Does he have many?"

"In truth, I suppose they are my father's, but he has given them to the priest's keeping." She grinned. "And Father Goddard shares them with me."

"I do not know another woman who reads Latin," he said quietly. "It somehow does not surprise me that when I find one, it is you."

She lifted one white shoulder, then shook her head

slowly. "I think it does me no good." Her expression sobered as she focused upon the dark blue spread of the Black Forest beyond the Rhine. "What will I do? If I were the son my father had wished for, perhaps he would have let me go to the university. For a woman, there is no such place."

Solomon chewed his bread slowly, studying her with a dawning sense of surprise. Several times she had made barbed comments about the opportunities afforded him. He had not realized how truly envious she was. "Is that what you wish for, Rica? To go to university?"

Her gaze flew to his face and he saw the suspicion there—she was afraid he was laughing at her. After a moment, when he did not break into teasing or laughter, her guard eased. "I would read everything that has ever been written," she said in a voice hushed with passion. "Instead I run the kitchens and tend my father and my sister . . ." She sighed. "Pay me no heed," she said quietly. "It is the foolish dream of a child. I know that."

Solomon saw the hunger for learning in her exquisitely beautiful face, saw once again the gleam of bright intelligence in her eyes. He touched her slim hand. "You would do well, I think."

"Do not patronize me."

By her downcast eyes, he could see she did not believe he meant what he said. She no doubt thought his words were just another form of seduction.

And somehow, the intellectual curiosity that so mirrored his own kindled his desire as keenly as the shimmer of her hair. The thought was so strange that he wanted to laugh, wanted to kiss her in exultation. "Ah, Rica," he said, and lifted her hand to his lips. With all the curbed passion he could not elsewise express, he kissed her fingers, closing his eyes. From the road came the sound of travelers, and faintly the mournful and celebratory song of the monks floated over the Rhine.

He opened his eyes to find her looking at him with sorrow and hunger. Feeling as if there were no other choice, as if all the planets and mysterious forces in the heavens had ordained this moment, he took her hand and placed it on his jaw.

"I can't," she whispered in protest. But her fingers traced the edge of his beard and feathered along the edge of his eye, exploring.

He shifted closer, smelling the warmth of her skin and the crushed grass beneath them. A humming began within him. "You are more beautiful than stars flung across a midnight sky," he whispered, touching her hair. "As brilliant as a blazing torch."

"A poet," she said with a tremulous smile. "Are we mad?"

"Utterly," he said in a raw whisper. A need welled up within him, rising until it broke the threads of restraint he'd held over himself. Moving slowly and deliberately, he pushed gently at her shoulders until she lay amid the grass and buttercups, her hair spread out below her like an Arabian carpet.

"I am mad," he murmured. "But I care not—for if madness brings visions such as these, I willingly leave the world."

Closer and closer he moved, until their bodies touched from shoulder to ankle. With a hand that trembled, he stroked her hair, looking into her beautiful eyes.

"Rica," he said and could think of no more. He touched her peach-colored cheek—only for a moment. One moment, stolen from all of time, was little enough to ask.

"My lord," she whispered weakly, "I do not—"

"Nor do I," he whispered, bending over her. "I do not kiss strange ladies, no matter how beautiful they are. But you have been no stranger to me since the moment I saw you in Helga's garden."

Overhead a grackle called in the blue, blue sky and a gentle, heated wind blew a lock of her hair over his shoulder, but Solomon felt only Rica's rich curves against his body. She smelled of gillyflowers.

"Please," she whispered, raising her hand to his face.

"Please?" he echoed. "Please do?" He bent his head closer, to whisper his words over her poised and waiting lips. "Or please do not?"

"Please kiss me, Solomon," she breathed, grabbing his shoulders, "or I shall die of wanting."

Yesterday, afraid he would frighten her, Solomon had only tasted lightly of this sweetness. Today, his control left him. He suckled her lips and thrust his tongue into her mouth to taste her. Her small teeth nipped sharply at his lips and a low cry escaped her throat, a sound that resonated through him, settling low in his groin.

After a moment, starved for breath, he lifted his head and touched her chin with his thumb. "No woman has ever made me willing to forget all that I am." He swallowed. "I dreamed such dreams of you last night that I thought I would weep upon waking, to find they were not true."

He kissed her again, longer now, more slowly. She eased against him. Solomon felt her hunger in the clutch of her fingers against his arms, in the protesting and passionate noises she made, in the fierceness with which she met him. She lifted a hand to his hair and he shuddered in reaction.

But after a moment, the madness of what they were doing seemed to strike her. "Solomon," she said urgently. "It is given to women to—" She made a slow sound as he trailed his tongue around her lips, her body going limp.

She pushed at him weakly, but lost in the taste of her, he would not be calmed. He kissed her cheek and her ear, and rubbed his wrists against the silk of her hair.

"You must stop," she whispered, but her hands trailed over his back and her eyes closed.

He lifted his head. "You do not wish me to stop, my love." He covered her white throat with his palm to feel the silky warmth, to touch the source of her murmurings. With his thumb, he followed the path of an artery and he felt the furious pounding of her heart. "And may God forgive me, Rica," he said against her mouth, "but I do not wish it either."

With a small cry, she opened to him again, pulling him closer to instinctively arch against him. He groaned at the pressure, groaned at the sweetness and passion mingled here in this beauty.

He tasted her jaw and throat and shoulder, feeling the gilded hair brush against his face.

The screech of a magpie overhead intruded momentarily. The sound served, for Solomon found himself at war even as he touched her. She was a virgin, the daughter of a powerful lord, a Christian. And until his touch, she had not known the carnal hungers of a man.

He had told her yesterday it was not lust. But this fierce and biting madness was evil, whatever he called it.

Yet even as he thought these things, he found himself suckling her throat and tasting the rise of her collarbone. His hands of their own accord roamed over her back, gauging the curves below her velvet surcoat.

Suddenly, she shoved him away and rolled free. "No!" she gasped, and stumbled in haste to her feet. "We must not!"

Flung backward into the grass, Solomon stared at her, breathing raggedly. As he sprawled there, stunned into sanity, he saw that her lips were swollen, that his beard had left marks on the tender flesh of her jaw and along her neck, that her hair was tangled and littered with bits of grass.

All at once, he was deeply ashamed. He fell to one knee and took her hand, pressing his forehead to her fingers. "Rica, forgive me."

Her free hand lit in his hair. For a moment, she said nothing, only stroked his head silently as he knelt before her. At last she said quietly, "The priest brought me the Bible last night, as instruction."

He lifted his eyes.

She sank down to her knees, to look at him face-to-face. "I made a confession to him that I had spent many hours thinking of a certain man in ways that were not chaste."

Solomon lifted his fingers, seared by this admission, but she caught his hand before he could touch her. "Father Goddard said there was more to God's world than prayers," she said, "and he brought me the Bible to read, with a place specially marked."

Her eyes softened. "It was," she said with an ironic smile, "the Song of Solomon."

"Ahhh." He closed his eyes and leaned forward to press his forehead against hers, feeling as if he might weep. "And yet, this is impossible, Rica. We cannot love each other."

"I know."

For a long moment, they simply remained as they were, their fingers tangled, foreheads pressed together, all else forgotten.

Solomon finally felt calm enough to stand, and tugged Rica to her feet. "We must take care of you before you return to your father," he said.

"Take care of me?"

He nodded, shame still pricking his belly, and

touched the reddened places on her chin. "Let me soothe these marks."

She blushed. "All right."

Growing nearby was a stand of comfrey. Drawing on the teachings of Helga, he dug a little of the root-stock and walked to the riverbank to rinse it clean, then bruised it with his fingers.

As he knelt before Rica, she lifted her face trustingly to his ministrations.

His heart caught and began anew its fierce pounding. With effort, he swallowed his desire and pressed the herb to her chin gently. She would see that he did not only wish to hold her splendid form in his arms; that his fascination for her stemmed from the nimble mind she owned as well as the lust of the flesh that carted away his reason.

But as he tended her, his hand shook with his restraint. After a moment, he paused and breathed deeply. Once, twice, three times. When he was calmer, he blotted her white cheeks with a bit of his tunic. "Tell me what you most like to study, Rica."

"I do not know," she said, and smiled at him. The gesture caused her dimple to flash, and the corners of her eyes turned upward. "In truth, I like the poems best, the stories of knights and ladies—there! Now you may laugh at me for the foolish woman I am."

He found his hands had steadied with the conversation. "That is not foolish," he said lightly, bending to retrieve the poultice. "Romance gives the world lightness and beauty. Even some of the great stories in the Bible your priest brings to you are stories of great love."

"They are?"

He smiled. "Of course. David and Bathsheba—do you know the tale?"

Rica slowly shook her head. "Will you tell it to me?"

He looked at her, then at the sky, which showed clear and blue as far as the eye could see. But he could not sit indefinitely with her. Soon or late he would yield again to temptation. "Another day, perhaps."

As if hearing his unspoken message, Rica stood and brushed loose grass from her skirts. "It is time I returned. Perhaps the astrologer has finished the task I set for him."

She turned to call for Leo. The dog came pounding through the woods, tongue lolling. Rica smiled. "Would that I were so carefree."

She settled her hat over her hair and tied it in place. For a moment she was silent. Then she lifted her chin and met his eyes. "This is a sin, Solomon," she said quietly.

He waited.

"It is given to women to be the stronger." She bit her lip. "I will not be alone with you again, my lord. Much as I want to see you, there is only tragedy ahead if we continue thus."

His heart plummeted. "I wish it were not so."

For one long moment more, she looked at him. He thought she would say something else. She opened her mouth—but then only closed it again. Turning away, she said, "Good day."

Solomon watched her go, longing for a word in any of the languages he had labored to learn that might call her back to him. There was none.

Instead he followed at a safe distance, to be certain she was not set upon by thieves. He trailed her past the lean-to village that clung to the city walls, and through the gates, then to the astrologer's. When she dipped inside there, he ached at the new loss of her.

Never once did she look back.

7

Rudolf paced the walk, looking toward Strassburg as the sun sank toward the tips of the Vosges. From the direction of the city rode Rica and her servant Olga. Leo, the fierce beast that gave Rica such unseemly freedom, trotted alongside the horses.

His eyes narrowed. He'd seen Rica leave this morn, and although it had been a little time before he could find leave to follow her, the delay had caused the girl to be swallowed up in the city's arms without a trace. He'd sought her horse, the dog, the servant, stopping in at the shops Rica most often patronized. None had seen the beautiful daughter of Charles der Esslingen.

Now here she rode, free as the wind, hair sailing out behind her, her chin high. When she was his wife, she would not go abroad so. He would teach her the manners and attitude befitting so highborn a lady, would show her the error of her ways.

The thought gave him some satisfaction, but he could not quite shake his annoyance over being unable to find her in Strassburg. It would have given him a chance to advance his suit—for the sooner she was his bride, the sooner he could begin her education.

As the pair neared the castle gates, he turned away. At supper tonight, perhaps he could learn where her errands had taken her.

Rica wearily climbed the stairs toward her chamber. She longed to change her gown, put behind her the tumultuous emotions of the day.

And yet even as she climbed the steep, twisting steps, her mind floated toward Solomon, toward the glory of his touch, the taste of his mouth, and the press of his broad, strong body against her own.

In the passage, she paused by a broad window cut into the thick stone walls. Below sat Etta, embroidering in the hazy late afternoon, her gown spread prettily over the grass, her hair caught demurely into a braid. Leo had found her and slept in the dead doze he deserved after his day.

Beware the change of season, the astrologer had said. *I see much ill fortune there.*

Rica stared at her sister. The alignment of their births made the stars say the same for both of them. Rica could see that her own foolishness might lead to tragedy if she did not keep her wits about her. But what of Etta?

Her sister looked as virtuous and still as a marble carving of the Virgin Mother. As if she sensed Rica's gaze, she looked up and lifted her hand in greeting. Rica waved back.

Etta gathered her basket of silks and made for the castle. Rica turned toward her chamber, knowing Etta would come to her.

Behind the heavy oak door, she stripped her surcoat and cotehardie, then poured a bowl of water from the pitcher. She scrubbed her face and neck and arms, sluicing away the dust and sweat of the journey.

As she lifted her palms to her face, a waft of Solomon's scent struck her nostrils.

A panicky sense of guilt clutched at her and she rubbed more fiercely at her flesh, trying to erase the aroma of him, that scent of male and frankincense and fresh bathing. A tactile memory of his black curls, hot from the sun and springy to the touch, rose up to haunt her. In her ears, his soft groan of hunger lingered.

Abruptly, she realized she was standing in her kirtle, with water dripping from her palms, her unfocused gaze fastened upon the whitewashed stone of her chamber walls.

She took a fresh tunic from her trunk, caring little for the cut or color. It had just settled about her ankles when Etta entered the room. "Hello, sister," Rica said. "How have you spent your day?"

"As always," she said and put aside her basket.

"I brought you something." Rica lifted a bangled belt. "Do you like it?"

"Aye." A gentle smile spread over Etta's face as she accepted the offering. "'Twill look well with the new green surcoat I have just embroidered. Rudolf likes green."

A pluck of foreboding pierced her, but Rica proceeded with caution. "How goes your pursuit of the fair Rudolf, sister?"

"I do not pursue him." Her chin lifted in queer arrogance. "I simply allow him to pursue me—or rather you. He kissed me last night, after the dancing."

"None too gently, I suspect." She touched a slightly swollen spot on her sister's lip, as casually as she would touch her own.

Etta pulled free. "'Twas not all his roughness."

There was something odd about Etta today,

something Rica could not quite place. Was it only the passion for Rudolf that had bloomed in her heart, or was there something more amiss? In a sudden fit of worry, she said, "Perhaps we should not play this game any longer, Etta. I am—"

Etta whirled, her eyes glittering. "Will you take this thing from me?"

"Etta, no! I am just—"

"You are jealous!"

Rica jumped to her feet, stunned. "No! I am only worried about what will happen."

"You think me simple, as all the others do." Etta straightened to a haughty posture. "I am not."

"I do not worry over simplemindedness, but over your innocence, Etta." With an imploring gesture, she extended one hand. "Please, let us end this spat. I do not care for arguing with you."

With a suddenness Rica found startling, Etta launched herself into her sister's arms. "I am sorry," she whispered. "Just do not take this one thing from me, I beg you. He is like the sun—when he appears, the world alights for me. I could not bear to—"

"If you so long for this man, Etta, then you will have him. I swear it." She lifted her head. "But there is something I must tell you."

"What is it?"

"Come. Sit with me." Rica mulled her words. She longed to spill the story of her turmoil over Solomon but did not dare, not even to Etta. "I have had a sense of evil coming—I knew not what. Today I went to the astrologer. The stars that govern us, sister, bode no good for the autumn. We must be very careful."

"What could happen?" Etta said with a soft smile.

Rica took a breath. "You are no virgin, Etta. How will—"

A strange, shuttered look crossed Etta's face. "'Tis cruel of you to mention it."

Exasperated, Rica squeezed Etta's hand and leaned forward. "You must prepare for that night. We must ask Helga."

Comprehension dawned. "Oh, yes. We should go tomorrow."

Again, a thick blossom of dread filled Rica's heart, and she stared at her sister, trying to pinpoint the source of her worry. A vision of Rudolf's tight, sharp lips passed through her mind. Perhaps it was Rudolf that frightened her—she would talk to Helga. "Perhaps," she said. "We'll see."

Rica could not remember whether Solomon said he would go mornings or afternoons. Could she bear to see him? Would Helga see the passion that had passed between them?

But Etta would not go abroad alone. Rica would have to go with her. Perhaps there was safety in their number.

Jacob ben Isaac watched his son Solomon all evening. When Solomon was a child, this strange mood had indicated trouble brewing; Jacob did not like to think there would be trouble now.

Solomon sat nearby the unshuttered window in the solar, staring off toward the line of mountains visible over the roofs of Strassburg. He sat unmoving, deep in a brooding frame of mind, sighing softly to himself.

A woman, Jacob thought. Yet Jacob had seen no hint of her. On Sabbath afternoons, Solomon did not linger in the courtyard of the temple; neither had he seen Solomon gazing overmuch at anyone in particular, though God knew he had a bold eye. Not entirely his own doing. Girls had flocked to this child since his earliest moments; even as a babe he'd had more than his share of attention—aunts fussing over his thick curls, neighbors clucking over the dimples in his cheeks as he grew, then girls and women of all walks eyeing him wherever he went.

Considering all, Jacob thought Solomon had done well for himself. The years at Montpellier had sobered him, and perhaps the bustle of those days now made Strassburg seem a dull hovel indeed. Not so strange.

As if he sensed his father's gaze, Solomon glanced up. A soft flush of color suddenly rose in his cheeks and he hurriedly glanced away.

Jacob frowned. A woman, then. One he should not be thinking of. Was it the wife of some neighbor? Miriam, the baker's wife, was a fine figure of a woman, too young for her fat, bad-tempered husband. Perhaps she had drawn Solomon's eye. Or perhaps it was the daughter of some peasant he'd met on his walks to the herbalist's cottage.

Jacob would watch. There was little he did not know about his children. This one was born with too much passion.

So why was he reluctant to force Solomon to marry? He was close to the age when many communities would not let him reside in them without a wife. It was his obligation and his duty.

But Jacob wanted his son to have his education, to go as far as his brilliant mind would carry him. He would, perhaps, be the finest physician the world had yet seen, and thus bring glory to his Maker and his people.

Pushing the subject aside, Jacob promised himself he would keep his eyes upon this youth. It was only a few months until he could return to Montpellier, surely. And Solomon, though passionate, was also wise. He would not err too greatly with so much at stake.

*   *   *

The visitors came the next morning.

Rica was bathing in the warm room behind the
kitchen, where a fire had been laid. The water was
warm, scented with lavender flowers freshly plucked
and set to float with rose petals on the surface. Etta
stood nearby, silently waiting to rinse her sister's
hair.

Last night Rudolf had been aloof at dinner, speaking
only with brief courtesy to the twins before gathering
with their father to discuss some matter of state. Rica,
with narrowed eyes, had realized this was some sort of
punishment, but Etta seemed to blame her twin—Etta
had been sullen and withdrawn all morning.

"Etta," she said, soaping her arms and neck, "had I
wished for silence, I would have invited Leo in for
company."

Etta only looked at her.

Rica rinsed the soap from her skin. "Men often
have concerns other than women, you know. In fact,
'tis likely you have a greater share of his attention
now than you will ever have again once he beds you."

Etta turned her back, almost rudely, and took up a
comb to unsnarl her hair.

Exasperated, Rica dipped her head and soaped her
hair, scrubbing furiously. Etta dutifully rinsed it with
a pail until it squeaked and handed her a length of
linen for drying when she stood up.

"Ignore me, then," Rica said, snatching the towel.
"Run back to your little shell and say nothing. I don't
know why I bother!"

Etta gazed at her serenely. There was a small edge of
triumph in the pale eyes, and a knowing expression
around her mouth. It marred the perfection of virtue

that only weeks before had made Etta seem a Madonna to her sister's eye.

The trill of a horn from the walk, sounding long and loud, announced visitors. Etta ran from the room, leaving Rica behind to dry and dress alone.

"Etta!" she cried in annoyance.

But Etta did not pause. The horn trilled again, and Rica could hear the sound of voices and excitement rising in the courtyard. In her haste, she tried to don her tunic before her arms were completely dry. The tight sleeves stuck fast her flesh, and a tendril of hair got tangled inside. In her present humor, it took several moments to extract the tresses from within the sleeve, then settle her gown properly.

Meanwhile, from the yard came the sound of several horses and the hale shouts of guards in cheerful greeting and the flurry of voices. The horn rang out again in announcement, calling the castle inhabitants to the bailey.

She squared her chin as she headed for the yard, lifting her skirts to move quickly.

The scene that greeted her was one of mass confusion and excitement. Seven or eight well-appointed horses stepped restlessly in a small herd just inside the gates. A cluster of vassals and men-at-arms gathered on the walk above, chattering among themselves. Scullery maids peeked from the doors of the kitchen until Cook shoved them out of the way to get a look herself. Chickens flapped and screeched warnings to one another.

The morning sun had risen just above the wall and lit the arriving party from behind—Rica could not even make out how many had come. But there were women's voices amid the expected lower booms of the men.

It was only as her father emerged from the hall that Rica realized who it must be—her uncle from the borderlands to the south, along with his wife and daughters.

Their appearance was unannounced; not even a messenger had been sent ahead. Rica paused, remembering her talk with Solomon the day before, and knew without a doubt that the grim pestilence so scouring the land had chased her uncle and his family north.

"Rica!" squealed a high, sweet female voice, and Rica found her arms filled with the weight and mass of her cousin Lorraine's body. She smelled of the length of her journey and Rica unwillingly caught her breath in defense.

Rica bit back a sigh. Under the best of circumstances, this cousin was a sore trial—and her mama was worse. The third woman in the party, Lorraine's younger sister Minna, had been only eight the last time the families had come together. Rica had no idea what she might be like but didn't hold much hope.

Her aunt came forward smoothly, richly dressed below her traveling cloak, and eyed Rica with a shrewd gaze. "'Tis plain to see you have at last grown from a colt to a girl," she said.

Humphrey, her father's brother, pushed into the group and scooped Rica into a bear hug. "This is no *girl*," he bellowed roundly as he settled her back to her feet. "Our little wild Frederica has turned into a woman of fine proportions."

Rica kissed him, laughing. Older than his brother by a year, Humphrey was a monster of a man with a black beard and thick black hair. His laugh could fill the great hall and drown an entire chorus of troubadours. "I am so glad to see you, Uncle," she said.

Charles came forward, his hawk on his arm in a jess. "Humphrey!"

They embraced and eased away from the knot of women. Charles looked over his shoulder toward Rica. "See that a feast is prepared, daughter." He scanned the milling group for a moment and signaled to Rudolf, then followed the men inside.

Rica busied herself giving orders to various servants—for the manor rooms to be readied, for a pig to be slaughtered and new greens to be plucked. There were berries aplenty growing in the fields, perhaps even a few cherries yet. Rica herself would see to them.

When the women were settled and preparations for the feast well underway, Rica headed purposefully for her father's solar, carrying as her excuse a loaf of bread and thick slices of cheese along with a tankard of ale.

The oak door stood ajar and Rica entered quietly. Humphrey and Charles sat on a bench in the sunlight while Rudolf stood nearby the window, staring grimly toward the courtyard below, his hands clasped loosely behind his back.

"'Tis madness," said Humphrey. "The stench rises up from the earth like a vile poison. There are whole villages stricken and empty. The beasts lie dead in the fields."

Rica lowered her eyes, thinking of the insects about which she had complained yesterday.

"We shall not trouble you overlong, brother," Humphrey said, and gratefully accepted the wooden cup Rica put in his hand. "We head north to my wife's manor near Nürnberg, and there will stay until the threat is passed."

"I am glad to know you are well, and your daughters are good company for my own."

Humphrey looked at Rica. "Your sister seems much improved."

"That she is." Charles sipped his ale and eyed Rica. "I trust, daughter, we will have no games from the pair of you?"

"Games?" Humphrey echoed.

"You will soon see there are hours you cannot tell which is Rica, which is Etta."

Humphrey snorted. "I will always know Rica."

Rica glanced toward Rudolf, who frowned at this. Did he guess that he had been fooled? In recklessness, she said to her father, "I will go to the orchards to gather cherries for your supper, Papa."

Charles nodded and gave his brother a rueful twist of his lips. "She nags me like a wife, keeping all the good meat from my table, feeding me scraps like an old woman." To take the sting from his words, he patted her hand. "That would be a treat, daughter. It will be a sore trial to watch the rest of you feasting."

She kissed his broad brow. "I will prepare something myself," she said and left them. She smiled as she heard Rudolf ask permission to take his leave as well, the hearty chuckle of her uncle ring into the passageway. "I'd go after her, too, my boy!"

Lifting her skirts, Rica ran down the twisting stairs on light feet and ducked into the pantry off the great hall. She startled a maid with a fresh armful of rushes as she hurried through and nearly bumped a boy who followed with another.

In the bailey, she rushed into the swell of activity. The rich scent of baking white bread rose on clouds from the ovens, and everywhere pages and servants scurried to make ready the hall for the feast. Rica heard the screech of a poorly played horn and took enough time to stop a black-haired vassal. "Lewis, send to Strassburg for musicians. Yesterday, there was a troupe in the square by the new cathedral—I would have them come to us."

"And if they have traveled on?"

"Then hire others. But go, quickly. I will not have our guests insulted by that—" She glanced over her shoulder as the screech sounded out once more.

The vassal laughed. "Consider it done, my lady." With a devilish wink, he added, "I will seek you out when they are here, and dance with you wildly."

Rica shrugged coyly. "If you can fight your way through the hordes surrounding me, perhaps I will favor you."

Again he laughed good-naturedly and turned to seek a boy to accompany him. Rica glanced behind her and saw Rudolf watching them from the stairs that led to the hall, his blond head gleaming. The rigid line of his body spoke of his displeasure. Rica lifted her chin. A pox on him. She whirled and rushed away.

Leo was nowhere to be found and Rica did not wish to confront her sister again just yet. Let her stew a little, as well. She left through the gates and made for the orchards.

Once there, she found a narrow path that led to the forest. If she followed it to its end, she would find herself in Helga's garden. With a longing glance down the path, she settled instead beneath a great old pine. A brown spider tried to climb into her skirts and she brushed it away.

She did not have long to wait. Rudolf strode through the trees with as much noise as a boar. In the orchard, he paused. "Rica!" There was command in his tone.

Calmly, she plucked a strand of grass from its sheath and chewed on the end, watching him stomp in circles around the trees as if his temper could conjure her from the shadows. If he only stopped to look around himself, he would see her.

But when it became plain his temper could stand no more, when his face was flushed, his lips a thin white line, Rica stood up and shook her skirts, sending the bells at her wrists and waist ringing into the still noon forest.

Rudolf spun around. "There you are."

At the fury in his eyes, Rica clutched fingers

together in fear, but said sardonically, "What a surprise to see you here in the orchard. Have you come to pick cherries for my father?"

"I weary of your games, Rica."

She met his gaze with disbelief. "Do you?" Stepping forward, she clutched her skirts. "I weary of yours. You think to punish me when I do not behave as you wish."

"Rica—"

"Am I Rica? Or am I Etta? Do you know which you kissed in the hallway and which you followed? Do you know, my lord?"

Arrogance thinned his nostrils. "Does it matter? One is the same as the other." He took a step closer to her, and with a snake-quick gesture he snared her arm above the elbow.

Rica felt a ripple of fear and cursed her foolish temper, the pique she had allowed to overrule her common sense. Little had she known of passion before the past few weeks, but saw it now on his face, sharp-edged as obsidian. She tugged at her arm, but his fingers tightened.

His voice was low when he spoke again. "Which of you did I see bathing in the river? Which of you walked nude as the day of your birth for any passerby to witness? Which of you is the whore, which is the maiden?"

Rica swallowed, a coppery taste in her mouth. His fingers bit hard into her flesh and she knew she'd carry the marks on the morrow.

After a moment, he let her go. "Do not mistake me for a fool," he warned quietly.

Watching him depart, Rica fingered the tooth of the saint in a small pouch at her belt, praying silently— for common sense, for a level head.

Beware the change of the seasons.

8

Rica sought out her sister before going to
the hall for the feast. Etta was dressed in a rich tunic
trimmed with minever, her hair woven with flowers.
As if in forgiveness, she gave Rica a gentle smile.
"Your present was well timed," she said, as Olga
fastened the bangled belt on her hips.

"I see." She smiled at Olga. "I know you are weary,
Olga, with all this activity. I will help her finish now."

Olga sighed mightily and nodded. "Thank you, my
lady."

When she had gone, Rica said, "Papa has forbidden us
to pretend to be each other while our cousins are here."

Etta smoothed her surcoat and reached for a casket
of jewels. She extracted a circlet of gold to settle
around her hair.

"Did you not hear?"

"I am not deaf."

Rica sighed. "Then tell me you hear! I will not risk
Papa's wrath."

"How will he know?" Etta asked calmly.

"You cannot be me! You cannot run the kitchens
and order the servants and see to the accounting. You

have no knowledge of such. Am I to turn my back on all so that you are not jealous for a day or two?"

"To run the household of my lord, I will need to learn such things, will I not?"

"Etta, 'tis not so simple as that."

"You think I cannot do it."

Rica's heart plummeted, for that was, indeed, the truth. She did not believe Etta *could* oversee the myriad tasks required of the mistress of a castle. For all that she seemed to be healing, it was too sudden and startling a change for Rica to quite take in—she feared it was no permanent shift.

Rica fingered a ruby brooch. "I will be glad to teach you what I know, sister, but let us wait until our cousins have gone to Nürnberg."

Etta stared at her for a long, long moment with no expression whatever in her wide violet eyes. At last she said, "We will do as Papa wishes."

Rica hugged her. "Good."

"You will teach me?"

"Everything. I promise." She slipped her hand through the crook of her sister's elbow. "Come. A feast awaits."

Etta moved forward, then stopped abruptly. "Rica."

She turned quizzically.

"Do not kiss him. Please."

"Nay, sister." In truth, the idea revolted her. For a fleeting second, she wondered how her sister could be so passionate about a man Rica could not imagine kissing. How would Etta regard Solomon, if she saw him?

Solomon. At the thought of him, she tensed and then forced him from her mind. "Let's hurry. I am hungry after so much work today."

They met Lorraine and Minna in the courtyard,

coming from the manor. Minna squealed over their finery, touching the gold net over Rica's hair and the bangles on Etta's belt.

"How can you both be so beautiful?" she exclaimed. At twelve, she had not yet begun to think of herself as such, although it was plain she had inherited her father's rich, robust good looks. Amid the three blondes, she stood out more fully than she knew.

Rica hugged her. "And how can you still be so sweet?"

A bevy of servants rushed through the bailey, carrying tankards of ale and Rhenish wine and trenchers for the guests to share. A knot of vassals and men-at-arms, some from Humphrey's household, some from Charles's, stood nearby the steps to the hall. They had donned velvets and colorful hose and soft shoes with pointed toes. Several had curled their hair in elaborate preparation. The group of them admired the girls frankly.

Lorraine spied them and preened, twining a finger through her riot of natural ringlets. Rica nudged her. "Do not ask for more than you can handle. There will be much drinking tonight."

"Pah. None of them interests me." Arching her painted brows, she lifted her chin. "Now, *there* is a man."

Etta made a quick sound of dismay, for it was to Rudolf, dressed in sea-blue velvet, that Lorraine pointed.

"Ah," Lorraine said with a sharp smile. "I see I am not alone in admiring him. Has he spoken, my little dove?"

"Your conceit is boring," Minna said, and took Etta's arm protectively. "Pray do not weary us so all evening."

Lorraine flushed and seemed about to make an angry retort, but Rica smoothly tugged her forward. "It is no wonder the men are enchanted," she said tongue in cheek. Had the cut of Lorraine's gown fallen any lower, her breasts would have spilled free, and the

tunic was so closely cut Rica could make out her cousin's
hip bones. Pretty she was, but there was no question she
would run to fat before too many years had passed.

Rica's comment mollified her, however, and they
took their places at the trestle tables arranged around
the hall. Rica sat with Etta. "Do not worry, *liebling*,"
she murmured in her ear. "Lorraine is too coarse by
far for Rudolf's tastes."

Etta gave her a grateful smile.

Cook had outdone herself. The tables were filled
with brewets and pasties and meat tiles together with
jellies and fritters and plentiful ale. Rica, from long
habit, dished their trencher full of the brewet, stab-
bing a choice bit of mutton from the carmeline sauce
with her knife. She made a sound of pleasure and
nudged her sister. "Don't be so stubborn you starve,
sister. Cinnamon is your favorite spice."

Etta took up her knife and began to eat. Rica let go
of a little breath and settled in to feast and forget.

As the meal wound down and the musicians began
to make tuning noises on their instruments, Rudolf
studied the tables through narrowed eyes. His stomach burned and he sipped a little ale to digest the
heavy meal he'd gulped. Charles, in good spirits
today, ate lightly of the berries Rica had collected,
and nibbled cabbage in a clear broth, but left the
meats and sauces alone.

Next to Charles, Humphrey's face was greasy with
his feasting—he ate everything with hale enjoyment,
his great laugh booming out repeatedly.

In coarse Humphrey, Rudolf saw the peasant
blood that ran through the family. In Etta and Rica,
the blood had been thinned to nearly nothing, for

they were as fair as any noble maids, thanks to the brilliant marriage Charles had made.

Charles and Humphrey had fought well and married well, but they were not far removed from the crass burghers flaunting their wealth garishly in the streets of the cities. Rudolf wondered if the coarseness would show in the offspring of his match with Rica.

If, indeed, he could ever learn which twin was which. His stomach increased its grumbling burn as he stared at the pair. Impossible to tell.

One dressed in rich rose with miniver on her surcoat and embroidery on her tight, buttoned sleeves. Her hair was loose and woven with flowers, and a ruby gleamed in the hollow of her throat. Her demeanor was calm.

The other wore vivid blue and an excess of bells at her wrists and girdle and sewn to her gown. Her surcoat was lined with fur that seemed to caress the elegance of her creamy flesh, and her mouth, as Rudolf watched, seemed as lustful as a rutting dog's—red and lush. As he studied her, her pink tongue snaked out to lick a bit of sauce from her bottom lip, and the vassal next to her leaned in close, hunger in his eyes.

Once he would have named the belled girl Rica, the other Etta. But the game they played confused him. Did Rica play herself more coarsely or was that Etta overplaying her sister?

And which, no matter the names, did he wish to own? His eyes strayed back to the wide mouth of the belled girl. A welter of distaste rose in his throat. A whore's mouth.

Next to her sat her sister, who nibbled delicately at her portion and sipped lightly from the cup. She seemed oblivious to the chaos around her, and her bearing was straight and noble as a queen's.

Now he saw a small difference in them, something

hard to pinpoint; not a single detail, but a dozen tiny things. The slight tilt of an eye, the slight difference in the breadth of their shoulders, the graceful movements of one's hand. As he looked at the more delicate twin, she happened to look at him. Catching his gaze upon her, she blushed with sudden, painful intensity. He smiled.

The memory of her warm lips whispered through him. Her passion, though hidden under maidenly ways, was wide and deep and promised earthly delights so great he could barely wait till their marriage.

He thought broodingly upon their encounter this afternoon in the orchard, and his confusion returned. She had seemed to almost hate him in those moments. Perhaps she had regretted kissing him last night in the dark hall, and her shame had led to anger with him—a seemly emotion for a well-bred maid.

He frowned, still uncertain. Perhaps, he thought, lifting his cup, he would test them each. In that way, he would finally learn which was which.

The tables were dismantled, the shreds of the feast cleared away, and fresh tankards of ale were brought as the minstrels strummed to life in the gallery. They started with light tunes, meant for easy dancing, and Rica gave a smile and a nod to the vassal who'd arranged for the musicians to come from Strassburg. With a grin, he crossed the rushes and held out his hand. "Seems I've beat the teeming hordes to your side, my lady."

Laughing, Rica stood up to dance with him, taking pleasure in the cheery light in his black eyes and the easy humor with which he treated her.

Lewis had come to the castle as a child and now had worked through page to squire to vassal. He had been part of the scenery of her childhood.

But as Rica danced with him now, she realized with a start that he was of a size and coloring of Solomon. His hair was thick and glossy, although it did not curl. His eyes were dark, though not quite black. His face was handsome, though perhaps not quite as strongly carved as Solomon's, and tanned from working outside.

And yet as he held her loosely, his broad hands warm on her back, his laughing mouth only a small space from her own, she felt no tingling, no rush of hunger, no aching need to tumble with him in naked passion.

It pierced her. Had her heart been snared by the curve of this man's lip, she might have wed him freely, might have borne him sons and laughed late into her old age with him.

Catching some glimpse of her thoughts on her face, Lewis smiled gently. "Come now, my lady. Am I so clumsy as that?"

"Nay. You are as graceful as a young stag."

He inclined his head with mock arrogance. "There are those who have made their comparisons."

Rica laughed, as she was meant to.

"Tell me, lady," he said in a more sober tone. "What know you of the young lass your uncle brought today? Is she his daughter?"

"Lorraine?"

He glanced at her, grinning. "I am no fool. The other one."

Rica looked toward Minna, who sat on the sidelines with her hands clasped in her lap, a longing expression on her clear young features. Her dark hair spilled over her shoulders and pooled on the bench beside her. "She is not yet thirteen summers."

"That is plain." He lifted a dark brow. "'Tis also plain she will bloom into rare beauty—if I wait to speak my suit, someone with more to offer will claim her first."

"She is no more than a sweet child," Rica protested. "Would you bed her so soon and steal that child's innocence from her?"

He laughed outright. "Ah, my sweet maid, are you jealous? Perhaps I should be seeking your hand instead!"

She gave him a rueful smile. "I seek only to keep her protected a bit longer—fathers have been known to throw their daughters into the clutches of the first man to ask."

"I would not take her so young, my lady. And I am not an old wrinkled man looking to warm my bed with the pleasures of a child—but I like the strength of her. She would make me a good wife."

"And you would make her a fine husband."

He grinned and released her as the music stopped. "Thank you."

As she turned to leave him, Rudolf appeared at her side. "Will you do me the honor?" he asked.

Rica glanced toward Etta, who stared miserably toward them, then toward her father, who was also looking at her.

She nodded, but vowed to keep her distance henceforth.

"I sought you in the city yesterday, Rica," he said softly as he took her into his embrace.

Startled, she looked at him. A flush of guilt heated her face. "I did not see you," she said. A roughness marked her voice.

"Nay. Nor did I find you." There was a dangerous silk in his words and Rica saw belatedly the brightness of drink in his eyes. "Where did you go?"

She lifted one shoulder as if in disdain, but her heart beat a painful tattoo. What if his luck had not been so thin and he had seen her leave the gates with Solomon?

Worse, what if he had seen them kissing in the grass?

In a moment of weak terror, she closed her eyes. She had no doubt how Rudolf would have reacted to such a scene. He would have raged and screamed and dragged them both to the square of Strassburg to be publicly beheaded for their crime.

With a calm she did not feel, she forced herself to speak. "I tarried with Olga at her sister's house, and saw an astrologer and found a belt for Etta. Nothing so wild as you seem to imagine."

"Oh, I imagined nothing untoward. I only wished to find you so that we might spend an hour or two alone." His eyes swept over her lips and he pressed a little closer. His voice softened, became a gentle whisper. "Perhaps we might have shared a quiet kiss or two."

Rica lowered her eyes, assailed with sharp visions of Solomon, whose mouth had tasted of things she'd only dreamt of, Solomon who was so beautiful and was forever denied her. With a sharp, plucking pain she wished it was he who held her and spoke to her now. Feeling weak with the longing, she clutched without thought at Rudolf's arms.

"Ah, my sweet, you are too much a lady to say it, but you wish it, too. Tonight, I will walk with you to your chamber if you wish."

"No!" Her answer was so vehement, she saw him blink and flush as if embarrassed. "I mean we should not, with so many about. 'Tis not seemly."

"We are—" he began, and broke off. Stiffly, he released her. "As you wish."

Rica nearly sagged with relief. Her head suddenly ached with the smell of the fire and the lingering odors of the food and the stale scent of so many bodies. It had been a long day and she wished only for her bed.

But she could not retreat. Instead, she took her place next to her sister, relieved that at least her promise to Etta had been kept.

Together they sat and listened to ballads of lost love and thwarted dreams. Rica glanced once at Etta and saw the same haunted emotion of her heart reflected there in her sister's eyes.

Etta reached for Rica's hand and gently squeezed her fingers. "All will be well, sister," she said.

Rica nodded, but she knew it was a lie. Nothing would be well, not ever again.

By the fourth day, Rica could not bear another instant of Lorraine's boasting, Etta's misery, or the preening superiority of her aunt. When the men went out to hunt, Rica seized her chance.

Leaving Etta and their cousins to their stitchery in the fine early summer light of the lower bailey, Rica took Leo and set out for Helga's, claiming a need for herbs.

The day was clear and mild. Barges moved on the Rhine and a soft wind blew freshness into the heavy summer air. It was good to be free of the castle, to be alone with only Leo, to gaze toward the splendid beauty of the blue Vosges and listen to the monks singing their dirgeful prayers. The sound hung thin and melancholy on the breeze.

It disturbed her vaguely. This morning she had been shriven in the small confessional and done her penance, but it had not cleansed her soul as it ought. Even if she had been able to confess kissing Solomon, she could not have truly repented. It had been too joyful a moment to regret.

For a moment, she wished she had never set eyes upon him, that she could turn back the days to before their encounter and return to her innocent ways. Her greatest sins had once been a dream of avenging her mother and taking off her hat in the sunshine of a late spring day.

From the moment of her meeting with Solomon, it seemed everything in her life had shifted. Was it only the demand of the stars? Was there nothing she could do to halt the forward spin of events?

As she approached the cottage, she saw Helga laughing with the peddler in the yard. "Round back, my pretty," Helga called. "I will join you anon."

Rica smiled. At least one thing would remain as it had been. Helga and the peddler would flirt over cups of ale and tease each other and pass an idle hour in harmless play.

Rounding the cottage, she tugged off her hat and shook her hair loose, smelling dill and thyme as her skirts brushed the plants. The scent, so married to the peace this cottage had brought to her life, gave her surcease.

As she came around the corner of the cottage, that peace was abruptly shattered. For there she saw the source of her restless discontent. Solomon stood by a waist-high tree stump, his jupon shed in the thick heat of the day, his tunic loose at his throat to show his neck and chest. His sleeves were rolled to the elbows; his hair tumbled loose around his sensual face. The details flooded through her as she stared at him, frozen in fear and longing.

But as she drank in the sight of him, her body seemed to swell. She felt at once pained and yearning and overly full, as if she would burst. Dreamlike, she moved forward, drawn against her will to the shining lure of him.

He'd been absorbed in his task, but at the sound of the bells on her wrists, he glanced up. He dropped a bundle of herbs, glanced at them where they fell by his foot, then back to Rica.

He did not speak. There was no need, for in his eyes there leapt a blaze of joy. Rica's careful control dissolved in the heat of it like melting honeycomb.

Crossing the grassy space between them, she bent to retrieve the bundle of herbs he had dropped, and held it out toward him.

For a long, silent moment, he only stared at her hungrily. Slowly, then, he reached out and took the tied bundle from her, his fingers lingering over the heart of her palm, caressing softly before they closed around the bundle. All the while, his dark eyes burned into hers.

And though Rica tried, she could not stop the response of her own fingers, which curled to touch his knuckles as they withdrew.

They moved apart, by unspoken agreement putting the broad stump between them. Solomon glanced toward the back door of the cottage. "I could not remember whether I was to come mornings or afternoons," he said.

"Nor could I."

His hands stilled and he looked at her. "Ah, Rica, you've bewitched me. I think of naught but you."

She wanted to weep. How much her life had shifted! "Solomon!" she whispered, but whether in supplication or protest, she did not know.

Over the rings of the stump's surface, he touched her hand. "Rica—I mean you no pain. Forgive me."

He moved away and snatched his jupon from a bench nearby the oak tree. Rica stared at him. "Oh, do not go!" she cried softly. "You give more pleasure than sorrow, though I should not say it."

Still he stood there, his coat clutched in his fist. All at once, he moved forward. "I have been taught a man should be always moral, Rica. We study this—we are taught from childhood." He shook his head slowly, regretfully. "And I know it is my nature to be weak in this way, but I do not know how to keep you from my thoughts."

His words were uttered in a fierce low voice, and he leaned intently over the stump toward her. "In truth," he said at last, "I have lost my wish to resist you."

It seemed he would kiss her, there in the dappled light falling through the branches of the oak, with the scents of Helga's garden filling the air with spice. "I know not how to manage this untoward passion!" she said quietly.

His features were harsh and closed for a moment. "It is forbidden," he agreed. "Yet I know a little of the world—it is not so strange." Again he glanced at the cottage. "Will you trust me?"

"I should say nay," she said, and sighed.

A gentle, teasing smile touched his lips. "Is it so terrible to tell me yes?"

"No," she whispered, her eyes snared in his. She had the strangest feeling of being drawn close, drawn into him somehow. Not against her will, but with it. "I thought of nothing but you these past days, Solomon. I have begun to care little whether it is good or right."

"Then meet me tomorrow," he said, and touched her fingers discreetly. "By the Ill, where before we met. Can you find leave to do so?"

She swallowed. "I'll try."

A soft, glad sound came from his throat. "I'll wait from Sext to Nones, and if you have not come, then I will know you have not found leave."

Her throat was too dry for words. Slowly, feeling as if her head were bobbing on a string, she nodded.

His fingers traced the tops of her fingernails. "You need fear nothing, Rica. I will be mindful of our places."

By which he meant he would leave her a virgin. Rica solemnly gazed at him. "I wish it were not so," she whispered, and touched his fingers in return.

For a long, quiet minute they stood thus, only their

eyes and fingertips touching in anticipation and a certain sweet sorrow. He smiled. Rica smiled in return.

He straightened. "Now, my lady," he said with a somehow rakish grin, "allow me to give you a lesson in the fine art of medicine."

By the time Helga joined them, Rica was laughing at his jests, his easy storytelling. He had a gift for mimicry that he used to imitate the physicians at his school and the customers and merchants in his father's shop.

Somehow laughing eased the swollen longing in her body. By the time Helga joined them, guffawing over the end of Solomon's story, Rica felt more herself.

"I see you've amused yourselves this day." Helga's face glowed red with perspiration as she settled herself on the bench. Baldly, she hiked her skirts up over her knees.

Solomon shot an amused glance toward Rica. "Do you think she tries to seduce me?"

"Of course I do!" Helga cried. "More fool I, if I did not!" With a great heaving sigh, she leaned back. "'Tis the right of a woman of my years."

Rica settled next to her on the bench, plucking the heads from a basket of dried chamomile stalks. "I will see, one day. I will flirt with peddlers and aging knights"—she nudged Helga ribaldly—"dreaming of bed sport no longer mine."

The midwife closed her eyes, a smile hovering about her mouth. "I would not be so quick to dismiss the pastimes of an old woman."

"Oooh!" Rica returned mockingly. "Do you hear her?" she said to Solomon.

"Aye." He grinned easily and a loose bevy of curls fell on his forehead. "Bawdy old thing."

"You will see, my tender young ones. Inside does not change."

Rica grinned at Solomon. "Perhaps you'll prey on sickly young girls."

He laughed, showing his white teeth. "Nay. I will be rich and fat and will no longer care for nubile young figures."

Helga snorted. "Pah!" Abruptly, she sat up and slapped Rica's thigh. "How fares your sister, my girl?"

Rica frowned and she glanced through her lashes at Solomon. "It is she I came to speak of today."

With good grace, Solomon fetched his jupon. "There are tasks I must tend for my father," he said and dipped his head in a courtly, mocking gesture. "Another time we will laugh again."

"Good day," Rica said, grinning.

"Ah, lad, I will teach you proper birthings if you show yourself by Saint Peter's and Paul's Day," Helga said.

"A birthing, *fräu?*" His tone was clearly shocked. "I am no midwife!"

"So be it." She waved him out of her yard. "Be gone then if ye have no use for midwifery."

Quizzically, he looked at her. "I see no point, but I will come if it will take that tone from your voice. You see I am your humble student and I will do as I am bid."

"Saint Peter's and Paul's Day," she repeated and gazed at the sky.

The notion of teaching a man the art of midwifery shocked Rica, and she nearly questioned the old woman. Then she thought better of it. Helga was wise. Whatever her reasoning, Rica knew she had given the matter considered thought and found need to give Solomon some lesson related to her legendary skill at midwifery.

Solomon walked off toward a hidden path in the forest that led to Strassburg. Rica forced herself to look at the basket of apple-scented chamomile in her lap rather than at his retreating back, but it took all the control she owned.

"So, my pretty, tell me about it."

Thinking at first Helga meant the secret longing she felt for Solomon, Rica started guiltily. For a long moment, she simply stared at the old woman, dumbstruck, her mind a whirl.

"Well, girl? What worries have you over your sister?"

"Oh." Rica breathed out softly. "That."

"That. What *that?*"

Absently, Rica put a small round blossom in her mouth to suck on. "It is less a matter of Etta than it is of Rudolf, my father's vassal. You know of him?"

Helga pursed her lips, her eyes unreadable. "What of him? Does he chase her?"

With relief, Rica spilled the whole story, from the moments in the forest when she'd tempted him, to Etta's longing for the knight, to the sense she had that Rudolf might be dangerous somehow, in ways she could not always pinpoint. "Now my father speaks of Hugh, the squire's son, for Etta and I know not what to tell him."

An odd, shuttered expression bled the animation from Helga's ruddy face. "Let it lie."

She stood up, as if ending the subject, and picked through a basket with an air of dismissal. Rica, frowning, jumped up. "I come and spill my heart to you and all you can say is, 'Let it lie'?"

"I have not the answers you wish, Rica."

"What answers do I wish?" she asked in frustration, taking hold of one fleshy arm. "I am frightened, Helga. Think you that Etta is well and truly healed? Think you she can make a wife to Rudolf if I teach her the duties of a goodwife? Think you he is dangerous and I should not let him seduce her?" In her agitation, she shook the arm minutely. "What?"

Helga lifted one work-roughed hand to Rica's cheek. "You have been blessed, child. More than you know. Your papa dotes on you, the times have been peaceful—you have beauty and youth and laughter."

A ripple of foreboding whispered over Rica's flesh.

"But now you've grown to a woman strong and must take your place."

"What has that to do with my sister?"

"You will be parted soon or late, sweet. You must let her make her own way." She took her hand away and pushed a basket into Rica's arms. "Help me carry these inside. I smell a storm brewing."

With a small noise of irritation, Rica hurried after her. Inside the cottage, filled with its perfume of herbs, she spoke sharply. "Helga!"

Abruptly, Helga turned. Her face in the dim light looked suddenly old. Her pale eyes showed bleakness. "The portents are ill for the coming year. Ask me no more, girl."

Then as if regretting her words, she kissed Rica's forehead gently. "You are a worry, sweet, and I would spare you suffering, were I able, but I cannot. You must marry and take your place and there is naught I can do. Enjoy the last days of your girlhood, for they are numbered."

Rica wanted to weep. Instead, she straightened, knowing the midwife echoed her own thoughts of this morning. Changes were afoot—she had felt them herself.

"I will teach Etta as well as I can, then." She reached out and took Helga's hand. "Pray for us all."

Then, afraid she would disgrace herself with weeping for the ephemeral pleasures of childhood, she fled.

9

In the evening, Rica climbed the circular tower stairs to her father's solar, her heart heavy. She did not go to unburden herself, but to seek the rote security she found in his presence.

It was no surprise to find him abed, his hawk hooded and sleeping on a perch nearby the embrasure. Charles's cheeks were an unhealthy red and his breath came in labored weights, as if he were very fat.

At his side sat Humphrey, speaking in his booming voice. He was a little drunk, Rica thought with a frown.

"Mark my words, Charles," he said and belched. "There will be nary a Jew left when this pestilence is spent. Those overlooked by the plague will be hanged or worse."

Fighting the terror his words struck through her, Rica hurried forward with a frown. "Uncle, are you blind? Can you not see you weary him?" She plucked the wooden cup from his fingers and slammed it on the table. "Off with you! Go join the merriment in the hall and leave my father to his rest."

Chuckling, Humphrey tugged his beard, his dark eyes shining with laughter. "What a fine woman you've grown to be, Rica! Charles, why is she yet a maid?"

"Off, I said." With a swish of her skirts, Rica nudged his shoulder none too gently. Laughing, he bid Charles farewell and took his leave.

"Ah, Pappi," she said, dipping a cloth in cool water. "You have been overburdened these last days."

"I need only a little rest, *liebling*."

"Why do you let him stay and weary you so?"

He only shook his head.

Rica pressed the cloth to his brow, leaving it there to cool the feverish look of his face. Settling at his side, she hummed a soft tune for his pleasure, a soothing melody meant for babes.

After a few moments, when his color seemed more to her liking, she took his hand in her own. "Is it true, what Humphrey says about the Jews?"

"Yes," he said with a sad grimace. "You are too young to recall the *Judenschlägen*." He took the cloth away and shifted restlessly in his bed. "We found a boy, only ten or eleven, beaten to death by their number. 'Twas only a week after your mother died. It sickened me." He closed his eyes. "He was only a child, and what could he have done to them? Like Etta."

Rica frowned in concern at this odd trail of conversation, although she thought she understood it. The two events were tangled together in his mind.

He roused himself. "'Tis their ilk—the *Judenschlägen*—that stalk Europe now, killing the innocent the pestilence leaves behind."

Again an icy finger snaked through her. "Is there no protection from the Church? Surely the emperor—?"

His eyes were grave when he looked at her, and weary beyond measure. "There is no force that can stop fear, *liebling*. Remember that."

Seeing he was tired, Rica said no more. But as she sat beside his bed, humming to quiet him until he slept, she stared at the fire, sick with fear.

How long? How long until the pestilence swept in from France? How long till it was borne to Strassburg on an ill wind and the madness descended?

She tried to tell herself that Solomon could be right, that perhaps the city would be untouched, but daily the reports grew longer and grimmer. She heard the gossip of the servants, saw the fear in her cousins' eyes when they spoke of it.

And when it came, it would bring with it the madness of fear and hatred. A voice deep in her soul gave up a little cry: *Solomon!*

Tomorrow she would meet him in the glade by the river and tell him what she had heard. Perhaps there was something he could do if he were warned in time.

Solomon gathered food stealthily from his mother's kitchen while she quarreled with a serving girl in the courtyard over the placement of summer vegetables. Into a large pouch went a skin of wine, a Sabbath cake freshly baked for the next day, a round of cheese, and a new loaf of bread.

Frowning, he stood back, wondering if his theft would be noticed—then he smiled to himself. Yes, his mother would notice, but she would only groan over the appetites of her sons, an exasperated edge of love in her words.

Quickly, he wrapped the food and tied it to his belt. Trying to recall how he exited the house when he was only innocently heading toward Helga's, he passed through his father's shop.

Jacob was bent over a table with an abacus and

his books. "Off to the midwife again?" he said.

"Yes."

Jacob settled back in his chair, his dark jupon falling open to show a silk lining. His eyes were sharp as he raised a knowing brow. "She saves you from the trouble of idle hands?"

Solomon felt a guilty start in his chest, but with effort he smiled. "She is no youthful wench, Papa— but round and wise."

"Well, it is to that very boredom I have given much thought these past days. My traders tell me the pestilence is spent southward—it rages now to the north." He picked up his quill. "In the autumn you will return to your studies at Montpellier."

"As you wish." Solomon, relieved the conversation seemed at an end, moved toward the door.

"See that you mind yourself between now and then," Jacob said, beginning to write.

For a moment, Solomon paused, wondering what his father knew. Jacob's black eyes were too sharp.

Solomon turned and hurried out, disturbed. But for all of that, his feet could not carry him quickly enough to the meadow by the Ill.

Finding it empty, he sat on a rock by the water, tossing pebbles absently. In the autumn, his father would send him away, back to his studies. A part of him embraced the notion with gladness. Although he had learned much at Helga's hands, he knew he'd nearly reached the limits of her knowledge. He was a quick and eager student, a fact he accepted without undue modesty or arrogance, and he had missed serious study these many months away. He longed for the exhilaration of intense instruction that filled his days at Montpellier.

And yet, the thought of leaving Rica pierced him. It made this day seem all the more precious.

But the afternoon heated and the sun moved inexorably toward the mountains in the west and Rica did not appear. Restlessly, Solomon began to pace. Perhaps she'd been unable to find leave at all. Helga had told him there were guests at the castle; perhaps her duties bound her to the castle for the day.

His waiting would likely prove futile, but neither could he make himself go. With longing he gazed toward the path down which she would come, then he walked toward the river again. Each little noise caused him to whirl, then settle again in disappointment.

Finally he heard the bells for Nones ring out through the hazy air. He bent to gather the food he had not eaten, then thought better of it.

Rica had not come, but the river still ran. There was something to be salvaged from the day. He stripped and dove into the cold water, taking pleasure through his acute disappointment in the sharp fingers of the water in his hair and on his shoulders. They cooled the ache of his hunger.

It was good to remember there were things in life he cared about. Good to remember he had a life beyond the strange, sharp attraction he had conceived for Rica.

For in the end, there was no hope for them.

The bells for Nones were already ringing by the time Rica found leave to go to the meadow. Her father, on some whim, had ordered a lavish meal prepared for their supper. He wanted dancing and drink and a feast, he said in a querulous tone from his bed. Rica, exasperated with trying to dissuade him, complied. To appease her sister, she also took Etta with her to the kitchens, and the instruction had cost her precious time.

Now she hurried through the forest, praying Solomon was not yet gone from the glade. Breathing hard from her rush, she paused on a hill overlooking the bend in the river. The glade was empty.

Her heart plummeted. She had told herself she wanted only to warn him of the trouble on the continent, but as she stood by an ancient pine, clutching her skirts in frustration, she knew it was not true. She had wished to look upon his face, to listen to his voice and glimpse the respect that lived in his eyes. She wanted to hear a story, to speak of ideas and thoughts to which no one else would allow her to give voice.

Feeling near tears, she began to turn away. A loud splash sounded on the water and she spun around, just in time to see his dark head break the water.

With a rush of excitement, she hurtled down the hill, her heart singing. "Solomon!" she cried out in exuberance as she stopped by the edge of the river. She waved to him.

He wiped his eyes and stared at her. Water streamed from his dark hair and glistened on his broad, well-formed shoulders. She suddenly thought there were things she didn't know, things she wished to learn. Things he might teach her.

He found his footing. "You surprised me!"

Rica mischievously fingered his clothes, hanging from the branch of a tree. "So I see!"

"Will you join me?" he called, spreading his arms in invitation.

Rica only smiled.

"I beg you turn then," he said, walking toward her.

The current fell lower and lower as he approached the bank, showing a strong chest covered with dark hair, and a lean waist. "Give a poor man a little dignity to dress."

Rica did not move, smiling instead as she eyed the length of his torso. "You have nothing I have not seen on the bodies of a hundred knights as they bathed, my lord."

"Ahhh," he said with a crooked and knowing grin. "Are you so certain?"

Rica tossed her head. In truth, he was marvelously well made. No softness marred his flesh. There was an astonishing array of beauties to admire—his hard, rounded arms and lean waist and wide shoulders.

Solomon grinned and stepped forward. The water dropped lower, to his hips. Rica only smiled.

But then he moved again, a measured expression of teasing in his dark eyes, and the silvery water sluiced away from his magnificent flesh. A razor of yearning sliced through her loins as images branded themselves in her mind: a nest of dark curls and lean hips and the shining length of a strong thigh—

With a little cry, she whirled away, slapping her hands over her face. Behind her, Solomon laughed. She scurried away from the tree where his clothes hung, still hiding her face.

In a moment, he grabbed her from behind, his arms decently draped in his tunic. "'You have nothing I have not seen,'" he mimicked in a high, falsetto voice, pulling her against him. He chuckled, bending to kiss the tender flesh of her neck. "Are you so shy, sweet lady?"

"No," she said sadly and turned in his embrace. "I fear I am too bold."

She flung her arms around his neck. His body was

damp and smelled of sunshine and cool water, and the smiling curve of his lips was only inches from her own. "Oh, by the saints," she said with a sigh, "I care not if it is sin to hold you thus. I have thought of nothing else since early morn."

She lifted herself on her toes and kissed him, kissed the smile from his mouth. Her body sang as he grabbed her close. There was fierce hunger in the noise he made low in his throat and she pressed upward, clutching his head between her hands.

In a moment, gasping, he took her arms gently. "I am only a man," he murmured, touching her face. "I cannot kiss you all day without pause or I will go well and truly mad."

His eyes were glazed, and his lower lip glistened with moisture from her mouth. Hesitantly, she touched the place with her thumb, and with a sudden move, he bit her playfully. "Come," he said with a smile. "I've brought food."

"I can stay only a little. My father is not well."

"Whatever it is will suit me."

Beneath a chestnut tree was a small bundle. He unwrapped it and took out a small cake, cheese, and a wineskin. He withdrew the last thing, hiding it a little with his hands, and Rica inclined her head curiously.

"What have you there?"

"A surprise." He held it out, a small painting rendered in vivid reds, blues, and sharp whites. "'Tis Cairo."

Rica, stunned, took the painting and stared at it with a feeling of awe. "Oh, Solomon."

There was the fierce Muslim warrior with his scimitar, and the slain Christian knight. Scarlet tipped the sword and flowered over the knight's breast. Behind rose white mushroom shapes. She pointed to them. "What is this?"

Solomon bent over her shoulder. "Mosques—the cathedrals of Islam."

"I wonder if they are as beautiful as they appear." She stared, transfixed, seeing in her mind this street and the women in their dark robes with their faces covered. A trill of excitement sounded over her nerves—the whole earth seemed suddenly a thousand times larger and vastly more seductive.

She looked up, clasping the painting to her breast. "This is a most precious gift, Solomon. I will treasure it always."

"I knew that you would." His fingers brushed her cheek and fell away. "Will you eat with me?"

Rica kept the painting close by her leg. "I wonder how the air smells there."

"I don't know. But there are spice markets—perhaps it smells of cloves and cinnamon."

"Perhaps it does!" Rica laughed, then cocked her head. "What interests you about the place, Solomon?"

"The physicians," he said without hesitation. "If not for the Moors, we would all still be barbarians." He broke a bit of cheese. "One day, I will study with them."

"You sound very sure."

He chewed a bit of bread before he answered. "One day, I will go."

The words plucked at her, for they brought too much reality into the stolen day. "It seems strange I will miss you so much," she said quietly.

He didn't speak for a moment, his head bent. After a little time, he lifted his eyes and met hers with a clear, honest expression. "My father is sending me to Montpellier in the autumn."

Rica swallowed, then stretched out her hand to touch his face. "You have become important to me so quickly," she whispered and stroked his jaw where a light beard grew.

He looked at her, his black eyes fathomless and full of sorrow and yearning. Urgently, he reached for her, his hands circling her head below her hair. "I care not if it is impossible," he whispered. "For now, for today, we are here." He kissed her.

A turbulent gladness welled in her at the taste of his mouth, at the feel of his form against her, at the press of his stomach against her own. His lips moved over her face and touched her chin, then her neck, and trailed a line over her collarbone. Sunlight fell through tree branches to create dapplings of light and shadow on the lids of her closed eyes, and from the forest came the sound of crickets whirring and sparrows singing. Grass brushed her calves.

Solomon lifted his head, shifting so that her thighs straddled his legs. There was ruddy color in his cheeks. He kissed her again, differently this time. He suckled the edge of her mouth and tasted the corners and teased her tongue, and his hands roved over her arms.

Rica felt a rightness in the moment, a dizzy power. His hands moved on her shoulders, then over her chest above her gown.

She stilled, thinking of her forbidden dreams of him, but even as she went rigid, his hands slipped down over her breasts.

A quivering rippled through her at the pleasure this new thing gave her. Startled, she looked up and found herself snared in his black eyes. His gaze held her as his thumbs stroked over her nipples, back and forth slowly. And still she stared at him in wonder, shimmering with the pleasure that radiated through her from the gentle motions.

She smiled a little, and he closed the inches between them to kiss her fiercely, engulfing her with his silky hot tongue. Against her belly was a rigidness, and, caught in the shivery thrill of the moment, Rica reached down instinctively to take it in her hands.

"Ah, lady," he said with a strangled sound in his throat. "Ah—Rica, no." He grabbed her wrists in a hard grip.

Still overflowing with pleasure, Rica did not listen. Though he held her hands, his position was vulnerable, and with a laugh, she launched herself forward, tumbling him back into the grass. They landed in a tangle, her arms caught in his hands, their thighs interlocked.

She laughed as they struggled, the laughter gentling in her throat as she bent to kiss him and felt his lips grow soft and giving and sensual. His grip eased on her wrists.

But at the moment she thought she had tamed him, he gave a triumphant little cry and rolled her to her back, trapping her there in the grass with his thighs and powerful arms.

"I am only a man, Rica," he warned, his voice ragged. "I will not sully you for this dalliance that can lead nowhere, but you must abide by the limits I set."

Rica smiled up at him, in spite of the serious tone of his words. "I will try."

"*Oy Gotenyu!* You will drive me mad." He fell upon her, kissing her neck and ear, her jaw and eyelids and lips. "In all God's kingdom, there is no woman like you," he said against her neck. "No woman."

He reverently kissed the swell of her breasts over her gown. His hair brushed her chin. "'Tis torture, Rica. More torture than I have ever known."

All at once, as if dragging himself, he shifted away from her. He sat upright, taking her with him. He touched her cheek. "I said once I would give much to teach you passion, Rica, but there is much I think you would teach me."

Rica buried her face against his neck. He stroked her back. "The world is not fair," he whispered.

His words reminded her of Humphrey's conversation with her father. Abruptly, she raised her head. "Solomon! My uncle says they are hanging Jews in France for this plague. He says there will be no Jews left in the empire when it is all spent."

He made a soft, low noise, something between a laugh and a groan. "I know." He looked away from her. "It is an old story. When the world goes awry for others, it is always the Jews who are punished."

"How foolish I am," Rica said, feeling a flush steal into her cheeks. "I thought to warn you."

A sad smile touched his mouth. "What could you know of such things? You are young and rich and the daughter of a powerful lord."

Rica bent her head, disturbed in some unnamed and uncomfortable way. "My father said—" She broke off and frowned. "Ah, it is no matter."

"What did he say, Rica?" A sharp bitterness edged his words. "That it is only fitting for Christ-killers to die in such ways?"

"No!" She shifted, inclining her head in fury. "Think you all lords are vain and ignorant? My father is a good man. He grieves for the killings."

A dusky color stained his cheekbones. "Forgive me," he said with his eyes downcast. "The world is no more his doing than it is yours or mine." He took her hand and quoted softly,

"Ah, Love! could you and I with Him conspire
To grasp this sorry Scheme of Things entire,

*Would not we shatter it to bits—and then
Remould it nearer to the Heart's Desire!"*

Rica bent her head to kiss his fingers. As her lips touched his palm, she felt him touch her hair gently.

"I have not heard those words before," she said. "The priest would call them blasphemous, but they comfort me today."

"Holy men of all ilks think Omar Khayyam a blasphemous poet." His hand moved in her hair. "I think that is why I find so much comfort in his words."

Rica lifted her head. "Do you not believe, Solomon?"

"Believe in what?" A fury blazed now in his black eyes. "In the loss of you so I might gain God's favor? Should I deprive myself of all that is rich in life—for what?" He shook his head. "I wish I did not believe, for I think it cruel of God to give you to me and snatch you away."

Alarmed, Rica covered his lips. "Say no more!"

He grasped her fingers. Closing his eyes, he moved her hand over his mouth and the light fur of his beard, and settled a kiss to her palm. Deeply touched, Rica allowed it.

Finally he sighed. "The hour grows late and my bad temper will ruin this sweet time if I stay longer."

Rica nodded. "Soon I will be missed."

She stood up, brushing grass from her skirts, and helped Solomon gather the leavings of their meal. He broke the bread and cake into crumbs, scattering them along the riverbank, then came to stand beside her. She hugged the small painting to her breast.

"When will you come to me again, sweet Rica?"

She stared at him, loath to leave. A restlessness moved in her, a restlessness she knew would only worsen. With a small, worn cry, she pitched herself forward and kissed his tempting mouth one more time.

She thought of her father, and the bustling presence of her relatives, and knew it would not be soon. "I will be missed if I come often." She frowned. "I'll find you at Helga's when I am able."

He nodded soberly, and Rica could see his disappointment. A cloud shadowed the sun abruptly and she shivered, taking it as an ill omen. In dread, she stared at the darkness for a moment. How dared they break all the laws of God and man thus? "Solomon—"

He stilled her words by placing his fingers over her lips, as she had done moments before. "Do not speak it, Rica, I beg you." His eyes were bleak. "There is so little joy in any life, I will take this time with you until I must go." He smoothed a lock of hair from her face. "In our old age, we'll remember and be glad."

Her eyes filled with bittersweet tears. She wanted to rage against the certain loss of him, and yet could not deny there was beauty in his words, in the small hope he gave them. "So it shall be," she whispered.

He stepped back. "Go now, before you are missed."

10

A spell of bad weather plagued the valley, and after several days of rain and drizzle, Rica grew weary. The men-at-arms were restless, and Charles was in fading health.

The vassals and guests played cards by day and drank heavily by night. Rain muddied the baileys and stables. Humphrey had today arranged a hunt, even in the wet weather, and the men had brought back a deer, which Cook dressed and served with great flourish. Maidservants had cleared it away now, and Rica sat with her sister and cousins on a bench in the great hall. The trestle tables had been moved aside, and dancers moved to the tune of a haunting lute.

Smoke from the fires and lack of exercise made Rica irritable. She cast a jaundiced eye over the room. In a corner, one of Humphrey's men leaned over the buxom figure of a maidservant who blushed and giggled at his drunken whispers.

Rica shifted, looking the other way. She had warned the maids to steer clear of the drunken men late in the evenings, but they paid her little heed. Nine months hence, there would no doubt be a new crop of babes for Helga to deliver into the world.

But as long as there were no fights, Rica chose to ignore it all, although she kept a sharp eye on her cousin Lorraine, who teased and strutted much too boldly. Already there had been arguments over her, and her parents seemed not to notice the girl's wantonness.

Even now she bent low over Rudolf's shoulder, her breasts nearly spilling free of her low tunic. She smiled ripely. Next to Rica, Etta made a low noise.

Rica patted her hand. "Fear not, sister," she said. "See how Rudolf turns away? He likes not that forwardness." Rudolf had flushed a dusky red and he shot the twins a glance, as if to see if they noticed. Shaking Lorraine's hand from his velvet-clad shoulder, he crossed the room. He bowed before Etta.

"I would dance, if you would grant my favor," he said.

Etta smiled and gave him her hand. As the two whirled away, Rica nodded in satisfaction, lifting her brows toward Lorraine, who shrugged and turned her attentions to a more willing partner.

Humphrey, who should have censured the girl, snored loudly, slumped in his place. His wife, pinch-mouthed, watched Etta and Rudolf dance.

"Minna," Rica said, "I have had enough of this place. Will you walk with me?"

"I had best stay," she said with a grim glance toward her sister. "Else Lorraine will likely bring the castle walls down with her games."

Rica kissed her with a smile. "You're a brave girl."

She made for the winding stairs in the west tower, which led to the dark walk over her own chamber. Huddling deep into the folds of her cloak, she pulled up the hood and stepped into the soft, drizzling rain.

To one side, two men-at-arms chatted lazily. One of them was Lewis, who had his eye on Minna. "The weather's foul for a walk, my lady," he said.

"And below the air is foul with drunkenness," Rica returned sharply.

He laughed and stepped aside to let her pass.

The two men murmured as she walked toward the end of the square over which they stood guard. At the edge, she stopped and gazed out into the wet darkness in the direction of Strassburg. It was not so late there were not glimmers of lights left burning beyond the city walls, though the tiny orange flickers were only twinkles in the darkness. She crossed her arms.

Which of those lights might lead her to Solomon? What might he be doing at such an hour? He had many brothers, he'd told her. Did he play chess with them on rainy evenings or did he study by the light of the fire?

Did he, she wondered, think of Rica, as she thought of him?

She shifted, lifting her face momentarily to the cool rain, letting it wet her skin.

For the past few days, in each spare moment, she haunted the priest. It was, in part, a need to escape the endless chores the extra guests put upon her time, and a way to feel more than a workhorse, carrying and fetching for others. In his little rooms nearby the chapel, she pored over his small collection of books, seeking knowledge of the Jews.

What little she found only made her hunger to learn more. All of her life, the streets of Strassburg had been populated with the Jews, the merchants and moneylenders who made the building of cathedrals and cities possible, they with their yellow circles and strange customs and separate lives. Yet, till now, she'd had no cause to wonder over them.

Because of Solomon, she longed to learn. She wanted to know what he ate and how he slept and what songs he sang. She wished to know all the things that made his life his own.

From the embrasures of the great hall, left open in spite of the rain to let the stench of food and too many bodies out into the night, came the robust sound of drums and a pipe and a lilting horn. A shout of many voices cried out in greeting, and in her mind's eye, Rica saw the revelers jump up to the new dance.

She turned back toward the city. Solomon could never be a part of the merrymaking in that great hall, so it held no interest for her.

Lewis walked up behind her, his scabbard clinking against the waist-high wall along the walk. "Lady, the hour grows late, and I fear you will be ill if you remain in this rain."

She nodded. "You're right," she said, and put a hand on his arm in gratitude as she turned.

"It saddens me to see your lightness descend to such worry, pretty Rica," he said with a smile. "Is there aught I can do to put the mischief back in your eye?"

For a moment, Rica said nothing as she stared out toward the city. Then, softly she said, "Only if you can start the world anew."

Puzzled, the vassal looked at her. She sighed. Solomon alone seemed to see there was more to her than a pretty smile, that she had a hunger for things beyond herself.

"There is naught you can do," she said gently. "But I can ease your worry by retreating from this cold spot. Good even."

She steered clear of the noise of the great hall and went instead to her chamber. The tedious, endless details of feeding and housing so many, of entertaining them all while the skies poured days of rain, wearied her. And since Rica had been teaching Etta what she could, the tasks became doubly draining.

A knock sounded at the heavy oak door, and for one moment, Rica was tempted to pretend she was already abed. It was bound to be Etta or Lorraine—the one whining, the other preening—and Rica did not wish to listen to either tonight.

But she called out and the door opened to reveal Minna on the threshold, the stub of a tallow candle in her hand. "I hope I do not disturb you," she said in a small voice.

"No, cousin." Rica drew the girl into the room. Around her eyes were deep hollows of strain, as if she had not been sleeping well. "What disturbs you?"

Minna began to cry. "I cannot sleep for fear of dreaming!" she said and pressed her face into Rica's breast. "I dream of them over and over and wake up screaming. Lorraine only shouts at me and my mother thinks I am foolish, but Rica, I am so afraid of dreaming again!"

"Shh, shh." Rica held the trembling girl and stroked her hair and hummed quietly. When Minna had settled a little, Rica drew her to a bench beneath the rushlight. They sat side by side and Rica took her hands. "Tell me what so frightens you, little Minna."

"The pestilence." Her fingers tightened painfully on Rica's. "There were such horrors as we came that I could not bear it. . . . We had to tie cloths over our mouths for the stench. Whole villages, Rica, where nothing moved at all. Not even the birds sang, as if they knew some horror—"

She bowed her head, and tears began to run over her face. "Even the cats and the dogs and the babies just lay there with no one to bury them."

Rica made a low, sympathetic noise and drew Minna back into her arms. "Ah, those are nightmares indeed. And there is naught I can say to take away the things you have seen."

"Why has God let this happen? Are we so terrible to be punished thus?"

Clasping the child's head, Rica stared at the shadows flickering on the wall. There was no answer to give her. "I think it is not God, Minna," she said at last. "I think it is not a punishment, only some natural thing that has run wild."

"I do not wish to live in a world where such things are natural."

"Ah, but you have no choice." She lifted her head and pinched the wet cheek gently. "You are here now. There is naught you can do."

"May I stay and sleep with you, cousin?" she asked, and bit her lip. "Just for tonight—and perhaps tomorrow?"

Rica smiled. "I will be glad of the company. If your dreams still plague you, I will fetch a potion from the midwife tomorrow."

"Thank you." Minna breathed more easily and laid her head on Rica's shoulder. She was asleep almost instantly.

Holding the slim body of the girl against her, with the cold of the stone wall behind her and the hiss of the burning rushlight overhead, Rica felt oddly calmed. There had been so little time the past few days to think or breathe or take a moment to sit quietly.

Her eyes fell upon a silver crucifix fixed to the wall. The now familiar mix of joy and shame washed through her. It was shameful to kneel in the confessional and hear the prayers of penance Father Goddard gave her when she knew she lied by omission. She had even felt a flush of guilt yesterday when taking honey from the hives, for the scent of beeswax reminded her sharply of that wooden confessional in the chapel.

She sighed. It would be easier if she could regret her actions, but she did not. How could she repent of something that gave her such sweet and piercing joy?

In the autumn, Solomon would be sent away. Then Rica could go to the cathedral in Strassburg for full confession. Until then she would avoid the communion table as well as possible, and pray to Mary, who understood the needs of women. Mary, virgin or not, surely knew more of a woman's heart than priests who were only men.

Autumn—when the stars and portents said evil would befall them. Idly stroking Minna's hair, Rica thought now it was the pestilence toward which those ill omens pointed. Perhaps this was the last season any of them would see.

In that light, her love for Solomon seemed a precious gift, not the guilty secret she thought it. Tomorrow, she would go to Helga's on the excuse of procuring a sleeping draught for Minna.

One by one, the vassals and maids and guests filtered out of the hall, and when there were only a few left, gaming in one corner, Rudolf took his lady's hand. "Rica," he said, "let me walk with you to your chamber."

The girl blushed delicately, and whispered her assent. Next to her, Lorraine inclined her head toward Rudolf, leaning over to kiss Rica good night. "Sweet dreams," she said, and laughed as she caught Rudolf's eyes on her neckline, a neckline cut so low her nipples nearly showed. Nay, he could see the dark crest when she bent, and she knew it—

Whore, he thought violently. If he'd not had so much to drink, he could control the carnal leap of his flesh, but after so much mead, he felt only a hazy anger. With more force than he meant, he grabbed Rica's hand, crushing her fingers in his own as he tugged her toward the stairs.

At the small noise of pain she made, he slowed and loosened his grip. In the shadowy recesses of the circular stairs, her blond hair seemed to catch all the light, and her wide lavender eyes were as innocent as Lorraine's were knowing. Before Lorraine, Rudolf had thought Rica to be lusty. Now he knew differently.

"Did I hurt you?" he asked.

She did not speak as he moved closer, but her eyes grew even larger as he lifted her hands to his mouth and kissed them.

The sounds of the hall reached them, boisterous and shrill, as if to emphasize the quiet here in this dark, silent stairwell. Across his vision flashed the heavy breasts of Lorraine, obscuring the virtuous beauty before him. Angrily, Rudolf bent to kiss Rica's mouth.

He kissed her hard, needing the taste so long denied to remove the evil taunting him. Passively, she allowed it. It fueled his frustration. How dare she? How dare she walk so boldly through the streets of Strassburg and wander the countryside and challenge his judgment and yet kiss him like some fainting maid?

Roughly, he pushed her against the stone wall and pressed into her. A small frightened noise escaped her throat. The sound inflamed him. He tasted blood on her lips and felt the push of her hands against his chest. A panicky movement in her body made him think of a frightened bird. Still he held her and kissed her, and somehow his hands were at the shoulders of her tunic. He fumbled, his member engorged and pressing into the folds of her skirt, seeking the heat between those long white thighs. He tore her tunic in his hurry to touch her breasts.

Rica made a noise of horror at the sound and her fighting passed frightened, moved to frantic. She scratched at his face and neck as his hands kneaded the fullness of those naked breasts below the tatters of silk, and he met the pain with exultation—now she suffered as he did. Now she knew the punishment a man could inflict. Now she would begin to learn who was master, as ordained by God.

Once before it had been like this; once before he had tangled with her in a dark passage, but it had not been so violent then. Now she pulled at his hair and bit his lip and he shook with his need to have her.

Struggling, he lifted her skirts and grabbed the supple flesh of her bottom. All at once, she froze and beat at him fiercely. "No, my lord!" she whispered. "We cannot!" She shoved at him at a vulnerable moment and he lost hold, slamming against the opposite wall in the narrow stairwell. "No!"

Blinking, he stared at her, her hair wild with his caresses, her tunic torn to expose one white breast, her lips swollen and one bleeding. To his horror, the sight nearly made him lose control, and he left her, stalking through the darkness to his chamber, sure she was a demon.

Just as Rica settled Minna on her bed, another knock sounded at the door of the chamber. "God's teeth," Rica muttered under her breath and went to open the door.

There stood Lewis with Etta leaning on him, her

lip bloody. "Forgive me, my lady, but I thought it would be better to bring her to you than to your father."

"What happened?"

"I know not." His mouth hardened. "I found her weeping on the steps nearby here when I went to fetch the new guard. No doubt some drunken louse mistook her in the darkness for a serving wench."

Gently, Rica took Etta from him and led her into the room. There was an alarming pallor in Etta's cheeks, but when she looked up at Rica, there was no vacant look about her eyes, only an abject misery. A sharp ripple of relief passed through Rica's chest—and she realized anew how tenuous Etta's recovery was.

As Rica settled her on the bench, she slumped against the wall.

Rica made a low, furious sound. "Seek him out who did this to her," she said in a harsh voice. "Say naught to my father. I will avenge my sister this mistreatment."

Lewis, standing uncertainly by the door, narrowed his eyes. "I cannot leave such work to you."

"Do you doubt me? Will you trust me thus far and no farther? Think you I am incapable of wreaking justice for my sister?"

He only stood, implacable, for a moment. Then he shifted, glancing once to limp Etta, then away. "I do not doubt you. When I learn the beast's name, you will have it, but you must promise to give me the pleasure of witnessing your vengeance."

"I swear it."

As he caught sight of Minna asleep on the pallet, a gentleness came on his face. "Ah, she is a young one," he said quietly and looked at Rica with a rueful smile. "I would that she were older so I had not so long to wait." He sighed and touched Rica's arm. "Good night."

As she closed the door, Etta cried out, then burst into tears. Rica rushed to her and took her in her arms, as she had done with Minna only minutes before. "Shhh, little one," she murmured. "All is well."

Etta wept as if her heart would burst, but in a little while, she seemed calmer. There was no damage Rica could see—only a small cut on her lip, as if she'd been kissed brutally. Etta quietly allowed the ministrations, clutching her cloak about her.

At last she said, "I would go to my own chamber now."

"You will not tell me what happened, sister?"

Etta shook the hair from her eyes. "'Twas nothing— naught but a drunken soldier. I was only frightened, not hurt."

"You must tell me who it was—so that he may be disciplined."

Etta got to her feet, studiously avoiding Rica's eyes. "I didn't see him. 'Twas dark on the stairs." She reached for the door and her cloak fell open, showing the torn bodice of her gown and a bruise purpling on her breast. Dismayed, she quickly grabbed it closed again, but not before Rica could take her arm.

"Let me see," she said.

Head lowered, Etta let the fabric fall away. The elegant embroidered tunic was torn, the silk frayed. The imprints of a man's fingers showed dark against her pale skin, and it was plain she had been roughly treated.

Rica looked from the bruises to her sister's miserable face. "Why did you not tell me?"

"I did not wish to be so humiliated," she whispered, her eyes closed tight.

"Etta, you did not do this. You have no need to be ashamed." Gently she closed the cloak. "Men are often beasts, as now you have learned. I will not say more unless you ask it."

Etta nodded. The movement set the ruby in the hollow of her throat afire with light, a deep glowing red that looked like blood.

A terrible thought crossed Rica's mind. "Etta," she said. "It was not Rudolf who did this?"

"Nay!" Etta protested, her eyes flashing. "Nay! How can you say such things? He would never handle me so."

There was such shock in her expression that Rica believed her. Still, as her sister left and made for her own chamber, Rica was filled with a deep uneasiness.

From behind her, Minna spoke quietly. "Your sister is mad."

Rica turned, head inclined, a protest on her lips. But Minna leaned soberly on one elbow, her intelligent young face quite serious, and the protest died. "Go to sleep, little Minna."

"You do not believe me because she's clever, but her mind is unhinged."

"Minna, why would you say that?"

The girl slumped to the mattress, her shiny dark hair spilling over her thin shift. "She speaks to those who are not there, like a witch. I hear her sometimes when I pass, giggling and chatting there in her chamber."

Gooseflesh rose on Rica's arms. In fear, she spoke sharply. "'Tis only the imagination of a solitary girl, Minna. It is unkind of you to call her mad." Roughly she doused the rushlight and climbed in next to her cousin. "Go to sleep."

Exhausted, Rica pushed away all thoughts of Etta and the plague and her father's illness. In the private darkness behind her closed eyes, she reached for visions of Solomon—Solomon laughing and kissing her and quoting poems. Thus were her worries purged, and she slept.

11

Through the unshuttered window of his chamber, Solomon could hear the patter of rain on the streets below. The fresh scent of it washed through the opening on a cool wind.

He hunched over a table, quill in hand. A single tallow spluttered and flickered, and the uncertain light cast shadows over his work on precious parchment. In his careful hand, he translated a poem into Latin, taking pleasure in the bitter words:

> *But helpless Pieces of the Game He plays*
> *Upon this Chequer-board of Nights and Days*
> *Hither and thither moves, and checks, and slays,*
> *And one by one back in the closet lays.*

For ten days he had faithfully gone to Helga's each afternoon, aside from Sabbath and Sunday. For ten days, he'd awakened each morning hopeful, his step light, his heart yearning. Each morning he thought, perhaps today, she would come.

But each afternoon he walked home in disappointment, his mood dark, his only solace in the harsh and lovely poems of Omar Khayyam. In the evenings, as soon as he was able, he escaped to his chamber, where he laboriously copied the poems. He decorated the margins of the pages with drawings of the herbs with which he'd grown so intimate these past months—borage and lungwort, tansy and foxglove and pennyroyal.

He longed, as he mixed potions and cured herbs and ground rootstock for Helga, to ask the midwife how Rica fared. Of course he could not, and as if to thwart him further, she who had once babbled about the girl with pride and love at every chance, now fell silent and spoke of her not at all.

He sketched the graceful round heads of chamomile and remembered Rica nibbling them as she sat on a bench below the tree in Helga's garden. He thought of her laughter and teasing that day, and of the strange entrancing power of her smile the next afternoon by the river.

As if to underscore his imaginings, muted noises floated into his room. First, squeals and giggling and the low chuckle of his brother, then Raizel's soft womanly cries and the hoarseness of completion from his brother.

Solomon set his jaw and dipped his quill, trying vainly to ignore them. Was it not cruel enough that he had conceived a forbidden passion? Now he was forced to listen to the cooing sounds of his brother and new wife next door, had to see the shy, sly glances they exchanged with each other over meals. He saw them in the courtyard, sneaking kisses when they thought themselves unobserved.

Jacob, seeing Solomon's mood this evening and the glowering looks he shot toward his brother, had remarked with a grin, "They do make marriage look

an appealing state, do they not? 'Tis as it should be—
love and duty mixed together."

"They are rare."

"She has a sister," Jacob commented good-naturedly,
moving a pawn on the chessboard.

Solomon caught the teasing gleam in his father's
eye, but the suggestion irritated him nonetheless. "I
do not wish to marry yet."

"Aye. I have begun to wonder if you ever will,
beneleh. Maybe you think you're too good for the
girls around here, eh?"

"Ah, who wants a silly maid with nothing in her
head?" Solomon scowled and rashly moved his
queen. "When it's time, I'll take a wife, and she'll be
wise as well as beautiful."

Jacob laughed outright and took the queen. "That's
why I like to play chess with you! You lose your temper so easily that I can win if I tease you."

Ruefully, Solomon shook his head. "Tata, one
day—"

"One day—ha!" Soberly, Jacob raised his eyes and
slowly stroked his salt-and-pepper beard. "One day
you will grow up, Solomon. One day, you'll see passion is a small and fleeting thing."

"I have already learned that, Papa, at your hands.
It is not passion I seek."

"Ah, I forgot. You want a *wise* woman."

Earnestly, Solomon leaned forward. "My life has
been devoted to learning. How am I to find any contentment with a woman who cannot even read? What
will we talk about when the passion fades?"

"A woman is not for talking. You will find that
companionship with the men in the community—not
your wife."

Solomon said nothing, but over his father's shoulder,

he caught his mother's eye, and she smiled gently at him, shaking her head. All at once, he was grateful to her, for her fine, sharp intelligence, even though unschooled. She had been fascinated this summer with his talk of herbs and cures and the lore of the midwife.

Taking her cue, he told his father, "Perhaps you are right. There will be a woman for me here, but first I must finish my studies."

Hours later, in his chamber, alone but for the sleeping presence of his brother, with the spluttering candle casting a yellow light over his neatly written words, Solomon admitted to himself that he'd never dreamed a woman could be his equal intellectually. And yet Rica, whose schooling had been uncertain and unfocused, was certainly as hungry for knowledge as any man he'd ever known.

And whatever his father said, she was a woman who would talk with him in the evenings once their passion was spent. The cruelty was, now that he'd found a woman he would gladly take to wife, she was denied him—forever unattainable.

The next morning, he set out toward Helga's once again, but he'd lost his cheerfulness. He had no faith she would come to the cottage as she had promised. His mood was as thick as the mist. He wondered if Rica had gained her senses, had realized how dangerous their meetings were, and thus chosen to forget him. Had fear perhaps stolen the pleasure?

Abruptly he turned from the path that led to Helga's and struck out through the trees toward the castle. There was less than a mile between the cottage and the great stone fortress with its ancient keep. Once before, Solomon had hidden in the orchards on the chance Rica might go there.

Beneath his feet, twigs snapped and his soft boots

slipped on the wet leaves. His cloak caught on a branch, but in agitation, he did not care and ripped it free. At the edge of the thick trees, he paused, gazing toward the castle. In the mist, all that was visible were the walls of the bailey. It looked deserted.

His mind raced as he stared at those walls, raced with a tumble of wild plans—he would present himself as a pilgrim and beg food. Nay, a physician on a journey, bearing tidings of the pestilence and cures. Or—

In misery, he bowed his head. Madness.

Two months ago, he'd never seen the woman who now obsessed him. All the years of discipline, all the prudence and resistance he had practiced had come to naught in the face of his longing for Rica. He was ready to storm the castle to carry her away, ready to make a fool of himself to gain a glimpse of her in the bailey.

For what? The most he could hope for was a month or two of stolen afternoons, a kiss here and there, and a laugh in a glade. He could never lie with her, sleep next to her, walk in a public square. He could never sit with her over a meal and talk of the day's work, or take her hand in old age.

With a hard set of his jaw, he turned away. Nature and fate had made him a fool. His chest ached with it as he stumbled blindly toward the comfort of Helga's cottage, where at least there was work for his hands and a feeling of some purpose to his life.

A town official rode out to talk with Charles. Rica hovered nervously in the solar, having won her stay by glaring at the official and clucking about her father's health. Charles, rather than argue with her, allowed her to linger.

Now, as the men talked, she tended the fire, listening

with concern to the tales the burgher related. He had come on behalf of the council of Strassburg, to talk with Charles about the rumblings they had heard about the Jews.

The tales he told made her hands shake. In Carcassonne and Narbonne, Jews had been dragged from their houses and thrown onto raging bonfires. It stunned and terrified her.

"We do not wish to see such madness in the streets of Strassburg," the judge said in a prim tone of voice.

"No man of any common sense would wish such violence," answered Charles, dipping bread crusts into clear wine. "But our new emperor has vowed fines to cities who allow such violence." He wiped his face with his palm. "I know nothing else we can do right now."

Seeing the gesture of weariness, Rica bustled forward. "Papa, do not continue if it tires you." Over her shoulder, she glared at the judge. "Is there some assistance you would ask of him, or some purpose to your visit? If that be, state it and go. He has not been well."

The judge rose. "I meant only to warn you, my lord, of the concerns of the council. We wish to protect our citizens—"

"And their taxes," Charles said cynically.

"None will benefit from such a slaughter."

Charles lifted a hand. "There is truth enough in that. I thank you for coming out to tell me."

As the man left, Rica tucked her father's robe more closely about him. "I must go to Helga's today, Papa. I'll see if she has some remedy to speed your health."

"Time, child," he said, and settled under her ministrations. "Time and sleep are all I lack. Go you to Helga's for rest, but not for my sake." He closed his eyes. "Give her my regards."

Rica smiled, for she knew Helga often slipped in and out of the castle. Only two days before, Rica had seen her riding away from the castle at first light, on a mule given her by Charles. "That I will do."

She fetched her cloak and basket from her chamber, and paused there for a moment, cursing as a rumble of thunder sounded from afar. Hurrying, she found Etta in the kitchens and drew her into the bailey. "Think you can be mistress over the evening meal if I have not returned?"

Etta, recovered from her encounter on the stairs, smiled slyly. "I thought we were not to switch parts again till our cousins went away?"

"I am weary and wish to escape. The weather may prevent my early return, and I thought you might—"

"Etta is unwell today," she said, and kissed Rica's cheek. "You may stay as long as you like."

Rica smiled. Minna thought Etta mad, but it was only love and new awakening that made her seem so. Had she not ordered the meal for the evening herself? Nonetheless, she paused. "Take care in dark passages, sister."

A quick, shuttered look passed over Etta's face, then was gone. "That I will do."

Then Rica was through the gates, on the road, with Leo in her stead. She nearly flew along the path, aching to see her Solomon, to escape the confines of the castle, to be young and free, one more time.

It was a shock when a figure slipped from the trees, only a shadow in the mist at first. There was a stealthiness about him that frightened her, a kind of grim purpose to the steps. Next to her, Leo paused, alert. His tail began to move slowly back and forth, and the figure moved from the mist.

"Solomon!" she said with a glad cry, and rushed

forward, eager to hurl herself into his arms, to taste his lips and feel the power of his well-made form against her.

A harshness in his face halted her. His lips were set in an unsmiling line. The hood of his cloak hid his curls, reminding her once more that he was no youth, but a knowing man. Rica gazed at him in some fear.

He closed his eyes, then opened them and moved his head once side to side, as if to deny that she stood there. He lifted his hand toward her. "Rica," he said in a lost and ragged voice.

She stumbled to him and he caught her close. She buried her nose in the wool over his chest, smelling the exotic essence of his flesh. His chest was a warm, broad wall and his arms circled her so tightly she thought she would burst. "Oh, I have missed you."

Pressing his lips to her temple, he whispered, "I did not know if you would ever come to me again."

"My father is ill and there are guests and—"

"Shhh." He rested his cheek on her hair. "It matters not. For now, you are here and I am glad of it."

Encircled by the mist, in the holy silence of the day, Rica did not care so much now for kissing him and feeling his naked flesh against her own. All those sensual visions paled in comparison to the solidity of his arms wrapped around her, to the simple glory of being next to him. She felt dizzy, as if she were standing in the center of the world and all else would slip into harmony as long as Solomon held her.

He rocked her silently, holding her almost painfully close. "It does not seem an evil thing," he said with quiet wonder. "It seems as if I have held you thus for all of time, that I should go on doing so forever."

She pressed her cheek to his chest more tightly, closing her eyes to shut out all but the perfection of him warm against her and the richness of his voice in her ear.

Very gently, he lifted her chin with one finger. For a moment, he held her face on a level with his and his fathomless eyes glowed with passion. A soft smile curved his mouth. "I am so glad to see you, my love."

He bent his head and pressed his lips to hers. Her dizziness trebled. She swayed, her fingers curling to clutch at the fabric of his cloak.

As if to chide them for their indiscretion, the fog began suddenly to part, and from far off, a rumble of thunder rolled through the mountains.

Rica grinned up at him. "Is it chastisement, do you think?"

He laughed. "No doubt there are angels even now readying arrows of lightning to pierce us."

"Then we must hurry to the shelter of Helga's cottage."

"As long as I am with you," he said, taking her hand, "I care not where we go."

She met his gaze. "Nor do I."

He could not hold her hand on the road, but they walked closely together, and Rica took pleasure in the brush of his fingers from time to time.

Just out of sight from the cottage, she paused. "Helga is a wise woman. She'll guess what we are about if we do not take great care."

His expression sobered. "Yes. You go now. I will follow in a little." He touched her hand and melted into the forest.

At Helga's door, Rica rapped twice, then pushed inside to the sweetly scented gloom of the cottage. A pot boiled on the hearth, sending up a cloud of fragrant steam. "Helga! I ran away today. . . . Are you here?"

From a dark corner by her store of herbs, Helga emerged, her face shiny. "Oh-ho!" Her smile was

JOIN THE
TIMELESS ROMANCE READER SERVICE
AND GET FOUR OF TODAY'S
MOST EXCITING HISTORICAL
ROMANCES FREE,
WITHOUT OBLIGATION!

Imagine getting today's very best historical romances sent directly to your home – at a total savings of at least $2.00 a month. Now you can be among the first to be swept away by the latest from Candace Camp, Constance O'Banyon, Patricia Hagan, Parris Afton Bonds or Susan Wiggs. You get all that – and that's just the beginning.

PREVIEW AT HOME WITHOUT
OBLIGATION AND SAVE.

Each month, you'll receive four new romances to preview without obligation for 10 days. You'll pay the low subscriber price of just $4.00 per title – a total savings of at least $2.00 a month!

*Postage and handling is absolutely **free** and there is no minimum number of books you must buy. You may cancel your subscription at any time with no obligation.*

GET YOUR FOUR FREE BOOKS TODAY ($20.49 VALUE)

FILL IN THE ORDER FORM BELOW NOW!

YES! *I want to join the Timeless Romance Reader Service. Please send me my 4 FREE HarperMonogram historical romances. Then each month send me 4 new historical romances to preview without obligation for 10 days. I'll pay the low subscription price of $4.00 for every book I choose to keep – a total savings of at least $2.00 each month – and home delivery is free! I understand that I may return any title within 10 days without obligation and I may cancel this subscription at any time without obligation. There is no minimum number of books to purchase.*

NAME_____

ADDRESS _____

CITY_____STATE_____ZIP_____

TELEPHONE_____

SIGNATURE _____

(If under 18 parent or guardian must sign. Program, price, terms, and conditions subject to cancellation and change. Orders subject to acceptance by HarperMonogram.)

GET
4
FREE
BOOKS
(A $20.49
VALUE)

TIMELESS ROMANCE
READER SERVICE

120 Brighton Road
P.O. Box 5069
Clifton, NJ 07015-5069

AFFIX
STAMP
HERE

broad and happy. "I've missed you, my pretty—but now you'll be stuck here, for there's a terrible storm brewing and I won't let you go."

Rica hugged her, taking a fierce gladness in the round, soft contours of the woman who had filled the motherless places in her life. "What a pity," she said, smiling. "Perhaps it will rage all night and all my father's silly guests will have to fend for themselves."

Helga waved her toward a bench nearby the wall. "Sit. I've got stew boiling and some fresh milk. We'll have a nice chat." As she bustled toward the hearth, she asked, "How is your sister?"

"She is well," Rica said, shedding her cloak. "I have been teaching her the kitchen arts and even a little of the books."

Helga turned, her cornflower eyes showing surprise. "Can she read?"

"A little. Not as much as she will need."

A knock sounded at the back door of the neat little cottage and a giddy shiver made Rica's hands shake. She folded them together so Helga would not see.

Wiping her fingers on her apron, Helga muttered about the inconvenience of babies and opened the door. Seeing Solomon, she made a noise of surprise. "I did not think to see you on so foul a day."

Solomon ducked under the threshold. In the small room, with its low rafters hung with herbs, he seemed a giant. He did not look at Rica, but instead smiled at Helga. "I could not stay away. There is much to learn and so little time left."

"Pah!" Helga returned. "You know all I have to teach. 'Tis a mystery why you still come to me each day."

Rica stared at him greedily. At Helga's words, it was as if he could not help himself—he turned and looked at Rica. Her heart leapt as he gave her a slow, seductive smile. "Why, it is your young friend that I long to see, old woman." He threw back his hood, freeing the riot of curls that graced his head. His voice lowered, sweetened. "And today I am rewarded."

Rica blushed and glanced at her hands, delighted at his open flirtation. Much better by far than attempting to hide the raging attraction between them. At least this way, there was some outlet for play.

"How weary I am of men who see only this fleshly shell," Rica said airily. "You are all a boring lot."

He laughed. "That we are."

A great crack of thunder shattered the sky overhead and Rica jumped, squealing a little over the suddenness.

Helga cackled. "There's a punishment for your boldness, lass."

"What about his?" Rica asked in protest.

"The heavens only punish women," she said, bending over her pot.

Rica heard a note in the words that jarred in the teasing light of their conversation. Helga straightened and gave Rica a direct, penetrating stare. As loudly as if she had spoken, Rica heard Helga's warning from early in the summer: *It only takes one man to make a woman a fool.*

12

Sneaking a glance at Solomon, Rica realized he, too, felt chastened at Helga's subtle warning. Without looking toward Rica, he sank down next to her.

It wasn't long before the usual light-heartedness returned, however. It was as if Helga, having issued her warning, felt free to relax. She was full of gossip gleaned while tending the birth of a noble's child in the city. She entertained her guests with speculations and rumors, and had both Solomon and Rica laughing in no time.

She had brought out dice for them when yet another knock sounded into the cottage, this one pounding and frantic. "Mistress! Midwife!"

Helga glanced at Solomon. "'Tis the birthing I spoke of." She flung open the door. "I'm here, son," she said, touching the shoulder of the peasant man kindly. "I only need fetch my cloak."

"Hurry!" the man said. "She's screaming like a demon."

Rica saw the tightening of Helga's jaw. A hard birth, then. Suddenly she knew that the very difficulty of it was why Helga had chosen it for Solomon's education.

He stood up. "It is unseemly," he said, "but I am willing to learn whatever you have to teach."

Helga, rushing to don her cloak and gather her mysterious potions and herbs, stopped long enough to give him a measured look, one of pride. "A fine physician you'll be one day, Solomon." Pursing her lips, she reached out to the badge of Jewry on his cloak. "Tear that off. I will sew it back later."

He frowned, but did as he was told.

Rica, watching, felt bereft. For so many days, she had longed to see Solomon, to escape the castle confines and be free, and now not only Solomon, but Helga, too, would be swept away. She felt an unreasonable irritation toward the laboring woman.

Helga bent to kiss her head before she left. "We may not return for many hours. Do not go until you must, and do not leave while the storm yet rages. I will send to your father, if you wish."

Rica nodded sadly. As they left, Solomon turned at the door to give her a single, wistful glance. But even in the wistfulness, she saw his eagerness to tend the birth, and smiled at him.

His eyes blazed, then he was gone, and Rica was alone amid the herbs as rain began to fall.

In the dark storm, Solomon made his way back to the cottage. His mind whirled with images—the screams of the mother as her body convulsed gruesomely, the violent ripping of her flesh, the patience of Helga as she used her hands to take the babe when the mother could no longer work to free her body of its burden.

And more, as if that weren't enough—the tears of joy on the mother's white face as her babe was laid at her breast; the endless bleeding that left her dead in an hour; the lonely whimpering of the babe, as if he knew his mother was gone.

The healer within him had always sensed Helga's latent power. Tonight he had seen it. Her hands, so veined and old, moved with surety and strength. Her voice, so rough and bawdy, held a thousand notes for encouragement and sympathy and command.

He understood why she had insisted he go with her to this birth.

Now she had sent him back to her cottage, and though his father would worry, he could not go without letting her finish her lesson. For that was what it had been—a cruel and illuminating lesson in the challenges of treating women. A sorrowful gladness touched him. He was blessed indeed to have found her as a teacher.

Wearily, he pushed open the door of the cottage, his cloak sodden, his face and hair wet.

A fire burned low in the hearth, and the smell of the mutton stew still lingered, reminding him it had been many hours since his last meal. In a fog of exhaustion and loss, he sank on a bench, dropping his cloak on the floor to bury his face in his hands. At the warmth of the room and the sudden release of his muscles, his body tingled from feet to shoulders.

And then, there was Rica, soft around him. Her arms circled his shoulders as she knelt before him, and he smelled gillyflowers in her hair. With a noise of anguish and pain, he grabbed her close, burying his face against her breasts. There was comfort in her warmth and silent sympathy. She pressed her cheek into his hair and stroked his back.

Solomon wept.

It was a release, an aching kind of grief for the

peasant woman who had died, for all the women in the world who must endure such travail to give men their sons. He wept for his ignorance and his helplessness, his uselessness as a healer in the face of all that violence.

Rica said nothing. And he could not have found words for the pulsing new knowledge he'd gained of a woman's lot. He was too moved and too exhausted.

He lifted his head. Pulling her into his lap, he wrapped her close against him and kissed her. Deeply, holding her head between his hands, needing to feel the pulsing of life in her veins and the heat of her cheeks against his palms.

After a moment, she stood up to take a kettle from the stove. She poured hot liquid into a cup, then handed it to him. "Drink this before you take a chill." She smiled.

He found a small answering peace as he took the wooden cup from her fingers, to drink gratefully of the pungent mulled wine.

It slipped inside of him, warming his throat and belly. Rica took a length of linen and dried his hair, her hands efficient and ungentle. Her vigorous scrubbing sent blood rushing to his scalp.

"Where is Helga?" she asked, at last, pausing in her ministrations.

"She stayed to see to the babe. I know not why she sent me back."

Rica laughed gently and tugged at his hair, playing in the curls as if he were a beloved child. "You would not wonder if you had seen your face." Her tone sobered as she leaned over to look at him, her hands on his shoulders. "Was it so terrible?"

"Yes." He put his cup down and took her hand. "Sit with me."

Moving aside a little, he drew her down next to him on the bench. As she sat, he drank in the contours of her face once again, memorizing it for the days when he'd no longer have the face and only his sweet dreams of these days.

Rica stroked his fingers. "Do you wish to speak of what you saw?"

He closed his eyes. "Not yet."

"Then I will tell you what I have learned these days away from you," she said with a smile.

He raised his eyebrows. "Have you been studying?"

"Yes." She brushed a heavy hank of hair over her shoulder, still holding his hand. "I found the story of David and Bathsheba."

"Ahh. And what did you think?"

"It was beautiful," she said softly. "As lovely as any of the troubadours' stories, or the poems of the knights." She laughed. "And poor Father Goddard could hardly deny me a story contained within that holy writ, though I know he wished to."

He smiled, and moved his thumb over her palm, a palm callused with the hard work of her days. "I always believed a lady would have hands as delicate as spider webs."

"Perhaps they do," she said, and he could see he injured her. "I seem to not be much of a great lady."

"I like these calluses, Rica. You are not idle." To prove it, he lifted the palm to his lips and kissed it. "They are strong, like you."

"You are the most unusual man I have ever met, Solomon. Men don't talk this way to me." She inclined her head and asked shyly, "Are other Jews like you?"

At this, Solomon remembered his conversation with his father the night before and laughed. "I wish I could tell you yes, but I cannot. Not even I have ever spoken to a woman as I speak with you, Rica." He looked at her hand, cradled in his own. "I never wished to."

"And yet," she said quietly, "perhaps there are dozens of women all around you who have longed to have someone listen as if they had some thought in their minds besides coupling and cleaning and standing like a queen in perfect shining beauty."

"But," he responded with a grin, "had I given one of them my ear, perhaps I would not be here now, listening to you."

She leaned over and kissed his mouth. "I am glad, then, that you found them all silly."

The temptation to tease her was irresistible. "Did I say they were silly? No, I just thought them more interesting for other things."

Her blue eyes narrowed. "So you are like all the rest."

"I am a man," he said with a deliberately casual shrug.

Her silence stretched so long he looked up and found a puzzled frown on her brow. "Have you had so many women?"

For a moment he did not reply, unsure what answer she sought. But to now, he had not hidden any part of himself from her.

"Yes," he said at last. "I do not like to say it, because it seems boastful, but there were many willing even when I was quite young." He gave her a rueful smile. "A boy thinks women are magic."

Her lashes swept down. "The day I saw you in the city, they all stared at you. Young and old, rich and poor. All of them." She lifted one white shoulder in a half shrug. "It made me jealous."

He shook his head slowly and touched her jaw, aware that Helga might return at any moment, but unable to resist touching her for a little while. "Know this, Rica," he said in a low voice. "In all those women there is not one to match you. They have known my flesh. You have known my heart, and stolen my soul."

He kissed her, felt her fingers fall in his hair. Her mouth was like a pot of honey, dark and sweet and infinitely delicious. He wanted to stay, supping it, for all of time.

She pulled away, lowering her head. "Helga will come and find us this way and I will never be able to see you at all." Her eyes glowed a blue as dark as the mountains. "I could not bear it." She stood up. "Are you hungry?"

His stomach clawed him at the thought. "I had forgotten—but yes, I would eat."

As she bent over the pot, he admired her long, sleek arms and the strength in her back. "Tell me what else you studied, Rica," he said to distract himself.

"What else I studied," she echoed and gave him the wooden bowl of stew. Settling on a three-legged stool, she sipped her mulled wine. A rosy tint stained her cheeks.

"Ahh!" he said with a chuckle. "It embarrasses you. Now I am even more curious."

"'Twas nothing very much."

Amused by her reticence, he ventured a guess. "Was it some forbidden text of the womanly arts?"

She looked at him, her embarrassment forgotten, a gleam of eagerness and surprise mingled on the intelligent brow. "Do such things exist?"

His mouth was full and he could not answer for a moment. He nodded. "So I have been told."

"Now there is a book I would be pleased to see."

"If you are so curious, I could teach you what you wish to know of such arts."

"I have no doubt you could, but it is not for myself I would wish to read such a thing."

"No?"

Primly, she lifted her chin. "'Twould be for the education of my sister, who will soon be wed."

Solomon frowned, thinking of the vacant expression in the young woman's eyes. Rica's twin, and yet not Rica at all. "I thought she was not"—he stumbled here—"er, well enough to marry."

"Have I not told you of the miracle of my sister?" A brilliant smile curved Rica's lips and she leaned forward eagerly.

Much as he struggled to pay the view—so innocently exposed—no heed, Solomon found his gaze drawn to the swell of milk-white breasts above her gown, to the velvety sheen of her skin. He remembered the softness against his face from the day beside the Ill, and for a moment he ached to reach out.

When he lifted his eyes, he found her looking at him. Ashamed, he shook his head slightly. "Forgive me." Ruefully, he smiled. "I am showing myself again to be like all men."

"From you I do not mind it," she said quietly. Her eyes darkened. "When I cannot sleep," she whispered, staring intently at him from her stool, "I think of the way your hands felt upon me." As if to illustrate, she placed her palm flat on the rise of her breasts over her tunic. "It comforts me."

"Comfort," he echoed ironically. Slowly, he moved close, and pressed his mouth to the curved places above her bodice. She sighed against him, regretful, but full of longing. He drew back. Kneeling there, he put his hands around her waist and kissed her mouth once more. "I think of my hands on you, Rica, but it gives me no comfort. When can you meet me again?"

She laughed, touching his chin. "I think it should be soon."

"I will look for you every day."

Jauntily, she lifted her cup in a toast. "To that day when I may join you."

He chuckled and reached around for his own cup, touching the rim against hers. "To that day."

They drank together, and then unaccountably, both of them laughed. "Ah, Rica," he said, "you are good for my dark soul. You remind me to laugh."

"And you remind me that I am more than a slave to the whims of others."

With effort, he returned to his place on the bench, mindful of Helga's near return. "Tell me of your sister and the miracle."

Helga rode a mule through the forest to her cottage. She had taken the babe to the hut of another woman deprived days before of her own child. The woman's milk had begun to dry, but would come back quickly. It was as well, she muttered to herself. In a few months, the babe could be weaned to sops if it survived, and by then the papa would be recovered from his deep grief.

The rain had ceased. The first light of morning stained the sky, and it looked as if the storm might at last move on.

Outside her cottage, Helga paused, afraid of what she might find inside. Her choice to send Solomon back here had been a measured one—she had seen the depth of his distress and had known Rica would comfort him.

Helga snorted, thinking on the silliness between the two of them that afternoon. As if she were blind! Pah! Rica's face shone like a jewel when he appeared, had since the first time she had met him, there in the garden.

Not that Helga could blame the girl. His virility crackled around him like a hot light. The most ordinary acts, when given life by Solomon, were imbued with a sensual grace even innocent girls could sense.

And Rica, though innocent, had always been possessed of passion. The pair of them, that first day, had ignited each other. Helga, wise to the acts of men and women, had watched the flame grow and blaze more with each meeting.

Had she wished to halt it, she could have. She might have forbidden Solomon to come to her again. She was not always entirely certain why she did not— except that she knew a little of forbidden passions herself. She had loved Charles der Esslingen for nigh on twenty-five years, since the first time she had laid eyes upon him. It was a source of grief to know he was dying, that even the small times she spent with him would soon be taken.

She prayed now that Solomon had shown wisdom, and she would not enter her cottage to find the young lovers entwined in forbidden embrace.

Outside the cottage, her courage deserted her, and creeping around to one side, she peeked in the shutters.

In the orange light of the fire sat Rica on a stool, her gilded hair streaming around her like silk ribbons. She held a cup in her hands. As Helga watched, Rica laughed, showing pretty white teeth and the dimple deep in her cheek. Solomon sat opposite, leaning forward, an answering smile on his red mouth. His hair tumbled in black curls around his strong face.

But it was their eyes Helga saw, their eyes that plucked at her heart and made her sorrow for the future. For in twin pairs of eyes she saw not the lust she had believed, but love. Adoration, given and received. As Helga watched, Solomon's smile gentled and he stood up to pour himself more wine from the pot by the stove. He paused before Rica, his hand on her shoulder. He said something Helga could not hear, then knelt and kissed her so gently, so sweetly, so longingly, Helga was moved to her soul. Tears welled in her throat—for there was no hope for that gentle love. Doomed they were, and damned, too.

Turning away, she pressed a hand to her pinched heart. "Sweet Mother of God," she whispered. "Oh, help them. Help them."

13

The last week in July, Humphrey, together with his wife and daughters and their party, assembled in the bailey with first light. Rica, up since long before dawn helping to prepare the baskets of food they would take with them, stood next to Minna as slivers of gold sunlight began to shine over the wall into the damp, cool courtyard.

Nearby, Lorraine flirtatiously bid farewell to a pair of Charles's vassals. Rica rolled her eyes. "Your father would do well to get her married—quickly," she commented.

"Yes." Minna made a face. "But I fear she is smarter than my father. She twists him about her finger like a piece of string."

"So I have seen." Touching Minna's cheek, Rica paused, looking deep into the girl's eyes. "And you? Do you have thoughts of love as yet? For there is a vassal here who thinks much of your beauty. He will speak to your father, I think, before much time has passed."

Minna frowned perplexedly. "He has been most discreet—I cannot think who you must mean."

Rica smiled at this sweetness. She glanced around the bailey and spied Lewis standing near the gate, deep in conversation with another man. "'Tis Lewis, there, who has been smitten."

Minna glanced cautiously over her shoulder. "Him?" she squeaked. Her cheeks flooded with color. "But he is the most beautiful of your father's men. How can it be he would not claim you? Or your sister?"

Lewis spied them looking at him. With a sure grin, he plucked a rose from a vine climbing the bailey wall and crossed the grass. Holding out the pale pink flower, still beaded with dew, he bowed. "A token, my lady, to carry with you on your travels."

Speechless, Minna stared at him. The flower shivered in her fingers.

Gently, Lewis lifted the trembling hand and kissed it. "May God keep you well."

Again he bowed and turned away, but not before Rica caught the good-humored wink he sent her way.

All at once, harnesses jingled as men began to mount. The horses milled restlessly, their hooves making soft thumping sounds against the earth. Minna turned to Rica with a small cry and hugged her. "Why do I fear I will never see you again, dear cousin?"

With foreboding, Rica thought of the warnings of the stars for the coming autumn. Against her lips, Minna's hair was fragrant and cool, her body slight and precious. "We will meet again, Minna," she whispered. Impulsively, she added, "Pray for me."

"Yes, as I have done," she said fiercely against Rica's ear. "As I always will." She released her and allowed herself to be helped atop her palfrey. "Take care, Frederica der Esslingen."

Rica lifted her hand in farewell. The party turned

and, with a shout, rode without hurry through the gates just as the sun lifted above the castle walls to splash yellow into the churned yard.

In their wake, the party left silence. The priest, called out to give blessing, wandered back to the chapel, yawning. Kitchen maids, their attention stolen for a moment by the grandeur of so many horses and men-at-arms, giggled to one another and made for the gardens and scullery and bakehouse. Castle guards, too, departed to their tasks, and Rica heard one chuckle in the still morning.

Standing alone, his hawk on his arm, was Charles. In the gentle morning light, he appeared much as he might have in his youth. His hair was gilded, the silver strands invisible, and his bearing was steady. His belly was flat—for he had lost much weight these last weeks.

Smiling gently, Rica crossed to him. "Does it sadden you to see them go, Papa?"

"There is danger now in travel. I worry a little over their safety." He shook his head and gave Rica a grin. "But, no. My brother has always made too much noise for my liking—and that daughter of his nearly started a war with her games."

It seemed an age since last she'd had her father's attention. She realized with a start that she had missed him. Impulsively, she took his arm. "Will you walk with me awhile, Pappi? We can sit by the peach trees and break our fast."

"A man would be a fool to turn down the company of so beautiful a maiden on so glorious a morning." He called to Olga, coming out of the kitchen. "Send sops and ale to the lower bailey."

"And fruit!" Rica added happily.

They walked past the gardens slowly. Rica, her

hand tucked into the crook of her father's arm, admired the rich abundance—late cabbages and thick onions; greens and herbs. Bees clustered around the lips of flowers. A pair of sparrows flitted from the wall to the garden, seeking worms.

Leo, gnawing on an enormous bone beneath a tree, looked up as Rica passed. His tail wagged lazily, but Rica could see he had no desire to leave his prize, so she did not call him.

"You are fond of that dog," Charles commented.

"He lends me freedom."

"Ah, yes. Your precious freedom." He smiled. "I pity the husband who must tame you."

"Since it is you who must say aye or nay to my betrothal, I trust you will not saddle me with a man who wills me to be tame."

A faintly troubled expression furrowed Charles's brow for a moment. "So Helga warns me, too."

They reached the peach orchard and settled on a stone bench surrounded on three sides with gillyflowers, blooming red and pink and white in the warming sunshine. Their spicy scent perfumed the air.

"Ah, I am glad it is no longer raining," Rica said with a sigh, shaking her hair from her face as she leaned back on her palms. She tilted her face toward the sunshine and closed her eyes. "It seemed it would go on forever."

"As it did the night you stayed so long at Helga's cottage?"

Startled, Rica looked at him. Seeing the teasing light in his eyes, she smiled. "And Etta thought she did so well to fool you."

He laughed. The sound was husky and warm, and it was only as it fell into Rica's ears that she realized how long it had been since she had heard it. "In truth, *liebling,* if you are more than five paces from me, I cannot tell the difference." He touched her hand. "But if Etta speaks, I know it is she."

"She will be disappointed."

"So do not tell her." He shrugged. "There's little enough harm in the game. It is a miracle, Rica, all that she does now. I see her in the kitchens and hurrying about the baileys and I always think to call your name."

"I am teaching her letters, now, too."

"I never thought . . ." He trailed off, then shook his head. Abruptly, he faced Rica, close and intent. "You must marry, both of you."

Rica thought instantly of Solomon and lowered her eyes to hide their expression. If only she could say to her father, "There *is* a man I would take to spouse . . ."

But she could not. Instead, she must forestall her father's wish to find her a husband until at least that time Solomon departed for his studies. Even that thought made her feel somehow diminished. "I do not wish to marry yet, Papa," she said quietly. "It would suit me more to wait another year."

"No." The word brooked no argument.

In alarm, Rica looked at him. "But I am not ready! Will you marry me against my will?"

"If need be." His eyes, ordinarily so gentle, were a clear, implacable blue. "It would grieve me to do so, but there is much danger in the air. I would see you settled—and soon."

"Will you wait at least until the equinox? It is you I do not wish to leave. And my sister needs me yet."

"That may be—but you will marry by All Saints' Day. Look about you."

Head lowered, Rica whispered, "Yes, Papa." Then

frowning, she looked at him. "Have you a mate in mind?"

He stroked the breast feathers of his bird. "Perhaps."

"And for Etta, too?"

"Hugh, the horseman, will do for Etta. Especially now she has grown so strong."

The servant appeared with sops and ale. Rica stared at the food with a bleak heart. Once again, time crept up on her. Now she would not only lose her love, she would be forced to marry.

She also had to find a way to bring the alliance between Etta and Rudolf to her father's attention before it was too late and Etta was firmly betrothed to Hugh.

A dull ache sprang to life between her eyes. If only all could remain as it was this summer!

But time would not let it be so.

Rudolf knelt in the confessional. Against his knees, the flags were unkindly cold, and he took satisfaction in the discomfort, as he did in the rough hair shirt he wore hidden beneath his tunic. "Forgive me, Father, for I have sinned."

At the priest's murmured invitation to confide those sins, Rudolf's guilt rose like bile in his throat, clouding his vision with a red haze. "My carnal appetites have led me to sins of the flesh," he said in a harsh voice.

"Do we speak of fornication?"

"Nay, Father. I have only handled roughly a woman who should be more gently treated. I cannot think what madness overtook me." He shifted in discomfort at the memory of Rica on the circular staircase and his drunken, lustful frenzy. He'd seen bruises on her the next day. "Now I fear I have lost my suit for all time."

The old priest chuckled. "Oh, surely it is not so dire as that, my son?"

"She speaks not to me, Father, and when I speak to her, she stares through me as if I am a wraith." He rested his forehead on the wooden wall. "I know not how to make amends to her."

"You handled her roughly, you say?"

"In my passion, I frightened her. She is yet a maid. I was a fool."

"Did Ric—er—this maid seem to show fondness before your mishandling of her?"

"I believe she was growing very fond."

The priest grunted. "Then all you need do is show her you can be gentle as well as harsh. Women must be sweetly wooed. Read to her of poetry, perhaps."

Rudolf frowned. "I cannot read."

"Oh, yes. Well, collect flowers and baubles, then—things that will please her."

"That I can do."

"And do not be overly harsh with yourself, my son. 'Tis a man's nature to hunger for the flesh of a woman, and your virtue speaks well of you."

Rudolf lifted his chin as pride in this recognition pushed away his guilt. Women were temptresses, all of them—even Saint Paul exhorted them to keep themselves covered so as not to draw the eyes of men. "Thank you, Father."

His penance was not harsh. He said the prayers by rote, then begged a healing lotion from the cook and went to a private place. There he shed the hair shirt and rubbed lotion over his reddened flesh. Dressed once more, his sins absolved, he made for the gardens to gather flowers for his love.

* * *

Solomon knelt in the beds of herbs in front of Helga's cottage, ostensibly weeding. Nearby Helga, too, weeded the neat rows, her face perspiring. She talked sporadically of the properties of various plants, quizzing him in their uses. He answered by rote, his attention focused on the narrow road down which Rica would come if she found leave.

More days than not she came. Solomon had given up all pretense of believing anything else in his life mattered. He lived for the hours she sat with him in Helga's yard or cottage, when they talked of poets and natural law and the structure of society. He could discuss anything with her, and if she did not know the subject, she was eager to learn.

She liked to hear his stories of Montpellier and travel tales and the stories of faraway lands he'd heard told by the merchants in his father's shop all his life. Her eyes gleamed with excitement as she listened.

She was also deeply curious about his religion, although at first her questions had been offered shyly. She wanted to know about it because it was his—but he also saw that it fascinated her.

In turn, he asked about the ordering of a castle, the feeding and housing of so many who depended upon the lord. She also had a great store of legends and fairy tales she shared with him.

Talking. He had never talked so much, so hungrily with anyone. Her mind was like a thick and fascinating book, one which he longed to study again and again. It seemed he could never talk enough with her.

He glanced up desultorily and straightened, blinking. There on the road was not one Rica, but two.

He gaped unabashedly at the twins. From twenty

paces, there was no difference in them whatever. One wore yellow, the other rose. Identical, endless hair tumbled over matching white shoulders.

Next to him, Helga made a soft noise of disbelief. "I cannot see which is which," she said.

The girls stopped before them, smiling identical smiles of secretive mischief. And yet, once they came close, Solomon knew instantly which was Rica—in spite of the similarity of their features, he knew his love. The color of her eyes was a bit deeper than that of her sister's, her mouth a little fuller, her figure a little more robust. It was a hundred tiny details that made the difference, but he knew.

Helga seemed not to see those tiny details, and looked from one to the other with an almost comically baffled expression. "Sweet Mother of God, 'tis a miracle! I cannot tell which is my Rica, which is my Etta!"

Before they could speak, Solomon grinned and stepped forward, looking deep into Rica's eyes in secret hunger and joy before he turned. He took her hand and drew her forward. "This is Rica."

She laughed. "Well done, Herr Jacob! Only the priest can tell if we do not speak!"

Helga reached for Etta, her cornflower eyes sparkling with tears. "Ah, my pretty. You are healing! I did not think it could be so quick!"

"Love can heal any wound," Rica said teasingly and nudged her sister.

Etta blushed, but her chin lifted. "As she is the one who loved me so well, she should know."

Even her voice was much the same as Rica's, Solomon thought, narrowing his eyes. Etta's was a little higher, a bit lighter, somehow. He stared at her intently, trying to pinpoint the differences in her face. In his hand, Rica's fingers wiggled and he looked at her.

The dark blue irises blazed with approval. "I am impressed, my lord," she said quietly.

Etta drew a small package from the pouch at her waist. "I have brought you a present, Helga," she said quietly. "And I have a petition for you, if you might give me a minute or two."

"Pah!" Helga grabbed the girl's hand. "Such formality from a babe I brought to the world!" She waved a hand toward Solomon and Rica. "These two can go make bawdy jokes in the gardens. You and I will have a cup of ale and chat alone."

Etta smiled.

Solomon and Rica stood on the road watching them disappear into the cottage. Suddenly, Rica lifted her skirts and ran for the back garden, laughing impishly. "I will beat you!" she cried.

His heart light, he laughed and ran after her, catching up as they reached the side path. He grabbed her arm, and she laughed, nearly stumbling in the hem of her too-long skirts.

"You win, my lord," she said, and slumped against the warm wall of the cottage.

She was tousled from the little scuffle, and in the warmth of the day, her skin was dewy. All at once, Solomon was struck deeply by the fragile beauty of her white throat, and leaning in close, he tasted the delicate hollow at the base. Against his tongue, her skin was slick and salty.

The unexpected pleasure of touching her burst through his veins with a sizzling madness. "Oh, Rica," he breathed against her, and took small sups of her throat, following the graceful line to her chin.

They were hidden from the road here, and Solomon knew they'd hear Helga before she appeared. He circled Rica's waist with his hands, stroking the sweet curve. He smiled. "This must be the prize I've won."

Her eyes were mischievous. "If you like." Her head fell back a little, and a bar of sunlight struck the blue pupils, making them seem blazing jewels set in her rosy face. Overcome, he kissed her, falling deep into her mouth. And Rica met him eagerly, her lips succulent and giving and playful against his own, her tongue dancing and parrying until she made a deep, slow sound. He felt her fingers on his wrist, urging his hand higher. He chuckled and followed her bidding, creeping up over her rib cage until her breast, soft and full, pressed into his palm.

Even through the layers of clothes, he could feel the hard nub of her nipple against his palm, and he rubbed it slowly, plucking at her lips with his teeth. She wriggled deliciously against him, and again he chuckled, tantalizing her flesh with his thumb.

Against her lips, he whispered, "Wouldn't you like to feel my mouth here, Rica? Like this." He captured her lower lip, suckling in illustration. "And like this." With his tongue, he traced tiny circles over her mouth, over the tip of her tongue.

Then, somehow, he was lost. His passion, until that instant a leashed creature, leapt beyond his restraints. He kissed her violently, pressing her against the wall of the cottage, vaguely aware of the heat of the day, of the sound of insects around them. Rica instinctively moved against him, and her hands roved over his back, and lower, and crept—

The door banged in back. Solomon tore himself away and straightened, pulling his tunic down. Quickly, he reached out to brush a lock of hair from Rica's damp mouth.

"Oh-ho!" Helga called.

Rica shot him a panicky glance. He shook his head minutely and bent over the beds nearby their feet. "Over here!" he called, and plucked a cluster of blue flowers from a borage plant.

Helga looked around the corner curiously. Rica had recovered herself enough to kneel next to him in the dirt, and he handed her the borage. "She's proving an apt student," he said, repressing his amusement over the irony. "Perhaps she just needed a better teacher."

But the joke didn't ease Helga's expression. "Come grind these spices for me, in the back," she said brusquely.

They hurried to do her bidding. As they settled in their usual places, Solomon noticed for the first time they were in full view of Helga.

"Do you think she guesses?" Rica said after a moment.

"Oh, yes." He grinned at her. "I'm sure of it."

"Why does she not stop us, then?"

He looked toward the cottage, then back to Rica. "Perhaps she has a romantic heart." To change the subject, which would only lead to solemnity, he asked, "What is your sister about today?"

"She wouldn't tell me." Rica grinned. "In truth, I think she seeks a love potion."

"Ahhh." He laughed. "So, is that how you've captured my heart? With magic spells and potions?"

"You are the one who is so well versed in herbs and the like," she said archly. "My mind was pure before you."

"And now?"

"And now I will not tell you." She smiled without looking at him.

He grinned, feeling a gentle heat surge through him. "Put your hand alongside of you," he said and when she complied, he drew light circles over the heart of her palm. "I am dying for want of you, Rica."

Her gaze sobered.

Solomon glanced toward the cottage and saw Helga bent over the hearth. Looking back to Rica, he said, "I think of nothing but being with you, naked, touching you."

She blushed.

"Do I embarrass you, *mein herz?*"

"No." Her fingers tightened on his, and she closed her eyes. "I am just afraid."

"We'll meet in a hidden place—no one need know where we are." His heart pounded with both arousal and love. "It would be more beautiful to love you that way than anything I can think of."

"Once we begin—"

"Shhh." He smiled. "You must trust me, Rica. I know—" He shook his head. "Never mind. You must trust me. Will you do that?"

Her expression blazed as she lifted her eyes. She smiled, shaking her head. "You know I will say yes."

He laughed. "Good. Tomorrow?"

"Yes." For a moment, she clutched his hand. "It's so hard not to kiss you when you are so close."

He let her hand go and glanced toward the cottage. "But for now we must work, or Helga might find ways to put us on separate tasks."

As the twins walked home, Rica again asked Etta what business she had wanted to discuss with Helga.

"It was nothing," Etta insisted again. "A private question I wanted to ask."

"I am curious, that's all. You've never kept anything from me before."

"None that you know."

Rica glanced at her, laughing. "Etta!"

"Well, you do not tell me all."

"Yes, I do." Guiltily she thought of Solomon, but that was a different manner. Dangerous.

"You have secrets now, Rica." Etta gazed at her steadily. "I see them in your eyes."

Rica said nothing.

After a moment, Etta said, "Who is that man you were with?"

"Solomon," she said casually. "He is Helga's student. Remember? We met him once before."

"I dislike men who are so bold," Etta said with a curl of her lip.

"Bold?" Rica echoed. "I have not seen that."

With a sigh, Etta frowned. "That is not what I mean, exactly. I do not think I have words for it."

Nostrils quivering with amusement, Rica said, "Please try."

"He makes me think of a stallion. His teeth and something about how he does things—everything is so—passionate. Did you not see his mouth? And his hands?"

"I did not notice," Rica said, swallowing her giggle.

Etta straightened her shoulders. "I like men who are pious."

With a strangled snort, Rica's laugh emerged. To cover it up, she coughed, as if choking.

"Are you all right?"

Rica looked up. "It was a bug. It flew in my throat." But at the absurdity of this lie, she could no longer hold back the welling laughter. It wasn't a reaction to anything Etta had said, exactly, but a wave of giddiness that bloomed in her veins whenever

Solomon was near, and the clear silliness of preferring a man who would spend his life on his knees like a priest, rather than tangling with a woman, as men should.

She restrained her giggles. "I'm sorry," she said.

Etta was rigid with rage. Her hands shook at her sides, and her mouth was drawn tight over her teeth. "You make sport of me, because you think me simple and ignorant, but I will turn the tables on you one day, sister."

"Etta! I am only a little silly—do not be so serious."

But Etta whirled and stormed away. Leo trotted along behind her but looked over his shoulder in concern when Rica did not follow. Grabbing her skirts, she hurried to catch up.

But as she made up the lost space, she heard the muttering grumble of her sister as she stomped up the road—a wild singsong spill of words that struck Rica with a strange chill.

Perhaps Minna had not been so wrong, after all. Perhaps Etta truly was mad.

14

Jacob watched his son Solomon more warily with each passing day. The young man was flushed with healthy color since his night with the midwife, and he returned from her cottage with bemused smiles and sparkling eyes. In the evenings, he hid away translating profane poetry into Latin, or sat staring into the fire like a lost dreamer.

Solomon was in love.

For a week the knowledge had weighed in Jacob's chest like a rock, a rock that grew thicker and more solid with each passing hour. Little clues fell into place: it was not a woman he could claim openly; it was a woman who could read and think, the only kind of woman Solomon said he would wed.

There were no women Jacob knew who could read. Girls were not given such instruction, although boys, even poor ones, went very early to study in the temple school.

So this woman was a Gentile and no peasant.

Each time he thought this, Jacob's bowels turned to water. His prayers these past days had been for this willful, passionate man who was his son, who had always been his favorite, though Jacob tried never to show it.

It was with heavy heart that Jacob set out after Solomon one afternoon. He followed at a discreet distance, through the narrow streets of Strassburg and the west gate, into the forest. As they made their way through the woods, twice Solomon stopped and glanced around. Jacob was forced to lag farther behind.

At the road that led to the midwife's cottage, Jacob crept forward to see what direction Solomon would take.

But as he gained the road, he found Solomon had vanished. Although he peered hard in all directions, there was no sign of the dark blue jupon Solomon wore, not anywhere.

For long moments Jacob stood there, frustrated and at a loss. With a defeated sigh, he turned back up the road, choosing it instead of the back paths he had followed in pursuit of Solomon. Little more than a horse path here, it joined the road toward Strassburg nearby the river.

As he neared the castle, movement caught his eye. There, dancing down the hill with a monstrous dog behind her, was a woman. Even from some distance, he could see she was richly dressed in a yellow tunic with a deep green surcoat, cut away to show her lush form. Hair the color of light tumbled over her shoulders and back, and there was about her a leaping joy. She held her skirts in her hands to run through the trees.

To an assignation? Was she running to meet her lover? The rock in Jacob's chest grew to the size of a boulder as he watched the girl disappear into the forest.

Shaken, he stepped forward with one foot, thinking to follow her to see if it was Solomon to whom she ran so joyously. But one step was all he managed.

All at once, he was afraid of the truth. As he turned

toward the city, his mouth was grim. Der Esslingen's daughter! The very thought made him cold.

Henceforth, Solomon would have no leisure. Jacob would see to that. It was only a few weeks until he could return to his studies. Until then, Jacob would see that he had no chance—

Gotenyu! Der Esslingen's daughter.

Rica rushed to the place where she had agreed to meet Solomon. It was on a hill that had a copse of trees, like a crown, at its crest. From between the trees, the whole of the Rhine valley could be seen, shimmering in blue and gold.

She ran in exuberance, her feet fleet and light in their soft boots. She danced over small branches and tree roots in her path, feeling the wind of hurry in her hair and on her ankles.

And when she arrived on the hill, there was Solomon already, looking toward the path eagerly, his smile broad and welcoming. As if he could not wait, he rushed forward to snatch her—nearly mid-step—into his arms. His mouth was hot and sweet on her own. She laughed against his mouth. "Did you miss me?"

"Yes," he growled, and pulled her hard against him. "As do I each day." His kiss was forceful, deep, overwhelming. "I am a madman, Rica—I can think of nothing but you."

There was about him today a peculiar intensity, as if he were only thinly tethered to reason. A little alarmed, Rica eased free of him to go stand by the water.

He followed her. "Are you afraid of me, Rica?" His voice, low and strong, purred over her muscles. He bent close to press a kiss to her shoulder. Needles of sensation shot through her muscles from the spot, and she shuddered.

She didn't look at him. Squatting down next to the spring, she dabbled her fingers in the water. It was cold and silvery, and she could see leaves in many layers pressed to the bottom. And even with her attention so carefully trained on the pool, she felt Solomon all through her. His scent filled her nose, and his heat brushed her arms, and there were deep, quivering feelings in places she didn't want to name.

Abruptly, she knelt and splashed water on her face, taking perverse satisfaction in the gasping shock of it.

Solomon, standing beside her, said, "It won't help, my love."

Sluicing water from her cheeks, she stood up, facing him with a tangle of emotions rising in her breast. "Nor will anything else!" She shook droplets of water from her fingers. "I do my chores, and talk to the servants and to my father, and below it all, I feel like an overripe plum about to burst!"

His eyes glittered, and he stepped forward with the same heat and purpose she had felt a few moments before. "You must trust me," he said, and gave her his rich smile, his red lips and white teeth like the flesh and skin of an apple—an apple she most achingly wished to devour. But when he took her arm, she yanked away.

"Do not!" she said, and the frustration was like a wild beast in her belly and her thighs. She whirled and ducked under a low-hanging branch, trying desperately to reclaim her sanity.

Solomon snagged her from behind, moving so quietly she didn't know he was there until his arm looped around her waist. He dragged her against him. "Be still," he said.

Her thighs grew rigid at the feel of him against her back. "Solomon!" she said, half protesting, half distraught.

His mouth fell again on her bare shoulder, a touch as sweet and pale as the first light of morning. It grew thicker, wetter, until his lips and teeth and tongue settled below her ear, and there stayed, suckling with exquisite pressure at that tender place.

Against her ear, he murmured, "I know what ails you, my love. It tortures me in the night and upon waking. It nearly shreds my soul when I am with you."

His hand moved on her belly below her surcoat, spreading heat with spiraling movements. Higher and lower he went with each sweeping circle, until he brushed her breasts slowly on the top swirl, and the soft aching place between her thighs on the lower.

"I wish to please you," he said, and his voice, too, was like a touch, like the thick honey flavor of mead. She trembled and leaned back into him, resting her head backward on his shoulder as his hand swept again over her breasts.

He shifted a little, and touched her nipples with his fingers, caressing them with both hands through the thin linen of her tunic as his mouth trailed heat over her cheek and the corner of her lips and along the curve of her jaw.

There was no protest left in her, only a rising urgency. Her palms itched with the need to feel his skin.

She turned and caught his face in her hands and lifted on her toes to kiss him. Over these past golden months, she had learned about kissing. She tasted each lip in turn, each edge and corner, every tiny portion; she urged him to open his mouth and thus explored the heat and lingering salty taste of her neck on his tongue.

His reaction was violent. He grabbed her close

and dipped her nearly backward to kiss her with all the passion she now realized he'd held in check. His hands moved with power over her body, over her buttocks and thighs and sides.

He pushed the loose surcoat from her body and Rica felt the weight pool around her feet; she kicked it away as she worked the buttons of his jupon free, still kissing him—his hard jaw and rough chin and sensual mouth.

But when he reached for the laces on her tunic, tugging them loose with a single, practiced gesture, she froze, catching the tunic close in sudden, unaccountable terror. In the warm day, she wore no kirtle and would be naked if the tunic followed her surcoat to the ground. The thought made her pause in embarrassment. He had known many women. Would he find her pleasing?

He lifted his head. A haze of sensual longing softened his forbidding black eyes, and his cheeks were ruddy with arousal, his hair tousled around his face with the restless combing of her fingers.

Inclining his head, he lifted an eyebrow and shed his jupon, tossing it carelessly toward Rica's surcoat, then unlaced his white shirt. A gentle, teasing smile spread over his lips as he took the edges of tunic from Rica's clutching fingers. "You will be glad," he said, and gently pulled the fabric away, his hands skimming over her.

Rica closed her eyes tight as the linen slid down, freeing her skin to the kiss of sunlight and a playful breeze.

And Solomon's eyes.

He didn't speak, and Rica stood there in an agony of waiting, her eyes closed, naked in the grove.

"Oh, God," he whispered raggedly, and Rica felt him kneeling before her, his curls brushing her breasts as he planted kisses on her belly, his hands lightly stroking her sides and back and legs. "I have dreamed of touching you this way from the first day I saw you in Helga's garden."

He took her hands and tugged her down to kneel with him. Staring with penetrating hunger into her eyes, he cupped her bare breasts with his hands. "Do you remember what I said I wanted to do?"

A quiver shook her. "Yes," she whispered.

He bent his head and took her nipple into his mouth.

"Oh!" She sighed, stunned. She had imagined this, imagined what his beautiful, rich mouth would feel like upon her breasts—

His tongue flickered and Rica made a noise. Nothing had ever felt so luxurious as the plucking, swirling glide of his tongue against that sensitive peak. Another soft, surprised sound escaped her lips, and she grabbed his shoulders to steady herself.

He chuckled, but the sound thinned to a low rolling groan. His fingers dug hard into her sides. She sagged, feeling the fabric of his shirt against the front of her thighs.

He steadied her but did not stop. He seemed lost, his mouth leaping and teasing, his fingers curling and caressing. He supped as if all the time in the world was theirs to expend on this one thing, this wild and searing pleasure.

The rising heat in her loins seemed as if it would burn her to death. "Stop, Solomon!" she finally cried. "I will burst."

He lifted his head, smiling a promise. "Yes."

He kissed her. Rica tugged at his shirt, and he willingly lifted his arms so she could pull it off, and then he was as naked as she.

Soft, golden light poured over him, gilding his beauty. For a moment, Rica only looked at him in wonder. His flesh was elegant, with a sheen and texture like flowing amber silk. The angles of his shoulder and jaw meshed in perfect symmetry; his limbs and torso were straight and loosely jointed.

As if he might disappear, she stretched out her hands and placed her palms on his chest. The heat of him surprised her and she looked up.

He smiled, a sultry but somehow enveloping expression. She sketched the firm roundness of his shoulders and arms with her fingertips, and he allowed her exploration, lifting his hands to her body in return. She molded his chest, the neat, light triangle of black hair over walnut skin; he stroked the curve of her breasts. She touched the tiny nipples; he grazed hers with his thumbs. She brushed the flat, hard stretch of his belly; he smoothed his palm over her navel.

Then, boldly, Rica looked down to the proud flesh nudging her thigh, and she reached for it, thrilling at the leap it took toward her hand and the curiously velvet feel of it against her palm.

In surprise, she looked at him, and found his eyes upon her. Their hands and bodies were so tangled that the shock of looking at him—so close—was nearly overpowering, but she did not waver. It was raw and honest and somehow thrilling.

He touched her cheek. "With all that I am, Rica," he said, "I know this is not wrong."

Then he reached for his cloak and flung it sideways, and tumbled Rica backward to it. Stretching himself over her, he kissed her and pressed his body into hers. There was at first a glorious shock as his supple flesh moved over her, the crisp hair on his chest and legs a rough luxury against her skin. She flung her arms around his shoulders, pulling him closer. "Oh, Solomon, I do like this."

He chuckled. "I somehow knew you would." He kissed her in his elaborate, thorough way. "There's more."

He shifted and stroked her leg, deepening his kiss as his hand moved higher and higher. A new, intense kind of heat flooded her, as if in anticipation. She closed her eyes and felt herself open to him.

"This is all I have to give you, my love," he said against her jaw, and his hand settled in the folds of her womanhood. With slow power, his graceful fingers coaxed a swelling pressure from her body, until she felt herself damp and hot and aching for something she could not name. At the very instant she was certain she could not bear another second of the torture, he bent over and suckled her breast while his fingers danced their clever steps.

With a cry, she burst.

But it was not the quick, sharp thing she had imagined. It was slow and deep and nearly endless, a rippling, swelling pleasure so intense she lost herself in it.

And then Solomon knelt over her. His mouth took hers with bruising hunger, and with uncontrolled movements, he shifted her legs close together. "I cannot go away from you today like this."

In the lost and glorious moment, she would have done anything, given him her very life if he asked it. Instead, she felt his member move in tight against the heat he had touched with his hands, and he began to slide against her. Not in her, where she wished him to be, where he no doubt longed to settle, but safely outside.

Then it didn't matter that the joining was not exactly what they would have wished. A wild rhythm built between them. Rica clutched him and writhed and arched. Solomon grasped her and shivered and pressed. And all at once, together, they tumbled into blessed release, an explosion of love and consummation.

He fell against her, his head nestled into the crook of her shoulder, his hair spilling over her jaw and mouth. His hands were clutched hard at her shoulders. Rica held him close, trying to gather into memory the heat and silk of his back, the sweaty press of his chest on her breasts, the pressure of him between her legs.

And suddenly, she found herself bereft and weeping for the loss that would come. She turned her face into his jaw, feeling his ear grow damp with the seeping tears.

He lifted his head and cupped her scalp in his palms. "Ahh, my Rica," he whispered, and caught a tear on his lips.

He kissed her eyelids and mouth. "I love you," he said fiercely. "It matters not who we are forced to wed by church or family—you and I now belong to each other forever."

She stared at his beloved and familiar face. In wonder, she touched his mouth. "You have not said that to me before."

"That I love you?" A grimness twisted his mouth. "For love only would I risk all that I have, *ahuvati*. For love, I risk death." He kissed her reverently. "Never doubt it."

No, she did not doubt, looking into the passion of his black eyes. With a trembling hand, she smoothed curls from his forehead. "And I love you," she said quietly, as soberly as he had. "No matter what man holds the power of husband over me by church, you are the spouse of my heart."

He kissed her, as if sealing the words forever between them. Rica felt their souls passing lip to lip, melding and mingling until naught could part them.

* * *

Rica lingered much later than usual. Even when
the sun had nearly settled over the mountain and
they had dressed again, she stood with Solomon
against a tree, kissing him. She had nearly left three
times, but each time, one or the other would think of
something to say, and they would stand a little
longer, sharing soft kisses and murmurings.

"I must go," Rica said at last. She sighed and
moved a little, her limbs lazy with the delights uncov-
ered this day. "If I do not return soon, my father will
not let me out again for a long time."

"At what hour shall I look for you tomorrow?" he
asked, tangling his fingers with hers.

"At Sext, by the Ill."

He squeezed her fingers and kissed her lightly
once more. "I will be there."

This time, she gathered herself and pushed away
from the tree and away from Solomon and began to
walk down the hill. She turned once to wave to him,
and he grinned, then blew a kiss toward her. Rica
laughingly caught it and pressed it to her lips. Then
he was gone, disappearing into the trees.

It was only then that the lateness of the hour
struck her. With a clutch of terror, she saw the
lowering sun and wondered just how long she had
lingered with him in the meadow. Had she been
missed?

She thought of the naked tangling on the forest
bed and grabbed up her skirts as she began to run.
What if someone had seen them?

As the castle walls came into view, she slowed her
pace, brushed back her hair, straightened her gown.
Her lips felt swollen, her skin ruddy with the last

hours—how could anyone look at her and not know what had just transpired?

Rudolf sat in his customary place next to Charles on the bench in the hall, eating with pleasure the meat he had denied himself these past days. There was mead on the table, and wine, and good ale, but Rudolf carefully left these alone, opting instead for weak beer.

So when one of the twins came through the doors with a serving maid, his senses were still alert. He watched her as she made her way along the edges of the room, keeping to the shadows. In spite of her lowered head and the expressionless blank of her face, there was an agitation about her Rudolf thought interesting.

As she settled next to her sister, he saw once again how very different they were. Etta was by far more the peasant than Rica. Rica's figure was slim, her bearing more delicate. Even her eyes and her voice were lighter. Etta, next to her, was disheveled, as if she'd taken no time to neaten herself before coming to the table, and as he watched, she ate with the appetite of a wolf, as if she were starving.

Rudolf lifted an eyebrow, smiling to himself. When his Rica was yet a slim, lovely goodwife in his castle, this sister would be a broad-hipped matron, doubtless missing a front tooth or two. He shuddered to imagine it.

His eyes washed over the long neck of his Rica, with whom he'd spent the afternoon in the bailey. The neck of her gown had been low enough that when she bent for a flower, he saw the yellowing traces of his fingers on her breast. Appalled all over again, he knelt at her feet to beg forgiveness. She had only laughed lightly and touched his shoulder. "I tempted you overmuch."

How he had longed to kiss her! Instead, he'd contented himself with kissing her fingers. Preparations had begun for the Feast of the Assumption—summer was all but gone. Soon, he felt confident, he could speak to Charles about a day for the wedding. His suit was all but won.

He glanced once more toward Rica's pitiful, peasant sister Etta—and found her staring at him with the most evil eye he had ever seen. Her nostrils flared in a gesture of disgust, and she looked toward his neck, then back to his face.

Before he could stop himself, he guiltily touched the remnants of the rash his hair shirt had left like a blazing collar around his neck. Realizing what he'd done, he snatched his hand away. Too late.

Etta's eyes narrowed. For a moment, Rudolf felt sure that it was not the gaze of a woman slightly befuddled. No, there was fierce intelligence in the cunning hatred he saw, and it chilled him.

With a hand that trembled the faintest bit, he poured another cupful of beer. When he looked up, the peasant sister was gone, leaving only his shining, soft Rica at the table once more. He smiled and took pleasure in her gentle blush.

All would be well. A few weeks—that was all the time he needed. Then they would be safely wed, and out of the reach of this evil sister.

15

Solomon walked toward home. He wandered, really, lost in his thoughts, wrapped in the magic that was Rica. His flesh glowed with the imprint of her body, and his heart seemed a bright fire. He ducked below the low-hanging arms of pine trees, unmindful of the lateness of the hour.

He reached the gates of the city just after sunset. The bells for Vespers were ringing. In the narrow purpling gloom of the streets, he heard men making merry in alehouses along the way, and the shrill cry of a babe from the rooms above a furrier's shop.

Some noble's dog had escaped its tether and the cheerful beast loped along behind Solomon for a bit, stopping now and again to snuffle at refuse. Solomon paused in the face of the creature's relentless good humor to scratch his ears. The dog sniffed eagerly at Solomon's sleeve. "You smell Leo, eh?" he said. "But he would never let a stranger coddle him. You are a spoiled thing."

The dog licked his palm, then, seemingly satisfied, headed back the way he had come. Solomon smiled, watching him. Who could fathom the mind of such creatures? He'd never owned a dog—there were ordinances against any but the elite having them in the city—but he had grown fond of Leo.

Unease prickled the hairs at his neck. Alerted, he turned slowly, scanning the shadows. Nothing moved. A mean-faced shopkeeper stood in the doorway of his shop, staring with hatred, his arms folded over his chest.

Solomon looked at him for an instant, then walked quickly away, his dagger ready in his sleeve. He felt the malevolent eyes bore into his back as he walked, but the man did not follow. Solomon's lips twisted bitterly—there would have had to be a gang of them if beating was their intent. Against a group, the dagger would have been little help.

There was in the air now an evil sentiment toward Jews, as if they were to blame for the horrors of the plague. Solomon shook his head. He had seen his own people lying dead of the scourge with the rest. God had not protected Catholic or Jew, child or bride.

But the facts mattered little in the face of terror. Rumors of hangings, thin at first, gathered weight with the passing months and the swelling of the plague. The list of towns and cities fallen to the blight grew longer daily—Bordeaux, Lyon, Paris. So grew the reports of the burning and hanging of Jews.

How long could Strassburg hope to be free of it?

These were his thoughts as he stepped through the doors of his father's house. "At last you wander in," Jacob said, and nodded toward a chair. "Sit."

Still tangled in his thoughts, Solomon said, "Papa, there are things—"

Jacob interrupted. "You will not go again to the midwife."

Solomon stared at his father, stunned for a moment into silence. The old man's black eyes bore a hole through him, burning down to the secrets of this day.

Against his will, Solomon flushed, even as he gathered his arguments. "But we are making such progress!" he protested and leaned forward earnestly. "I am learning the science of these plants, Papa. I am beginning to see how they mesh, and what properties there are. The possibilities are endless!"

A flicker of doubt broke the harsh aspect of Jacob's face. Solomon seized upon it. "If you need me here more, I will not go so often." He spread his hands, as if in easy compromise, lifting his brows. The ruse shamed him, but he could not bear the thought of seeing Rica no more. They had so little time as it was.

"No. You will go no more. There are others with the midwife's lore. Seek them out."

"Papa!"

"No more!" he roared. "I have spoken."

Sullenly, Solomon sank into his chair. There was no breaching that voice.

"Go," Jacob said harshly. "Your mother has bread and meat for you."

His mother smiled as Solomon came to the room where she sat, embroidering by the fire. He kissed her head. "I am not hungry," he said, "though I thank you for remembering me."

She squeezed his hand in silent sympathy. Asher had gone to Mainz, so Solomon was alone when he retreated to his chamber. His mind awhirl, he sank to the stool before his table, where the poems he had transcribed were spread. With a bitter twist of his lips, he stared at them.

His body still rippled with the sense of her, of his Rica, all around him. He had only to close his eyes to see the shimmer of her hair falling around them, to see her standing by the tree, her cheeks flushed with their play, her eyes soft with love as she kissed him.

A bolt of yearning shot through him and he buried his face in his hands. For all the women there had been in his life, he had not loved till now. He had not known it would be so broad and wide a thing, so engulfing.

With a moan he cursed himself. There was no greater fool than he, no one who had loved so unwisely as this.

Rousing himself, he shed his cloak and set to work on the poems. Somehow, though all else was lost, he would find leave to get them to her.

In her chamber, Rica lit a tallow and sat with a sigh on the bench, throwing open the shutters to let in the clean evening air.

As she leaned back against the cool damp wall, she smelled the coppery water of the Rhine mingled with new growth. She closed her eyes.

All at once, the long, long day caught up with her. In the morning, there had been chores and household accounts, and a lesson in overseeing the brewhouse for Etta.

And now, there was Rudolf to think on; Rudolf, who bore the marks of a hair shirt around his neck; Rudolf, whose guilt had betrayed him when he caught her gaze upon him; Rudolf, who had treated Etta like a whore.

There was Etta, who had lied to protect him. Or had she? Perhaps not all was well in the mysterious mind of her sister. Perhaps she had believed some version of the story she told to protect him.

Rica shifted and a host of sore muscles protested

the movement. The best part of the day flooded back through her, not only in her mind, but in the palms of her hands and the small bones in her spine and in her mouth. She lifted her hands to her face, smelling Solomon on her palms, and smiled.

Solomon had fiercely said there was no evil in their joining, and she swore it was true. Where this morning had lived a restlessness in her spirit, there now glowed pleasure, lush and glowing. As if he were the pen and she the page, Solomon had written a new life for her.

A fragment of poetry wafted through her. "'As the apple tree among the trees of the wood, so is my beloved,'" she whispered aloud, shifting to look up to the sky. To the stars, she murmured, "'I sat down under his shadow with great delight, and his fruit was sweet to my taste.'"

Leaning her arms on the embrasure, she laughed. Tomorrow they would meet again, and the day after and the day after. Until—

No. She would think only of what was, not what was to come.

Humming under her breath, she touched her cheek with the hand that smelled of frankincense, hearing in her mind the sound of his voice and seeing the sparkle of his eyes. "Oh, love!" she whispered.

The knock at her door startled her. Snatching her hand from her face as if someone might guess her thoughts, she made a small sound of dismay.

It was Olga who entered. "Your father would see you in his chamber, my lady."

"Is he ill?"

"Not that I see."

Rica nodded. "I will go to him in a moment."

The servant departed and Rica combed her hair,

braiding it quickly. She brushed her surcoat and splashed her face with water, rubbing hard to give it a rosy gleam when she was done.

Her father. Guilt flooded back through her. Her *pappi* would be deeply wounded if he learned of her times with Solomon. She did not think she could bear to see the disappointment in his eyes. Nor did she like to think of the beating he would no doubt administer.

Taking up an iron candlestick, she headed through the narrow passageways to his solar in the highest part of the castle. Just before she reached the door, she suddenly thought of the rough play of the afternoon and wondered if her skin showed signs of it.

With nervous fingers, she loosened the braid only just woven. Candlelight cast her shadow on the wall, making a mockery of her duplicity, and pricklings of shame bred in a thousand lectures and sermons arose in her breast. By all the laws of Church and state, she had sinned mortally.

But what choice had she?

Forcing a smile to her lips, she entered the solar. "Papa, you wished to see me?"

He was not abed, as she had half expected, but sat instead by his table, a tankard of ale at his elbow. "'Twas not so urgent you needed to rush, *liebling*," he said. "I have seen little of you these last days and thought to visit awhile is all."

A distinct rippling of relief passed through her limbs, and weakly she sank to a stool nearby him. "You know I am always glad of your company." Orange-tinted light from the candles set in iron sconces flickered over his cheeks, lending him a good color. "You look well tonight, Papa. The absence of our guests improved your health quickly."

He grinned. "Indeed." He plucked a piece of parchment from the table and passed it to her. "Your cousin writes that all is well with them. A messenger brought it this afternoon."

Rica read the short note quickly, taking pleasure in Minna's neat hand and precise German. "I will have to write to her soon," she said. "I fear I miss her a great deal."

"A sweet child."

"Not so long a child, Papa," Rica said with a laugh. "Your own vassal, Lewis, thinks to take her to wife before much time has passed."

His mouth turned down in surprise. "She is a beauty," he said, nodding. "'Tis not a bad match."

"I think he would be kind to her."

A small silence fell and Rica watched as her father fed bits of bread to the hawk on his perch. "I had news from other quarters today as well."

A demon of guilt screamed in her heart. She could not speak.

As if he did not notice, Charles spoke again after a moment, his voice grim. "Some of the shopkeepers in Strassburg have refused to serve the Jews there. I worry there will be trouble. It seems they will not wait for this pestilence."

Rica stared at the edging of gold around her sleeve, a rush of blood pounding in her ears. Had he guessed that she might harbor love for the Jew who came to Helga? Was he warning her?

She sat very quietly, afraid even to look at him.

But his silence stretched so long she was forced to look up. He still stared toward the darkness, his hands clasped loosely behind his back. Only his profile was visible, and it showed a tightness about the mouth, nothing else. "Papa?"

"It never changes," he said, his voice grim. "We make war for this lord or that king, plunder the land and the people, fight for new order." He turned slightly. "And always it is everyone but the knights who pays." He looked at her. "I am weary of it all."

"You are not God, Papa. You cannot make pure a sinful world." She smiled and coaxed him back to his bench. "You are not a prophet, sent to change the terrors of a thousand years."

He clutched her hand. "A single man affects little, when all is said. I look back over the years I have been given and wonder what God had for me to do."

Dropping the bantering tone of a moment before, Rica shook her head. "I have no wisdom, but surely all thinking people must ask themselves much the same questions?"

"Do you, daughter?"

Rica frowned. "Perhaps not those very ones," she said after a moment. Ruefully she lifted her brows. "I think I'd quarrel with God's choice of sex for me. Do you not think I would have been better born a man?"

He chuckled. "Nay. To cheat the men of the world of your beauty and light would have been tragedy indeed." Cocking his head, he asked, "Do you mind so much?"

She lowered her gaze to the aging hand that clasped hers so firmly. It was a powerful hand, broad and strong with stubby, fierce fingers and thick veins risen in the flesh. Her own was slim and white, the nails round, the fingers very long. One seemed strong, the other weak. "It is not being a woman I mind so much," she said slowly. "'Tis the way men seem to always order my life."

She leaned earnestly toward him. "Your hand, Papa, has wielded a sword and cradled a child and held power over hundreds of men." She held up her own hand. "This one has far fewer adventures before it."

In his gray eyes, there was a flicker of understanding, then swift regret. "I should not have given you so much freedom, *liebling*. It has led to unhappiness for you." ʹ

"Oh, no! I am not unhappy—"

"I see your restlessness, Rica. I feel it stirring you up, have felt it all summer. I see you staring off with your head in your hands when the troubadours sing. I see you pacing the walk and drifting through the baileys. I am not blind."

"So I am restless—there are many changes afoot. Is it so strange?"

He stared at her, as if to peer through her skull to see her thoughts. "Is it only the restless wish for adventure you seek, my little one? Some dream of grand romance?"

Rica began to answer, found no words, and shrugged.

"There are no grand passions in life like your poems, Rica. A man and a woman can find peace with each other, but there is nothing like what you dream of."

She wanted to protest, *but I have found it!* Instead she asked quietly, "Did you not love my mother so?"

Charles swallowed and did not answer for a moment. "I did," he said roughly. "And she was taken. That's what I mean, daughter—better the peace of a comfortable match than the loss of a great love to mourn all the rest of your days."

Rica smiled with the bitterness so new and yet so familiar to her now. "Not for me, Papa. I would rather love with all my heart and soul and mind for one hour than to suffer all my life with the lack."

As she spoke, she felt the power of her union with Solomon move through her, growing and gathering fire, so that her words were passionate with knowledge, not curiosity or hope. And she felt him moving in her, as if he were with her.

Her father stared at her with a strange expression on his face, as if he saw her in some new way. Rica lowered her eyes, suddenly afraid he might guess at her secret.

"Perhaps," he said at last, and touched her hair. "Now play dice with me. I am weary of the world and all its problems. I would forget them for a time."

Rica smiled. "That we can do."

The next day, she went to the glade by the Ill and waited there for two hours. Solomon did not come.

Again she went the next day and the next, sure he had been somehow detained, that he could not find leave, that soon he would come to her.

The fourth day, she went to Helga's, hoping to find him there, working. The yard was empty—and Helga had been called to some birth. Only the cat came to greet Rica.

She bent to lift the soft, sturdy creature into her arms, ignoring the low whine of Leo beside her. Holding the warm body close, she wandered toward the back of the cottage, where she had sat with her love so often these last weeks.

"Where is he?" she murmured to the cat.

Each day, her hopes fell a little more. Each day her doubt grew. From the tangle of yearning and guilt rose a new fear—what if he had only seduced her for his amusement?

She buried her face in the plush fur of the cat.

Helga had tried to warn her. "It only takes one man to make a woman a fool," she'd said. And how many times had Rica heard that refrain in her mind since?

She had never behaved with him in a seemly manner—from the first day she had been frank with him, and flirted. Even her repeated warnings to him could be seen as the ruse they had become—a teasing request for more vigorous pursuit.

Embarrassed heat crawled up her cheeks. A vision of him walking in the streets of Strassburg filled her mind. The gaze of women had followed him that day as if he were some magnificent king, as if there were more promises arrayed in the air about him than in all the knights in Christendom.

Rica, who had resisted with sophisticated banter the wiles of many a man, had fallen like a rotten tree at his first glance. Now he'd had his way with her and would come no more.

In her arms, the cat purred and bumped his head against her chin, oblivious to the torturous thoughts whirling in her mind. Rica rubbed her cheek in the soft fur. "I think I'd like better being a cat," she said. "You do what you like, catch mice for your supper, take love where you find it." She sighed. "It would be easier to be anything but a woman."

The sound of running steps reached her ears. Alarmed, Rica clutched the cat to her breast, gentling the low growl of Leo next to her. Quietly, she waited.

And then, there was Solomon, his hair mussed, his jupon unbuttoned and askew, his breath coming in great gulps, as if he'd run all the way from Strassburg. "Rica!"

In that fleeting frame of seconds, as she took in the beloved face and the worry in his eyes, she knew her story of willful seduction was false. With a little cry, she jumped up and ran to him.

He caught her close and urgently, raining kisses upon her face. Then he enveloped her and pressed his face into her shoulder and held her so tightly she could scarce breathe. "Ah, Rica," he whispered.

"I thought you would not come again," she said. "I thought it was only seduction and—"

He lifted his head. There was misery in his dark eyes as he touched her face. "My father has forbidden me to come here."

"But why?"

"I think he might have followed me the last time."

Horrified, she gripped his coat. "But wouldn't he have done something to stop us?"

"I don't think he followed all the way. He has not accused me of anything—he would not do so without proof." Solomon shook his head. "It is the only reason I can find. I thought I heard someone behind me that day, but in my rush to be with you . . ."

She let her head fall forward, pressing her forehead to his chest. "Oh, Solomon, I cannot bear to think it is already ended."

"Nor can I, love, but I am here today only through deceit, and must quickly return. Can you find leave to come to Strassburg at all?"

"It is not so simple to go to the city—I must take my servant, Olga." She frowned, afraid and yet unwilling to believe the joy they had found together could be so suddenly snatched away. Not yet. "If I am able, how will I leave word for you when I come?"

He glanced toward the trees, his eyes narrowing in thought. "I can think of no one I trust."

She clutched his tunic. "But it is not so long before you leave—I would have one more day, at least."

"Know you where the Jewish shops stand?"

She nodded. "I think so."

"When you find leave, walk there as long as you dare. Linger and shop if you may. I will see you if you stay long. We are not far from the temple. Do you know where it is?"

"Yes."

"When you have walked as long as you dare, go to the square by the astrologer's house and wait. I will come to you there." He took a breath and pressed his forehead to hers. "It is not what I wished for us, Rica. But it is all I can think of."

"I will not complain, my lord." With all the hunger built from the last four days, she kissed him, tasting the shape of his mouth and the silkiness of his tongue. She pressed against his dear and familiar form. "In truth," she whispered, "it will be hard to wait. I so wished to practice pleasing you."

With a fierce sound, he kissed her passionately, caressing her jaw and hair and shoulder. After a moment, as if dragging himself, he pulled away. "I must go, Rica."

She nodded and stepped away a little, but his hand snagged hers. He pulled her close again and kissed her cheek. "Be well, my love."

Then he was gone, into the forest, running again as if for his life. As he disappeared, Rica realized their idyll was gone. Except for one day—perhaps two if fortune smiled—their time had fled.

Once he left her, she did not know how she would go on with her life.

16

The day before Assumption, Etta fell ill. There was no fever or spotting, to Rica's great relief, but Etta could keep nothing but a little water in her belly. It was sudden and violent, but by the time for the evening meal, she had settled into a deep sleep and Rica felt confident she could leave the girl in the care of a servant. "If she worsens, send word," Rica said.

"Ja, fräulein." The servant was calm. "There was a lot of it last week—she'll sleep now till morning, and waken fresh and new. You'll see."

Rica paused in her chamber to brush out her hair and wash her face. It was as she bent over the bowl that the idea struck her—now she might learn how Rudolf courted Etta, might learn what ill thoughts lurked behind his overly pious face.

There was no doubt that it was Rudolf who had accosted Etta that night on the stairs. He had done penance for the act, severe penance if she were to judge by the rough red rash that had circled his throat. The act of his penance stayed her wish for vengeance—for the moment.

From the first there had been something akilter in

the blaze of lust through his piety. The mix disturbed her in some way she could not name.

Straightening, she dried her face and removed her belt and the bangles at her wrists and found a simple leather girdle to circle her waist. Tonight Rica would become Etta, to see what she might learn. Etta would no doubt be furious if she learned of this duplicity, so Rica would not risk going to her chamber for a surcoat Rudolf would recognize as Etta's—whom he believed to be Rica.

Instead, she smoothed her tunic and wore it alone with only the simple belt.

As she descended the stairs in the tower toward the hall, she felt a strange, sudden worry.

Where would this duplicity end? And how would Rudolf, so proud and pious, take the news of their dishonesty?

She paused a moment in the gloom. Perhaps it was past time to end the ruse, to spread the game before Rudolf and let fate take its course.

But Rica could not do that to her sister without Etta's consent. Whether Rudolf was good or evil, Etta loved him now. In light of that love, Rica could only act in protection—she could not damage whatever chance Etta might have with him.

In the hall, a simple meal had been laid and servants scurried quickly to finish their chores before the bells rang at sundown, freeing them from their duties for the Feast of the Assumption. Tomorrow the priests would wander the fields and pastures, blessing animals and crops. Herbs would be gathered for their greater medicinal properties.

Rica, sitting down to her meal, was struck suddenly with a way to see Solomon. She would take herbs from Helga's garden to him, as if Helga had sent them. She smiled to herself in satisfaction—she would not even be forced to take Olga, since she was freed from her duties for the day. Amidst the wandering peasants and priests and burghers celebrating the glorious feast, no one would notice another woman, more or less.

So happy did the thought make her that she nearly forgot to pick lightly over her food as Etta would do—and even when she realized she must, it was no small task. She had tended Etta nearly all the day, and her stomach growled over the rich scent of the roasted quail set before her.

Still, conscious of Rudolf's watchful gaze, she sipped delicately of her cup of ale and nibbled a shred of meat and broke a hank of bread in half. In the corner, a lute player strummed a soft tune.

She was rewarded when the meal was cleared. Rudolf bent over her. "Will you walk with me this night, my lady?"

Rica inclined her head demurely in assent and accepted his hand to stand. From the corner of her eye, she saw her father nod to himself in satisfaction. Charles knew Etta was ill, so correctly assumed it was Rica who took Rudolf's arm.

With suddenness and clarity, the truth struck her. In horror, she looked back at her father's smile, then looked at Rudolf, who tucked her fingers in the crook of his elbow.

It was Rudolf her father wished her to marry! How had she been so blind?

Somehow she moved her stiffened limbs in a semblance of walking. Waves of horror washed through her, over and over.

Mocking flashes of memory pointed to the signs that had been there all along—if only she'd been wise enough to see them. With a rising sense of panic, she remembered conversations with her father, and with Rudolf.

Rudolf spoke little, seemingly content to press her fingers to the crook of his elbow. As they walked, Rica felt a wild fear growing. The deception she and Etta had indulged all these weeks now seemed a terrible, terrible tangle from which there was no escape; a tangle with grave consequences.

Silently she walked with Rudolf past the kitchens and brewhouse, past the stables and hives, toward the orchard. The sun was low, and just as it slipped behind the jagged line of mountains to the west, bells began to toll to free the servants. Rica watched a cluster of stableboys run for the gates, headed for hardier pursuits in the clusters of peasant dwellings beyond the walls.

"And so the rabble departs once more for sin," Rudolf said.

"They are only boys," Rica replied mildly.

Beneath her fingers, Rudolf's arm went rigid. "'Tis as boys they learn the lustful habits of a lifetime."

Rica wondered what Etta would have said to that, and stayed silent.

"'Tis not our concern," he said with a shrug, and led her to the stone bench beneath the peach trees where Etta so often sat to do her embroidery. As Rica settled, he added, "In truth, I would speak of happier things this night."

A cold break of sweat traveled down her spine. "Happier things?"

He smiled down at her, as if infinitely patient. "You have forgiven my lapse, Rica, but we have spoken little of it."

It was that very lapse she had wished to speak of, but it seemed prelude now, and Rica was eager to squelch it. "We need not! I would forget, and have you do the same."

Earnestly, he sank beside her on the bench and

took her hand in both of his. His fingers were cold. Rica forced herself not to yank away. "It was my love for you that made me mad in that moment." He lifted her fingers to his thin, sharp lips. "In truth, fair lady, I think of nothing but our wedding night."

Rica had thought herself a wanton. She had feared that Solomon's touch had forever unleashed a beast of lust within her. But though her breath came quickly now, it was dismay that made it so. Her flesh shrank from his touch. His breath smelled of onions, and his tunic, upon close examination, was none too clean. Beneath his nails was a thin grime. If she embraced him he'd smell of sourness and old ale.

She snatched her hand from his. "Marriage?"

He laughed, as if she were teasing him. "Surely you do not think my courting would lead to some unseemly end? I wish not a mistress, but a wife."

She stood up, putting her back to him in order to collect her thoughts. It mattered not what she, Rica, thought of this moment. It mattered what Etta would think and feel.

Or did it? The masquerade now seemed absurdly unworkable, unless she were to pretend to be Etta for all of time, even for her father. Untenable.

"A wife?" she echoed, stalling for time.

"Do you worry about your father?" he asked.

"Yes." Rica turned, tossing her hair over her shoulder. From a foot or two away, it was not so hard to act the shy but besotted maiden. From this distance, she saw the shine of his blond hair and the evenness of his teeth. Earnestly she clasped her hands before her. "He may not wish for me to leave him— he is not well, as you know."

Rudolf smiled, and it was a gentle expression, but amused, also. "He already granted my petition, Rica."

She closed her eyes and pressed her fist to the sudden new pain below her ribs. "When?"

"What does it matter?" he asked. "I asked, he answered—a woman needs no more than that."

She bit her lip. "I only wish to know, my lord," she said silkily, "so that I might celebrate that day through the years before us."

He preened and she knew a swift, sharp need to slap him. Instead, she folded her hands, taking a measure of calm from the pain of knuckles pressed too tightly together.

"I cannot think of the date, my love," he said slowly, then brightened. "But it was the day your sister cut her hand with the scissors—do you remember?"

The day she cut her hand with the scissors. Rica glanced toward the mountains rising above the castle walls and willed herself to remain straight and unmoving.

"Yes," she said softly. "I remember." She had walked with Etta to Helga's cottage. As if the day were written on the blue hills, she saw it clearly—the bandage on Etta's hand as she bent to speak for the first time to someone other than Rica herself; the joy. . . .

Rica remembered.

In the yard at Helga's that day there had been a young man with curls shimmering like a raven's tail, and a mouth red as apples and eyes that said he knew her every thought.

It was the day Etta had begun to speak so clearly, the day she had begun to heal.

Because she had been sitting in the solar and had overheard Charles give his blessing to a betrothal between Rica and Rudolf. Etta wanted Rudolf for herself.

And Rica had helped her.

In place of horror, Rica now felt rage build and

rush through her at the tangle of betrayals—her father had betrayed her by promising her to this vassal without even asking if she had a wish or a choice in the matter. Helga, no doubt, had known of it and thus had urged Rica to experience the last days of her youth.

But the worst of it was Etta, who seemed pure and gentle and had shown herself to be more conniving than a thief. Ah, yes, Rica had underestimated her.

With a bitter smile, she looked at Rudolf. "It seems, my lord, there is naught for me to say but that it is time. Let us marry quickly."

So great was her anger that she suffered the quick, eager hug Rudolf bestowed upon her without flinching. After a moment, she stepped back. "We shall announce to him tomorrow that it is done, when my sister is well again and can hear."

"As you wish," Rudolf murmured, and kissed her hand.

When Rudolf left her, Rica raced through the passages toward her sister's chamber. Anger spurred her feet; it sucked the breath from her chest. Her gown was caught in tight fists, and when she burst through the door of Etta's chamber, the door flung back and struck the trunk behind with a crack.

The servant, startled and frightened, looked up. "Go," Rica said. "Leave me and go to your family."

The girl scurried out. With narrowed eyes, Rica approached her sister, who slept peacefully wrapped in the bedclothes. Her color, so wan earlier, had returned, and her long braid snaked from below the sheets like a gold serpent.

She looked so innocent, Rica thought. Like a carving of the Virgin, her features so clear and virtuous.

And yet if Rica had but seen, the signs had all been there—the strange triumph in Etta's eyes when they'd argued over Rudolf upon the arrival of their cousins; the quick recovery from her long quiet; the steadfast denial that Rudolf had been the one to mistreat her.

Abruptly, Rica sank down on the three-legged stool the servant had vacated. What a tangle it all was! Now that she thought on it, it seemed impossible. How could it be only three months since that day Etta had cut her hand, the day she had met Solomon, that Rudolf had petitioned for her hand? How could life change so quickly?

It made her dizzy.

She had come to this chamber fully prepared to drag Etta from her sleep and demand explanations, but the longer she sat, the less inclined she was to disturb Etta.

Instead, all through the night she sat on the little stool, trying to puzzle through the mess that the deceptions and tangled passions had created, seeking an answer to it all. In the morning, she would face her father and Etta and Rudolf. By then, there had to be some kind of plan.

Just before dawn, she slipped through the passages and out to the courtyard. It was oddly still without the clatter of pans from the kitchen and the sound of servants at work. There was a hush of waiting in the still lavender morning. Rica paused, staring around her, seeking signs of what the day would hold.

The chapel was empty, for it was well known Father Goddard waited until the last minute before rising to ring the bells for Prime. It was dark within, illuminated only by a host of flickering candles lit to the Virgin for her holy day. Each candle represented a prayer, and for a moment, Rica stared at the small flames. With swift and sudden compassion for the troubles of others, she breathed, "Oh, Holy Mother, grant them all."

In the cool silence, she knelt on the stones before the statue. "Mary, Mother of God, hear my prayer. I have no one else—only you can grant this petition I lay before you. Grant me courage in what I am to do today—and grant protection for my love."

The words seemed too small in light of what she faced. For long moments, she struggled with some offering she might make to speed her prayer. No material thing she owned seemed enough, nor could she offer herself to a nunnery.

She closed her eyes, knowing the one thing she could give. "Oh, Mary, if you will see us all safely through this, I swear I will not kiss my love again. I will be as women should, and discourage the natural passion of my Solomon."

The promise left her bereft. For a long time, she knelt there, weeping and whispering Hail Marys until the first rays of the sun struck the precious colored window high on the chapel wall.

Even in prayer, she felt no peace. There was a loose, reckless feeling in her, as if events had already been set in motion and nothing she did would influence the outcome.

And yet, she had to try. Rica stood and gathered her cloak about her, squaring her shoulders. The rest of her life, and her sister's, hung in the balance of this day's events.

In his chamber, Charles stood by the wide embrasure, sipping at his wooden cup of ale. Since Humphrey and his group's departure, Charles had felt his strength returning. He no longer resented the diet of light foods

Rica and Helga insisted upon, for he had seen how
much healthier he was when he abided by it.

So from the carved bowl he had settled before
him, he plucked a handful of the early raspberries
Rica had collected for him this week and watched the
bustling in the fields beyond the castle. Already the
priests were about, riding mules from plot to plot to
bless the crops and creatures. Clusters of peasants
walked toward the waters of the Ill, there to bathe for
healing. Charles thought to do the same himself later.
Rivers were blessed on Assumption. Perhaps he could
find a measure of health in them.

His hawk cocked an eager eye toward the berries
in the bowl. With a chuckle, Charles held out his
palm to the bird. Delicately, as if the beak were not
designed to shred the flesh of hapless rodents, the
bird picked one out and swallowed it. He made a soft
noise of approval and bent his head again.

"Ah, my friend, you, too, are growing old. What
will we do without each other?"

Rica came in. Her arms were laden with a pitcher
of fresh ale and a basket filled with fruit, bread, and
cheese. "What's this, daughter?"

She raised her brows. "A celebration."

Without looking at him, she shook a linen cloth
from her basket and spread it over the small table he
kept in his room. There was harsh efficiency in her
movements and a tightness around her lips.

"Rica, is something amiss?"

She looked at him. In her eyes was a blaze of anger
he had not first spied. "What could possibly be amiss,
Papa?" The words were bitter.

"I'll not play some guessing game. Tell me or keep
it to yourself, but curb your teasing." As if he did not
care, he fed the bird another berry.

"You have not long to wait. My sister joins us in a moment."

The first pricklings of unease slid down his spine. There was more than a little anger in her voice. This was a black fury, and not the temper of a child, either. Charles pursed his lips.

Rica slammed food and tankard and cups on the table. Her cheeks were flushed. For once, she wore not the bangles and bells of which she was so fond, and her hair was demurely braided away from her face. The tunic was simple, unadorned but for the leather girdle that carried her purse and keys.

Before he could comment, however, Etta appeared. Her surcoat was richly embroidered with red and purple and gold. Her hair was loose in waves around her shoulders and arms. "Good morning, Papa," she said, then kissed his cheek. She spied the food. "What's this?"

Rica did not pause to answer. With exaggerated care, she brushed crumbs from the cloth, then raised her eyes to Etta. It was upon her sister the fierce anger found focus. "A celebration."

Etta only plucked a berry from the bowl on the embrasure and settled herself on the bench. "Pray tell, sister," she said calmly. "What do we celebrate?"

Then Rudolf came into the chamber, his handsome face flushed, his hair combed wet into place. "Ah!" he said, smiling. "I see I am the last to arrive."

Charles instinctively glanced at Rica. Her body drew up, taut as a bowstring. "Please, my lord," she said in a gentle voice. "Sit awhile."

Etta, too, had gone rigid. Her eyes narrowed upon her sister, and Charles felt another prickling of foreboding. He frowned. "I weary of this game," he said harshly. "Show your hand."

For a moment, it seemed Rica did not know what her game was. She looked at him with sorrow and pleading in her eyes. Before he could speak, she whirled.

"Tell me, Rudolf," she said sweetly, standing beside her sister, "which is Etta and which is Rica?"

Rudolf rose, smiling. "I have come to know the difference these last weeks. The heart can see what the eye cannot."

Charles watched him cross the room and kneel before Etta in her rich red coat. He kissed her hand. "This is my betrothed, my Rica. The woman who will bear my children."

Rica looked at her father with a triumphant tilt to her chin.

For a moment, the trio was frozen before his eyes—Etta awash with love for the blond and courtly knight, Rudolf kneeling in the most perfect pose, Rica standing like an avenging queen beside the two.

A thready pain passed through Charles's chest.

By the saints, he should have seen how weak the foppish Rudolf was, should have seen what now was clear—he was no match for Rica.

Charles pressed a palm to his chest, where the thready pain gained power. His breath felt short. His heart pounded twice its usual speed.

Rudolf thought he had won his prize. And if Charles withdrew the betrothal now—after word had been sent to his family—war would be the result. The proud der Brumaths would not take the game of these two girls lightly.

Gasping, Charles grabbed his left arm, where a bolt of pain shimmered through.

"You idiot, der Brumath. That is Etta!" he cried, and collapsed.

17

Rica watched her father fall. "Papa!" she screamed, and ran to his side. His face was mottled, his lips bluish. Urgently she opened his jupon around the throat and loosened the laces below. He breathed in labored gasps, his eyes open as if to hang on to his life.

After a moment, his pain seemed to ease, but the bluish look of his lips did not. She had seen a man die in just such a way only last year after dancing with a wild young girl in the great hall. "Papa!" she said fiercely. "Be still. I'll run for Helga!"

He made a noise.

She jumped to her feet. "Etta, sit with him—no, Rudolf, you stay. Wash his face with cool water. Etta, go you to the kitchens and mix the tisane—exactly as I showed you. Come quickly back and give it to him."

They stared at her dully. "Do what I say!" she shouted.

They moved. Rica raced through the passages to the stables and found her horse. She'd never ridden without her saddle, but there was no time to do it now. Making do with a blanket tossed over the palfrey's back, she struggled astride with the help of a low gate, then urged the horse into a run.

The priest was in Helga's yard, scattering holy water and blessings over the broad plots of herbs. "Helga!" Rica cried. "It is my father! You must come quickly."

Helga whirled instantly, lifting her skirts to dash into the cottage. In a trice, she was back, her basket in hand. "Help me," she ordered the priest harshly.

He struggled to help her mount. With a whoosh of breath, Helga was astride, and Rica urged the horse into a run once more. It was less than a mile each way, but the horse was unused to such weight, and refused to run. Grunting with frustration, Rica settled for a canter.

"Tell me all," Helga said over her shoulder.

"He collapsed, holding to his arm as if in great pain. His lips were blue." She fought tears and nudged her horse with her heels.

"What did you do?"

"I loosened his clothes, then sent Etta to get his tea. Rudolf stayed with him."

"Good child, good." Helga squeezed her arm. "Was he still in pain when you left him?"

"No. He seemed better, but his color was poor . . . that terrible blue."

A guard saw them coming from the walk and called orders for the gate to be opened. They rode through to the bailey. "How is he?" Rica said to the vassal waiting to take her horse.

"I know not, lady."

Rica gave Helga a terrified look. On the way up, she said, "Solomon told me it is his heart."

Helga nodded.

"He seemed better!" Rica said.

"Aye, that he did." Helga grunted as they made the long climb to the solar, winding around and around on the stone steps. Breathing hard, she asked, "Was there some news this morning to upset him?"

Rica swallowed, thought to answer, then could not. "I will explain all later," she said.

Until they entered the solar, to find Rudolf standing stiffly by the embrasure as Etta tended her father, Rica not thought of the twist this hour had put on her fate.

Now Rudolf swiveled around to stare at her, his proud, haughty face blazing with arrogant fury. "Ah, *Rica*," he said with a sneer. "You have returned."

Etta met her gaze with misery.

Ignoring them both, Rica pushed through to see her father. "How are you feeling now, Pappi?"

He, too, looked at her for a long moment. Rica was chilled by the narrowing of his eyes, and a pang of regret arrowed through her when he removed his hand from hers. "Helga," he said.

The midwife bustled forward, her stout figure in its rough homespun reassuring. Rica stepped back, watching as Helga touched Charles's forehead and cheeks. She pressed a hand to his chest and closed her eyes as she felt the beats. "No more pain?" she asked.

"No."

Helga turned to the trio awaiting her pronouncement. "He will come round. I will stay with him." With a wave of her hand, she shooed them out.

Rica reluctantly turned away, wishing to put things right somehow, both with her father and with Helga, who must now guess she was responsible for her father's bad turn. As if sensing this, Helga said, "Rica, you must go to the apothecary."

Rudolf made a noise of disbelief. "But there are no servants to take her!" he protested. "She cannot go abroad so alone."

"I will take Lewis with me," Rica said impulsively before she was stuck with Rudolf himself. "He can guard me as well as any."

Rudolf glared at her.

Rica lifted her chin and opened her mouth to tell him he was not yet her husband, but mindful of her father, she closed it again. "What shall I fetch for you, Helga?" she asked.

Rudolf stormed out of the room. Rica glanced over her shoulder to watch him go, hating him with every fiber of her being. When she turned, she found both her father and Helga looking at her. On Helga's face was sympathy and sorrow. Only anger showed in her father's face.

She knelt at his side. "Papa, I am sorry—"

"Leave me," he said, his voice weary.

Stricken, Rica rose. Tears stung her eyes. Blinking, she turned to go, but Helga stopped her at the door.

Murmuring so quietly Charles could not hear, she said, "I warned you, sweet. Do not be overly hard on yourself—he will forgive you in time. Go now to the apothecary and fetch me a tincture of foxglove."

Neither tears nor guilt would give any help. Lifting her skirts, Rica went in search of Lewis to ride with her to Strassburg.

Rudolf strode through the passages toward Etta's chamber, his sword clinking at his side, his spurs jingling on the stone passages.

The door was slightly ajar, and he slammed it with his open palm. The sting of the blow gave him satisfaction, as did the noise, which startled Etta. She turned in fear.

"I cannot think what God made that is more evil than woman," he said without preamble.

"My lord," she said, stepping forward with imploring hands outstretched. "Do not be angry, I pray you. 'Twas Rica insisted we deceive you. She wishes not to marry yet."

"You have made me a fool, both of you."

"Truly, my lord, I did not pretend to love you." Her words seemed to embarrass her—she flushed.

The virtue of her demeanor, coupled with the richness of her flesh spilling over her gown, lit the familiar lust in his loins. And yet this girl was not even a virgin! Without thinking, he lifted his hand to strike her. She saw the blow coming and flinched, but did not try to move away.

He caught himself in time. This was not the one he wished to punish. She had been ill used—by not only her sister but himself. "Get up from there," he said harshly.

She rose from her knees.

"It will give me no pleasure to wed your sister, for it is your heart I have learned to love these past months."

A great joy lit her features. Hope. He crushed it with a bitter smile—some small punishment was due this girl, too. "But wed her I will, and see that she pays for this duplicity."

Etta cried out, "But—"

"Enough! You were sullied early for what purpose God only knows. Take yourself to a nunnery and there pray for His purpose. I see no other use for you."

Without waiting for her reply, he turned with a military click of spurs and walked out, shutting the door behind him. It was no surprise to hear something hit the wood behind him, something thrown with fury at his head.

He smiled in bitter satisfaction. One punished. One to go.

* * *

Lewis rode soberly with Rica into the city. Leo ran beside them. As they traveled through the gold-and-blue morning, Rica tried desperately to keep her thoughts from Solomon. It seemed evil beyond measure even to imagine him while her father lay ill because of her duplicity, and the storm of this morning's revelations had yet to gather fully. She had made her vow to Mary, too, and it must be honored.

And yet, because of the sudden new blots on her life, the thought of her love was doubly enticing. She had not, after all, promised never to think of him, but only not to kiss him.

To comfort herself, she thought of him laughing so merrily in the glade by the Ill, thought of his strong hands and the shining respect in his eyes.

Next to her, Lewis asked, "What puts so sweet a smile on your face, my lady?"

She flushed. "Oh, I know not. For all the trouble this day, it is beautiful weather, is it not?"

To her surprise, he laughed. "Nay, that was no weather smile." His gaze was trained on the approaching gates of the city. "I have watched you this summer. You are in love."

"Lewis!"

"Can you deny it?" Jovially, he lifted one brow. "Think on it. I have seen you walking the baileys and rushing off to the woods and glowing and sighing."

"Oh, 'tis only restlessness," she said, as she had to her father. Was she so easily read?

Lewis shook his head. "'Tis love. I think, too, 'tis he that puts that smile on your lips—perhaps it is the son of some noble in the city?"

Terror struck through her heart and she closed her

eyes, banishing thoughts of Solomon. "I tell you there is no one."

He slowed. "Rica, your words to your father about Minna will help my suit. He has said he will speak to Humphrey in my behalf."

"That is good news indeed," Rica said with a smile.

"In return, I would help you if you will allow it." He paused, as if considering his next words. "I dislike Rudolf der Brumath and am loath to see you linked forever to him."

"God's teeth! How know you of this betrothal? Did everyone know except me?"

Lewis again lifted a careless shoulder. "He bragged to his underlings. They gossip."

"He is evil," Rica said with passion. "I cannot prove it, neither will I convince my father, but I feel it."

"Yes." He reined his horse and reached for hers. "So will you not let me help you in some small way, my lady? In gratitude for what you have done for me?"

In misery, Rica stared at him. She wanted to weep but simply shook her head. "I thank you, but believe me when I say there is no hope."

"Then I will pray."

At the gates of the city, they paused. Hordes of people lined the streets, and a procession honoring Mary wound past.

"Ah, no!" Rica cried out. "How will we find the apothecary in this mess?"

"All we can do is try."

But as she feared, the shop was empty.

They stood there a moment, staring about them. Leo slurped water from a puddle by the wall. The sun beat down on Rica's head, reminding her urgently of time passing. "I cannot wait until the morrow!" she said in frustration.

"There is a Jew who sells tinctures, nearby the temple."

Rica stared at him without speaking.

Mistaking her look, Lewis lifted his hands. "I do not mean to offend, my lady, but it seems the matter is pressing, and your father will not know if 'twas a Jew who made the tincture."

"Neither would he care," Rica said fiercely. "Let's find him."

The Jewish sector was outwardly plain, and here the noise of the Assumption feasts and games was not heard. Shopkeepers visited with one another quietly, watching with curiosity the two mounted riders passing by.

Rica stared straight ahead, her heart pounding in her chest. She prayed silently that Solomon would not see her and mistake the reason for her presence here.

Leo trotted alongside the horses cheerfully, snuffling at this and that, running to catch up. When he suddenly barked, Rica nearly jumped from her skin. Before she could catch him, he dashed through the open door into a shop on a corner. "Leo!" she cried out, furiously. He did not reappear.

She glanced at Lewis, not knowing what to do. Lewis grinned. "'Tis not like him to be so ill behaved. There must be a bitch within."

Rica stared at the shop. Her heart shivered. Nay, it was no bitch but Solomon that Leo sought; she would lay her life on it. Frozen in fear, she simply stared. Her limbs trembled.

"My lady," Lewis prompted. "He will not come to me. Are you so frightened to go in?"

Rica did not trust her voice. She shook her head and slipped from her horse. Her legs nearly buckled. Her senses seemed extraordinarily heightened; across the street, she saw a bearded man with a long face stare at her with suspicion. The air was filled with an assortment of scents, garlic and roasting poultry and cinnamon. From an open casement above the shop, she heard a woman's laugh ring out, teasing and somehow ardent. A child chased another into a courtyard down the street, both of them screeching.

It seemed she stood there an eternity, building her courage to walk into the shop of Solomon's father. "Lady," Lewis said. "Shall I go with you?"

She looked at him and steadied herself. "No. I will return in a moment."

But when she turned back, there was Solomon. He had been working—his sleeves were rolled back on his lean arms, and water yet glistened on the flesh. On his head was a small round hat made of velvet and embroidered simply around the edges. He held Leo by the scruff of the neck.

And here, Rica saw him anew again. Not a boyish rogue or a forbidding man or her passionate lover, but the son of a Jewish merchant, who had a life so different from her own, a life he'd owned before she came into it, a life with which he would continue when the storm of this day passed.

As if nothing at all were strange, she forced a smile to her lips and stepped forward. "Forgive us, sir. He is not so ill behaved most days. Did he cause you trouble?"

He gave her a blazing smile. "No trouble, *fräulein!*" he said. Then he bent his head toward the dog, whispering so only Rica could hear, "My love, I ache to see you. Can you tarry an hour?"

Rica made to take Leo, leaning close enough to Solomon that she felt his heat and smelled his unique aroma. She nearly swooned. "I cannot!" she whispered back. "My father is ill and I must return quickly."

His eyes were bleak. "When?" he asked in a low voice.

It was unbearable to look into his face. Unbearable to think she would never taste his lips again, listen to him laughing with her, feel his hands in her own.

Knowing it was a sin, that she would be punished, she nonetheless met his gaze. "Monday, by the Ill," she said. "You *must* come."

"I will." He bent close to look at the dog. His arm brushed hers. She looked at him. For a brief second, he held her gaze. Under his breath, so quiet not even Leo, had he cared, could hear, he said, "Rica, I love you."

She swallowed, biting back tears. A movement in the doorway caught her eye and she started.

There, appearing like the avenging God of all the terrifying texts, was a man with a long gray-and-black beard. His features were stern. The deep eyes and thick hair were repeated in the son who stood before him, and in the power of his bearing, she saw what Solomon would one day be.

He glared at Rica. She suddenly felt there were no secrets from this man, that somehow he knew of what had passed between her and Solomon.

One word from his lips sent Solomon back into the shop. Rica called Leo firmly and mounted again. "I apologize, sir, for any trouble he caused."

Solomon's father did not reply—only stared with dark knowledge until she set her horse forward.

They found the apothecary's shop and purchased the tincture and rode silently away from the Jewish sector. Once past the gates of the city again, Lewis spoke.

"I see you need more than prayers, my lady."

She stared ahead of her, afraid to speak. Her voice would betray her.

Lewis seemed not to mind her silence. "Love can be cruel. . . . I have seen it tear the life from a woman. Do not let such be true of you."

He had somehow become her friend these past months. Her need to confide in someone overpowered her caution. "I am a fool, Lewis. A foolish, foolish woman."

"No." The word was strong and sure. "As witness to that moment on the street, I wish but for a fraction of the love I saw there between you. It may be fleeting, but it is sweet."

The castle loomed closer, the whitewashed walls serene in the still August afternoon. Heat shimmered around the base, making it seem to float on the hill. How could it look so much the same, when all else had changed?

Just before they passed through the gates, Lewis paused. "Rica, you have my word that no tales will pass through my lips. And should you need an ally, know that I am he."

"Thank you, sweet Lewis." She shook her head. "Be kind to my cousin—that is all I ask of you. At least one of us will find happiness thus."

"On that you may depend."

They spurred the horses and went through the gates.

18

Solomon worried through Sabbath and the day after how he would manage to free himself of his father in order to sneak away to the Ill.

It was madness to think on it, madness to still dream of Rica, but he could not stop. It was as if she had somehow become a part of him, like an arm or a leg, and without her he felt less complete. Less himself, less a scholar, less of everything.

At night, he dreamed of her laughing as she wound herself around him, frowning as she disputed some point of learning with him, sighing as she kissed him.

And there had been about her words an urgency. "You *must* come," she had said, as fiercely as she was able in a whisper.

But Jacob watched him continually, endlessly. If he left on some errand, Hershel and Asher watched in Jacob's place. From daybreak to sunset, Solomon found his hands and back busy at some task.

So it was on Monday, as the morning passed. Anxiously Solomon conceived of one plan, then another, then another. All of them were foolhardy, not worthy of his thought.

He grew desperate. One last day with her was all he asked. One day to savor as he walked the rest of his life without her.

His mother called down the stairs for the men to come eat. Jacob put down his books and rose. "Come, my sons."

Solomon looked up, as if distracted. "In a moment, Papa." He bent his head again over the figures he had been copying, as if still adding.

The three went up the stairs—Jacob, Hershel, then Asher, who looked over his shoulder. "The figures will wait, Solomon. We are always kept hungry till you finish writing."

Without looking up, Solomon scribbled a meaningless number, then lifted his quill and looked at a number higher on the page. He turned to the abacus. "Do not wait—tell Mama I will come when I finish. If I do not complete the series, I will have to begin anew."

"If you tarry long, I will eat your portion."

Solomon ignored him. Asher could eat a king's share and still want more.

He did not look up again but counted the steps as Asher climbed. Overhead, he heard murmurings as Asher relayed his message, a higher *tsk*ing from his mother.

It was then he bolted through the open door of the shop, leaving the servant behind the counter to stare agape. Without coat or proper hat, he ran full speed through the winding streets of the city, headed for the west gate.

Once through the gates, he paused for an instant to catch his breath, then keeping to the cover of trees growing alongside the Rhine, ran toward the castle. It was a roundabout route, but his father would not think to look here.

Just before he reached the castle, he detoured

through the vineyards, waving toward peasants at work testing the grapes. He walked more easily now, although he could not stop himself from glancing over his shoulder once or twice. The way behind him was clear.

When Solomon returned home today, his father would beat him, but the knowledge did nothing to dim his excitement. As he drew nearer the meadow by the Ill River, his heart leapt with anticipation.

And when he saw Rica, standing morose beneath a chestnut tree, his breath left him. Her hair streamed over her blue tunic, and a circlet of bells girdled her slim waist. He approached slowly, drinking in the sight of her, letting his love and anticipation build until he could not bear it. When he spoke, his voice was rough with emotion. "Rica."

She turned with a glad cry and launched herself into his arms. He caught her hard against him, wishing they could somehow meld so they would never be parted again. Burying his face in the silk of her hair, feeling her breasts and belly press into him, her arms locked around his neck, he felt faint with bittersweet joy. This moment was worth any beating.

"God, I have missed you," he whispered. "I am not whole without you." He closed his eyes to feel the smooth curve of her cheek against his own and the shape of her ribs below his fingers.

Rica buried her nose in his neck, squeezing him close. "Solomon," she whispered. "I was afraid you would not come."

"I am here, my love. Is there something amiss?"

Slowly she lifted her head. In her face was a new sorrow. "I am to be wed."

"What? When?"

"I know not the date. Soon." Grimly, she clutched his sleeves. "To Rudolf der Brumath."

Jealousy sucked the air from Solomon's lungs. He gripped her shoulders. "Who is he?"

"The one who watched me bathe." She pointed toward the bluff. "There."

From the beginning, Solomon had known there was no future for them. From the beginning, he had fought against loving her. Now he found he could not bear the thought of another man touching her, when he—who loved her—had barely tasted the edges of her desire.

He kissed her urgently, as if he could keep her there with his lips. "I cannot think on it, Rica," he whispered. "I cannot think of never seeing you again."

"Take me with you, then." She clasped his face in her hands. "To Montpellier." When he did not immediately reply, she rushed forward with a torrent of words. "I will do whatever I must—be your mistress, anything. Just do not leave me here to marry him."

"A whore is what you would be, Rica."

"I care not."

He made a soft low sound. "'Tis I that could not bear it."

"It matters not where I live or how. I am clever, I will find a way—and as long as I am with you, I do not care."

He shook his head. "Rica, you have been so protected! You know not what you ask."

A little of the earnest expression bled away from her eyes. "You do not think me equal to it."

It wounded her. He could see that, but he had been honest from the beginning. "No, Rica. I don't think you can do this. I think our love would not be enough to sustain you for long."

"But Solomon!" She curled her hands into his sleeves. "Think of it! You can teach me of philosophers and mathematics and all the things you are learning.

Perhaps I can do copying work. I have a very fine hand."

He stared at her, taking in the passionate and eager pleading in her mountain-blue eyes. The curve of her lip and the intelligence on her brow struck a cord of hunger through him, a yearning so deep he could not breathe. He pressed his forehead to hers. "Let me think on it," he said at last.

"There is no time!" she cried. Falling to her knees, she bent her head over his hand. Warm tears fell on his fingers. "I cannot bear for you to go away and leave me here. I cannot think of living my life without you." Her voice fell to a whisper. "Please, Solomon."

A bar of sunlight arrowed through the leaves above them and danced on the crown of her head. Solomon thought of the tight-lipped vassal with the strange, carnal air he'd seen the day she bathed in the river. There had been something unholy about the knight. Solomon suddenly imagined Rica nude and rigid, with the hands of that man upon her breasts.

In sudden, sharp decision, he pulled her to her feet and into his arms. At the sweetness of her soft form against him, he knew it would be worth whatever struggles lay ahead. Together, they could face them down. "I have no wish to leave you, Rica. I am mad with love for you."

A shimmer of joy washed over her face. "Oh, Solomon!" she cried. "Think of all that you can teach me!"

"I have things to teach you," he said, half-teasing, and kissed her. "No more talking, for I swear I am half starved with want for you."

There was no gentleness or ease in his movements today. With fingers made clumsy with haste and hunger, he unlaced her cotehardie and tugged the fabric away from her arms and planted kisses along her shoulder. She tasted of sunlight and her hair smelled of lavender. He kissed the smooth flesh in a rush of joy and love, reveling in the sheer splendor that was Rica.

She laughed lightly and buried her hands in his hair, gasping when he freed her breast to suckle one rosy tip. She kissed his temple and tugged his hair to bring his mouth to her lips.

Then he was lost in her, in the dark honey taste of her mouth, his hands rounding the supple weight of her breasts. She loosened the buttons of his jupon and pushed her hands below, touching his thighs and hips, her fingers bold and—

The first blow struck his ear and shoulder with a force that nearly knocked him senseless. He grabbed for something to steady himself. For a moment, he had Rica's gown in his hand. A second blow landed against his arm and caught the side of his jaw. Rica was torn from him, and he heard her scream.

Before he could find his footing, another blow struck his shoulders with the force of a falling tree. Solomon fell to the grass, blinking.

In quick succession, two more hit him, across the legs and back.

"You fool!"

His father. Solomon went cold. Slowly he turned and saw Jacob standing over him, a cane in his upraised arm. Before he could move away, it struck him across the shoulders again.

He struggled to rise, to get away from Jacob's wrath and the litany of punishment spilling from his lips. But the rise and fall of the stout cane seemed to anticipate his every dodge.

"How many times have I beat you for this ill-guided passion?" Jacob roared. "How many times? How long until you learn?"

The blows rained down on his head, on his shoulders,

his back, and legs. Solomon tasted blood. His head seemed full of noise.

"Stop!" Rica screamed. "You'll kill him!"

And still the blows fell until Solomon could no more raise his hands to ward them off. His body throbbed with pain.

All at once, the beating ended. Solomon heard Jacob breathing in gasps, and Rica weeping. He heard the cane fall to the leaves.

"Get up," Jacob said, his voice weary.

Rica was there, helping him to his feet. She had gathered her tunic, but it hung loose around her shoulders. Solomon reached protectively toward her, to pull the fabric over her collarbone.

His father slapped him, and only Rica's determined grip kept him from falling. On rubbery legs, he found his footing. "I am no boy, Papa," he said, and wiped his mouth with a trembling hand.

A sharp drumming pain pounded over his left eye, and he felt a swirl of blood coming from the place, but he faced his father squarely. "This is not lust, Papa," he said. "This woman is my life."

Jacob only stared at him, fury and sorrow and pain in the black eyes.

The pounding pain intensified, and Solomon stumbled, raising a hand uncertainly. Unable to stave off the dizziness any longer, he dropped to his knees.

"You are a fool," Jacob said.

Solomon whispered, "Yes." Darkness swallowed him.

Solomon slumped to the ground and Rica whirled, a sharp accusation on her lips. As she faced the fierce man with his black-and-gray beard, however, terror struck through her. She stepped backward.

He lifted a finger, pointing at her. "If anyone else had found you two, they would have dragged you to the square in Strassburg and beheaded you!"

Clutching her gown to her breasts, she nodded. "I know."

"Why did you come after my son? Was there no knight who sought your fancy or did you just wish to dally with someone strange?"

She lifted her chin, tugging her gown over her shoulder. "Nay! He told you—we are in love." Tears of reaction rose in her throat, and she swallowed them. "I promised the Holy Mother I would kiss him no more. It was I you should have beaten!" she cried. "It is given to women to—" her throat filled so thickly with remorse she could barely speak, "to avoid tempting men. You could have killed him."

The man looked dispassionately at Solomon. "He will not die . . . not today." His eyes narrowed. "To save him from death I beat him. And you, too."

Solomon groaned and Rica knelt beside him. He struggled again to rise. Blood stuck his shirt to his back and trickled from a split in his fine mouth and one over his eye. Purpling showed along his smooth brown shoulder and on one side of his face. He lifted his hand toward her. "Go, Rica. Leave me with my father."

His eyes were fierce. She swallowed and gathered her skirts.

As she rose, Solomon's father said, "Wait!"

The command was unmistakable. Rica turned around.

"Look at your love now," he said in a rough voice, "and remember I am his father. He sat on my knee as a babe and chanted his figures to me before he lost his first tooth."

There was deep sorrow in his voice. "I beg you,

stay away. If I who love him can do this, think what those who hate him will do."

Rica closed her eyes, then before she could do more to humiliate herself, whirled, and ran back through the forest.

Charles felt better. The weather was calm. His chest had given him no more pain. In her customary alcove, a subdued Etta embroidered the tapestry that had seen so little of her attention this summer.

With kindness, he inquired, "Where will you hang your stitchery when it is finished, my dutiful daughter?"

"I have not yet thought, Papa." She smoothed the brightly colored folds, which showed a detailed scene of a hunt. "Do you have some wish for it?"

"Perhaps on that wall there." He pointed. "To cheer me on gloomy winter days."

She smiled sweetly, and for an instant, Charles was sharply reminded of his long-dead wife, who in temperament resembled this Etta who had bloomed this summer. For all the trouble the games had caused, he could not regret the change in Etta.

He frowned, thinking on his other daughter, who in temperament far more resembled him, stubborn and willful and as passionate as a thunderstorm. He had no doubt he would be forced to tie her up and gag her in order to wed her to Rudolf.

Helga tapped his shoulder, not unkindly. "Do not begin your brooding, my sweet. 'Twill only make you ill."

Rudolf appeared at the door. "My lord, a word with you, if you will."

"Did I not tell you to give the man a rest!" Helga said. "Must you run to him for every little thing?"

Rudolf gave Charles a disapproving look. He did

not like the midwife, thought she was a witch, he said, or her cures would likely fail as others did.

But to his credit, he used his head. "You do not mind if I sit awhile?"

"No work," Helga warned.

Shoving a tankard of ale toward the young knight, Charles chuckled. "Rest a bit. You'll find it pleasant enough on a hot afternoon."

Helga moved away to shake the linens outside a window. Charles heard her cluck. "Ah, there's my girl! In a temper, too, by the look of her."

Charles twitched his lips, suppressing a smile. He was still furious with Rica but had missed her company these last days. In truth, he would welcome one of her tiffs with the brewhouse staff or some indignant huff over Cook. He reached for the chessboard. "Will you play?"

"I will, my lord."

Rica burst into the room. One look at her was all Charles needed to know that the peace of the day was shattered. Her hair was uncombed and fell in loose tangles over her shoulders. Her tunic was soiled. A smear of blood stained her neck.

He stood up. "Rica! Are you wounded?"

Into the room she moved, alight with some fire. Her cheeks glowed with it, and her eyes held an almost unholy shine.

"Mother of God," Helga whispered.

"Wounded?" Rica said. "Oh, yes. I am wounded—by your betrayal, and Helga's and my sister's."

"Are you still wallowing in all your self-deceptions?" Charles said with a frown. "For I'll have none today."

With the same strange passion, she advanced. "I will not marry, Papa. Not *him*"—she threw a disdainful glance toward Rudolf—"not anyone."

"You *will* marry, girl, and when and who I say!"

He leaned on the table. "If need be, I will tie you to the church doors!"

She stared at him and he saw her breath came hard, as if she were winded. "I am no virgin, Papa!" she cried out in triumph. "Who will take me?"

"I will." Rudolf leapt to his feet. "I care not, my lord, if she be virgin or not. I will still take her as my bride."

Rica smiled and glanced toward Etta, and Charles turned quickly enough to see the shuttered look that passed between the sisters.

"Oh, no," he said, and came around the table. "Oh, you will not try it again, you—"

He whirled toward Helga. "Take her and see if she tells the truth. There will be no more games from you, girl. You've been spoiled long enough!"

Rica stared back at him, and he saw there were tears running over her cheeks, and that her fists were white at the knuckles where she clutched her gown. So close, he saw the marks of love upon her flesh, and his heart plummeted. It was true—she had taken a lover to spite him. His lips thinned. "You disgust me," he said. "Leave me. I will not look upon your face until you wed willingly as I say you will."

"Then look your last," she flung back. "For I will never marry of my own will. Never!"

She ran out, and Charles sank down to his bench, touching his chest. But there was no physical pain, only the sorrowing endlessness of loss. Today, his daughter was no more.

Suddenly, he became aware of the hush surrounding him and looked up to see all three pairs of eyes trained with concern upon him.

"Helga," he shouted, "go after her and do as I say." He waved a hand to the other two. "Go away."

* * *

In her chamber, Rica fell to the bed and buried her face in the linens. A deep, raw ache tore through her chest, so wide and painful she felt she had no breath. Over and over in her mind's eye she saw Solomon's blood and torn clothes; over and over she felt him snatched from her embrace.

Forever. Never again would she meet him in the meadow or by the river or amid the beds of herbs and spices spread around Helga's cottage. Never would she listen to the sound of his rich voice telling her the wonders of places she had not seen. Never again would his eyes shine for her with love and respect and hope. Never again would he bend tenderly over her to touch his beautiful mouth to hers.

It was punishment from God. Rica had made a vow and broken it within only days.

She felt crazed with loss and sorrow, beyond tears or reason or thought. She lifted her head with a cry and clutched the pillow in her fists.

Then Helga was there, sitting next to her, tugging her at her wrist until Rica sat up. The sturdy arms wrapped her in a sympathetic embrace. "Oh, love," Helga whispered. "Oh, my sweet."

And then Rica did weep, in great gulping sobs, her body shuddering as she gasped for air to fuel more tears. She wept so long she thought she would never cease, and through it, Helga stroked her hair, murmuring endearments and soft comfort.

Finally, hiccupping and exhausted, Rica lifted her head. "I will die without him," she whispered, and a new trail of tears seeped down her cheeks.

"No, child." With the corner of her rough homespun apron, she blotted Rica's cheeks. "Life is not nearly so kind. Live you will and suffer, too, until time takes the pain."

Rica closed her eyes, fighting off a vision of her life—stretching dark and dreary without the light of Solomon.

"Rica, you must speak the truth to me now. You are still a virgin, are you not?"

Rica bowed her head. "He did not take my maidenhead."

"I thought not."

"But in heart and soul and mind I am no virgin!" she cried. "In all things I belong to him and I will take no other!"

Helga sighed. "You *will* take another, my sweet. You'll take Rudolf as your father says—because he will tie you to the church doors if he sees you go not freely."

"Why can Etta and I not trade again?" Rica grasped Helga's hands passionately. "No one will know until it is too late, until—"

"Stop being a foolish child. We have all indulged you far too much. You must do this thing—there will be war if this marriage does not take place. The betrothal was formal these three months past."

"I cannot bear to let him touch me!"

"You will—and more!"

Cut to the center of her new rawness that even her last ally had deserted her, Rica wailed, "I cannot!"

"Child, you must listen." Helga took a long breath and bent close. "Your sister was brutally handled by those soldiers. She will never have children—"

Rica frowned and sat up.

"No children," Helga repeated. "Nor even coupling. There are terrible scars."

"But it has been many years! Surely—"

Helga steadfastly shook her head. "No. It was a

great miracle that she survived such treatment, Rica. Believe me when I say I did not think she would live."

"Oh, my poor, poor sister." Rica buried her face in her hands. "Does she know?"

"Nay. 'Twould be unkind to say. I see her going now to a nunnery, where she will be happy when her passion for Rudolf has faded."

"She seems at peace with this turn of events, Helga. I do not think she will be a cause for worry."

"I have given her a sleeping draught to ease the time between now and the wedding. It makes her calm."

"It seems Fate has spun a web about me. I am to be devoured in her web like some hapless fly."

"Such drama!" Helga snorted.

Dully, Rica rubbed her grainy eyes. She felt emptied and hollow. "Tell my father he need not tie me to the church doors. I cannot bear to lose his goodwill when all else is gone."

Helga kissed her forehead. "There's my wise girl. You sleep now, and I will see that you do not stumble over your sister or Rudolf these next days."

Numbly, Rica nodded. "When is this wedding?"

"Saturday—at the cathedral."

Five days. Rica made no comment, and Helga softly moved toward the door. "Sleep, child," she said, and left her.

Rica curled into a ball, clasping her arms around her chest to staunch the raw ache, but nothing gave relief. Five days and she would be Rudolf der Brumath's wife while her love and heart rode for Montpellier.

Five days.

19

In his room in the city, Solomon, too, lay prone on his bed. Darkness had fallen and he had not risen to light a candle, nor had anyone come to do it for him.

He would not die of this beating, but each movement of eyelid or finger sent fresh reminders of it shooting through his bruised limbs and muscles. He had been prepared to be beaten, had known this night would be so, but foreknowledge made it little easier to endure.

His mother had silently tended his wounds, which were not, when all was finished, so terrible. A cut on his shoulder, one lower on his back, a split in his lip from hitting the ground. His legs and arms and shoulders were black and blue.

He would not die.

Nor would he trade the beating for the kisses he had shared today with Rica. He would go now to Montpellier with the feel of her soft flesh in his hands and the sound of her voice in his ear. Like pressed flowers, his memories would go with him always.

He drifted in and out of sleep. Beyond his locked door, his father raged, then all fell silent. He heard, once, his mother weeping. Solomon, unmoving on his pallet, dreamed of Rica swirling all around him like a being of light, gold and rose and smelling of lavender.

But as dawn filtered into the room, so too did the new reality of his days come into his mind. No more would he go to Helga's to laugh and tell bawdy tales. No more would he peer into the deep violet eyes of his love. The magical summer had disappeared into the mist, no more to be his. No more.

At the door, he heard the lock click and Jacob appeared in the wan light. He was haggard, the lines deep around his mouth. Hollows marked his cheeks above the thick beard. "So," he said.

Solomon waited, feeling his father's exhaustion and sorrow. Jacob nodded to himself and stepped into the room. "I did not see what was under my nose," he said. "The blushing and sighing—I should have known there was danger."

"Papa," Solomon whispered.

"One day, *beneleh,* you will be as wise as your namesake. I wish only it had come sooner."

Filled with unexpected shame and sorrow, Solomon struggled into a sitting position, groaning at the protest of his battered body. He knelt on the cold flags. "It grieves me to know I have given you pain. I beg your forgiveness."

"The heart of a young man speaks more loudly than all the wise words of all the wise men in all the world." He touched Solomon's head. "You will go to Montpellier in two days—my tradesmen tell me the pestilence is fading there, and you should return to your studies. Until then, you must eat and regain your strength. Your mother is bringing bread and stew."

Jacob turned as if to leave, then paused. "Grieve her now and be done with it. She marries in five days."

Solomon closed his eyes, overwhelmed by a vision of her weeping on the cathedral steps.

For a moment longer, Jacob paused. Then he turned without speaking and left Solomon alone. He locked the door behind him.

For a long time, Solomon did not move. Light crept in through the shutters and fell in slim shafts to the pages of the poems he had copied so laboriously for Rica this summer. He stared at them.

No greater fool than he had ever been born. How could he have believed for even a single moment that they might fly away from here together? Rica was strong and intelligent, but she would be no match for the life they would live together.

And yet, even now, he would risk it for a few more hours of loving her. For himself. To have her waiting when he had finished with his classes; to sleep entwined with her; to laugh before a fire on cold evenings . . .

He closed his eyes, sick with yearning. Oh, yes. In selfishness, he could do it.

For Rica's sake, he could not. As his mistress, she would be scorned and snubbed and called vile names. She was used to comfort and servants and the obsequious attention the nobility took for granted.

It would not be long before her starry-eyed passion faded. Then she would begin to blame him for the life of which she had begged him to make her part, and the shimmering thing that lived between them would die.

No. For Rica, and for himself, he would not take her to Montpellier. Better she should have the life she had always known. Better he should grieve now than lose her by degrees.

* * *

Rica awakened groggily to the urgent whisperings of Lewis, who shook her shoulder roughly. "My lady, come quickly."

"What?"

"Helga sent me—'tis your love riding away. If you hurry, you may bid him farewell."

With a cry, Rica sat up. "Turn around then, and let me rise."

"I will wait in the passage."

Rica dressed, her hands trembling as she rushed. A heavy velvet surcoat would keep her warm in the damp, early dawn. A cloak, tossed as afterthought over her shoulders, would shield her from the mist.

It was only as Lewis led her through the passages and out beyond the castle to the deserted road that her heart began to pound. She rubbed sleep from her eyes and crouched near a tree, her hands trembling violently.

Lewis said, "I will be waiting at the small door through which we escaped, to let you in."

"Perhaps I will never see you again, Lewis," she said, a bolt of joy swelling her grief-shrunken soul.

His eyes were sad. "Nonetheless, I will be waiting."

Rica turned back to wait, watching the road eagerly. A thick mist obscured all but a few feet of the hard-packed earth, and all sounds were muffled. Behind her on the hill rose the castle in grim splendor, the jail from which she would cheerfully flee.

A mule emerged from the mist, with a dark-cloaked figure riding on it. Rica stood up, peering to see if it was Solomon who rode so disguised. The man rode listlessly, his head bent. Was it he? She could not tell.

Not until he was nearly even with her did he look up. Rica gave a glad cry—for it *was* Solomon who came so despondently from Strassburg. "Oh, my love," she said, stretching out her hands, "did you think me so fickle as to let you go?"

No smile or sweet greeting came from his lips. He only stared from beneath his hood, his eyes grim. Rica let her arms fall, wondering if she had done the right thing. "Do not stare so," she protested. "You are frightening me."

"And you frighten me, Rica!" He dismounted and took a step toward her. "Are you mad? Was one beating not enough?"

"No!" She moved forward, imploring, unable to stop herself. "I mean, I do not wish you to be beaten—'tis only that I could not bear to see you go. I have been distraught these last days, wondering how you fared." With a hesitant hand, she touched the healing split in his lip. Softly, she asked, "How do you fare, my love?"

He stared at her, his eyes burning in his pale face. Abruptly, he grabbed her arms in a fierce grip. Rica, thinking he was drawing her close, clutched at his sleeves, nearly weak with relief. "I have little to take with me, Solomon, but I lay my life at your feet, and will gladly follow where you lead."

"Rica! You cannot go. There are those who will behead you, and hang me, for this passion." He gripped her arms with bruising strength. "At best, they will treat you as a whore."

She stroked his jaw, traced the line of his brow. "I have been the daughter of a petty lord these many years and it serves me not."

In his eyes she saw his weakening, saw his love shining and hungry. His gaze swept her lips. "You do not know what you say." There was a weary sound to the words.

In the distance, muted by the mist, came the sound of a horse. Solomon looked over his shoulder, then with a savage cry, he pushed Rica away. She stumbled on her cloak, landing ignobly in the grass at the side of the road. Stunned, she stared up at him.

"You are a witch!" he said in a low, angry voice. "You have cast some evil spell over my senses these last months. Leave me now!"

"Solomon, no!" She struggled to her feet, unmindful of the grass and dust clinging to her clothes. "You do not mean what you say. I love you."

The thudding hooves echoed more loudly, and Solomon glanced again over his shoulder. When he turned back, there was a cruel look in his eye. "You are not the first girl I have taken to amuse me, *fräulein.*" His lips twisted in a parody of a smile. "Nor will you be the last. Go marry your knight and live your silly noble life—I am done with you."

Rica stepped back. "You lie, Solomon," she said.

He laughed, the sound cold and mirthless. "Do I?"

Doubt wound through her, but she tossed her hair from her face. "You love me, and you will suffer for this."

For one long moment, he stared at her, his sensual mouth set in hard lines, his eyes glittering chips of obsidian. "Good day, my lady," he said, and rode into the mist.

Before the other rider could discover her there, Rica turned and ran through the trees toward the door where Lewis waited. He let her in without a word. Rica, smarting with humiliation, brushed by.

But back in her chamber, she collapsed. Her life was ended.

The night before the wedding, Olga brought word that Etta had asked for Rica's company. Wearily, Rica left her tasks and went to her chamber.

Rica had seen no one these last days. Olga and Helga, gentle guards, brought her food and helped her ready her clothing and belongings for the journey to Rudolf's fief to the east. Dangerous country, she'd heard, where still barbarians roamed. When Rica overheard Olga whispering this to a younger girl, Rica had only wished the barbarians would find them both and kill them before she had to endure a lifetime of Rudolf's caresses. As it was, she had stowed away a cache of herbs to drug herself with in order to endure her wedding night.

It was the only rational act she had been capable of these last days. She moved in a dull stupor, close to tears much of the time, and yet too weary to indulge them. Listlessly, she brushed velvets and mended linen, and in the evening, when at last her well-meaning guards left her, she dove into the refuge of sleep.

Even the walk to Etta's chamber wearied her. She wondered if the evil spell would ever lift.

Etta sat nearby her bed, adorned prettily in her rose surcoat with its rich embroidery. A gilded circlet shone round her forehead, and her hair hung in loose waves over her shoulders. A bath had been laid, and Rica could see steam yet rising from the scented water.

Etta smiled and rose to kiss Rica's cheek. "Let me bathe you, sister, this one more time."

Rica closed her eyes and pressed cold fingertips to the lids. "I do not wish to bathe. I have no joy in this marriage—nor should you."

A bright strange light bloomed over Etta's face. "I am only a subject of the Lord's will." She rounded Rica's unmoving form to untie the laces at the back of her gown. "I have found joy these past days in prayer."

Rica caught the gown. "Etta. I have *not* prayed, nor will I. I go unclean to Rudolf der Brumath." She pulled away. "'Tis the only rebellion I have."

"Drink this wine with me then, sister. We have only tonight to be as we were for so many years." The color in her cheeks was high, and Rica thought she might already have been indulging a little in the wine. "I will miss you," Etta said. "They have said I will go to a nunnery."

Stung by her own selfishness, Rica took the cup from her sister's hand. "We have had our struggles this summer, but I feel cheated we are now to be parted."

Etta bowed her head. "I would change only the way this has ended." Her voice was hushed.

"As would I."

"'Tis unfair indeed that we should *both* lose all," Etta said, and lifted her eyes. Her pupils were overly large or perhaps only seemed so against the high flush of her cheeks. There was clarity in her words. "I know it was the Jew you loved, Rica."

Rica sank down to the bench and poured a cupful of sharp new wine. "How did you know?"

"I saw you kissing him at Helga's that day. Through the branches of a tree before I went inside."

"I could not tell you," she said.

"I know." She reached across and took Rica's hand. "I pray for him, too."

Briskly, she stood. "Now let me do this last sisterly thing for you," she said with a smile. "The bath is hot and sweetly scented. Drink your wine and let me wash your hair."

Rica drank deeply, draining the cup. Perhaps drunkenness would give peace to the grief so haunting her. At least for a little while.

She extended the cup and, as Etta refilled it, shed her clothes and stepped into the bath.

It was not without sorrow that Charles fetched Rica the next morning. She waited calmly in her chamber, her hair dressed with flowers, hands folded in her lap.

"Come," he said.

For a moment, she simply looked at him and he saw all the things she would not say. Pale blue circles below her eyes showed her weariness, and there was heaviness in the set of her shoulders, as if they carried some great weight.

But it was the resignation around her mouth that most pierced him. He felt as if he were sacrificing her to some terrible fate. "By the saints, Rica," he said fiercely, "he is no ogre, bent on devouring you. I am not long for this world. He will see you well cared for."

With dignity, she stood up. "I am ready."

They walked through the passageways without speaking. It was a silence Charles longed to fill with words of love and protest. How he would miss the child! She had been his most steadfast companion these many years.

Outside Etta's door, he nearly spoke these thoughts, but thought better of it. It would only make the parting more painful. He opened the door—and swore, for the girl was still abed.

Next to him, Rica touched his arm. "Leave her, Pappi," she whispered. "Do not force her to watch her beloved wed another."

Pierced, Charles nodded and closed the door gently.

The party traveled to Strassburg in the bright morning. Next to Charles, Rica rode nobly, without speaking. No animation lightened her features and he finally forced himself to stop looking for signs of acceptance in her. No matter to him if the day were more like a funeral than a wedding—the end result would be the same.

It wasn't until the vows were spoken and the deed was sealed that he realized he'd been holding his breath, afraid she would somehow rebel at the last moment.

Standing there in the sun, Charles felt a tight catch of foreboding as Rudolf bent to kiss the hand of his new bride. His heart fluttered in its cage of ribs. Had he erred in giving his blessing to this union? Had he been so stubborn in his own goals that he had overlooked some crucial detail?

He looked at the faces gathered around them. Lewis watched with a grim expression. Helga pressed her lips together. No joy lit the cheeks of any who knew the pair. Only the poor townsfolk, glad of any break in their routines, cheered.

But it was done—and could not be now undone.

She dreamed of barbarians with wild hair chasing her, raising bloody scimitars over their heads. She dreamed of scratching the face of a nameless rapist, and of lifting a dagger to avenge her mother's murder. Everywhere was blood and danger and terror. In her dreams she ran and ran, looking for something she couldn't find. Her sister. She couldn't find Etta anywhere—in her dreams, she chased through ominous dark forests, screaming Etta's name.

And she dreamed of Solomon, his bitter smile exaggerated as he told her she was only a diversion while he awaited his return to Montpellier.

In her dream, she cried out his name with sorrow and longing, and it was this cry that pulled her from sleep.

It was dark. She still felt the cry in her throat, felt her heart pounding and tears on her cheeks. In the soft darkness, she felt his loss anew.

As the first wave of grief passed, she rubbed her tired eyes, wondering how long she had slept. Her head felt thick, her limbs heavy, and she could not tell how long it was till dawn.

She shifted in the bed to look toward the embrasure, looking for signs of light beneath the shutters. None yet showed. She could sleep a little more then.

Nestling deeper into the linens, she closed her eyes and reached again for sleep. This time it settled around her like a soft net, comforting and peaceful.

When next she stirred, it was with a strange sense of urgency. She sat bolt upright in the bed, wincing as a pain rippled through her head. Disoriented, she pressed her palm to her temple.

She was in Etta's chamber. In the shadowy gloom, she saw the outline of the tub where she had bathed. Vaguely, she remembered climbing into the water, remembered Etta filling her cup with wine over and over as she soaked in the scented water. The images began to blur then—she thought she remembered Etta rinsing her hair, but could not be sure.

Faint light pressed at the shutters, and Rica could hear the sound of horses in the bailey, then beyond on the road. She blinked, her vision bleary, and pressed her fingers harder against the thick pain in her head.

It was her wedding day—still early or Olga would have awakened her. Rica flung the linens aside and tested her ability to stand. Her stomach roiled. An array of shooting lights crossed her vision.

She groaned at the price of drunkenness.

It was only then that the faint sounds of merrymaking reached her. Music and a wild, besotted laugh.

With a cry, she whirled toward the sound, blinking against the pain in her head and the fuzziness in her limbs. Dressed only in her kirtle, she ran for the door and flung it open.

She raced toward the sounds in the great hall, ignoring the throbbing in her head that seemed to derive from something other than only wine. . . .

Etta must have drugged her. Once again, she had underestimated her sister.

As she descended the curving stairs in the tower, hurting her feet on the cold stones, Helga's words floated mockingly through her mind. *No children . . . nor even coupling. There are terrible scars.*

Wild terror filled her. Rudolf would not learn he had married the wrong woman until he tried to fit his member into a place it would not go. He would be drunk by then, and that strange passion would be built to a roar and he would be thwarted—!

"Oh, Mary, do not let me be too late!" she cried, and burst into the hall.

The room was littered with the remains of a great feast. Knights slumped over the tables, snoring. A drunk musician continued to pluck his strings, his head bobbing in time to some internal sound. In one corner, two men-at-arms tossed dice, and as Rica stared at them in horror, one looked up as he lifted his cup. Wine spilled over his chin and he wiped it carelessly away with his sleeve.

His gaze raked over her. "Too late, little pigeon," he grated out, hoarse with all-night merrymaking. "But I'll comfort you if your—"

Rica ran toward him, unmindful of her undress or the tangles in her hair. "Where is my sister?!" she cried, grabbing his shirt front.

He laughed drunkenly. "Why she rode out not an hour ago, off to her new fief with her new husband!" He grabbed her. "Let me ease your broken heart. I don't care if you're a virgin or not."

Rica slapped him, backing away in horror. Little caring what they would think of her, she screamed in her anguish, then collapsed on the floor, weeping hysterically.

20

Rudolf waited until his men were busy with the setting of the tents and preparation of the meal before he took Rica's hand. "Come, my love," he said with a smile. "Walk with me."

She gave him a shy glance, and a blush rose on her cheeks. "Is it safe?"

He grinned, knowing her words were double-edged. He touched the sword at his side and winked. "I will protect you."

She laughed.

They walked in silence into the forest, away from the men. Rudolf could not speak for his desire, and each step deeper into the shadowy, sweet-smelling trees made him ache a little more.

At last they reached a thick stand of pines that stood in a circle around a bed of spicy needles. With ceremony, Rudolf removed his cloak and spread it out. His new bride stood nearby, watching, and when he took her into his arms, she jumped.

"Do not be afraid, wife," he said, and kissed her.

All day, he had been waiting for this—nay, all year. Now he felt the madness of his long-stayed hunger welling up like a beast within him, the beast that had always frightened him hitherto, but now could be safely released with his wife.

He tugged up her skirts ungently. Last night, his drunkenness had left him unable to deflower the wife he'd so long waited to bed, and his need seemed trebled now.

Unlike last night, his member stood stiff and ready. With a growl, he freed himself and grabbed her, needing to show her his failure the night before was only too much drink and excitement.

She cried out a little as he tumbled her, shoving himself between her legs. "My lord, a virgin needs time—"

He covered her mouth, nipping at her lips with his teeth, positioning himself to enter. Yes, last night she had been kind, wise even, pricking her finger to put blood on the sheets so none would be the wiser for his failure.

But now, he was hard and ready and had no wish to be gentle. She would know she had been loved today.

But he could not seem to find entrance. Over and over he prodded and pushed, and finally used his hand to seek his goal. He found it and began to ease in.

Again, he was obstructed, and with a cry of frustration, he shoved at her, gripping her shoulders and thrusting with his hips.

She screamed.

The sound infuriated him. He slapped her to make her still, and pushed. A flood of wet heat touched his thigh— ah! She was just a stubborn virgin. Not so long now.

He thrust and felt something give. She screamed again and began to fight him, biting and thrashing with her legs, striking him with her fists. He pinned her and kept at it.

But no matter what he did, he could move no farther. In fury, he pulled away and saw there was blood between them—on his legs and hers and on his cloak.

With a sickness in his belly, he stared at her, breathing hard. There was hatred in her eyes.

"You are a swine!" she cried, and hurtled forward to bite his chin, her nails tearing at his eyes.

He grabbed her arms, feeling new heat flood through his loins. "So be it." In a blind red haze, he took her, muffling her screams with one hand until they faded to whimpering, dull cries.

Jacob left his sleeping wife and headed with purpose to his desk. In the silence, he dipped his quill and began to write.

> *Dear Solomon,*
> *It grieves me to be the one to tell you these events, but elsewise you will not know and will perhaps wonder always about the girl.*

Here, Jacob paused, feeling slightly ill over the lies he must tell.

The talk these many weeks still buzzed with the tragic story of Frederica der Esslingen, whom all had seen married on the cathedral steps.

Then, only days later, they had crowded along the road to watch her carried home in a bier, killed by thieves. Her husband's body had not been found— and this above all gave cause for worry, for it could not be given proper burial.

Tragic, they said in the streets, shaking their heads. So beautiful a girl, violated and murdered so brutally by the barbarians still roaming the forests to the east. They all remembered her mother, and her end. Even those who hated the nobility felt sympathy for Charles der Esslingen over such adversity.

This morning, Jacob had had business with the council. As he walked back toward home, he passed the cathedral and glanced toward the steps, feeling a twinge of sadness himself over the fate of such a beautiful young girl. As if his thoughts had conjured her, she stepped through the doors.

Stunned, he stopped to stare.

No, he remembered, looking at the girl, this was not the one who had been killed, was not some ghost come to haunt him. It must be a sister, her twin.

But the girl, standing only a yard or two from the steps, saw him. Like a frightened deer, she froze. A deep flush of color crept through her cheeks as she stared at him, and all at once, tears welled in her eyes. She covered her mouth with her hand and ran away, a huge dog following behind her.

The same dog that had come into his shop one day not so long ago.

Jacob did not know how it had transpired, but the girl Solomon had risked so much to love had somehow survived. Her sister had never seen Jacob, would not have blushed or wept.

As long as she lived, she was a danger to his son.

He picked up his quill and prepared himself to lie.

Solomon carried the letter from his father up to the small rooms he kept. A cold wind blew outside the walls, lonely and bringing tidings of winter. A blessing the cold would be this year, Solomon thought grimly, for the pestilence seemed to freeze with the cold.

He broke the wax seal on the letter and settled by the fire to read. It told of Rica's wedding.

A great weight seemed to fall on Solomon's chest, and he put the letter down for a moment. It was cruel of his father to send him this news. A vision of the strange knight's hands on his love tormented him. Angrily, he stood up, pacing until his mood calmed. He smoothed the page.

And read of Rica's death.

In the loneliness of his room, Solomon cried out. He buried his face, guilt and grief searing him like a violent flame.

So this would be his punishment for his foolhardy and forbidden love—Rica dead because he had not taken her with him.

Rica dead. All the light in the world was gone. In despair, Solomon wept.

Part Two
Strassburg—Winter 1349

Thy wit is as pure as thy witchery,
And both in thy face are displayed;
Alas! mid the maze of thy pleasuance,
From the path to thy heart have I strayed.
—Abraham ben Meir ibn Ezra

21

Solomon rode home a week after Epiphany. As he approached Strassburg, thick flakes of snow fell gently around him and stuck to the branches of the pines alongside the road. Rising from the swirling snow was the walled city, looking like a magic kingdom alongside the river. All sounds were muffled.

He gazed at the tumbling of rooftops and the cathedral spire with little emotion. He felt hollowed out after his long, wandering journey these past months. There was a mild relief in him—tonight, he would sleep in his father's house, in warmth and luxury. Tonight he would eat well at his mother's table.

Perhaps the comfort of his family would ease the torment in his heart.

In the streets of his home city, all seemed well. Merchants and tradesmen went about their business with brisk and cheerful attitudes; goodwives shopped and haggled; beggars waited at the gates of great homes for scraps. Cats chased mice and slept lazily in sheltered alcoves. Children ran.

The normality of the scene stunned him. He stared with bleak eyes at the rosy cheeks of the good

Germans, hale and hearty in the streets of their safe
city. He breathed of the air; foul to be sure with the
dampening snow, but it was the familiar noisomeness
of ordinary garbage, of cooking and spices mixed
with the droppings of animals.

There were odors far worse.

It seemed all the world outside this little enclave had
gone mad with fear and horror. Everywhere in France,
tiny village or big city, plague dead littered the streets. The
stench of them hung over the silent countryside like the
breath of hell. Dressed as he was in his priest's garb, survivors fell on him, begging Christian burial for their lost
loved ones. At first, in good conscience, he refused.

He had spent only weeks in Montpellier—even
now the horrors of that city did not bear thinking of.
He heard it, more than saw it, in memory—the wild
doomed laughter ringing through sparsely populated
streets. A city once filled with doctors, and there were
none left. No priests or monks. No one. Solomon had
been only too glad to leave it behind when his father's
letter had told him of Rica's death.

In despair he wandered through those fear-mad
cities and villages, where now he did stop to bury the
dead he found. There was no healing or comfort he
could offer as a physician—as priest he could give
some peace to grieving widowers and mothers.

In a tiny village, he stopped at the petition of a young
girl, perhaps twelve, to bury her parents and baby
brother. He stepped from the mule and collapsed on
the road.

He had no idea how long he had lain ill, besieged
with a black despair so vast he cared not for life at all.
But the girl had dragged him to her mean little hut
and bathed him with cool water and sang strange
witchery songs over him.

Somehow, he lived. He had little memory of the days he had lain at the mouth of death, except a strange, exaggerated vision of the girl, her dirty face streaked with tears as the boil on his groin drained. She had known what it meant. In his stupor, he had not known or cared.

There in the mean little hut in a village deserted but for himself and the young girl, he stayed for two months to regain his strength. When he left, he took her with him and settled her with a widow he had met in another village.

Now, as he rode up to his father's house, he stared at it with new eyes. A lifetime had he lived these past months. The youth who had been beaten for his passion was dead. A man, weary and thin, rode home in his place.

It was nearly time for the evening meal, and through the glittering swirl of snow, Solomon looked to the upper windows. A smell of chicken and garlic reached him. He dismounted and rounded the house to the back entrance of the courtyard.

He surprised Raizel and Hershel stealing kisses in the soft twilight. It brought a smile to his lips. "Hershel," he said, "has she not learned to nag you yet?"

They turned in shock. "Solomon!"

Hershel reached him first and hugged him with burly arms, then held him back to examine his face. "You have been ill."

Solomon shrugged.

Raizel ran for the others, calling out the news of his return. His mother and brothers crowded down, hugging him, kissing his cheeks. In their eyes, he saw that he still did not look himself.

Then there was Jacob, standing in the doorway, his lips pressed together in some powerful emotion. Solomon stepped away from his mother.

"Papa," he said—and stood there, overcome. Only his father knew the truth of the many sorrows of Solomon's life these past months. Only Jacob knew.

Solomon was at once unutterably exhausted. He swayed, feeling the old sick hollowness flood through him.

His father took his arm firmly and waved the others away. "Leave him. He is weary from his journey. Let's all go in, eat, and let him rest. Tomorrow you may ask your questions."

For several days, Solomon gave himself up to luxury. Asher moved to another room, and Solomon slept alone and uncrowded in his chamber, on a bed covered with clean linen and scented with herbs. He slept there deep and long, and rose each morning a little stronger. He ate of good, wholesome food prepared under his mother's precise direction, and drank good Rhenish wine.

It was only after his physical needs had been attended that he began to notice the pall over his father's house. In the evenings, there was a low buzz of muttered conversation, and visitors in and out. The women stayed clear of the men but exchanged worried glances with one another.

At first, Solomon ignored it, but as he regained his strength, he began to understand the fear stalking the Jews. They feared for their lives.

And yet, it was still several days before he roused himself enough to care.

One afternoon he sat in the solar, warming his feet by the fire, a robe draped around his shoulders to stave off the chill of winter howling beyond the window. He ate an apple from the summer stores. It was mealy but still sweet and he looked at it as he chewed, amazed at the beauty of the brownish-red skin, dotted with dark spots, in contrast to the pale meat. He bit again and looked again. So small a thing, an apple—and yet so large. He closed his eyes and ate it slowly.

His father came in and dropped into his massive chair, piled with soft embroidered cushions. Solomon smiled. "You still make me think of a king, Papa."

Jacob chuckled. "You said that when you were a little boy."

"I remember."

Settling himself more comfortably, Jacob tugged off his shoes and stretched his toes toward the orange fire. "You did not have much to eat out there," he said, eyeing the core of the apple at which Solomon still sucked. "There are more apples. Let me call a servant for another."

Lazily, Solomon tossed the core toward the hearth and watched as it hissed in the flames. He shook his head. "No, Papa. 'Tis only greed now."

"You are feeling better?"

Solomon nodded.

"Good."

They sat for a while in silence.

Jacob made a noise in his throat after a time. "I would hear of your journey, if you would tell it."

Slowly, Solomon gathered his thoughts. He had known this moment would come. "When I rode through the gates here," he said to begin, "I could not believe how unchanged it was. It is not that way in other places."

"So we have heard."

"There is no tale as grim as the truth." He closed his eyes for a moment. "I thought I had seen the worst at Montpellier—there were none left there. It was terrible. And it seemed, once the stories of the burnings of the Jews began to come, not a safe place to be. So I left there."

And so he told his tale of wandering, told of the violence and stench and madness that seemed to follow the plague like a demon sibling.

Pacing, he shook his head. "God's world has order, does it not? What I saw was chaos—and no sense to who would live or die. A whole village dead with only the town drunk still alive?" He spread his hands. "Why?"

"It is the will of our Maker," Jacob said, ever steadfast in his faith.

Solomon pursed his lips. This he had heard, over and over, but he would not offend his father. "Perhaps," he said wearily. "Is it then God's will that so many die?"

Jacob lifted his brows.

"Papa, I had this plague. The boils and fever and—" He laced his fingers together. "It is a great puzzle why I am now alive. As a student of medicine, I long to know what secret is locked in this body to make it so."

"Hmmm." It was the only answer Jacob made when Solomon spoke of medicine. It indicated interest and ignorance at once.

Solomon sighed. "This has been puzzling me since before I came back in the summer. Why do some fall ill while others do not?" He paced toward the door, then back, thinking. "In the village where I did finally fall prey to the pestilence, there were none alive but the girl who nursed me. One cat wandered through. That was all. The bodies were piled in the square, waiting for someone to bury them."

Jacob muttered something under his breath.

Solomon touched his chin, caught once more in the puzzle. "Then I, too, fell ill after so long when I was well. Why did I get sick then? Was it breathing the air in that foul place? And if that is so, why did this girl not die, too?"

"This girl . . . she tended you?"

Solomon nodded. "Yes, and well. I could not travel for two months—I was too weak. She found us food and water and kept us both alive."

"May God's blessing always be upon her," Jacob said in a rough voice.

In surprise, Solomon looked up to see how white his father's face had gone. "Ah, Papa, I am sorry. I do not mean to trouble you. I am only puzzled over these things. I wish to know the answer, so perhaps there can be some order in the chaos—perhaps there is some answer to this plague, and if I am alert, I can see what to do."

Jacob lowered his eyes. He said nothing for long moments. Then he lifted his head. "When your letter came, telling us how Montpellier looked, I was afraid for you. When we did not hear for so long, I feared you were dead. I should not have sent you back there."

Solomon had gained some knowledge of guilt and regret these past months. He touched his father's shoulder. "It was God's will," he said. "And here I am, home again, and growing stronger."

Gently, Jacob covered Solomon's hand with his own. "I am sorry for your troubles, *beneleh*."

As if the words made her flesh, Solomon felt Rica all around him, smelling of lavender, her golden hair trailing over his arms, soft as silk. It was not a vision or a dream—he felt her. And with the vision came familiar grief and guilt, commingled until he was nearly as mad with it as he had been with passion.

He swallowed hard and turned away to hide his eyes. In a moment, the feeling faded to coals once more. "I led us from what you wished to say, Papa."

Jacob drew a long breath. "Ten days ago, the good

citizens of Basle took the Jews from their homes and burned them in a wooden house on an island in the Rhine."

Solomon closed his eyes. So it was in Carcassonne and Narbonne, and in fear-mad villages and towns throughout the Continent. But Basle was close by, less than two days' journey by horse. "Has there been trouble here?"

"Not so much. But there are things." Jacob shook his head. "I cannot name them exactly."

"We should go, Papa. Leave now before there is more terror."

"I have spent my life building a legacy for my sons," he said stubbornly. "Do you think I will abandon all?"

"Papa, think!" Solomon said.

A voice from the doorway broke into the conversation. "You see? Even your precious Solomon agrees, Papa," Asher said. "It will not matter if we are all dragged from our homes who gets what you built."

Jacob looked from one to the other, his chin jutting out like a shelf of granite. "I will think on it," he said, then shifted forward, grabbing the table with its chess pieces arranged on it. "Who will play?"

Asher shook his head, his mouth pinched tight. "You can't make it go away if you don't look, Papa," he said, and flung up his hands. "You try, Solomon. None of the rest of us can get through to him!"

With a chuckle he could not suppress, Solomon turned back to his father. "So, King Jacob has spoken, eh?"

For a moment, Jacob struggled with a scowl. He gave up and gave his son a reluctant grin. "I will think on it. Now, come. Play."

They arranged the pieces, whose long shadows were cast on the ceiling by the warming fire. From the kitchen came the sounds of women chattering together as they cooked, and one of them began to sing in a sweet high voice. A healing sound.

"There is a girl I want you to meet, Solomon," he said, moving a pawn. "She is the daughter of a merchant in Mainz. . . . I would much like the alliance."

Solomon grinned. "Papa, I have been home only a few days and already you will marry me off?"

"Just see her for me, eh?"

It was little enough to ask. And in truth, Solomon had formed no plan for his future. Perhaps a wife, at last, was what he needed. Children, a home. Peace.

There were worse things.

He inclined his head. "All right. I will see her."

Her name was Hilde. She stood in the courtyard of the temple, and Solomon knew at once why his father wished him to see her. Just see her. She was beautiful, even more than Asher's wife, Raizel, with eyes rich as an evening sky. On her mouth was a trembling, unawakened passion. She moved her body with grace; a body, he noted with a wry twist of his lips, that any man would be pleased to claim.

He glanced at Jacob, who chuckled. Solomon raised an eyebrow in capitulation. She was worth seeing.

But when they later spoke in his father's house, Solomon found nothing in him stirring. Not even a mild twinge of passion. He found her simple conversation boring, her gentle voice annoying. The longer they spoke, the less he liked her and the reaction set up a strange disquiet within him. As politely as he was able, he excused himself from the gathering and, taking his cloak from the hook, went out to walk.

It was snowing again, but it wasn't cold. No wind blew, and the thick, fat flakes drifted down to cover imperfections with a gentle white hand. He made his way through the twisting streets toward the west gate of the city and walked along the river.

This was the first time he had left the city since his return. It was oddly freeing to be out and feel the crisp air in his lungs. The cold eased the constricting bands he felt strangling him as he spoke to the pretty young girl his father wished him to marry.

Bitterly, he kicked at a stone in his path. He still could not look at a woman—any woman—without thinking first of Rica. He knew he could not be with another, not yet.

The all-too-familiar bleakness descended over him, that cloying hopelessness and guilt that had so dogged him these past months. How long until he recovered? And was it only the woman he missed, or had the heady, dangerous time ruined him? Would he end up a sick old lecher, seeking out dangerous affairs for their thrill? The idea repulsed him.

Balefully he stared at the castle on the hill. As if to underscore his mood, the monks sang out their afternoon prayers, the lilting and solemn sound Rica had so loved. How often she had clutched his hand over it, her eyes lifting toward something unseen. "Listen!"

Sharp grief ripped through him. He wanted to cover his ears to shut out the sound. He began to run. His strength was still small, and he was forced to stop after only a little way, but it was far enough that he outpaced the prayers.

He paused against a tree to rest. His breath came from his mouth in clouds on the frosty air, and snowflakes cooled his heated cheeks. In a minute, he was better and straightened.

Out of the snow came a girl with a dog. His heart jolted painfully, and he stared, transfixed as she moved closer, unaware of him. His limbs trembled so violently he reached for a crotch of the tree to brace himself.

Rica.

He would know the straight, swaying gait in a crowd of thousands, a crisp yet sensual walk, like the woman herself. From below her hood fell a streamer of blond hair.

He could not move, nor breathe. The dog barked sharply. Solomon still stared. The girl lifted her head, looking around in fear.

From the shelter of the tree, he stepped forward. "Rica," he said, and his voice was as ragged as the coat of a beggar.

She clutched her chest and stared across the distance that separated them. For a brief, fleeting second, Solomon glimpsed a ripple of bright emotion in the beautiful face.

Then it was gone. With a vacuous smile, the girl said in a light voice, "Are you not Helga's student?" Without waiting for an answer, she moved her head slowly side to side. "You must have been away. My sister was killed by thieves these many months past."

Fresh horror washed through him, and with a plummeting despair, Solomon saw it was not Rica at all.

Rica was dead. Gone from him forever. Feeling hollow, he turned away. He would marry this girl his father wished for him, and go away to Mainz.

At least there, he might find peace again. If he did not find some soon, he would go mad.

22

Rica watched the figure retreat, seeing the despair and sorrow in his shoulders, in his defeated walk. She wanted to cry out in love and forgiveness, *Wait!*

But he had not known her. He thought her to be dead, thought it was Etta he saw now like a ghost on the road. That he could no longer see the difference stung Rica deeply.

For a moment, filled with pointed yearning, she watched him go. Then she turned before she could weaken, and ran back toward the castle.

Alone in her chamber, she dug in her trunk. Deep, buried below everything, rested the small painting of Cairo. With a trembling finger, she traced the curve of the mosque, and a swelling went through her, almost as if he had touched her again.

With sorrow, she remembered the wildness that marked last summer. The memory came to her awash in gold, like the light that had surrounded them through the magical long days they had spent by the Ill—Solomon reaching for her, his eyes shining with desire.

She gave a low cry. Because of that wild, selfish pleasure Etta lay cold and worm-eaten in the crypt.

Rudolf had disappeared, never to be seen again, whether in shame for lack of defending his bride or because he was dead it seemed they would never know.

Swiping away the tears on her cheeks, Rica put the painting back in its place. This forbidden passion she had conceived for the beautiful Solomon had always been a selfish and shameful thing.

Last summer, she had been a foolish child, filled with the sweet poems of the courts, those wildly romantic tales of illicit love that ended so tragically.

Grimly, she flung open the shutter and stared at the snow with a jaw clenched so hard her teeth felt as if they'd break.

She had sacrificed everything—her pride, her sister, her father. Her pride still ached at the way Solomon had rebuffed her the last day. She knew he'd lied, would have known it even if she had not seen his grief so plainly today.

But he had not loved her enough to face what lay before them. When it came time to choose between his studies and his love, he'd chosen his studies. It stung.

Etta, in some ways, had brought about her own death. But if Rica had not been so selfishly engrossed through those months, she would have been able to see more clearly the dangers that cost Etta her life.

The worst of it all, even worse than Etta's death, was that the passions of the summer and the resulting tragedies had driven a wedge between Rica and her father.

Charles did not believe that Etta could maneuver so wild a plot as drugging her sister and taking her place on the altar. He did not believe for many weeks, until Helga made him listen to the stories of Etta collecting the herbs from the castle gardens.

Still, Charles did not speak to Rica except to give

an order or instruction about some detail of the household. Rica had all but given up. She did not know how to reach his heart, how to ask him to forgive her, how to make right all the things that had gone wrong. She lived now a grim life. She still ventured sometimes to Helga's cottage, but it was painful; Lewis remained in Charles's employ, but he knew too much of the humiliation Rica had suffered for her comfort.

She still walked when she could with Leo. Only one place she did not go—to the copse of trees where Solomon had magically awakened the sweltering of her blood, where his strong hands and good mouth had stoked and satisfied the passion she had conceived for him.

And it had not been only her body he had awakened and teased to bright life, but her mind, her thoughts, her will to reason. She missed talking with him more desperately than anything.

Did he ever remember?

Bitterly she covered her mouth to hold back the cry of anguish that would come out if she let it. Even through her guilt and sorrow, she was aware of something asleep stretching awake within her. Her body felt newly tender, as if the slightest brush would bruise her. Simply seeing his face today for one moment had been enough to awaken all the sleeping coals of her lust.

Lust. It was only lust, and would abate. For never again would she speak to Solomon ben Jacob. He thought her dead. It would remain so.

Five candles and the fire filled Charles's solar with flickering light and warmth, and still he huddled in a thick wool blanket. Wind whipped the shutters again and again, whistling through the cracks and sending the candle flames to spluttering. He hated winter. The damp cold seeped into his very bones, and his joints ached with it. The lonely sound of the wind chilled his heart.

Rica came in, head lowered, carrying a tray of hot mead and fresh bread. Without speaking, she put it on the table. From beneath his lids, he watched her settling things, shaking out a cloth to cover his rough table and pouring his mead, a drink that gave him oblivion these cold nights. It was the only way he could find rest unless Helga was there to rub his limbs and comfort him in her other, more pleasing ways. But she came to him little these days. She thought his treatment of his daughter too harsh.

With a mutter, he scratched his belly. Helga was stubborn, but he would not be bullied. Not by his willful child or by a midwife who—

"Pappi," Rica said in a quiet voice. "I cannot live this way, seeing you and never talking. I am lonely. Have I not paid long enough?"

He closed his eyes. "I should have sent you to a convent." In truth he did not know why he had not. Shifting, he looked at her. "Will you tell me what man it was that dishonored you?"

She sighed. "I have told you—I lied. Helga tells you, too. I am still a virgin." The softness left her voice. She glared at him. "Why are you so stubborn?"

"Because I know you have lain with a man, Rica. It may be you are still a virgin, but I saw the look of a man on you that day." It was the most he had said to her. "Will you tell me?"

Her chin lifted. "No."

"So be it." He turned back to the fire.

With a noise of irritation, she stalked out. He heard her skirts swishing over the rushes. When the sound faded, he sank lower in his chair. They would not bully him. Not her, or Helga, either.

Aching simply to escape the pall that clung now to the castle like mold, Rica took Olga with her to Strassburg two days before Lichtmess. She wanted to buy a special candle for Etta and find some new fabric with which to amuse herself. By the saints, it seemed the winter would never end!

"What's here?" Olga asked as they rode toward Olga's sister's house. The roads were crowded and ahead was some sort of procession.

"I don't know."

Townspeople shouted and stared and raced after a band of people moving through the center of the street. A high keening sound, coupled with cries and moans, rang out into the cold winter air. Rica tugged back on the reins of the horse, a rustle of unease whispering over her nerves.

After a moment, she sorted the crowds of townspeople from the band in the street. They walked barefoot on the icy ground, and a trail of blood followed them. Their clothes were ragged, filthy; their hair unclean and uncombed. They looked like a horde of beggars but for the whips they used to beat their naked backs.

"'Tis the flagellants," she said and could not keep the disgust from her voice. "They think to save us from this plague. Come, let's go around them. I do not care to watch this spectacle."

They detoured through an alleyway but found themselves blocked once more by the long trailing band as they emerged. The horses, spooked by the scent of blood, backed nervously and Rica was nearly crushed against the wall.

"Dismount!" she cried to Olga. "We must wait till they pass."

So in horror, they watched the ragged group. Along the street, the robust townsfolk moaned in sympathy and wept and tossed out pennies. Rica stared at them with dawning awareness of the petrifying fear that ate at them. A fat housewife screamed and fell to her knees, waving her hands as the flagellants cried, "God spare us!"

"Has all of mankind gone mad?" Rica whispered to Olga.

The servant woman shook her head, staring like the rest at the violent spectacle. Rica looked back.

And there, in the midst of the most violent scourging she had yet seen, was Rudolf.

His hair had not been cut or washed since the wedding by the look of him, and he still wore ragged bits of finery. Tatters of velvet hung down from a belt. Malignant wounds and tracings of scars showed over the emaciated, bared torso, and his beard was a dirty tangle hanging from his chin. His eyes were wild.

A tumult of emotions rose in Rica's breast—fear and horror and grief. As he stumbled down the street, she remembered the rash his hair shirt had given him.

Rica shoved the reins into Olga's hand, and without thought, moved forward, pushing furiously through the crowd, her gaze caught on Rudolf. People grabbed her arms and her gown; she violently pulled free, intent on her goal.

A boy, no more than twelve, took hold of her hair. "Lady, you must not enter the circle, or they will have to begin anew."

Rica slapped him. "I don't care."

Before anyone else could grab her, she raced into the moaning crowd, her fists upraised. She sliced through the throng like a sword, her mouth open to let free a scream she heard but did not know she made until her throat tore with the power of it.

She struck Rudolf with both fists, one landing with a thunk against his mouth, the other against his ear. "Murderer!"

A half-dozen hands grabbed her. Rica screamed, kicking and pummeling at all of them in her rage. An elbow caught her cheekbone with a jarring smash. Shaking off the pain, she landed a fierce kick and one more fist to Rudolf's face before the hands dragged her away. And still she screamed, "Murderer!" She pointed at him. "He killed my sister!"

The men who had grabbed her from the procession dumped her ignobly in front of a baker's shop. She banged her head on the wall as she fell, and the dizzying impact kept her down for a moment. When she jumped up to see where Rudolf had gone, all she saw was the swaying, moaning crowd.

Spent, she collapsed on the step and buried her face in her hands. Etta! She missed her desperately, with a searing, deep pain it seemed would never ease. She wanted to weep in loss and rage, but her eyes burned with dryness. Since the day of Etta's wedding, she had managed not a single easing tear. It was as if something had hardened inside of her.

After a moment, she straightened and brushed her skirts. Her barbette had been lost in the scuffle, and her cloak had suffered a great rent. With a sigh, she examined the damage, then gingerly touched her cheek.

She pushed her hair away from her face and turned to go back to Olga and the horses. So deep was she in her thoughts that she stumbled blindly into a stranger on the street, a man who reached out kindly to steady her.

A sharp waft of frankincense rose from the wool of

his cloak. Clutching her belly against the sudden pain, Rica looked up in shock.

Solomon.

For a long, suspended moment, they stared in silence at each other. Rica drank hungrily of his face, seeing the hollows in his cheeks that had not been there before, and a haunted look around his eyes. He had been ill. The knowledge bit through her with swift terror, and combined with the beloved scent enveloping her and the spent energy of the moments just past, Rica felt suddenly faint.

His firm grip held her steady. "I saw what happened and came to see if you are wounded."

His voice poured over her spine, familiar and beloved and even richer than she remembered. Rica stared at him, unable to speak for the roaring in her ears.

After a moment of hesitation, he lifted his hand and touched the edge of her cheek. "You will be bruised," he said, and gave her a small impersonal smile. "But you are not hurt elsewhere, are you?"

He *still* did not recognize her. Rica stepped away from his touch, fury rising up in her breast like a wild beast. "No," she said.

Only then did she see the tear at the edge of his eye, a tear he tried to blink away as she stood there staring at him. It escaped his eye and he swiped the pad of his thumb over his cheek to catch it. He backed away. "Do not go so close to them again," he warned. "There is madness in their number."

He grieved for her, Rica thought. Her emotions, so tangled and lost since the death of her sister, screamed his name—*Solomon!*

As if he'd heard her silent plea, he paused and a fierce expression crossed his face. It was puzzled and alarmed and grim at once.

In panic, Rica bowed her head and hurried away. It was best this way. He thought her dead, and they had been mad to begin the first time. She would not begin anew.

Solomon made his way back to his father's house, away from the flagellants who gathered in the square to beg God for deliverance and show their humility with more of the whipping and wailing and screaming. He had seen their number before and was appalled to see them here now. Their presence boded ill for the Jews.

But as he hurried back to warn his father, his mind was not on the danger, but upon the girl in the street. He had been walking along with the crowd, listening as well as he could to muttered conversations so he would be able to tell his father how the feeling went among the townsfolk. The spectacle sickened him, and he kept his eyes averted, but a great buzz had flown up from the crowd when the girl broke through their number to attack a ragged man.

She screamed and pummeled the beggar with her fists, wildly thrashing against arms that tried to restrain her. It was only then that Solomon had recognized her target as the knight from der Esslingen's employ.

It was Rica's husband, now mad as a rabid dog, with wild unseeing eyes. Even as the girl struck him and screamed at him, he did not cease in his actions. Fiercely he struck his body again and again with a leather thong tipped with metal ends.

As volunteers hauled the girl from her mission, Solomon was riveted. All of his body leapt in response to the flush in her cheeks, the power of her young, strong body, the passion in her attack. In sudden, searing hope, he'd run to reach her.

And by all he was, he knew it was Rica, not Etta.

Her voice today was not so light, and in her eyes, he had seen a swift yearning he could not have imagined. This girl was too much alive to be the passive and vacuous Etta. Had he not seen the difference between them in Helga's yard? Rica's eyes were darker, her lips fuller, her brow high and intelligent.

A spiral of intense hope rose in him as he stared at her, remembering, dreaming. He could not have forgotten so much in so short a time.

He passed a peddler leading a worn and dirty horse, and the bells on the harness brought Rica so clearly, so achingly to his heart he nearly wept.

Madness. He rubbed his face. She was dead. The plague and his turmoil these past months had sent him beyond reason. All his wishful imaginings could not make Etta into her sister.

With weary steps, he climbed the stairs in his father's house. Jacob waited by the hearth, his hands folded.

"Papa," he said without shedding his cloak, "we must leave Strassburg. The danger is too great to stay here any longer."

A mulish expression crossed Jacob's face. "I will not leave yet."

Solomon took a great breath and blew it out. "Then send away the women . . . and whoever will go with them. I will stay with you here until we can stay no longer."

"If the danger creeps so close here, then why will it not go to Mainz or Nürnberg?"

"It may. But perhaps there is a little more time, and that way we can make larger plans. Europe is mad."

Jacob glanced up sharply. "You would have us leave the Continent? To go where?"

"Cairo." He held up a hand to forestall his father's protests. "Jews are many there, and the Mamluks are said to be fair. You have heard the same tales, Papa."

Jacob stroked his beard, his black eyes thoughtful. He pursed his lips. "Very well. I will send away the family if you will stay until I can settle my business here."

"These flagellants are dangerous—there should be no delay."

"So it shall be." He stood up. "Come, we will tell the others."

He moved to leave. Solomon stopped him. "Papa."

Jacob turned, an eyebrow upraised.

Solomon felt his throat filled tight with words. He could not speak around them, around his doubt and hope that it might have been Etta, not Rica, who died. He shook his head. Roughly, he said, "Nothing."

He helped ready the family. All but Jacob and Solomon would go—Hershel and Asher to protect the women on the dangerous roads. They would go to Raizel's family in Mainz, and to their brother Simon, who lived with his wife and children there.

By morning it was all done. When the prayers and blessings had been uttered, the mules packed and the family seen through the gates, Solomon turned again to his father. "I have a wish to see the midwife."

Jacob turned stony-faced. "I will not allow it."

Solomon smiled, sadly, and touched his father's shoulder. "The danger there is cold and buried in a crypt." He glanced toward the rooftops of the city. "Helga is a wise healer, and I wish to talk with her about this plague." He sighed. "In truth, it would comfort me."

A strange expression crossed Jacob's eyes. Worry? "Do what you must." His voice was thick with disappointment. "But do not tarry long. I will need you if I am to finish my business here."

"An hour or two, no more."

23

Rica had developed an odd habit over the past few months. Much as she hated needlework, she had taken up Etta's silks and had been trying to finish the tapestry Etta had left behind. It was slow, frustrating work, and often she had to take out a whole afternoon's sewing when she looked upon it again.

But slowly, her clumsy fingers were learning to make neat, tiny stitches. As she learned, sitting in the stone alcove of her father's chamber, she understood why Etta had loved so to sit here. The light was good, even on cloudy winter days, and the fire was cheery. Her father muttered and mumbled to himself as he made notes and listened to accounts from his men-at-arms and vassals and squires. He heard the petitions of peasants and granted or denied requests. When alone, he talked with his hawk and fed him bits of food.

It was as if Rica did not exist, and yet there was some comfort in taking part in his days. She thought, perhaps, he harbored some guilt over Etta's tragic end, too, and liked to half believe it was still she sitting here, stitching away.

So it was the day she returned from Strassburg.

There were things she wanted to tell him, things she needed urgently to discuss, and she had made up her mind on the ride home that she would talk, whether he listened or not.

But when she arrived, he stood by the embrasure, listening to the words of a councilman from Strassburg, the same one who had come this summer. Ignoring the glare her father shot at her, she bustled over to the corner and took up the silks.

The councilman broke off when he saw Rica, and glanced at Charles.

Charles set his mouth. "Go on. If she hears what she should not, 'tis only her fault for her nosiness."

"Very well. We have confessions extracted at Chillon in September that seem to prove the truth of these accusations against the Jews."

"Bah!" Charles shouted. "A tortured man will say anything to end his pain. At least death brings peace! I know not why the artisans believe such a confession."

The councilman, a sober man in sober black, shrugged. "'Tis greed, my lord, as ever."

"Yes." The word was weary. "So what is to be done?"

"The council of Köln has written to us. There is some fear the country might be destroyed if the violence continues."

Rica looked up, alert. There was a bleakness about the man she had not seen before and he bowed his head as he spoke again. "The tragedy at Basle sickened me."

"Who stands with you, and who against?" Charles asked.

"The mayor and Judge Sturm are with me. The artisans stand against us—and they have much power. They also have much to gain."

"And the bishop?"

"He is under papal dominion," he said, "and the pope has repeatedly forbidden these massacres under pain of excommunication."

Charles sank into a chair, and Rica looked at him in alarm. His color had drained away, and he seemed to have trouble catching his breath. She stood up, but he glared at her and waved a hand. Rica sat back down.

"So, tell me, what is the plan?" Charles asked.

"There is to be a conference in Benfeld with the councils of Strassburg and Köln. The bishop and all the feudal lords will attend. It would be an honor if you would be there to support us, my lord. Your fairness is well known."

"Send to me the details and I will be there."

"Thank you, my lord." He dipped his head in a gesture of respect. "I pray it will end well."

"As do I."

The judge left, and Charles let go of a long breath, pressing a hand to his chest. His face was ghostly white. Rica leapt up. "Papa? Shall I send to Helga?"

With an abrupt movement, he nodded. "A potion of hers would not sit ill with me now."

She whirled and flew into the passageway and there waylaid a vassal. "Run to the midwife and tell her my father is unwell. Quickly—and tell her it is a matter of some urgency."

He bowed and hurried away.

Rica returned and knelt at her father's side. "Take off your jupon and lie down. She will come quickly if she is able. Between now and then, I will get your tea."

He allowed himself to be unbuttoned, his dress to be removed. In his shirt, he reclined on his bed. As

Rica made to go to the kitchens, he reached out for her hand. "Stay a little, child. It is a weariness of the spirit that plagues me, not ill health."

"Are you strong enough to go to this conference? Benfeld is a hard ride in such weather. How will you stay warm or dry?"

"Child—" He shook his head. "No, you are no child these days. I am glad of it." He held her hand close to his chest. "Listen. You have not heard the stories. I am ashamed such things could happen in my own land. I must go, Rica."

A vision of the flagellants, whipping themselves in the streets of Strassburg, passed over her eyes. "I am afraid, Papa," she whispered, and told him about the flagellants, though not about Rudolf. "It seemed everyone had gone mad. You can hear them talking, telling each other lies about the Jews." She swallowed, thinking of Solomon. "What will happen to them?"

"I don't know."

She went cold. "I will pray then," she said, and reaching for the blankets, she covered him. "You must rest."

He was only too willing.

Solomon felt a little faint as he climbed the stairs to Charles der Esslingen's chamber high in the old keep. He focused on the swaying of Helga's skirts in front of him, trying to catch his breath.

It was strange to be here, where he had imagined so many times. Rica herself had climbed these steps a thousand times, as a child and a young woman. Down them she had gone to ride away with her husband—to her death.

He had protested when Helga asked him to come, but she could be implacable. She thought he might know something more about this condition than she did, and he could see in her eyes that she loved the man.

So he had come with her. Now he wished he had not. At the top of the steps, he paused, putting his hand against the wall. "Helga, I am still not as well as I would like. Tarry a moment, if you will, and let me catch my breath."

She did not pause. "Catch your breath in the solar."

Solomon grinned at her. The world was falling apart all around them, but Helga had not changed. She was her sturdy, sensible self no matter what ills befell mankind. He had missed her.

She had said nothing about Rica. Following her lead, he had said nothing either, and now he braced himself for the sister, in case she was hovering somewhere about.

The lord lay on his bed. Hearing Helga enter, he opened his eyes and smiled at her. "I am in need of your medicine."

"I have brought someone today, my lord," Helga said, and turned toward Solomon, drawing him forward with her hand. "This is Solomon ben Jacob, who studied medicine in Montpellier."

Charles lifted a heavy brow. With a little pang, Solomon saw Rica had inherited his eyes. Not only the color, like the mountains on a warm day, but the light and passion, too.

"Know you how to cure me?" Charles asked.

"I am not yet a physician, but I have studied five years." Solomon's lips twitched. "Perhaps I may help a little."

There was a noise from one corner, and Solomon glanced over. He had not realized there was anyone else in the room.

Sitting on a bench, a tapestry spread over her lap, was the girl he had seen in Strassburg today. A purple mark stained her cheekbone. Once again the first thought in his mind was *Rica*.

"That is my daughter," Charles said. With an edge in his voice, he added, "She is simple. Pay her no mind."

Helga bustled over. "Oh, my pretty," she murmured. "Tell me what happened."

The girl—he could not bring himself to call her Etta—shook her head. In a breathy, quiet voice, she said, "'Tis nothing."

"Well?" Charles prompted. "Will you gaze all the day at my daughter, or examine me and tell me what I already know?"

Solomon chuckled at this. His own father put forth the same bluster.

The examination was not long—it did not need to be. There were telling signs at a simple glance. The lord's color was whitish, his skin clammy, and a bluish tinge edged his mouth. Solomon heard the labored sound of his breathing, and he leaned over to listen to his heart.

He rocked back on his heels and met der Esslingen's eyes. In that blue so like Rica's, in the broad and powerful face, Solomon read no regret, only a simple resignation. He was dying.

Wordlessly, Charles looked to the women, watching them with careful attention, and back to Solomon. "So," Charles said, "tell me what I know. I am an old man and must suffer along as best I can."

Solomon smiled. "You're an old man and must suffer along as best you can."

The girl, as if she could restrain herself no longer, rushed over to settle her father. Her movements were strong and sure, without the fluttering that women so often indulged. Her hair fell down to obscure her face, but Solomon was struck with the fullness of her hips as she leaned over. With a flip of her hair, she turned. The movement was so typically Rica, it scored his soul.

Transfixed, he stared at her. She cocked her head. "And Herr *Docktor*," she said with an ironic twist of her lips, shooting a glance toward her father, "what say you about a long journey to Benfeld?"

A swell of sweet joy filled him, and a yearning so bright and deep he thought it must flood the room. He had *not* lost his mind.

She lifted her chin in arrogance, but her eyes were dark with the same fury he had seen in her eyes the day he left her on the road to Montpellier.

And at last, the reason for her ruse penetrated his thick skull. She was angry—and with good reason—but if he had a little time with her, perhaps he could make her understand he had not left her for lack of love, but for the opposite.

Disdainfully, she lifted her brows. "Well? What say you?"

Solomon glanced at Charles, who watched the pair of them with a strange, musing look on his face. "I say it would be folly, my lord."

"See, Pappi?"

Charles straightened on his bed. "I am a knight, though an old one. I no more fight battles with swords, but there's still a battle left in this heart, and fight it, I will." He lifted a hand and pointed to Solomon. "It may very well be your life that hangs in the balance."

"It may be then, my lord," Solomon countered, "you give your life to save mine. I do not recommend you take this journey. The weather is yet harsh."

"Pah."

Solomon looked again at Rica, who still rigidly stood at the foot of her father's bed, glaring at him. "Stubborn, I see," he said slowly. "'Tis a habit that drives wedges through good intentions."

"Not so much as arrogance," she returned.

Solomon gathered his cloak, his heart near to brimming. "True enough," he said, and turned toward her father once more. "I urge you to send a letter in your place."

Charles cocked a brow and did not answer.

"I bid you all good day." He nodded to Helga, who had an odd gleam of satisfaction in her eye, and then finally toward Rica. She looked away.

Out on the road back to Strassburg, Solomon inhaled the cool wet air with a sense of exhilaration, a joy so vast he could barely comprehend it.

She was alive.

In the deep of the night, Charles stirred. He had not slept easily, in spite of the loving attentions of the woman at his side. Absently, he stroked her soft back and her fleshy arm for comfort. Helga nestled closer to his shoulder, her wealth of hair spilling over his chest.

"Trouble sleeping, my sweet?" she asked softly.

He sighed and kissed her hair. "Yes."

"Let me rub your back."

"No." He did not want to stop holding her. "I have missed you." He growled to hide his deep emotion, and stroked her breast.

"I am weary of staying away in temper," she admitted. "There is comfort for me here in these dark times."

"The times will be darker yet, I fear."

"Aye," she said quietly. "But you do not need to shoulder all of it, my lord. The plague will come and take who it likes and there is naught you can do."

"I can protect those in my house," he said. "When I return from Benfeld, we will shut the castle up as if for a siege. I would have you here then."

"I cannot promise you that. Plague or not, there is work I must do."

"Can you not find someone else to do it, woman?"

She chuckled. "None I would trust."

He let that settle, then came to the thing keeping him awake. "What of that young Jew?"

Next to him, Helga's body was not quite so pliant as a moment before. "What of him?"

"A handsome youth, is he not?"

She laughed, a bawdy, husky sound he loved. "Handsome is only the beginning!"

"Rica looked at him as if she would murder him," he said slowly, and waited.

Helga said nothing.

Charles scowled. "Why must you be so silent when I wish to hear your thoughts?"

She lifted up on one elbow. The moonlight creeping around the shutters was kind to her face. "I am only a woman, my lord," she said with an ironic twist to her lips. "What could you wish to hear from me?"

He grunted. "Perhaps I do not wish to hear the truth in this," he admitted. "What I saw today I did not like."

"What did you see?"

"Too much," he said, and remembered. Rica

unsettled and flushed and trying to get the man's attention, while trying to push it away. And then that single, blazing smile the Jew had given her. It was not the joyous smile of a man newly struck, but one deep with intimacy and knowledge. "It is he she loved," he said, and knew it to be truth.

Helga moved close and kissed him. "You must rest, my lord."

Charles closed his eyes. It was true, then, or Helga would have denied it. All this time, she had known and kept it to herself, when he might have done something to stop the tragedies that had befallen them. He clutched her arms. "Why did you not tell me?"

"There are things, my lord," she said and opened her palm along his jaw, "that women sometimes owe one another. Your daughter is a wise woman. You have not given her the trust she deserved. Trust her now."

With sorrow, he thought of Rica's protests that she choose someone more to her liking, her protests against Rudolf in particular. If only he had listened, perhaps his other daughter would not now be dead.

And yet—"She cannot wed a Jew!" he said.

Helga kissed him, as if to stop his talk. This time, he let himself be carried away by her strong, skillful hands. When they were finished, he finally slept.

24

For three days, Solomon left his father and went to walk on the paths he knew to be Rica's favored places. He slogged through the mud along the river Ill and climbed to the copse of trees overlooking the Rhine. He lingered in the winter-bare orchards nearby the castle walls and waited patiently along the path to Helga's.

On the fourth day, it was cold. He huddled deep into his cloak as he paced along the Ill, remembering with pleasure the days he had spent swimming there, and the time he had first kissed Rica. She had been bathing, and the thought of her naked in the river only moments before had made him wild.

But he did not regret that kiss, or any after. In finding Rica, he had somehow found himself, a self apart from all the things his family and religion and teachers had expected of him.

She was not there when he arrived, and somehow he did not mind. It seemed if fate had charted their paths so closely, then he only need be faithful.

And so he admired the dark trees with their frostings of snow and tapped branches to watch the glistening fall of flakes tumble in the cold, misty air. The river was frozen white at the sides, but the ice was thin as glass in the middle. He could see water running through it.

The silence was vast and clean, as if he were the only man on the earth. It made him feel large and calm.

When he heard the crack of branches in the forest behind him, he turned in the middle of this great silence, knowing it would be Rica at last.

She ducked through the branches, cloaked in blue wool, the hood up to cover her head. Leo bounded forward, racing for the edge of the river, and Rica cried out toward him, "No, Leo!"

He halted at Solomon's side and licked his hand.

Rica froze beneath the branches of a sheltering pine, her cloak dotted with snow fallen from the trees. She stared at him for a moment as if he were a huge dragon about to breathe fire and burn her to cinders, there in the forest.

Then, before he said a word, she turned and bolted through the trees.

"Rica!" he shouted. His voice rose like an explosion through the silence. Spurred by her flight, he ran after her.

She rushed headlong over the path, ducking beneath the low branches and dashing around shrubs. Her skirts nearly tripped her once and she made a sharp sound, then righted herself.

He caught up with her and reached out, snagging her arm. She screamed, trying to tear herself away from him.

"You are not Etta!" he said furiously.

With an abrupt, strong movement, she flung off his arm. Her hood fell away from her face. "No, I am not!" she cried. "But it matters not where you are concerned."

She had never looked more beautiful to him. He stepped forward. "Rica, forgive me. I meant to keep you safe. That's all."

"You are like all the rest of them." Tears sprung to her eyes and she brushed them away with her wrist.

"You say what pleases you, caring not for the wishes and passions of a woman."

Solomon frowned and took a step backward. What had he expected? That she would tumble, as she had before, into the circle of his arms? Yes. That he could coax her easily, as he had coaxed dozens of women to him in the past.

His own shallowness appalled him. The words and pleading he had composed fluttered away from him like leaves on a winter wind. "I have suffered for this arrogance, Rica, more than you will know." He straightened. "If you have no wish for me, so be it."

With a leaden heart, he turned away and began to walk back down the hill.

Rica gripped the trunk of a slender tree, watching him leave. She fought her need of him, fought the foolish woman weakness that rose in her breast, the same selfish foolishness that had led to so much disaster last summer. Her limbs trembled, and tears tumbled over her cheeks.

His head was bowed, and she remembered the passionate conversations they had once shared, remembered the perfect moment of melding she felt with him that day outside of Helga's cottage.

And all these bleak, long, lonely months without him, all these months she had dreamed of him, hungered for his touch—

"Solomon!" she cried on a sob.

He returned to her with a roar, his strong arms gathering her up so tightly she could scarce breathe. She flung her arms around his neck, weeping as he kissed her hair and her cheek and clasped her again, rocking her close in the cold. "Oh, Rica," he whispered, "I thought you were dead. I missed you so violently I wished to die myself."

She lifted her head, and before she could speak, he kissed her mouth with all that pent-up longing, with all the power of the months each had spent alone. Rica still could not halt her trembling or her tears. She felt as if she had come unfastened and would fall apart like a badly made gown. "Solomon," she said, grabbing to his arms in sheer emotion. "Sit with me. I . . . am . . ."

"Shhh." He sat and settled her over his knees. "My love, my love," he said against her neck. She felt his nose and eyelashes against her cheek, and his breath soughed over the hollow of her throat. "How could I have left you?"

She nestled her face into his shoulder, drawing strength from his solidness and the beloved feel of him against her. After a moment, her trembling eased and she trusted herself to speak. He dried her tears gently, and smiled. "You missed me a little, too, I think."

She smiled tremulously and shook her head, touching the wild disarray of his hair. "I felt I had lost my soul, Solomon. Truly."

He kissed her, intimately, passionately. Rica felt the swelling hunger rise up within her until her breath was gone.

Urgently, he released her. "Not this way," he said, pressing his forehead to hers.

"But—"

He touched her mouth. "I will be your husband," he said softly, and looked at her with a vulnerable expression in his dark eyes, "if you will be my wife." He tenderly tucked a lock of hair behind her ear. "Surely God will find it meet to grant us this small thing."

Rica's eyes filled with tears.

"So sad," he said with a smile.

"No," she whispered. "This is joy you see. For I can think of no greater joy than that. None." She moved her head. "But how?"

"We can only go forward one day, one hour, as we are able, Rica. Thinking too far ahead parted us. Let us just say we will marry, quickly, and once that is done, we will do the next thing."

Soberly, she nodded.

"I know we will have to flee this place. Will it frighten you?"

With a sure, simple smile, she said, "Where you go, I follow gladly."

"Good." He gently moved her to stand up. "I must go back to my father. He needs me now—the rest have gone to Mainz, and he will follow soon. But I will send to you when I find a place for us, and a time." It was his hand that trembled now. "And we will consummate this union, so forever we will be joined."

At the thought, so long forbidden, her hips went weak, and she pressed her lips to his palm.

He kissed her and made to go, then came back. "I am afraid to leave you," he said and caught her close. "I could not bear to lose you again, sweet Rica. I love you. I did not know how much."

Rica buried her face in his shoulder, breathing of the frankincense and heat of him. She squeezed him close, as if to pull him inside of her. "We do not have to wait," she suggested, thinking they could spread their cloaks on the ground.

He chuckled. "Ah, *mein herz,* do not tempt me." He bent and took her chin in his hand. "I have had enough of snatched moments with you." He bent over and touched his lips to hers reverently. "I will have you unhurried and without fear."

"You have changed," she said, struck less by his words than by his air of infinite patience. "The boy is gone. Now you are a man."

A wisp of sadness crossed his face. "So it is.

And the girl who was so joyful is gone, too."

"It seems many years since the summer."

He touched her cheek. "Now we will look forward to the spring."

"I love you, Solomon," she said, and tiptoed up to kiss him once more. Then she turned and flew through the trees, her feet light with joy and anticipation.

The conference was to take place on Monday in Benfeld, and Charles, despite protests, rode out early Sunday morning. The weather was cold but clear, and Rica, watching him ride through the castle gates with his entourage, prayed the weather would hold. As it was, she had seen to his dressing herself, making sure his neck was well covered and his head, and that he wore two pairs of stockings beneath his long jupon.

She had to admit, as she walked back toward the hall, his mood was high today. "With God as my witness," he said, "this is a battle worthy of my best." Then he kissed her. "Take care, daughter, and do not forget to pray well."

"That I will do."

Gathering her cloak about her, she climbed to the walk to watch them ride away until they were out of sight. Up so high, she could feel the new warmth of the sun, as if it could not wait for spring. A soft gray haze clung to the horizons.

In spite of the grimness of her father's journey, and the threat of plague hanging over them like a scythe poised to swing and cut them down, she felt a swell of hope and joy in her heart. As if to mirror the emotion, a trio of magpies swooped by, chasing each other on the wind, making all manner of noises. She laughed.

It was selfish to be so happy—but she could not

stop it. Her beloved was safe and well, and he loved
her. Soon, he would send word.

Late that day, Helga appeared in the great hall, a
strange smile on her face. "My lady," she said, "I have
news."

Rica grabbed her hands eagerly and glanced about
to be sure no one lingered too close. "What?" she
whispered urgently.

"Go you tomorrow to my cottage, before supper,
and you will find a kind and handsome man."

"You are our helper?" Tears sprung to Rica's eyes
and she hugged Helga close. "Thank you."

Helga chuckled. "I will stay here, and make the castle
ready for the closing your father wishes when he returns."

Puzzled but too filled with light to question, Rica
nodded. She stood up, then bent and kissed Helga
soundly. "I will forever be in your debt."

Helga swatted her bottom.

When she completed her chores the next day, Rica
went to the chapel. There she laid a special offering
for Mary and lit a candle for her father, then knelt in
the confessional.

"Forgive me, Father, for I have sinned," she said.

The priest heard her confession sleepily and
absolved her. Thus cleansed spiritually, Rica went to
bathe in water scented with a special packet of herbs
she had been saving. She washed her hair and rinsed
it with chamomile, then combed it dry by the fire. On
her nude body, she rubbed lavender-scented oil, to
give her skin sheen and softness.

Her hands shook as she dressed. First her best and
newest kirtle, made of snowy linen, then a close-fitting
cotehardie of soft green, patterned with paisleys in

peach and gold. Over this, she donned a forest-green velvet surcoat, open at the sides and lined with miniver. Into her hair she wove dried lavender flowers.

The last things were a bracelet and girdle with bells, for the old times, for music.

At last she bent over her trunk and withdrew the present she had found for Solomon on Friday in Strassburg. It was a bound copy of Maimonides' *Aphorismen Mosis,* one the bookseller had been pleased to sell at a good price. He had bought it before the current hatred toward Jews had risen again, and had not been able to find a buyer.

It had been carefully copied and illuminated, and as Rica wrapped it now in a length of blue linen, she imagined the pleasure it would give Solomon. She set it down and lifted her heaviest cloak, wrapping it about herself closely to hide her finery. The book she slipped beneath the engulfing wool.

Then, almost aching with excitement, she hurried from her room, into the bailey, and beyond, just as the sun slipped behind the mountains and the world was plunged into the pale, magical gloaming.

For two days, Solomon had been gathering things. He bought candied fruits and marzipan and two precious oranges at an outrageous price. There was good wine and fresh bread and hard-boiled eggs. He had taken Helga a kosher chicken and asked her to prepare it for him. She chuckled over the task, but agreed to it.

Outwardly, he behaved as if nothing were amiss. He and his father settled accounts and made an inventory of his goods. Some were boxed and shipped to Mainz, others distributed among the neighbors. Jacob grumbled over the losses he was forced to take, but when reminded of the alternatives, moved ahead with due haste.

The boy Solomon had secretly paid to deliver his urgent message came to the door just past Nones on Monday. He was a rough little peasant, but bright and quick; Solomon saw he wore new shoes when he breathlessly repeated the message Solomon had rehearsed with him. The midwife needed him for a most dire birth.

He rose, frowning, and told his father he would return when he was able.

He found Helga's cottage empty but swept clean. Through the windows spilled the last of the day's light, and a fire had been laid, awaiting a flint. On the hearth was a stew, rich with the scents of garlic and onion, and over the table Helga had spread a washed linen cloth, very old and very beautiful.

From the pouch he carried, he took a pair of silver candlesticks and put them on the table and fitted precious white wax candles into them. Helga had put out knives and spoons. Wrapped in cloth were trenchers and a loaf of new bread.

And there, set apart from everything, was a beautiful silver chalice, carved around the bowl with figures of women and men, bowing together and kissing and holding hands. Touched, Solomon settled it in the place of honor, next to the candlesticks. The gift he had brought for his bride—his bride!—he placed before the chalice.

Only then did he slip out of his plain clothes and brush smooth his black jupon and put on his good hat after combing his unruly hair into some sort of order.

Then, excited as a boy, he sat down by the fire to wait. It seemed hours before he heard a noise at the door, a scratching. He ran to it and flung it open.

And stopped, his heart soaring wildly through his breast, his stomach leaping out of control. She looked at him shyly from beneath her hood, her cheeks flushed from her walk. "Hello, my love," she said. Her voice was breathy.

"Rica," he said, drawing her inside.

She ducked in and put a package on the bench nearby the door, then looked around her as she loosened the ties to her cloak. "It looks beautiful," she said softly, and shed the cloak.

He took it from her as she turned, and stood holding it as he stared. "You are far more so." He stepped close and touched the velvet of her gown, brushed the miniver along the edges with his palm. "I have never seen you in such finery."

She took a step back and turned around slowly, her arms out to her sides, a teasing look in her eye. "'Tis all for you."

He lifted her hand and kissed it.

With a quizzical glance, she smiled at him. In her green gown, with her hair tumbling free and silky over her body, she made him think of the legends that a goddess of spring wandered through the valley, awakening the sleeping earth with kisses.

She stepped close and pressed her mouth to his. Her hands wound around his neck, and her breasts nestled softly against his chest. A rocking sense of rightness swelled in him, and he held her close for a moment, kissing her in return.

In a moment, he lifted his head. "First we shall make our blessing. I do not know your customs, only my own."

"Marriage is marriage in God's eyes."

He nodded soberly. "God will know our vows are true. Later, we will ask a rabbi to say it officially."

"I am willing," Rica said.

"Then, come, my love. Let us stand by the fire."

25

Rica followed him. He took her hand, his face sober and serious. "Rica, I must ask you a question."

She waited silently.

"The only thing I will ask of you in this is when we have children, I must know they will be raised as Jews. There are laws that say a woman who is not a Jew, if she be a good wife to her husband, she must be accepted. It will be this, more than anything, that will be necessary. Can you do this for our marriage?"

She did not need to think—the same thoughts had been in her mind. "Yes."

"In truth there will be no other place for us."

"I know."

He nodded, and she saw his throat move. Finally he lifted his eyes. "Are you sure you wish to marry me, Rica? It is not easy, living as a Jew."

She looked at him, at his black hair, grown a little long and unruly; at his broad shoulders; at his clean hands, holding hers so gently. Then she looked into his black eyes, where the soul of him shone, and she saw the intelligence and love and respect there, the respect she had never seen in another man's eyes in all of her life.

All at once, she was overcome. "If you were a beggar, I would tear my clothes and dirty my face to follow you."

As if in relief, he let go of a breath. "So be it."

He poured wine into a pottery cup, then put Rica on his right and turned them so they faced the south. Taking from his finger a silver ring carved with trees, he held it up. "My custom requires me to tell you this ring is made of silver, not gold. Do you see it?" He smiled, a little mockingly.

Rica smiled, too. "Yes, I see it."

He took her hand, and in a sober voice, said, "'Behold thou art consecrated unto me by this ring, according to the Law of Moses and of Israel.'"

He pushed it on her index finger. Looking into her eyes, holding both her hands, he said, "I must say these things in Hebrew, in God's language, but I will tell you after what they are."

She nodded, clasping his hands more tightly. Solomon closed his eyes and sang out in a strong voice, in a language unlike any she had ever heard. Rica stared at him, amazed at how tall he seemed when he spoke the strange words, how much his skin seemed to glow.

And as the words filled the room, the glow seemed to rise and shimmer between them, until Rica could feel it in her own body, as if a thousand candles were alight and shining.

Then he paused, and looking deeply into her eyes, he began to recite softly, "'O make the loved companions greatly to rejoice, even as of old Thou didst gladden Thy creature in the Garden of Eden.'"

Rica's heart ached with wonder. Tears of joy filled her eyes.

"'Thou didst create joy and gladness, bridegroom and bride, mirth and exultation, pleasure and delight, love and comradeship, peace and fellowship.'" A quaver moved through his voice. He swallowed, and Rica saw the bright sheen of emotion in his eyes. His next words were husky. "'Blessed art Thou, O Lord, who makest the bridegroom to rejoice with the bride."

He took the cup of wine and gave it to Rica, urging her to drink. He then drank of it himself, and with a smile, turned and threw it at the wall. It shattered and fell to the floor. He grinned. "Good luck," he explained.

"Am I your wife, then?"

Solomon took her hand. "Yes."

New tears gushed forth from her eyes, and she smiled through the blur. "I am so thankful!"

He bent close, and her vision was filled with his dark brows, so elegantly shaped against his high intelligent forehead, and his long-lashed eyes, starry now with firelight. Ever so slowly, his lips moved closer, until the moist warmth of them, tasting of wine, settled on hers.

She sighed and leaned into him, her hands falling on the broad expanse of his shoulders beneath the soft, expensive velvet. He kissed her slowly, thoroughly, his tongue swirling against her lips and then inside them.

He tugged her a little closer and lifted his head. "You cannot know, Rica, how I have longed for you these past months." He lifted the circlet from around her forehead and smoothed her hair down after. "I would remember your hair or your lips or your eyes"—he touched each in turn—"and it seemed I would never recover from the grief of your death."

Rica lowered her eyes and touched the new weight of the ring on her finger. "All the joy left my life the day you rode away. I thought—" she struggled for words, "I thought I could let you go and make my life again, but I could not."

"I love you," he murmured and bent to kiss her again. This time, his hands roved over her arms and slipped beneath her surcoat to trace the curve of her back. "It would be more proper for us to eat and drink, but I have waited too long for you. Do you mind if we partake of our marriage bed before our wedding meal?"

Rica laughed and caught his face in her hands. "Oh, no," she said. "I do not mind at all."

To illustrate, she reached up for the small round hat on his head and set it aside, then reached for the buttons of his jupon. He stood still, letting her skim the velvet from his arms until he stood only in his flowing white shirt sleeves, as beautiful as a fallen god.

Then it was his turn. He stepped close. "Lift your arms." When she complied, he lifted the surcoat over her head and gently settled it aside. Turning back, he reached out and smoothed a line from her shoulders, forward over her breasts, and down to her waist and hips. "You are so beautifully made," he breathed.

No more could Rica be patient. She swayed toward him, and touched the broad expanse of his chest, untying the laces at his throat to place her palms flat on his skin. Dark curls of hair spread over his torso, and she bent her head to press her mouth against the alluring sight. She tasted heat and crisp hair and supple skin.

In return, he spread his fingers over her back and traced the curves of her hips.

And little by little, in this way, they shed their ornaments and shields until they stood, face-to-face, in bare gleaming skin and firelight.

Rica stared at him, forgetting her own nakedness in her hunger. He was thinner than he had been, but still uncommonly virile and beautiful. He drew her close to him, until her breasts, so heavy with hunger, pressed against the silkiness of his flesh. He did not kiss her, but his eyes held hers as if he had cast some spell, and in his face, she saw the fever of his need. "For this, I have been waiting," he said in a low, raw voice. "For this, I would die."

And at last, he kissed her, and his hand touched her breast, and they tumbled together to the bed. Rica felt the strange, shimmering light of the ceremony return. It flooded the room, flooded her, as his hands sought the secret heat between her legs, and his mouth settled over her breasts. She slid her hands over his back, feeling each precious rise of bone in his spine as if it were something newly made.

At last, when she felt she could wait no more, he poised himself above her. In the firelight, his hair shone as it fell around his sensual face, and his eyes were burning and somehow tender at once. "I did not know I could feel this way, Rica." His voice was hoarse. "Now you will always be mine."

All of time gathered there—past and future mingled, and Rica felt a singular and shattering sense of harmony. His thighs, hard and strong, brushed her own, and then there was a nudging in that deep, secret place. His belly brushed hers, and his chest swept over hers, and then there was a wild filling, and a quick sharp pain, and then—

Rica cried out, lost in the slow, deep wonder of the feeling that coursed through her as he moved over her and with her and inside of her. He sought and found her mouth, and they were doubly joined, triply, for his hands tangled in her hair, and her arms were flung around his neck.

And still he moved, slow and strong, until Rica

could bear no more, and met his movements with thrusts of her hips until there were soft groans coming from his mouth, a rumbling through his chest into hers. A rocking, swollen tide built in her limbs and low in her belly, and she clutched him tighter.

A wide, bright shock moved through her, shattering her into a thousand shards. As if Solomon had been waiting, he grasped her hips in his hands and thrust deeply. He cried out and shivered within her and she kissed his neck, feeling him shudder as forcefully as she had. He made a noise, ragged and low. The muscles of his arms were rigid below her hands.

For a long time, they simply lay together, tangled and sweaty. The pulsing, shimmering light faded to a soft glow within her veins, and she slipped her fingers through his hair absently, over and over.

At last, he shifted his weight, groaning a little as her body gave him up. He tugged the blanket over them and pulled her close again.

Rica shifted to lean on her elbow. "'Tis lucky I did not learn how much more there was that day in the forest, or I would not have settled for so little."

"So now you must know it was not easy for me to walk away." He leaned forward to kiss her. His hand lingered on her face. "You are so beautiful, my Rica."

She slid near, until their bodies met chest to chest, hip to hip, and she slipped one leg between his. Lifting her face, she kissed his chin, reveling in the warmth of him, the scent, the glory that was Solomon. "I cannot think of anything I would rather do than lie here with you forever," she whispered, and stroked his side.

His hand moved on her shoulder, and he pressed his cheek to her hair. "Nor can I, my love. And for now, we need not do anything else."

Wrapped in the sacred comfort of their union, they dozed, tangled and satisfied.

After a time, Solomon stirred. He moved in drowsy contentment and felt at once the gentle weight of Rica curled close to him. A swelter of joy blazed in his heart, and he shifted to look at her asleep, feeling wonder at the pale blush on her cheek and the curve of her lip. Her hair spilled around them like magnificent cloth.

Thus he had dreamed of her a thousand times, alone in his room or on the road, or despairing in Montpellier. Tenderly, he brushed her jaw with his fingers and touched her silky shoulder where it lifted through her hair, then, feeling his passion rise again, he followed the path of that hair over her breast. So soft, so round and supple. The pink tip pearled against his fingers.

With a soft moan, he kissed her neck. She stirred. Her hands stroked his chest, and sinuously, her thigh moved against his. He kissed her neck and her shoulder, and pushed her hair away so he could take her taut nipple into his mouth.

Oh, the taste of her! He moved his hands over her sleek form, over the hollows of her back and the rise of her hips and the sweet curve of her bottom. She made a small noise, whispery and sweet, and he tasted the bow of her ribs and the hollow of her navel.

She began to move restlessly, as if she didn't know what next came, and Solomon, through his haze, smiled before he bent over the juncture of her thighs, and there placed the heat of his mouth.

But there had been too little time between them and he could not wait as long as he wished. Her little cries and impatient movements aroused him to a feverish state; the brush of her legs against him nearly hurtled him beyond the gates.

And so, he tasted again the hollow of her navel and the pert tips of her breasts and the lavender scent of her neck. He settled between her long white thighs and drove home.

He did not think it could be so shattering twice, so strange—that light moving around them, that shimmering melding. But it was the second time like the first, as if some magic, some power beyond them, had found expression here in this joining.

When he lay spent against her, catching his breath, she teased him with a soft laugh. "I can see I have much to learn, my love." She kissed his ear. "It will be a pleasure to be your student."

"It will be a pleasure to instruct you," he said, and chuckled wickedly. "Perhaps we can find those texts of instruction in which you were so interested."

Her eyebrows rose.

A rumbling growl from his stomach punctuated the moment. "I think I'm ready to feast. Are you?"

"I am famished."

"Good." He rose and slipped into his shirt, and found her kirtle for her to put on.

Rumpled and flushed with loving, she rose and donned the shift. It was a flowing garment, white linen with wide sleeves, and it made her look like an angel. "Ah, Rica," he said, shaking his head in wonder, "I am the most fortunate man in the world tonight."

She cut him a glance. "No, husband. I am the lucky one."

They ate hard-boiled eggs and chicken cooked in garlic. It was the most delicious meal Solomon had ever consumed.

"This is beautiful," Rica said, passing him the silver chalice filled with wine.

"Helga left it for us. Perhaps it was her wedding gift."

"Perhaps."

Darkness filled the room, and the candles were lit, and still they sat and talked of inconsequential things.

When they had finished the meal and sat over the shared cup of wine, Rica inclined her head. "Tell me about your illness, Solomon."

He frowned. "Did I tell you I was ill?"

"I am not blind. You are far thinner than you were. Although," she raised her eyebrows as she looked at the picked clean remnants of the bird, "your appetite seems to have returned full measure."

"See how good you are for me?"

"Truly, Solomon, I would hear your tale. Was it plague?"

He sobered. "Yes," he said on a sigh. He sipped the wine and repeated the story of the mad villages and the despair and the suddenness with which he'd fallen ill when the peasant girl stopped him.

"Oh, Solomon." She took his hand. "Who cared for you?"

"The girl." His memory of her was fragmented— barefooted and filthy and terrified that first day as she stood on the side of the road and shouted him down. The lingering images were flashes of her strange eyes, gray with darker circles around the iris, and her black hair, wild and tangled on her slim shoulders. "She was young, only twelve or thirteen, the only one left in her village. Everyone else had died."

"What was her name?"

He gave her a quizzical glance. "Why?"

"I want to burn a candle for her."

Solomon smiled and kissed her fingers. "Her name was Giselle."

She jumped up. "I forgot your present!"

She brought the package back to him, and he opened it and stared in surprise. "Rica, where did you find it?"

"Do you like it? I can take it to the bookseller again and find another if there is something you would rather have."

"No. I am pleased beyond measure. 'Tis a hard book to find these days." He looked at her. "But how did you know, Rica, to look for him?"

Her smile was secret and sweet. "You talk so much, and must forget what you say. I remembered when you spoke of him."

He kissed her. "Thank you." Then he tugged his own gift over from its hidden spot on the bench. "Tradition tells me I should give you a belt," he said with an ironic smile. "This seemed a better gift for you."

When she tugged off the wrappings to expose the gift, her face shone like a sky full of stars. It was the poems of Omar Khayyam he had copied for her last summer.

He watched her face intently as she traced a sketch of a chamomile blossom with her fingertip. "Is this your work?" she asked quietly.

"Yes. I wanted to leave it with you last summer, but—"

She raised her eyes and he saw in the vivid blue irises a tumult of emotion. "If you had given it me before, I would not have let you ride away to Montpellier without me."

There was subtle grief in her words. It reminded him that she, too, had suffered in their months apart. With one finger, he traced the curve of her cheek. "I would that I had it to do again, my love. I would spare you the sorrows you have known these months."

She launched herself forward into his arms. "I am so blessed to have found you, Solomon." She met his gaze. "Husband and lover, teacher and friend."

Deeply moved, he kissed her.

For all of that night and the next day, they were thus. Rica felt drunk with happiness as they laughed and played, and sometimes sat cozily side by side on the bed, reading their precious texts. They debated a little, but neither had much heart for true thought. The pleasure went too deep.

She thought she would never grow tired of looking at him. She opened her eyes when he moved inside of her to watch the dark hunger rise in his cheeks and soften his mouth, she watched his throat as he made luxurious sounds of satisfaction, she admired his mouth when it glistened from her kisses.

She watched him move, naked and without shame as he tended the fire, or poured watered wine into a cup for them. His muscles below his golden skin moved in perfect symmetry, as beautiful as fish gliding through water.

And when he bent, so serious, over his book, she watched him then, too, seeing the scholar, the thinker, who pursed his lips and frowned and absently plucked at a curl behind his ear.

It was this serious man who said to her, late on Tuesday, "In the morning, we go back. I wish to speak with you."

Rica nodded.

"I must help my father finish his business here," Solomon said. "It will take about six or seven days, I think. Then I will ride with him to Mainz and see him settled." He smiled, a glitter of mischief in his dark eyes. "Then I will return for you and we will go to Cairo."

Rica laughed in surprise and delight. "Cairo?"

"Does that please you, love?"

"Oh, yes." She thought of the painting, and of her longing, since she was a child, to see the lands to which the Crusaders had traveled. A prickle of gooseflesh rose on her arms. "Very much."

He nodded, then sighed a little. "I do not know the best way to speak with your father, Rica. You must know he is dying—he will not see this summer."

She lowered her eyes, resisting his words though she knew them to be true. "I have seen that he grows worse each day. But I don't like to think of his pain over this. Let me think on it a little, and ask Helga what would be best."

"So be it. I will send word as soon as my father is settled, and tell you a place to send to me as to what I should do."

Tears sprang to her eyes. "Oh, Solomon, I do not wish to leave here. I do not wish to be without you for even a few days."

His gaze softened. "Nor do I, Rica. But a few days now, and then we will be always together." He held out his hand to her. "Come. We must make the best of this little time left to us, yes?"

She laughed and rose to meet him.

A sudden sharp pounding came at the door. Rica whirled, her heart in her throat. In alarm she looked at Solomon, who had also got to his feet, and hastily donned his jupon, buttoning it a little.

The knock sounded again, and Helga's voice came through. "Rica! 'Tis me. Open the door. I must talk with you both."

Rica flew across the room. "Helga! You frightened me. What is it?"

The midwife bustled into the room, her hair slipping free of its braids, her breath coming in rushed little gasps. She looked at Solomon and her face was grim. "The mob has deposed the council and put new men in their places."

Solomon went white. "When?"

"This afternoon. They did not wait for the news from the conference, but acted while the bishop and mayor were gone."

While she spoke, Solomon dressed quickly. "Has there been any move toward the Jews?"

"Not yet." Helga looked at him miserably. "But there is talk that they are to be arrested."

Rica, bewildered, then dismayed, whirled toward Solomon. "You cannot mean to go!"

He looked at her sadly and touched her cheek. "My father is there, Rica." He bent and kissed her longingly, sweetly. "In a few days, I will send to you, and we will be gone forever from this place. Have faith, my love."

But she could not stop her tears. She clung to him for a moment, then stepped back and straightened her shoulders. "Go with God," she said.

Once more, he kissed her and then Helga, and he was gone, into the black and menacing night.

26

There was yet a light burning at his father's house. Solomon found Jacob in his shop, working feverishly by the light of a tallow. A stab of guilt touched him. "Papa, I came as soon as I heard."

Jacob looked up wearily. "So," he said in a dull voice, "you found her."

There were no lies left in him. Joy had burned them to dust. "Yes."

"My lie—it was only to protect you."

"I know, Papa."

"There is little enough joy in our lives," he said. "So little. I cannot be sorry if you have found a measure of it." Grimly he bent his head and pinched his nose at the bridge.

"Come, Papa, you are exhausted. Have you eaten?"

With a wave of his hand, Jacob dismissed the question. "I have been trying to make sense of all this, trying to find ways to—" He sighed. "All my years I have been in this city, and my father before me, and his before him. And now at the whim of evil men, I am forced to become an exile."

In the dark room, with the single tallow flickering

between them, Solomon leaned forward. "Why would you wish to be here amid all this hatred, when there are places so much better?"

"It is not better, Solomon, only hidden better." He roused himself and glanced toward the shuttered windows, as if seeing what lay beyond them. "This place is in my bones, *beneleh.* The way the mountains look on summer afternoons, and the way the river flows, and the smell of the forest, the sound of the bells and the monks and the square—all these things are *mine,* too." He slammed his fist on the table. "And because of foolish lies and fear, I am chased from my home and lose my business, a lifetime of work? What is there in Mainz for me?"

"Your wife," Solomon said, newly met with the word and its meaning. "Your sons and grandsons as they come."

Jacob nodded, but it was a weary gesture.

Gently, Solomon took his father's arm. "Come, King Jacob. I will fix you something to eat, and you must get some rest. In the morning, we will work out what to do."

Charles did not return until Thursday. Rica, who had been watching from the walk, raced down the twisting steps toward the bailey gates when she saw his small party returning on the road. Their defeat was plain from a single glance at their slow-moving band.

She met her father at the gates and gave a small cry at the gray color of his cheeks. "Help him dismount!" she cried to a nearby vassal. "Do you not see he is ill?"

Charles looked at her but was too spent even to speak. With a nod, he allowed himself to be taken from the horse, where only sheer stubbornness had evidently kept him.

They helped him to the hall, where Rica insisted they leave him for a time. "Stay close," she said. "He will need to be carried to his chamber."

She bent over her father and removed his cloak. His eyes were closed, his face an unholy shade of pale gray. His skin was cool and clammy.

A maid scurried in with tankards of ale and loaves of bread and cheese. "Get me water and a cloth, quickly," Rica said. The girl, wide-eyed, ran to comply.

Rica bent over him, loosening his overtunic at the throat. His breathing was labored and scratchy. "Oh, Papa," she whispered. "Try to drink some ale."

He seemed not to have the strength to lift the cup, and she held it to his lips so he might drink. He managed a few mouthfuls. The maid had returned with the water. Rica touched the girl's arm. "Thank you. Now tell Cook I must have my father's tisane. Quickly."

Then to a vassal, standing nearby in readiness, she said, "Go to Helga and bring her here."

"As you wish, my lady."

Rica washed her father's face with cool water and managed to get a little more ale in him and a few mouthfuls of the herbal infusion.

He started to speak, taking Rica's hand. "Shhh," she said, motioning to the waiting men to carry him up to his room. "First you rest, Papa," she said as they lifted him. "Then we will talk."

Helga could not be found. The vassal sent to fetch her had asked at all the peasant villages where she was known, and none had seen her.

Rica took up the watch herself, settling next to her father's massive bed. He slept, but not restfully. His breathing was too labored. She gave him another cup of the decoction and read aloud from Psalms, then stitched a little at the tapestry.

A brace of candles burned in the room and a fire kept it warm, and through the long, silent hours of the night, Rica watched her father sleep.

If she had borne any doubts about the limit to his days, this last bout cleared them away. And yet, she still did not know what to do or how to approach him.

She studied his face—even in such an unguarded moment there was fierceness and power in the cut of his jaw and the set of his mouth. And yet, she also remembered how he had once hidden apples in his pockets for her to find, and how he never left the castle without bringing back some treat to his daughters.

And she was his child, not only the child of his blood and loins, but of his heart. He had fostered within her the same powerful bent of mind he himself owned, had passed on to her his stalwart spirit. When she made her dangerous journey to Cairo with Solomon, it would be with her father's eyes that she would see the wonders of the world. It would be his heart, beating in her own chest, that gave her the courage to do it.

It grieved her deeply to know she must leave him to claim her own life. It seemed a steep and terrible price to pay. Her news would wound him deeply—and she'd only just found her way again into his good graces.

But she could not leave without bidding him farewell. Not for the world could she do such a thing. Not even for Solomon.

As if he heard the turmoil of her thoughts, he opened his eyes. "Ah, *liebling!* As usual you have cared well for me."

"Pappi!" She leaned forward to touch his brow and found the clamminess gone. His color, though poor, was improving. "How do you feel?"

"Old," he said. "It was all for naught. They deposed the council while we were yet meeting."

"Helga told me."

"How does she always know things?"

"She goes everywhere, sees everything. A midwife of her talents is privy to all secrets."

His smile was wan.

She took his hand, biting her lip against the cold fear in her heart. "Is there nothing we can do, Papa?"

"No," he said. "It is finished."

Solomon argued with his father through the night. "We cannot wait until after the Sabbath!" he cried.

Stubbornly, Jacob remained unmoved. "At least I will have the joy of a Sabbath meal to warm me on our journey."

Outside the house, there was a deep quiet, the still terror of the unknown threat that hung over all of them. One more day might be one day too many. There was madness alive in the streets of Strassburg.

But all day he had spoken thus, and Jacob was immovable. Solomon would not leave him.

He sighed. "All right, Papa," he said. "On Sunday early, we leave for Mainz."

On Friday, Helga left Strassburg sick at heart and rode directly to the castle. She found Rica in the solar with Charles, and the girl's face brightened in hope.

Biting back the sorrow the expression gave her, Helga said abruptly, "Leave us, girl. I have private matters to discuss," she said.

Rica seemed not to mind. She had been sitting there all night, no doubt. Kissing Helga's cheek, she drifted out.

Helga watched her go and swallowed the grief she

felt. Without preamble, she said to Charles, "They have arrested the Jews."

"So it begins," he said heavily and buried his face in his hands. "May God have mercy upon them."

Still Helga waited, staring at him, willing him to remember the young Jew who had come here only a week before.

And in time, he did. Lifting his head, he showed Helga bleak eyes. "Lock Rica in her room. Do not open the door for any reason."

"I will see to it myself."

Rica dozed on her bed. It was Helga, bearing a tray of ale and bread and cheese, who awakened her. The midwife put the food on a small table by the embrasure and said nothing.

Befuddled a little by sleep, Rica sat up. "What is it, Helga?"

Still Helga did not speak, but headed for the door, pausing only when she had reached the threshold. "I am sorry," she said, and Rica heard a break in her voice. "So very, very sorry."

Alarmed, Rica leapt from her bed, running for the door as Helga closed it. "Helga!"

She heard the lock slide home, and terror licked her heart. She pounded it with her fist. *"Helga!"*

There was no answer. Rica clutched her stomach, her mind racing through the reasons she would have been locked in her room. She had done no wrong—unless her father had somehow learned of her time with Solomon.

Frightened, she looked at the tray of food. Supplies, by the look of them. For a day, or more.

The order had come from her father, she was sure, after Helga had spoken to him "privately."

Helga knows everything, sees everything.

A bolt of pure horror weakened her knees, and Rica sank down before the crucifix on the wall of her chamber. "Oh, Mary!" she cried out. "Holy Mother, please do not let it be the Jews!"

She slept uneasily, waking suddenly through the night with a sense of panic strangling her. Each time, she rose and tried the door, only to find it still securely locked. Twice, she pounded on it, calling out in the darkness to be set free.

No one came.

At dawn, she opened the shutter and looked toward Strassburg. It looked ever the same, the rooftops struck with the first fingers of sunlight, the stone walls turning rosy. The Rhine ran by, serenely glistening in the morning.

Rica poured a cup of the ale, listening for sounds of life beyond her door. Her hands trembled a little, and she sighed, bowing her head. How could they have locked her in here, with no word of warning or a clue as to why?

She fought the knowledge that something had happened in the city, something Helga had witnessed, something unspeakable. Something, if Rica knew it, that would make her leave the castle walls in search of Solomon.

A long finger of sunlight angled through the embrasure and struck the silver-and-wood crucifix on her wall. The blaze of the metal caught her eye and she knelt before it. Sweet Jesus, himself a Jew, tortured unto death, his face weary with the weight of it. "Oh, dear Lord, can you not intervene?" she whispered, and pressed her lips together.

Again, she turned toward Strassburg, staring at the

city as if to see some clue as to what went on beyond the walls.

And she remembered, then, that it was the Feast of Saint Valentine. The saint of lovers. How she had hoped to be with Solomon today!

A ripple of dread touched her. Solomon. Out there, in the madness.

No. She could not bear that thought. Would not even think it.

Through the morning, she prayed for the others left in the city. She knelt piously, praying to Mary and Jesus. For good measure, she said prayers to Saint Valentine, too, because it was his feast day and because he symbolized love. Enough love could curb a mob, could it not?

The prayers somehow calmed her. At Sext, she heard the jingle of keys in the lock. She jumped up. Perhaps they would let her go now, and she could hear the news, hear what manner of madness had flooded the streets of Strassburg.

It was Helga again, and she bore another tray of food, this time more substantial. "I thought you might need a little hot food, too," she said.

Rica felt herself go still. "You have not come to let me go."

A burly guardsman stood on the threshold, his arms crossed. The sight of him struck new terror through her. "Helga, why am I locked here?"

Helga raised her eyes, and Rica saw in the red rims and the ravaged flesh below the evidence of much weeping.

Rica sank to a bench. "No," she whispered. "Please, Helga . . ."

The midwife only turned wearily away, her shoulders bent as if under a great weight, and she shuffled toward the door once more. Rica leapt on her, grabbing her arms. "No!" she cried. "Tell me what you have seen! Tell me what you know! Do not lock me away without even a word!"

A fresh glimmer of tears shone in the cornflower eyes as Helga turned. "Child, there is naught any of us can do." She struggled a moment, her lips trembling. "'Tis done."

In horror, Rica stared at her, trying to take it in. Helga nodded to the man, and he turned sideways to let her pass, then slammed closed the door.

Rica stood in the center of the room for a moment, stunned, unable to work her mind around the words. *'Tis done.*

Helga had been in the city, had seen something terrible. She had come here to tell Charles, and Charles had ordered her locked in her room, which Helga had done willingly.

She heard a strange noise on the wind and ran to the embrasure. And there, rippling like a demon into the clear blue sky, was a pillar of black smoke.

In Narbonne and Carcassonne, they are burning the Jews.

Rica screamed, clutching the stone embrasure until her fingers were bloody. "No!" she cried. "Oh, God, no!"

She stared at the billowing smoke and her mind was filled with the faces of the people she had seen there in the streets, the children chasing each other into an alleyway; the old man watching with amusement and guarded reserve as she dragged Leo out of the shop, the young women laughing together—

Now she could see a haze of heat bending the sky along the river. It was a monstrous fire, and the miasmatic smell of it blew toward her on a soft early spring breeze. The oily weight of it caught in her throat and burned her eyes.

She thought of Solomon's father, explaining why

he had beaten his son by telling how he'd held Solomon on his knee as a babe. "I do this to keep him alive, and you too."

Rica began to weep. The smoke caught in her mouth and her nose and stung her eyes and she breathed it all the more deeply into her, tears running so thick from her eyes she could not see. Still she stared at the flames and malignant smoke.

And through her sobs, she began to pray aloud, the prayer of absolution and deliverance, for all the souls now winging their way toward heaven. She cried the prayer in a loud, strong voice, as long as she could remain standing.

After a time, her legs no longer held her upright, and sobbing helplessly, she slid down the wall, her hands still stuck to the embrasure.

27

Rica did not know how long she had lain on the floor in her grief. At some point, spent, she must have tumbled into a world of half sleep, where the flames still belched into the bright sky. And somehow, those big flames had been transformed into tiny flickering lights that burned over a table that held the remains of her wedding feast.

Her eyes were grainy when she opened them, and there was something sharp pricking her cheek. The rushes. She struggled upright and rubbed the marks on her ear and jaw.

Night had fallen. The food sat untouched on her table. She stared at it with revulsion. Her throat was raw. Her fingers ached. Dully she spread out her hands to see that she'd broken several nails, and in three places, dried blood had caked onto her flesh.

There were no more tears left in her, only a wild, searing grief. Every corner of her was filled with it, an emotion black and sticky as tar. She could taste it against her tongue and smelled it thick in her nostrils. It held her, immobile, slumped against the wall in the darkness.

She did not know how long she sat there. A long

time. It was thirst that drove her unsteadily to her feet, and the movement made her so dizzy she nearly fell again. The tankard of ale seemed too heavy to lift; instead she drank what was left in her cup.

Beneath her kirtle, she felt something move against her breast. Sinking to the bench, she pulled out her silver ring from Solomon, which she could not wear until her father had been told of the marriage. It gleamed in the darkness and Rica brokenly pressed it to her mouth.

She had tried not to think of Solomon in those flames, but now it was impossible to keep the thought away. She screamed. Screamed and screamed, feeling it tear through her chest as sharply as a knife.

And finally someone came to let her out of her prison—Helga, who knelt before her and took her in her arms, and rocked her as she wept. "I am so sorry, Rica, my sweet. So, so sorry."

It was Helga who bathed her face with cool water, and gave her a sleeping draught to ease her, and stayed with her through the night, settling her back with cooing words when Rica bolted awake, over and over again. It was Helga who took the ring from around her neck and put it on her finger, patting her hand.

Rica awakened once, wild-eyed, and clutched Helga's shoulders. "He wanted to go to Cairo! Perhaps he escaped in time."

Helga only shook her head slowly, her lips pressed tight together.

In the aftermath of the disaster, Rica lost track of time. Day or night, she did not know and did not care. She could not eat; food stuck in her throat like pebbles. Matilda brewed possets and meat tiles to tempt her, but they remained untouched.

When people spoke to her, a vassal or a servant, Helga or her father, she stared at them blankly, unable to decipher what the words meant.

Only in sleep was there peace. In her dreams, Solomon lived to touch her sweetly. He teased her and kissed her and challenged her to long debates and laughed boldly.

In rare lucid moments, she prayed that she had conceived in those short, precious hours with Solomon. But even that hope was snatched from her. The flux came upon her with a violent rush one morning, so fierce Rica took to her bed.

Perhaps ten days after the burning of the Jews, the false spring disappeared and a dark sky moved in with foreboding bleakness over the countryside. Rica sat by the embrasure of her room, watching as it began to snow.

The return of winter cruelly echoed her life. It seemed particularly brutal of fate to have let Rica find Solomon again, only to take him away. What purpose could such torture serve?

All had been lost. Her sister, her love. And it would not be long for her father. The massacre had bled nearly as much life from him as it had from Rica.

And what did the future hold for her? She would not marry. To go to a nunnery when her faith had been so deeply shaken seemed a travesty.

She lifted her eyes toward the city, barely visible through the swirling snow. Never again would she set foot in those streets, unless it was to tear the stones apart, to dismantle in vengeance what had been built there.

A dark figure emerged from the snow—a priest on a mule. He bent against the wind, hunched miserably against the cold. Dispassionately, she watched him turn toward the castle gates, no doubt to seek shelter from the weather.

Grimly, she turned away, wishing for shelter from her own misery. But there was none. Her heart had turned to stone.

In his solar, Charles sat by the fire, struggling to breathe. It seemed each day the task grew more difficult, and at times he even felt lightheaded, as if there was not enough air in the world to feed his hungry lungs.

A page announced a priest who would see no one but Charles. "What does he want?"

"He will not say, my lord. Only that he must speak with you alone."

In his weariness, Charles could think of no excuse to avoid him. He nodded. "Bring him to me, but first check to be sure he has no sign of plague."

The priest came in a short time later, led by the page, who then departed. Charles waited.

The priest wore plain brown robes. He was quite tall and youthful as he moved into the room, but Charles could not see his face. "What is it you seek, good brother?" Charles said, pouring a cup of ale to give him. "I am not well and would ask you state your purpose quickly."

The priest pulled back his hood.

A jolt of painful shock ripped through Charles's heart, and he dropped the cup. "Dear God," he said.

The young Jew stood there without speaking, as sober as Job. Charles saw new grief in the hollow cheeks, and a weariness below his eyes. In the stillness, the pop of a log on the hearth was extraordinarily loud.

In his weakened state, Charles struggled to find meaning in the man's presence here, vainly tried to think of some word that would bring the matter clear to him. And the Jew did not help him, but only stood there, so grim.

"What do you want?" Charles finally asked.

The man hesitated only a moment. With a flourish, he knelt, crossing his hands on his knee. "I have come," he said solemnly, "to petition you for the hand of your daughter Rica, my lord."

The words were so quietly yet firmly uttered that Charles was dumbstruck. "You are a Jew," he said finally, but there was no roar in his voice.

"Yes."

Charles stared at him. "I could have you drawn and quartered for what you suggest, for what you have done to her."

"I know."

"You know." Charles frowned. "And yet you come here to ask me for her hand?" In astonishment, he shook his head. "What possible reason could you give me that would make me even consider such an absurdity?"

"I think you love her more than you love your own life," the Jew said quietly, "and you know you are dying."

"How dare you—"

"I love her, my lord," he interrupted, and now Charles saw the desperate and passionate light in the young man's eye. "She is my blood and my flesh and my soul. Without her, I have no more wish to live."

"You are a *Jew!*" Charles repeated.

"And you risked your life to save mine," he said quietly. He stood up. "I came to you because she loves you, my lord. I would ask your blessing upon our union. If you cannot give it, I will go away without her." He paused. "She thinks me dead. She need never know I came."

There was dignity and power in the man. On the broad brow, there was intelligence and passion; in the cut of his jaw and his firm mouth there was strength and steadfastness. But in his eyes, Charles saw tenderness, and the hands were strong enough to gentle the wild heart of his child.

"I wish she had loved more wisely," Charles said heavily, looking away. "How could she love you, knowing how dangerous it was? How could you let her?"

"We did not choose, my lord, not either of us."

Charles nodded. "How will you keep her? Where will you go? Do you have some plan?"

"I will study with the Arabian physicians, to become the surgeon I should be." He lifted the hem of his robe, settling the extraordinary weight of it into Charles's hand. "Money I have."

Charles bowed his head. His daughter seemed to be perched on the edge of a vast, yawning madness these past days. Her eyes were haunted, and he knew she had seen the flames from her chamber. If Charles sent this Jew away, Rica would wither and fade more with each passing day, until she was a parody of herself. He had it in his power to change that.

Charles stood up and opened the door. To the page in the passageway, he said, "Fetch my daughter from her chamber."

Rica had to be roused from sleep to go to her father. She'd been dreaming of revenge again. Only now instead of daggers she wielded fire like a mad witch, and burned all the houses of Strassburg.

She smoothed her hair, and a little disoriented, followed the page to her father's chamber. The boy stepped aside, and she brushed by him to go in.

Her father sat in his favored spot, and nearby the fire stood a priest. A bolt of alarm shot through her.

"Papa!" she said, going forward. "Is there something amiss?"

But before she reached him, the priest turned from the fire to look at her.

Rica closed her eyes hastily. He looked like Solomon—so much. These past days, she'd been poised on the brink of some terrible fall, and only through the most relentless discipline had she managed to hold to her sanity. When the panicky moment passed, she opened her eyes once more.

The priest still stared at her. His face had not changed. She cried out before she could stop herself and looked at her father, then back to the priest.

Solomon. Transfixed, she stared at him, unable to grasp the physical presence of him, standing here so plainly in her father's chamber, staring at her so soberly.

She fell to her knees, unable to speak. Tears washed down her face and she could not stop them. She bit her knuckle and tried to rise; looked to her father, who watched her—

Her shoulders shook with the effort of holding back her tears, and she found she could not speak or stand or do anything but hold up her arms in an imploring gesture, wordless, to her father, then to Solomon.

"My lord," Solomon said quietly.

"Rica," Charles said, his voice stronger than it had been in weeks, "I bid you take this man as your husband."

Rica stared at him, sure this was a dream and any moment she would awaken to find herself in her own bed, and the grief would be again a newly torn wound. She closed her eyes.

Then Solomon was bending to take her arms and a waft of frankincense came with him. Rica wanted to stare again into his fathomless eyes, whether it was dream or not, and she looked up at him.

He helped her to her feet. "All is well, my love," he whispered. "All is well."

She touched his beloved face, barely able to see

him though her tears. He lifted her hand and kissed the ring on her finger.

Rica cried out. It was real. She could feel the heat and moisture of his mouth on her fingers, and his hair brushed her chin as he bent his head. It was real, not a dream. He was alive—

Overcome, she fell against him, closing her eyes to feel the press of wool against her cheek and hear his heartbeat thudding hard and strong against her ear. "Oh, you're alive," she said, and found she was laughing through her tears.

Unmindful of her father, she pressed a passionate kiss against his lips.

Only then did she turn to her father, who watched her with a suspicious glimmer in his bright blue eyes. "So this is your choice?"

Wordlessly, she nodded, biting her lip.

He stared at her. "An hour, you said, of true love. Perhaps you will be lucky and have more."

Rica fell to her knees and hugged him tightly. Against her ear, his beard was scratchy, and she felt the new thinness in his body. Now she wept for him, for the knowledge that to have Solomon, she must leave her father. "Pappi—"

"Say no more, child," he said in a rough voice. He gripped her hard.

For a moment longer, Rica clung to him. "Thank you," she whispered at last.

"The journey will be a long one," he said, taking a breath. "And dangerous. Take what you need from here, and go with first light, before anyone knows."

"My lord, we must go tonight," Solomon said, not without regret. "I have made arrangements for us to travel with a party of pilgrims, so as not to arouse suspicion. It will be safer."

Charles looked stricken. In a moment, he nodded. "So be it."

Torn, Rica rocked back on her heels. "Tell Helga I love her."

He nodded. "That I will do." He gripped her hand tightly. "Send word when you have arrived safely, and tell me what wonders you have seen."

Rica nodded. "I will, Papa." She kissed him, knowing she would never see him again in this life. When she rose, she gazed at his face, rugged and strong and so dear, to press it into memory. "I love you," she said.

"Go with God," he said gruffly, and turned away.

Next to her, Solomon touched her arm. "Gather your things," he said quietly. "I will meet you in the yard."

Rica glanced around the room one more time, and spying the unfinished tapestry, took it from its frame. She glanced toward her father, and he nodded his understanding. Rica rolled it up.

Solomon smiled at her—and her heart swelled with joy. She raced to her room to make ready for the journey.

As Rica departed, Solomon turned back to the old man. From within his cloak, he took a small vial. "This will bring a quiet death when you are ready," he said slowly. "Put it in your wine before bed, and you will slip away in the night, peacefully."

"I would not like to think a knight should resort to such measures, but the pain is sometimes . . ."

"Yes." Solomon knelt and bowed his head. "My lord, you have given me my life tonight. And I wish to thank you—" His voice broke. He went silent a moment, then gathered his emotions and continued. "I wish to thank you for what you did in defense of my people."

"It was not enough." The words were weary. "There is an unholy stench to this place." He shook his head. "How did you escape? Helga saw you."

Solomon closed his eyes against the memory. It was too raw, still. "My father pretended he would leave with me on Friday. I dressed as you see me now, to travel. When the mob came to arrest us with the others, he screamed that I was trying to convert him." Solomon raised his eyes, unable to quell his grief. "He would not come with me. He screamed that he'd rather die a Jew than—" Overcome, Solomon bent his head. "And die he did."

"One day," said Charles slowly, "you will know the love a father has for his children, and there will be no more question in your heart." He touched his shoulder. "Go plant the seeds of children in my daughter's womb. Thereby will your father's blood live on, and mine, too. Perhaps there is some good in the horror if such a thing can come about."

Solomon nodded soberly. "So it shall be."

There was nothing left to say and Solomon made to go. "Thank you, my lord."

There were tears in the old man's mountain-blue eyes, and he looked suddenly small in his chair. "Take care of her," he whispered.

"I will." Solomon bowed and left.

In the courtyard, he found Rica, cloaked in heaviest wool, already waiting next to her horse. Next to her was Leo, whose tail started to wag as Solomon came up. She smiled at him. "He will not listen to me when I say this adventure is only for us."

Solomon, still aching over the moment in the

solar, bent to scratch a spot just below Leo's ear. The animal licked his wrist and barked softly. "He would make a good protector. We will take him."

He sighed and took Rica into his arms, pressing his forehead to hers. For a long time, they stood there in the swirling snow, brow to brow. The tumultuous events of the last months echoed in him, and he could feel them in Rica, too. But slowly, a wide shimmering began to glow in Solomon's veins. He felt it pass through him to Rica, until he knew there was illumination all around them, all through them, a light that would lead the way to the future.

"Are you ready, wife?"

"Yes."

Together they rode through the gates of Esslingen Castle, leaving it behind in the swirling snow. Once Rica paused and looked behind her. Diamond droplets of snow clung to her lashes, and the soberness of her look pierced him. He waited, a touch of fear in his breast that she would find herself unable to go after all.

When she looked at him, silvery tears washed over her face. "I told Lewis to fetch Helga for my father." She swallowed. "I will miss him very much."

Solomon thought of his own father with the new rawness of his grief. He took her hand. "We will remember them together," he said.

She gave him a wistful smile, her fingers gripping his almost painfully. "On to Cairo."

He smiled and kissed her. "To Cairo."

Holding hands in the swirling snow, they rode away.

28

Cairo—Autumn 1349

Rica lit a candle in her room. "Forgive me, Father, for I have sinned," she whispered to the small flame. Resting her hands on the round swell of her belly, she spilled the pockets of wickedness from her soul. She could not seem to keep her temper with a wicked neighbor who babbled insults at Rica in a conglomeration of languages, and she had sworn evilly at a merchant who sold her bad fish.

There was no priest, so she composed a punishment for herself to cleanse the black spots from her heart, then crossed herself and stood up.

When she turned, Solomon was standing respectfully at the door. With a grin he asked, "Is it such a trial for you to give up your old habits, my love?"

Rica smiled and shook her head. "No. Only confession."

"I have a letter," he said, coming forward. "It's from Helga."

Rica rushed forward to take it from him. "She must have paid a scribe to write it for her," she said, and held it up. "Look how beautiful the writing is."

"Read it," he said. "I am anxious for news."

"'My pretty Rica,'" she began, and grinned at Solomon. "'I am writing to tell you that your father has died. It was a peaceful departure; in his sleep he passed away, never waking again to the pain that was so terrible these last months. I am glad he is now at rest. He lies now with your sister and mother.'"

Tears blurred Rica's vision. Wordlessly she handed the paper to Solomon, who drew her down next to him and held her hand as he read the rest.

"'The plague seems now spent, though you would not know Strassburg now, so empty it is, and strange. I like it not. There is little food, for the harvest was so disrupted, and bandits roam freely, unchecked.

"'And that is all I have to tell you except that I will take you up on your wish for me to come to you. This place is only sad memories now and I wish no more to be here. All I have loved are gone. Lewis will travel with me.'"

Rica squealed, and unable to curb her excitement, she gave Solomon a hug. She touched the rise of her belly and murmured a soft word to the babe, too.

Solomon smiled. "I will rest much easier, knowing she will be here when the babe comes," he said.

She chuckled. "You will see, Solomon. I keep telling you I am well made for birth."

"All the same . . ."

Beyond the window came the sound of prayers being called. Rica went to look, as she always did. It thrilled her to see the bright, sharp light, so different from home, and the pyramids on the horizon, and the sudden ceasing of all activity as everyone bent toward Mecca to pray.

Solomon joined her, and looped an arm around her shoulders. "Is it what you thought it would be?"

A waft of the city's particular odor reached them—animals and heat and spices. "Oh, yes." She turned in his arms, delighting in the freedom she had to embrace him openly, whenever she wished, even after so many months. "There is no need to ask you," she said with a grin. "I have never seen anyone so happy with learning as you are."

He grinned. "Well, there are a few things I like better." Wickedly he traced the curve of her breast, and pressed his palm to her belly. "But only a few."

Rica stared up at him, so beautiful and strong— and now, at peace. All at once, she was filled with an odd, swirling sense of eternity, as if she had known him always, would know him forever. "I had not thought," she said softly, touching his cheek, "that marriage would bring such joy."

"Nor did I," he said, his eyes burning and serious. "You are everything to me, *ahuvati*. My whole world."

He tugged her close and kissed her deeply. The babe within Rica kicked in joy, and together she and Solomon laughed as the sounds of Cairo began anew.

LORD OF THE NIGHT by Susan Wiggs

Much loved historical romance author Susan Wiggs turns to the rich, sensual atmosphere of sixteenth-century Venice for another enthralling, unforgettable romance. "Susan Wiggs is truly magical."—Laura Kinsale, bestselling author of *Flowers from the Storm*.

CHOICES by Marie Ferrarella

The compelling story of a woman from a powerful political family who courageously gives up a loveless marriage and pursues her own dreams, finding romance, heartbreak, and difficult choices along the way.

THE SECRET by Penelope Thomas

A long-buried secret overshadowed the love of an innocent governess and her master. Left with no family, Jessamy Lane agreed to move into Lord Wolfeburne's house and care for his young daughter. But when Jessamy suspected something sinister in his past, whom could she trust?

WILDCAT by Sharon Ihle

A fiery romance that brings the Old West back to life. When prim and proper Ann Marie Cannary went in search of her sister, Martha Jane, what she found instead was a hellion known as "Calamity Jane." Annie was powerless to change her sister's rough ways, but the small Dakota town of Deadwood changed Annie as she adapted to life in the Wild West and fell in love with a man who was full of surprises.

MURPHY'S RAINBOW by Carolyn Lampman

While traveling on the Oregon Trail, newly widowed Kate Murphy found herself stranded in a tiny town in Wyoming Territory. Handsome, enigmatic Jonathan Cantrell needed a housekeeper and nanny for his two sons. But living together in a small cabin on an isolated ranch soon became too close for comfort . . . and falling in love grew difficult to resist. Book I of the Cheyenne Trilogy.

TAME THE WIND by Katherine Kilgore

A sizzling story of forbidden love between a young Cherokee man and a Southern belle in antebellum Georgia. "Katherine Kilgore's passionate lovers and the struggles of the Cherokee nation are spellbinding. Pure enjoyment!"—Katherine Deauxville, bestselling author of *Daggers of Gold*.

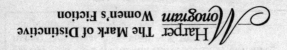

Harper *Monogram* **The Mark of Distinctive Women's Fiction**